THE AWAKENING

A Novel of Intrigue, Seduction, and Redemption

ALLEN JOHNSON

YUCCA

Yucca Publishing books may be purchased in bulk at special discounts for sales promotion, corporate gifts, fund-raising, or educational purposes. Special editions can also be created to specifications. For details, contact the Special Sales Department, Yucca Publishing, 307 West 36th Street, 11th Floor, New York, NY 10018 or yucca@skyhorsepublishing.com.

Yucca Publishing® is an imprint of Skyhorse Publishing, Inc.®, a Delaware corporation.

Visit our website at www.yuccapub.com.

10 9 8 7 6 5 4 3 2 1

Library of Congress Cataloging-in-Publication Data is available on file.

Cover design by Yucca Publishing

Print ISBN: 978-1-63158-009-3
Ebook ISBN: 978-1-63158-022-2

Printed in the United States of America

For
My adopted brother,
Who has been a victim of tyranny
And a model of forgiveness and integrity:
Juanito Garcia Oliver

Acknowledgments

My heartfelt thanks to my literary agent, Peter Riva, who, from the beginning, offered unflagging counsel, encouragement, and commitment in the writing, editing, and publishing of *The Awakening.*

I would also like to thank my dear friends—Judy Clem, Patricia Johnson, and Carl Van Hoff—all of whom graciously and meticulously lent their insightful comments and proofreading skills.

Your vision will become clear
Only when you look into your heart.
Who looks outside, dreams.
Who looks inside, awakens.

—Carl Jung

Although few acknowledge and even fewer accept, there is a time in every person's life when he or she is invited to be awakened.

For Anthony Rossi that time was September 1990 through January 1991. For Diego Garcia it was fifty-five years earlier in the teeth of the Spanish Civil War.

This is the story of their respective invitations and the ultimate merging of their destinities.

THE AWAKENING

I

THE OLIVE TREES OF ANDALUSIA

Saturday, September 8, 1990.

It was nearly midnight. Lupita Garcia was at the kitchen table expanding the medical notes she had scribbled in her patients' files throughout the long day. She had received her first patient at seven in the morning, and the young physician was looking forward to finishing her notes and collapsing into bed.

Finally, she closed the last file with authority, arched her back, peeled off her reading glasses, and gently massaged her eyelids with thumb and forefinger.

"There. That does it," she said, unpinning her glistening black hair, allowing it to cascade down her back.

Then it happened.

Lupita's body tensed at the unmistakable whine of her grandfather's van careening up the narrow cobblestone street and grinding to a stop at the front door of the house.

She was moving to the door when Diego stormed into the living room like a man possessed: "Lupita! Lupita!"

She was only a few feet away, and yet Diego acted like she was invisible.

She was terrified by the frenzy of her grandfather's booming voice. "Tito! I am right here! *¿Que pasa?*"

Diego whipped around to the sound of her voice and finally focused on his granddaughter. "Come!" he shouted, and then again, "Come!" He barreled out the front door like a man running for his life.

Lupita was on her grandfather's heels. The battered work van was still running, the front wheel perched at an angle on the sidewalk. Diego slid the side panel door open.

Lupita gasped.

There, crumpled among a jumble of shovels, hoes, plastic tubing, and olive tree seedlings, was the body of a man, a stranger, his head and torso drenched in blood. Lupita felt for the carotid pulse; it was beating, but only faintly.

"My God, Tito, we have to get this man to the hospital in Córdoba!"

Diego faced his granddaughter and clutched her firmly by both shoulders. "You know I cannot do that!" he bellowed. His eyes were scalding, his mouth trembling with emotion. Lupita had seen that look before and knew that any protest was futile.

"All right," she conceded, "but you have to understand he could die."

"He is more likely to die on his way to Córdoba."

Lupita was now in charge, as Diego knew she must be. After all, this was not new territory for his granddaughter; at thirty-two years of age, she was already a respected general practitioner and surgeon in the Córdoba province.

"Get the blanket from my bed," she commanded.

While Diego hurried into the house, Lupita tentatively examined the bandanna that Diego had tied around the stranger's neck to slow the bleeding; the blood was already dry; no artery had been compromised. Then she ripped open the stranger's shirt and located a puncture wound at his left shoulder. The wound was still slowly oozing blood. She tore off her blouse, rolled the garment into a compress, and firmly pressed the wad against the open lesion. The stranger did not stir.

As her grandfather returned with the blanket, she unhooked her bra and cinched it tightly around the makeshift compress. She caught her grandfather's gaze, which was not disapproval, but rather pride in his granddaughter's unconstrained ingenuity—at a time when speed and execution were more important than propriety.

Lupita rolled the stranger to his side. "Tuck the blanket underneath him."

Once centered on the improvised stretcher, they carried the man into the house.

"The dining room table," Lupita said, straining under the load.

They eased the stranger's body onto the century-old oak table, sending a vase with fresh flowers crashing to the terracotta tile floor.

"Get my bag," Lupita said. Then, mindful that she was still naked from the waist up, added, "And a shirt."

The young doctor seized a table lamp from the living room and planted it next to the stranger's side. She immediately began examining the shoulder wound, a deep three-centimeter-diameter puncture, which would need to be stitched. She breathed a sigh of relief when she saw that the laceration had narrowly missed both the axillary artery and the lung.

After treating and dressing the patient's shoulder, she turned to the gash at his throat and the abrasion on his forehead. Both required a thorough cleaning and several stitches.

During the examination and treatment, Diego stood beside his granddaughter, responding swiftly to every command. He was awestruck by her surgical skills.

Lupita did an ABO test to determine the man's blood type. She mixed a drop of her patient's blood with the anti-A antibody serum and then with the anti-B serum. The anti-A sample agglutinated; the anti-B did not. He was type A. Thank God for that. Diego was also type A; he could be the blood donor. Hematologic procedure called for two additional reagent blood tests to absolutely confirm her results, but time was unforgiving. Without an immediate transfusion, the stranger could die from hemorrhagic shock. Her eyes narrowed. "*Al diablo con eso*," she said to herself. The hell with it. Better to act now than risk losing her patient.

She called her grandfather by his pet name. "Tito, I have to do a blood transfusion. You have the right type. Are you willing?"

Diego was already rolling up his sleeve. "Take as much as you need."

Lupita smiled. "I think a pint will do it, Tito."

"I am ready."

"I am not," she said, moving swiftly to the door. "I need some things from the clinic."

Lupita jumped into Diego's van and raced to the small clinic down the hill near the entrance of Espejo, which housed Lupita's office and a bare-essentials emergency room. She quickly gathered hydration fluid, anti-tetanus serum, catheters, syringes, and two IV pole stands. Treating the patient at the clinic would have been easier, but the doctor knew that Diego would never stand for it; it smelled too much like a hospital. She loaded the supplies into the van and sped up the hill.

When Lupita rushed through the door, she almost burst out laughing. Diego had moved the stranger to one side of the table and was now lying stoically beside him, his sleeve rolled up, and his eyes fixed on the pin-and-mortise oak beams overhead.

Lupita quickly set up the IV pole stands and started the blood transfusion.

"I am glad I am giving my blood."

"Yes, Tito."

"I realize he is not Juanito, but it is still a good thing."

"It is a very good thing."

When they had done everything possible, it was two o'clock in the morning. Both Lupita and Diego were exhausted. Lupita decided to leave the stranger overnight on the dining room table. For security, she wrapped a rope three times around the table, crossing the stranger's legs, hips, and sternum. The next morning, when he was more stable, they would transfer him to her bed.

Lupita kissed her grandfather on his forehead. "You did well, Tito."

The two sat down in the living room, speaking quietly, almost in a whisper.

"*Gracias*, Lupita. You were unbelievable. I am so proud of you."

Lupita smiled lovingly at her grandfather. "Where did you find the man, Tito?"

"The Arab Quarter in Granada."

The Garcias lived in the village of Espejo, 130 kilometers northwest of Granada. It was a foolhardy journey, one that could have easily taken the life of the stranger.

"And you decided to bring him here."

"You know how I feel about hospitals."

"Yes, Tito."

A pause.

"You understand, of course, that we will have to call Miguel."

"Yes, I know," Diego said, "but not tonight."

"No, not tonight," she said, her eyes beginning to weigh heavy for want of sleep.

Lupita stood up and caressed the back of her grandfather's head. "Goodnight, Tito. You are an angel." She took one last look at the stranger and went to bed.

Diego did not get up; he was too restless, too stirred up to sleep now. Not that falling asleep was a problem for Diego; unlike many people his age, seventy-four, he could nod off at will. But sleep was not on his mind this night. He ran images of Juanito in his head, timeworn memories, yellow and dim, that made him smile, then cringe, then sigh with grudging resolution. Finally, just before drifting off, his thoughts turned to someone more immediate: Miguel. He wondered what trouble the Espejo chief of police might make for them.

Lupita was up at daybreak. She immediately stepped quietly into the dining room, where she found Diego. He was sprawled in an armchair that he had moved from the living room to be closer to the stranger. Lupita's stethoscope was draped around her grandfather's neck. When she entered the room, he awakened with a start and rubbed the sleep from his eyes.

"Did you hold vigil all night?"

"I wanted to make sure that he was all right."

"And is he, Doctor Tito?" she asked, glancing at the stethoscope.

Diego looked askance at his granddaughter. "He has not moved a muscle all night, but I have observed that his chest routinely rises and falls. I think that is a good sign. Would you not agree, doctor?"

Lupita kissed her grandfather on the top of his head. "Yes, doctor. Excellent prognosis. May I?" she asked, unhooking the stethoscope from Diego's neck.

Lupita listened to her patient's heart and lungs. Although he was still unconscious, his vital signs had dramatically improved. She was hopeful. She and Diego transferred the stranger to her bed.

At eight o'clock, Lupita telephoned the chief of police. "Miguel, I think you need to pay us a visit."

"Are you all right?" Miguel asked uneasily.

"I am fine."

"And Diego?"

"He is fine too. It is something I cannot talk about over the phone."

"I understand. I will be there in ten minutes."

Lupita heard Miguel's patrol car come to a stop. She met him at the door and invited him in. Miguel stood with his cap perched on the crown of his head. There was a look of concern in his eyes. Lupita, who was a stickler when it came to courtesy, regardless of the situation, stared at Miguel's cap.

"Huh?"

Lupita looked even more fiercely at the cap.

Miguel finally caught on, snatched the hat, and tucked it under his arm. His expression was half annoyance and half embarrassment.

"Now, do not go *loco*, Miguel. Everything is under control." Lupita led the police chief to her bedroom, where the stranger lay motionless—his shoulder, head, neck, and throat scrupulously bandaged. Two intravenous tubes were still dripping life-sustaining fluid into his arm and chest.

"*Caramba*! Who in the world is that?"

"I told you not to go *loco*."

"All right, all right, but who is he?"

"We do not know."

"What do you mean, 'you do not know'?"

"I mean, we do not know. We do not know who he is."

"Is he sleeping?"

"He is unconscious."

"Holy mother of God, you have an unconscious man in your bed, Lupita, and you do not know who he is?"

"Exactly."

Miguel ran his hand though his hair in total frustration and unthinkingly donned his cap.

Again Lupita glared at the hat.

"What?"

Lupita pointed with her nose at the offending cap, which Miguel again snapped off his head.

"Lupita!"

The doctor was not sure if Miguel's exasperation was linked to the errant cap or the mysterious man or both. "What?"

"How did he get here?"

"Tito brought him here from Granada."

"From Granada!"

"That is what I just said, Miguel. Stop repeating after me."

Miguel expanded his barrel chest, making him look even more bear-like than usual. "Sit down, Lupita," he said, motioning to a straight-back chair at the side of the bed. He fetched a second chair from the dining room and plopped down facing her. He spoke slowly, trying to control his emotions. "Where is Diego?"

"He is on the terrace," she said, starting to get up.

"No, you stay where you are. I will get him." He stood up and put his hand to his temple. "I could really use some coffee."

"You know where to find it."

Miguel turned, hitched up his gun belt, and made his way through the living room to the kitchen. He found a mug from the cupboard and filled it to the brim. Then he passed through the living room again to the sliding door that opened onto the balcony terrace.

Diego was leaning over the railing, looking to the south at the olive orchards that extended up and over the hills all the way to the horizon. Their home, a white-stucco row house at the top of the hill in the shadow of the church steeple, offered a perfect view of the village rooftops and the orchards beyond.

Diego turned when he heard the sliding door open.

"Ah, Miguel, *hola*! *¿Como esta usted*?" Diego recognized Miguel's coffee mug—it was his favorite—so, out of mischief, he added, "Can we get you a cup of coffee?"

"*Buenos días*, Diego. No, thank you. I have already helped myself." He raised his mug in a salute.

"So you have."

"Good coffee too."

"Glad you like it. So, tell me, what good fortune brings you here?" Diego asked, his eyes still transfixed on the hills.

Miguel pulled on his face and neck. "It seems you have a stranger in the house."

"Yes, we do."

"Well, then?"

"Have you met him?"

"I cannot say I have really met him. I have *seen* him."

"*Si*. He is not very chatty right now, is he?"

"No, he is not. And he is awfully busted up."

"I noticed that too."

"Hmm. So, would you like to tell me about him?"

During this conversation, Lupita made her way to the terrace; it was not an interview she wanted to miss. Diego could be merciless with Miguel. He did not dislike the chief of police; in fact, he was rather fond of him, as he was fond of all his neighbors. More than anything, it was his uniform that he could not stomach. It was not personal; Diego was repelled by all vestiges of authority. When talking to anyone with conferred power—policemen, priests, soldiers, doctors (with the noted exception of his granddaughter)—Diego took his own sweet time.

All three stood at the railing, Miguel and Lupita flanking Diego.

There was a lull in the conversation.

"Diego?"

"Yes, Miguel."

"Did you want to tell me about the man?"

Diego swept back a wisp of hair. "I am sorry, Miguel. I thought I already told you. There is a busted-up man in Lupita's bed."

"I know that, Diego. I would like to know how he got there."

"I can explain that."

"Good."

Diego remained silent, while Miguel waited with dwindling patience. Lupita bit her bottom lip to stop from laughing.

"Diego?"

"Yes, Miguel."

"You were going to tell me how the stranger got here."

"Yes, I was. Well, it is quite simple. I brought him here."

Miguel looked down the hillside and started counting housetops. When he got to ten, he spoke again. "Diego, I know you brought him here. Lupita told me you brought him here. What I want to know is *why* you brought him here."

"Oh, I see, Miguel. You want to know the whole story."

"Yes, Diego, the whole story."

"Well, we probably should sit down for that."

Following Diego's lead, the three sat down around a small circular patio table, and Diego began his story.

"Miguel, did you know I was born in Espejo?"

It was true. Diego was born in Espejo—in 1916 to be exact. Although according to the church records, he was born one year earlier, which can be explained. When Diego entered the world, his father could not afford the registration fee, a day's wages, to have his newborn son baptized by the village priest.

Years later, when Diego needed proof of his birth, he went to the priest, who searched the church records.

"You do not exist," the priest said, looking over his glasses at Diego. "You are not registered."

"But clearly I do exist."

"Clearly." The priest reexamined the registry again and saw that in 1915 Diego's mother had given birth to another son, also named Diego, who died of influenza before the infant was one month old. "Yes, we can do that," the priest said.

"We can do what?"

"You can take the birthdate of your brother who was born one year before you, almost to the day. You both have the same name. And, what is more, it is a way to honor your brother. *Now* you exist."

Diego's father, Francisco, worked for a rich nobleman from Córdoba who, deciding to diversify his holdings, purchased a thousand-acre olive orchard consisting of nearly 75,000 trees. The nobleman was very fond of Francisco, and for good reason: he was a tireless field hand.

Francisco's fifth year of faithful service was marked by a record harvest. As a result, the landowner felt particularly grateful and made Francisco an amazing offer. On the last day of harvest, the landowner placed his hand on Francisco's shoulder and said, "My good man, you are too valuable to me to lose. I want to make you a promise. You are my foreman. You have a job on my land twelve months a year for as long as you are willing and able to work. And, to seal the bargain, I have a special gift for you: A young burro. Does this bargain suit you?"

A smile overtook Francisco's face. "Yes, sir. It suits me very well."

The nobleman's gesture, though not completely altruistic, was still a godsend. Although the wages were low, Francisco was now assured that he could provide for his family. And the burro was a welcomed prize; Francisco called him "Regalo," the Spanish word for "gift," and grew to love the animal as if he were part of the family.

Years later, to celebrate Francisco's sixtieth birthday, the nobleman, now seventy-five years old himself, deeded a twenty-acre parcel to his loyal foreman. It was a stretch of land that encompassed 1,500 prime olive trees, an unimaginable fortune for Francisco and a magnificent inheritance for his family.

Francisco fathered three sons. The first, also christened Francisco, was called Paco to avoid confusion. Seven years after the birth of Paco, and one year after the infant death of the first Diego, the second Diego was born—a happy and hardy baby with an insistent voice when he was hungry. The grief that Francisco guarded for the first Diego evolved into an ineffable love for his third son. He called the boy his "miracle child," and although he tried not to favor one youngster over the other, it was true he held a special place in his heart for little Diego—a unique kinship that was sealed when Francisco's wife died of tuberculosis two years after Diego's birth.

Now, raising the infant fell to his care. Every day, when Paco left the house to go to school, Francisco placed his youngest son on Regalo's back, and together—father, son, and burro—made the forty-five-minute trek to the orchards. Diego played in the dirt and, when older, climbed the trees, while his father worked the fields. That was the beginning of their bonding.

Then, in the winter of his fifth year, Diego complained of abdominal pain. His forehead was burning. Two days later his back was covered with small red bumps like insect bites. A doctor was called. It was chickenpox. The doctor explained that the disease was both deadly and highly contagious; the child must be isolated for over a month.

There was no hospital for such cases, so Francisco did what was for him unimaginable: He moved the child to a shed in an open field near the house. Diego did not see another human being for forty days. His only constant companion was Regalo; Francisco tied the burro to a nail at the window of the shack.

Four times a day, Francisco went to the shed: First, to deliver the boy's meals through a crack in the door and then, at the end of the day, to wish his son goodnight. Night after night, Francisco would awaken in tears; he would make his way to the shed, sit down with his back to the door, and listen to his son breathe.

For thirty days little Diego cried; for thirty days Francisco cried with him.

On the thirty-first day, Diego stopped sobbing.

"Only ten more days," Francisco said to his son through the door.

"I know, Papa."

"Are you frightened?"

"Not anymore."

"I love you, my son."

"I love you, Papa."

On the forty-first day, Francisco opened the door to the shed and held his little boy in his arms.

After that, Francisco and Diego were in some ways more like brothers than father and son. The love they felt for each other was distinguished, not only by tenderness, but by a profound respect, like prizefighters of equal heart and strength. It was a bond that would never be breached.

The forty days in the shed had two other consequences: For Diego, it created the will to endure any adversity; for Paco, it planted the seeds of jealousy.

Although he never spoke of it, Paco deeply resented the bond between his father and brother. He falsely interpreted the alliance as the extinction of his father's affection for him and, consequently, sought a way to recapture his father's love. Eventually, he fell on the idea of his studies. It was a natural fit; where Diego was intuitive, Paco tended to be more intellectual, more analytical. From that point on, he poured all of his energy into his books.

When Paco was twelve years old, the village priest chose him as an altar boy, which was a great honor for the family. Two years later, the priest, who was now charmed by Paco's academic alacrity, recommended the boy be accepted at a private Catholic school in Córdoba. "It will be excellent preparation for the priesthood," the curé said.

The family proudly accepted. From then on, Paco was to be called Francisco, a nobler name for an aspiring priest.

For the young scholar, the move to Córdoba was the definitive moment of his life. He was not close to the earth—not like his father or even his little brother, who considered the orchards his personal playground.

Francisco would prove to the world, and especially to his father, that he was made for greater things. His head was full of the glory and majesty of the church. He secretly dreamed of one day becoming a bishop or perhaps even a cardinal. Sometimes, when he allowed his pride to overtake him, he saw himself in a flowing black and red cape, matching skullcap, and pectoral cross, blessing his flock with the wave of a golden crosier. It was an insistent vision—surely prophetical, he thought—and so he would pray, his hands held tightly against his forehead, "Oh, God, make me worthy."

Francisco's religious fervor was eventually rewarded. At twenty-four, he was ordained. One year later, he was assigned a post as administrator and spiritual guide at the Granada hospital near the old Arab Quarter. It was not a position that he coveted. He longed to be in the cathedral: to hear confession, conduct weddings, but, especially, lead the parish in mass. He had so much to say. The congregation of Granada was so often guilty of all the deadly sins—pride, envy, sloth—but, particularly, lust. How many times had he heard their sordid stories of flesh and carnal knowledge? How often had he seen the young girls batting their eyes at the hot-blooded boys who made kissing sounds when the girls strutted by like dogs in heat? It was all lust, and it sickened him.

Diego was now eighteen years old. It was harvest time. The boy worked alongside his father as always—marking the eighth working harvest of his young life. But this year was different. This year Diego admired a beautiful, barefooted Moroccan girl, thrashing the trees with a long stick to drop the fruit to the ground. He could see that the dark-skinned girl was conscientious, but mostly he was enchanted by her beauty. His preoccupation began to show in his work.

"What are you looking at?" Francisco asked.

"Do you see, Papa, how beautiful she is?"

"Who?"

"There," he said, pointing with the side of his head. "The barefooted girl."

"Oh, yes, I see. She is very beautiful. You have good taste in women, my son. But she is Arab and very dark. Does that concern you?"

"No, of course not. Does that trouble you?"

"Not in the least. It is not the color of her skin that counts, but the state of her heart."

"I agree. I am sure that she has a very good heart."

"You may be right, my son. Perhaps you should speak to her."

But Diego was too timid to talk to the girl, so he admired her from a distance. But then one day, the young beauty caught him staring at her, and she smiled. That was all the encouragement that Diego needed. At noon, when all the workers stopped for lunch, Diego whispered to his father, "I am going to talk to the girl."

"What girl?" Francisco asked.

"You know very well what girl. She is only the most beautiful girl in all of Spain."

"Oh, *that* girl," Francisco chuckled.

"Wish me luck."

"I do not think you will need luck, not if you are polite," his father counseled.

"Yes, of course, Papa. I am not as smart as Paco, but I was not born yesterday either."

"I know that, my son. Go quickly, before a less timid *hombre* steals her away when you are not looking."

Diego's eyes widened. "What? What do you mean by that?"

"I'm teasing," Franciso said with a smile. "Don't you know when I'm teasing? Now go."

Diego slowly approached the Moroccan beauty, picking up a small twig along the way and snapping it in one hand, but when the girl looked up and smiled, Diego suddenly lost courage, turned, and hurried back toward his father.

When Francisco saw his son reverse course, he frowned and flicked his hands at him.

Diego hesitated for only an instant. He whipped around and walked directly to the girl, talking off his straw hat and bowing his head to the girl's parents and then again to the barefooted princess.

"*Buenos días*," the girl's parents said.

"*Buenos días*."

Then the girl looked into Diego's eyes, and the young suitor thought his legs would give out under him. "*Hola*."

"*Hola*. My name is Diego."

The girl's father looked up at Diego, shading his eyes from the sun. "Please sit down. Let us have a good look at you."

Diego squatted cross-legged. "*Gracias*."

"Yes," the girl's father said to his daughter. "It is as you have said, Lupe. He is a very handsome young man."

The girl immediately blushed and looked down. "Father!" she said under her breath.

The father's words gave Diego an unfair advantage over the girl, and suddenly he was brimming with confidence. "Your name is 'Lupe' then. It is a very beautiful name, but it is not Arab."

"My parents were born in Morocco," the girl said, "but I was born in Granada. My father gave me the Spanish name, Guadalupe." She leaned her face into the sun. "Everyone calls me Lupe."

"My wife and I are Muslim," the father offered, "but our strong-minded daughter has converted to Christianity."

"That is very unusual, is it not?" Diego asked.

"Extremely unusual," Lupe said, "but we are a most unusual family."

Diego turned to the girl. What a brave thing to have said, he thought. It showed great pride and self-assurance. "I can see that."

Lupe smiled. "Do you like figs, Diego?"

"I adore figs."

"Then have this one," she said, extending her hand. "It comes from Morocco. They are the best, you know."

Diego, feeling braver with each moment, reached for the fig with both hands, placing one hand under the hand of Lupe, the other touching the palm of her hand as he swept up the fruit. He smiled as he held Lupe's hand for one second too long, and so she withdrew it, which would have pained Diego had it not been for her timid and telling smile.

Diego's eyes were flirting. "I am not at all sure that Moroccan figs are the best. Spanish figs are also quiet good, you know."

"That is true," Lupe said. "But Moroccan figs are sweet and luscious; it is almost impossible to eat only one."

Suddenly, Diego was not sure that they were still talking about figs, and he blushed despite himself.

After lunch, Diego worked again with his father.

"So what do you think of the girl?" Francisco asked.

"I am going to marry her," he said grinning and, with that, took the long stick in hand, gripped it firmly, and struck the olive branches with all the passion and joy that his heart could hold.

Increasingly throughout the harvest, Diego and Lupe worked side by side. Sometimes they would brush past each other when they raised their sticks and swiped at the olive branches, and Diego would catch a scent of Lupe's hair, which rendered him useless for an instant. Lupe knew she had this beguiling effect on the handsome Diego, and it secretly delighted her.

Francisco noticed this courting dance from time to time and smiled, as he remembered his own amorous awakening. "Sometimes I wonder whose family you belong to these days," Francisco said teasingly.

But Diego did not take his father's words lightly. "Papa, I am a Garcia, of course. But my heart has been captured by Lupe. Would you want me to abandon her?"

"No, I do not want you to abandon her, my son. Nor do I want you to abandon your father when he has need of a helping hand." Francisco gave his son a mock slap across the face.

"I would never do that, Papa."

Diego could see the twinkle in his father's eyes—testament that he understood his son's state of distraction.

At the end of the harvest, Lupe and her family were to return to Morocco to visit family and, Allah willing, work the crops. They were to be gone for six months. For Diego, the thought of Lupe leaving for a day weighed heavy; for her to be away for half a year was torment.

When they said goodbye, Diego took Lupe's hands and kissed her fingers. Lupe's father saw this and turned his back, not in disapproval, but in respect for youthful passion.

"I will miss you, Lupe. I miss you already," Diego sighed, his eyes looking like a dog that was left behind.

"That is what you say, Diego Garcia. But I have seen the way you gawk at the girls from the village who rustle their skirts when they walk past the orchard."

"If I look at them, Lupe, it is only out of pity, for their crude manners cannot compete with your beauty."

"Are those the sweet words that you string together for all the village girls?"

"No, it is the way I talk to the woman I intend to marry."

Lupe broke into a smile and then caught herself. "Are you implying that I am that woman?" Lupe said haughtily, her fists punched into her hips.

"No, I am not implying anything; I am telling you: You will be my wife."

"And when did you plan to do this thing?"

"At the end of next year's harvest."

"I see. Well, thank you for letting me in on this little secret," she said in a voice that was, at once, surly and flirtatious.

"You are welcome."

She turned and walked away to join her family and then looked over her shoulder to see if Diego was watching her retreat. He was. She stopped, turned on her heels, and walked back to Diego—leaning over at the waist to whisper in his ear. "Everyone should have a grand ambition."

In the long half year to follow—a sentence that Diego thought would never end—the sweethearts wrote constantly. When Diego received a letter from Lupe, he held it in his breast pocket, until he could be alone in his room and slowly savor the nuance of every phrase.

At first Lupe's letters were little more than travel guides about the landscape and villages of Morocco, which Diego read with a quiet annoyance. Or, at times, she talked about her many cousins or her ten-year-old brother, Zavier, whom she found increasingly irksome. Those early letters ended with "Your Friend" or "Fondly" or, in one case, "Sincerely," which made Diego drop his mouth in bewilderment.

But, little by little, the letters became warmer, more intimate, and those were the letters that Diego devoured. Finally, on the last line of the last letter that Diego read in the privacy of his room, she wrote "Your Loving Lupe," and Diego leapt from his bed and danced a kind of frenetic flamenco gambol, until his father asked what in the world was happening, and he collapsed on his bed and buried his face in the glorious letter.

Lupe and her family returned to Espejo in late August. As was their custom, they stayed with a cousin in a small house near the town square. On the first day of their return, Diego worked all day with his father, greasing the wheels of the olive wagons, and oiling the mule harnesses. A workday had never plodded along so slowly.

Toward the end of the day, Diego and his father were in the stable. Francisco was seated on a three-legged stool, while Diego sat cross-legged on the ground. Both were hunched over harnesses, though Diego's hands hardly moved across the leather straps. "What time is it now?" he asked his father in a tone usually reserved for funerals.

Francisco shook his head. "It is fifteen minutes since the last time you asked me. You are no good to me anymore, Diego. Go to your darling Lupe and leave me in peace."

Diego leapt from the ground without the benefit of his hands, hung the harness on a peg on the stable wall, and embraced his father. "Thank you, Papa. I love you, but not as much as I love Lupe."

"Get out of here, before I give you a taste of my sabot," he laughed, leaning back and punching his foot toward his son's backside.

Diego countered by throwing his hips forward. Francisco's foot only caught air, which almost sent him tumbling off the stool.

"You will have to be faster than that," Diego taunted, dashing out of the stable.

Francisco looked at Regalo, whose head was draped over a stable gate. "What? You think I do not know? Of course I know. There will be a wedding and then a celebration. And you and I will have to figure out a way to make it happen."

The burro redirected his ears to better understand Francisco's discourse and, deciding it had nothing to do with feed and water, gave a little snort.

Diego ran all the way home. He changed into his best trousers and hurried into the kitchen to wash his face and torso in a fresh basin of water. But when he looked in the mirror that hung over the basin, he scowled. There was a cowlick that sprung up like a rooster's tail from the crown of his head. He wetted the errant tuft of hair and pressed it down against his skull. He examined himself again and smiled, but the smile turned into consternation when the cowlick popped up, recovering its natural bearing. Again he pressed down on the patch of hair, and again it sprang out of place.

Diego's brain whirled through a series of solutions. Then, landing on one, he retrieved a bottle of olive oil from the cupboard. He gave it a sniff, and, it was true, it smelled a little rancid, but it was the only bottle in the house, and he had no choice. He tipped the open bottle over his head, and the oil poured out slowly—too slowly to please Diego, so he increased the angle, which let loose a torrent of the thick liquid. Diego sopped up the mess as best he could with a dishtowel and then, not knowing what to do with the soiled cloth, tossed it under his bed.

He reexamined his profile in the mirror with satisfaction; the cowlick was finally tamed. He put on his best white shirt, quickly tucking the tail into his trousers, and flew out of the house.

Diego was half way to Lupe's home when he remembered the coin purse on his bedroom dresser. "Aye!" he said, snapping his fingers. He hurried back to the house and retrieved the purse. It did not contain a fortune, only three pesetas, but it was more than enough to treat Lupe to a sweet cake and a cup of coffee. Again, he scampered off to Lupe's home, his arms outstretched like a bird on wing to keep his armpits dry.

Lupe's father answered the door. He embraced the young man and invited him into the house. There she was. Lupe was sitting at the kitchen table, darning a pair of her father's socks. A yellow glow from the table lantern fell across her face. She was heaven: her black eyes, her shimmering hair, the turn of her lips smiling softly. It was a scene that Diego would remember that moment for the rest of his life.

"*Hola*, Lupe," Diego said, wanting to say so much more, but not in the company of Lupe's parents and the snickering eyes of her little brother Zavier.

"*Hola*, Diego. I am enchanted to see you again."

"I am enchanted to see you again," Zavier sang out, mocking his sister.

"Hush now," Lupe's mother said, tapping the boy on the side of the head.

Diego bowed to Lupe's parents. "I wonder if I might invite Lupe for a walk on the square. I thought she might enjoy the cool evening air."

Lupe's father responded. "I think the evening air would be very good for Lupe."

Diego grinned.

"And Zavier," Lupe's mother added.

Diego's grin fell off his face. "Yes, of course." He smiled weakly at Zavier, who was playing imaginary maracas, his shoulders gyrating to the silent rhythm.

The three left the house and slowly strolled toward the square, Zavier sandwiched between the sweethearts.

Suddenly, Zavier sniffed the air. "What is that awful smell?" He leaned toward Diego and filled his nostrils. "It is you!" he howled. He jumped onto Diego's back and poked his nose into his hair. "Yuck! What is that?"

"It is nothing," Diego snapped, swinging the small boy off his back.

"No, it is something all right. It is olive oil! Your head is a salad," the urchin jeered.

"You be quiet," Lupe scolded, shaking her brother by the arm.

"Lupe loves a salad bowl. Lupe loves a salad bowl," the boy chanted, skipping out of arm's reach.

When the three reached the café in the village square, Diego had an idea.

"Your talking about salad makes me wonder if you are hungry," Diego said to the boy.

"Yes, I am hungry, I am hungry," Zavier said, bouncing straight-legged.

"How would you like hot chocolate and a big plate of churros?"

"Oh, yes! Churros, churros, churros."

"Good," Diego said, opening the door to the café. "They make the best churros here with extra sugar and cinnamon. You will love them."

Diego would have normally chosen an outside table to watch the people pass by, but that did not fit in with his plan. Instead, he seated Lupe and Zavier at the table in the back corner of the room. Then he walked to the bar where his schoolboy friend, César, was wiping down the counter. He leaned over the bar, seizing his friend by the shoulder. "César, you have to help me."

César was always a bit of a rascal himself, and he was intrigued by the urgency in Diego's voice. He raised his eyebrows. "What did you have in mind, Diego?"

Diego whispered his plan into César's ear and emptied his purse of the three pesetas to seal the bargain. Then he returned to the table.

In a few moments, César arrived with three hot chocolates and an enormous stack of churros, all freshly deep-fried and sugar coated.

"These look wonderful," Diego said. "Do you not think so, Zavier?"

The boy was preoccupied. He had already dunked the first churro in hot chocolate and stuffed it into his mouth.

"Oh, look, Lupe. There is Amando," Diego exclaimed, pointing toward the front window at an imaginary friend.

"I do not see anyone," Zavier said with a mouthful of dough.

"He just now walked by," Diego adlibbed. "I know he would love to see you, Lupe." Diego hooked Lupe by the arm. "We will be right back, Zavier."

The two rushed out of the café and darted across the long square, holding their sides with laughter. When they came to the fountain, they were both out of breath. They sat on a bench on the opposite side of the pool, hidden from direct view of the café.

"When do you think my brother will realize that we have tricked him?"

"Not until he has devoured the last churro."

"But he will be sick if he eats all of them."

"Oh, it is worse than that. I told César to serve a second platter when he was down to his last churro."

"You are terrible."

"Do you forgive me? I had to be alone with you, Lupe."

Lupe blushed. "Yes. To be honest, I wanted to be alone with you too."

Diego leaned back against the bench, stuck his legs straight out, crossing them at the ankles, and eased his arm around Lupe. At that moment of perfect bliss, all was right with the world.

"I am so happy you are here, Lupe. I thought the day would never come."

"Me too. I thought about you constantly. Did you think about me?"

"Oh, let me see. I remember one day last March you came to mind. But then I thought about a much prettier girl, and the feeling went away."

Lupe gave Diego a rabbit punch to his thigh.

"Hey, easy. I am a fragile guy."

Lupe put her fist under Diego's chin. "How would you like a sock to your fragile jaw?"

"No thank you. I like my jaw the way it is."

"So do I," Lupe said, giving Diego a peck on the end of his chin.

Diego straightened up and turned his body toward Lupe, placing his hand behind the small of her back. "I love you, Lupe, and I think you love me."

Lupe tilted her head up, her lips just a breath away from Diego's mouth. "I do love you."

The sweethearts kissed. Both were reeling with passion. Diego held Lupe tighter against his chest, and Lupe put her hand on the back of his head to press his mouth onto hers. And then she laughed.

"What? What is it?"

"It is the olive oil. My hand is full of olive oil."

Diego took Lupe's hand and ineffectively tried to wipe it clean with the palm of his hand. "I am sorry, Lupe. I have a patch of hair that refuses to lie down."

"It does not matter. In fact, I love you for it. I adore that sprig of hair."

She walked to the fountain and dipped her hand into the basin, and, to wipe the excess oil off her hand, she drew out a handkerchief from the hollow between her breasts. Diego's chest collapsed with longing. Then, she turned to Diego and wiped his hand with the handkerchief; he silently watched her work, and thought he had never seen a more graceful and tender gesture.

The time passed quickly. There were sweet exchanges and lingering gazes. Then, Lupe said, "We have to get back. Zavier will be sicker than a dog."

"It will be a good lesson for him."

"What lesson? Not to eat too many churros? Or not to be tricked by your sister?"

"Maybe both."

When they walked into the café, César gave a knowing nod. Zavier was still at the table, finishing up the last churro from the second platter. All three cups of the hot chocolate had been drained. He looked a little green.

"Oh, that Amando is a real talker," Diego said. "Did you enjoy the churros?"

Zavier wobbled his head. His stomach retched, and he quickly covered his mouth.

"You need some fresh air," Diego said, lifting the boy out of the chair.

Diego led the way to the front door, his arm around Zavier, who was holding his stomach with both hands. "Thank you, César."

"Anytime," the bartender said, drying a wine glass with a towel that was draped over his shoulder.

On the way back to Lupe's home, Zavier was groaning.

"My, those were good churros," Diego said, rubbing it in.

Zavier looked up at Diego. His eyes were swimming in agony. And then he threw up on Diego's sabots.

"Not on my shoes," Diego bemoaned, shaking the remnants of partially digested churros from his sabots.

When they had reached the house, Zavier entered first, and Lupe quickly kissed Diego goodnight.

"You might want to wash your head and shoes when you get home. You smell . . . Well, you have smelled . . . better."

Diego pointed to himself in self-mockery.

Lupe smiled. "Uh-huh."

It was a strange thing to Diego. Lupe could talk about rancid olive oil and vomit, and still make it sound like music. He breathed a long sigh of utter contentment and marched home, his arms swinging high.

Diego and Lupe worked the harvest side by side. Sometimes they swatted the olive branches; sometimes they swatted each other, playing their own lover's version of tag among the olive trees. Francisco would smile and raise his eyes to heaven as if to say, "It is all in your hands now, God."

By the end of harvest, Diego and Lupe knew that they would be married; there was no question in their minds. But Diego still had to present himself to Lupe's father and formally ask for his daughter's hand in marriage. It was not a task that Diego relished, and Lupe's father did not make it any easier.

"My daughter is my dearest possession—a gift from Allah," her father said. "Why should I give her to you?"

"Because I will love her more than I love myself."

"Is that wise?" her father asked, convinced that the young man was right for his daughter, but still savoring the moment to make him sweat.

"Is what wise, *señor*?"

"Is it wise to love another more than yourself? For if you do not love yourself, how can you love another?"

"But if I do not value the life of my wife over my own, how can I expect her to love me? And I do not think I could live without her love—not for one day, not for one minute."

"Very well said, young man."

"Thank you, *señor*. It is easy to speak when you tell the truth."

"Excellent. Excellent. You have my blessings."

Both families were delighted with the choice that their children had made. Yes, they were both very young and practically penniless, but Diego was a strong, hard-working young man with an exceptional heart. As for

Lupe, she was not only a ravishing *señorita*, but also undaunted in spirit, something that would serve the couple well in the hard times to come.

There was one bright spot in their impoverished condition. Lupe's parents owned a very small one-room apartment in the Arab Quarter of Granada and, although in shambles, it was vacant and was offered as a wedding present to the young couple.

Excitement mounted as the wedding day approached. And, yet, there was one who secretly disapproved of the marriage: Diego's brother, Francisco. When he saw the beautiful Lupe—her smooth, caramel-toned skin, the sensuality of her mouth, the curve of her breasts—he was overtaken with desire. It was unbearable. Naturally, he could not have her—she was to be his brother's bride—but, more, he was now an ordained priest and wedded only to the Savior.

And, yet, Francisco could not stop thinking about Lupe. He once saw her lift up her skirt and wash her legs on the bank of the Rio Guadalquivir at a family picnic, and, from that moment on, he longed to caress those legs. In his bed at night, he imagined the dark-skinned girl wrapping her limbs around his waist and, with her hands clasping the metal tubing of the bedrail, draw him into her below the crucifix above her head. And each time, when he had come, he would muffle a scream and fall to his knees, begging God for forgiveness. But the temporary relief from God's grace was not nearly as powerful as the pulsating current of his sexual imagination, and again he would give in to the seduction of her call.

Two weeks before the wedding, Francisco traveled from Granada to visit his father and brother in Espejo. One evening after dinner, he and Diego walked to the town plaza. Francisco was wearing his priestly black cassock, which pleased Diego; he was proud to be seen by the villagers with his brother, the handsome young priest. Diego knew nothing of Francisco's secret resentments and passions; he thought of him only as a wise and compassionate older brother, someone to be trusted wholeheartedly.

When they reached the fountain, Francisco laid his hand on his brother's shoulder and spoke to Diego in muted tones. "You know, little brother, that you cannot marry this woman."

Diego half laughed at the statement, thinking it was an awkward attempt at humor. But then he studied his brother's face and saw only a hardening of the eyes. "What are you talking about? I can and will marry her."

Francisco took his brother's arm and pulled him down to the ledge that circled the base of the fountain. "Yes, you can marry her. But if you do, it will be a sin against God and all that is holy."

Diego stared at his brother, completely baffled by his harsh words. "But why? Why would you say such an ugly thing?"

"Because it is God's truth. And you know I am bound by my vows to speak only the truth."

"What truth are you talking about?"

"She is Muslim."

"She is not Muslim; she is a Christian."

"Yes, that is what she claims. But her parents are Muslim—as are her grandparents and her great grandparents before them. Her roots are Muslim; that is not something she can change with a perfunctory conversion to the Holy Church."

Diego's eyes were brimming with tears. "I have always loved you, Francisco, and I thought I knew you, but I have discovered tonight that I know nothing about you."

"Then know this: It was the blessed Saint Paul who said to the Corinthians, 'Be ye not unequally yoked with unbelievers: for what fellowship hath righteousness with unrighteousness? and what communion hath light with darkness?' That is the truth. You must not copulate with this whore of darkness."

Without thinking and without hesitation, Diego slapped his brother hard across the right side of his face. He stood, trembling with fury and grief, and turned to walk away.

Francisco called out to him. "Christ has commanded us: 'Whosoever shall smite thee on thy right cheek, turn to him the other also.'"

Diego circled back and squared up on his brother, who sat upright, offering the left side of his face as a target. "I will never speak to you again," Diego said. "You are dead to me." He turned his back on his brother, took two steps, froze for an instant, and returned to Francisco who was still seated at the fountain ledge.

"If you want my forgiveness, you have it," Francisco said.

Diego was trembling. He slapped his brother so hard across his other cheek, the momentum of the blow sent Francisco to his hands and knees.

Two weeks later, Diego and Lupe were married, not by his brother, which had been Diego's dream for as long as Francisco talked of becoming a priest, but by the curé of Espejo. His brother was not present at the ceremony; Diego did not want him there.

But nothing—not even the condemnation of Diego's brother—could taint the joy of their wedding day. Diego wore the suit that his father had worn at his wedding and, for all he knew, the suit his grandfather had worn. It was a little snug across the chest, and the sleeves were two inches too short, but Diego's father, surprisingly nimble with a needle and thread, let out the sleeves and the back panel, and, in the end, Diego was very handsome indeed.

At the ceremony, the groom stood shiny and bright, a sturdy, straight-backed young man, but his good looks were overshadowed by the radiance of his bride. Lupe amazed everyone. She wore her mother's Muslim wedding dress. It was spectacular: red and wine with heavy gold beading and ribbon trimmings. At her neck was a wide, intricately ornate costume necklace with matching three-inch pendant earrings. Her long black hair was held back with a red ribbon, which was elegantly woven in an impossible pattern.

Despite some whispering among wedding guests that her dress should, after all, be white, signifying purity, no one could dispute her beauty.

As much as Lupe adored her dress, she was even more thrilled with her bouquet: white lilies—her absolute favorite and almost impossible to find, requiring a long horseback ride by her father to Córdoba. When she saw them for the first time, she kissed her father and said that she did not merit so much love.

"You merit more than I could ever give you, my sweet daughter."

The ceremony was distinguished by one other detail: Diego's father served as the best man, a duty he at first protested.

"The best man should be your closest friend."

Diego clutched his father's shoulders. "That is why I have chosen you Papa."

After the ceremony, the entire wedding party, over twenty-five in all, was invited to a dinner. Respectful of Muslim traditions, two fat lambs—seasoned in a marinade of olive oil, lemon juice, pepper, and oregano—were skewed and roasted over an open fire.

There were speeches to be made and songs to be sung and dances to be danced. The guests lingered until the morning light, and, with the exception of Lupe's parents, all were a little drunk.

Diego's father beamed throughout the evening. He had a crisp 100-peseta bill in his pocket. It was an enormous sum: a month's salary for a farm hand in 1935. He had to sell his beloved burro, Regalo, to raise the sum. It was true; he would miss his old friend, but it was a fair exchange to honorably celebrate the marriage of his son.

In the first morning light, when the music and laughter finally began to lull, Francisco hooked the arms of Diego and Lupe and walked them to the burning embers of the roasting pit. The lovers' faces shone in the combined light of the hot coals and the morning sun—a soft yellow-orange hue, so beautiful that it tore at Francisco's heart. He put his arms around the bride and groom, and for that moment the trio became one, like the trunks of three olive trees grown together.

"How I wish your mother could see you now," Francisco said with tears in his eyes.

"She does, Papa."

"And your beautiful bride. How proud she would be."

Francisco took the face of his son in his hands and kissed him long and passionately on both cheeks. "You are my blessed son." Then he turned to Lupe and kissed her. "And you are my blessed daughter. I am the happiest man on earth."

"No happier than I, Papa," Diego said.

"Nor I," Lupe added.

Francisco gave his son a two-handed handshake and slipped the 100-peseta bill into his palm. "This is for you, my son. It will help a little in the beginning."

Diego looked at the bill, and his eyes widened. "Papa, I cannot accept this. It is too much."

"Would you deny your father this moment of happiness? Are you that unfeeling? Did I not raise you better than that?"

Diego gave his father a fierce hug. "Yes, Papa, you have raised me much better than that. Thank you. I am proud to be your son, and I promise to bring you honor."

"That promise you have already fulfilled."

Finally, Diego and Lupe said goodnight to all their guests and made their way to Diego's room, which was little more than a narrow bed on a noisy spring frame, separated from the rest of the small house by an orange-and-blue-striped piece of cloth.

Lupe undid her hair and with the red ribbon attached the lily bouquet to the footboard of the bed.

"These lilies will bless our marriage," she said.

On that early morning, the young lovers silently undressed and explored each other's body with trembling hands for the first time. They took in the scent of each other's perspiration. Diego inhaled the breath of Lupe, and Lupe consumed the breath of Diego. They were two souls, once incomplete, now made whole. They were wind and dune, tree and earth, Christian and Moslem interlaced in perfect peace now and forever.

The days that followed were lost in a dreamy mist of lovemaking and giggles and tussles with sheets and pillows. During one exuberant love battle, one leg of the bed gave in to the assault and sent the lovers crashing to the floor. Even that was funny, the newlyweds giggling as they fabricated a bed support out of a short piece of firewood.

Francisco was in the house when the bed collapsed. He raised his eyebrows and scratched the back of his ear, an expression, all at once, of belief and disbelief and total contentment.

Then, two weeks after the wedding, Diego and Lupe knew it was time to make their way to the apartment in Granada. It seemed to be the best plan. It was January, and the harvest was over; there was no more money to be made. It was true that Diego did not have many skills outside of tending to olive trees. But he did know how to work, and he was sure he could find a job in a city as grand as Granada.

In 1935, there were few vehicles on the dusty road between Espejo and Granada. So, when Diego and Lupe set out with two small suitcases for the medieval city, they calculated it would take three to four days to walk the 138-kilometer route. But on the afternoon of the first day, they were lucky: A trucker with a load of sheep pulled off to the side of the road.

The driver was a jovial sort. He had a dark, round face accented by a thin mustache and a three-day beard. "*Hola.* You two look like you could use a lift."

"We sure could," Diego said. "We are headed for Granada."

"You are in luck. That is where I am taking this load of mutton chops."

The two climbed aboard, Lupe sitting between the driver and her husband.

Lupe noticed that the man was wearing a crisp black fedora racked over one eye. "That is a handsome hat."

The driver ran his fingers around the brim of his hat and then snapped it like ringing a bell. "You like this? This is my lucky hat. It cost me three-days' pay, but I think it was worth it." He turned to Lupe and gave her a wink. "It makes me look rather dashing, do you not think so?"

"It certainly does," Lupe said with conviction.

"You are nice people. I like you. My name is Juan, but all my friends call me Juanito. And, since you are my new friends, you can call me Juanito too."

Diego introduced himself and his bride to the driver. He told Juanito about their recent marriage and their dream of starting a life for themselves in Granada.

"So you are newlyweds. I knew that already, of course."

"How did you know?" Lupe asked.

"It is in your eyes. 'Love is a smoke made with the fumes of sighs; being purged, a fire sparkling in lovers' eyes.'"

"That is beautiful. Did you just make that up?" Lupe asked.

"Ah, that I could be so clever. No, my sweet, those are the words of William Shakespeare. My words are much more clumsy."

"You seem very intelligent," Lupe offered.

"I like to read. Sometimes I read books; sometimes I read people. You, for example. You are in love. When you are in love, you need nothing, except perhaps the moonlight and a few twinkling stars. Am I right?"

"Yes, Juanito. You are right," Lupe said, sharing a smile with Diego.

"Ah! That is wonderful, but is love enough? After all, with time a hungry stomach can speak louder than any declaration of love. Tell me, young lovers, do you have a job?"

Diego took charge of this question. "No, we do not have work. But I am very strong and willing to do anything. I am not afraid of hard work."

"I believe you," Juanito said. "Maybe I can help you. We have a truckers' union in Granada, and they take good care of us. It is the right of the people to organize and throw off the chains of bondage. If we do not stand together, the rich will trample us into the ground."

Diego and Lupe exchanged a look, not sure what to make of the driver's peculiar fashion of speaking.

"Are you a communist?" Juanito asked.

"No, I am nothing. I am a simple laborer. All I know about are olive trees. I am not political. It is not something that I understand."

"But you must understand, if you are to survive."

"That may be true," Diego conceded.

"I will take you to one of our meetings and introduce you to my comrades. If providence is on our side, you may find a job on the loading docks. It is strenuous work, but . . ."

"I am not afraid of hard work!"

Juanito laughed a series of hoots. "Yes, yes, I know that about you already, my friend."

The truck rumbled into the Granada stockyard in the late afternoon. After Juanito had unloaded his cargo of sheep, he suggested the three of them pay a visit to the stockyard foreman, who had a small office on the far end of the docks.

"*Hola*, José," Juanito called out, crashing into the office like a bull out of a chute and draping over a long three-foot high counter.

José scarcely looked up from a stack of papers at his desk. "*Hola*, Juanito. Did you get that load in from Córdoba?"

"José, you surprise me. Have I ever let you down? Of course not. It is not in my character—never has been, never will be. I am a man of honor. My word is my bond."

José ignored the oration. "Who have you got there with you?"

"I am glad you asked, *mi capitán*. This is Diego and Lupe. They have just arrived in Granada, and, as luck would have it, Diego is at this very moment at liberty."

"What does that mean?"

"In the language of the people, it means he needs a job." Juanito slapped his hand on the counter. "What have you got?"

"Yesterday, I had nothing. But today a worker fell off the loading dock and broke his foot. He is no good to me now, and I could use a hand." José looked over Diego. "Let me see your hands young man."

Diego presented his hands palms down. The foreman turned them over and rubbed his thumbs into the calluses. He smiled. "You are no stranger to work."

"No, sir."

"Can you work six days a week from dawn to dusk?"

"Yes, sir."

"The wage is seventy-five cents a day. Does that suit you?"

Diego only earned fifty cents a day in the olive orchards. Seventy-five cents seemed like a fortune. "Yes, sir."

"Are you union?"

"I am nothing."

"Then you are union. Can you start work tomorrow?"

"Yes, sir. I sure can."

"Good. Be here at six in the morning."

"Yes, sir." Diego offered his hand to the foreman. "*Gracias*."

The foreman shook his hand. "We will see if you thank me at the end of the week."

"I will."

"Oh, one other thing. We have a union meeting once a month. You are expected to be there."

"Yes, sir."

When the three left José's office, Diego thanked Juanito for his kindness, vigorously shaking his hand. "I will not forget this."

The young couple took up their suitcases and began the last leg of their journey, a five-mile trek to their new apartment in the Arab Quarter, the Albaicín. The two talked non-stop, excited about the turn of events—certain that it was the first sign of good things to come.

Tired as they were, Diego was grateful that Lupe knew the way to the apartment. When they approached the center of town, she warned her husband that the flat was not a palace. Diego said it did not matter, but when they finally arrived, the setting was even more grim than he had imagined. The apartment looked out on a narrow side street, barely wide enough for a horse and wagon to pass. The doorway was darkened, and the steps up to the third-floor flat were both uncovered and uneven, crackling underneath them at each step.

The apartment itself was a single darkened room, completely bare except for two straight-back chairs, a small wooden table, and a stained mattress folded in half on the floor in the corner of the room. There was no bed frame. Diego unfolded the mattress, and a rat scampered out from its hiding place.

Lupe screamed. "Get him, get him."

Diego flung his suitcase at the rat. It hit its mark, stunning the rat. Diego finished the job with two stomps of his heel. Then he turned to Lupe, who was now standing on her suitcase in the middle of the room.

"It is over." Diego took his bride in his arms. She was trembling. "Shh. You are all right now."

"I am sorry I am such a baby, but I hate rats. I really hate rats."

"I will make sure we have no rats."

Lupe calmed down and again surveyed the room. When she looked again at the worn mattress, she said, "Oh, I wish we had a bed frame. I know that is awful of me. We have so much, but would it not be nice?"

"Yes, Lupe."

Although there was no electricity, there was a potbelly woodstove, a kitchen sink, and, to the lovers' delight, a small bathroom with a toilet and a cold-water hand basin. There was much work to be done, but that would wait for another day. That night Diego and Lupe ate from their dwindling supply of bread and dried sausage and fell into bed, exhausted, but terribly happy. As they lay there in each other's arms, Diego hummed José Padilla's beautiful melody, "*La Violetera*," a tender song about a flower girl from Madrid with happy eyes who enflames the heart of every man who buys a violet for his buttonhole. And before the melody resolved, Lupe was fast asleep.

"I do not think Miguel wants to hear this story," Diego said.

Miguel's chin was on his chest. His mouth was open, and he was snoring.

"Would you like me to wake him up?" Lupita asked.

"No, let him rest. It is not easy being the chief of police. So many naps and so little time. And then there are all those aggravating cups of coffee to drink; the work must be grueling."

"You should not be so hard on him, Tito."

"You are right. He cannot help it. He thinks that the secret to life is following the rules."

"It gives him a purpose, Tito."

"I understand that, but there is so much more."

"Like your love for Lupe?"

Diego smiled. "There is no greater joy, Lupita: to touch the soul of the person you love. I hope you experience that for yourself one day."

"So do I, Tito."

Miguel snorted.

"He must be rounding up the desperados," Diego said.

"I will give him a nudge."

"We could put a fly in his mouth."

"Tito."

"Or unzip his pants and pull his shirttail out."

"I do not think so."

"Or how about tying his shoe laces together and shouting 'fire'?"

"You are cruel, Tito. I think I will just give him a nudge."

"Where is the fun in that?"

Lupita tugged Miguel's sleeve, and the police chief woke up with a start, both feet coming off the floor.

"So, you gave Lupe's brother two plates of churros," Miguel said, rubbing the back of his neck.

"We are a little bit beyond that point in the story, Miguel. But not to worry; I will fill you in on all the details later."

"Did you get to the part about the stranger?"

"Not yet, Miguel."

"Good." Miguel took a deep breath and blinked the sleep out of his eyes. "All right. I am ready now."

THE SHOP FOREMAN WAS RIGHT: The work was hard. Most of the day, Diego loaded sacks of grain and fertilizer from warehouse to truck and truck to warehouse. But occasionally, he worked the livestock—running sheep, pigs, and cattle in and out of the corral—a welcomed job that made him think of Espejo and the olive orchards. All in all, he was thankful for the work and certainly up to the task. In time, his muscles responded to the strain, becoming even more firm and defined.

He liked the other men. They generously shared their tricks of the trade, like how to twist the tail of a wayward steer or lift a 35-kilo sack of cement without breaking your back. Sometimes, over lunch, they would play dominos and joke with Diego about his beautiful new wife.

But of all the men, Diego felt closest to Juanito. At the end of a day's run, the merry poet would find Diego, slap him on his back, and ask, "So tell me, my boy, how are things in Camelot?"

Although Diego understood only half of what Juanito said, he knew one thing for certain: He was a good man with an enormous heart. He was someone he wanted as a friend.

In early February, Diego decided to visit Juanito at his home, who, as Diego had discovered, also lived in the Arab Quarter. It was where nearly all the poor working-class people lived. Like Diego and Lupe, Juanito occupied a small cold-water, upstairs apartment.

Juanito greeted Diego in his distinctive whimsical style. "Ah, it is my good friend, Diego. Enter my humble home, my brother."

Juanito's apartment was dominated by stacks of books scattered on a small desk and along the walls. Diego had never seen so many books.

"I know," Juanito apologized. "Order may be heaven's first law, but here it is chaos that rules."

"You must like to read very much."

"These are my friends," Juanito said, picking up three books at random. "This is Voltaire. This is Cervantes. This is Hardy. I also have Marx and Descartes and Plato somewhere in this hovel," he said, waving his arm across his body.

"How can you afford so many books?"

"I am not married," Juanito laughed. "These are my concubines. They are not as warm in the night, but their words can inflame your imagination. How else can you enter the minds of the most evolved men of antiquity?"

The two men sat and drank a cup of Juanito's exceptionally strong coffee. "If it is not robust, it will leave you hairless," Juanito chuckled, reaching over and tapping Diego along the side of his smooth cheek.

As was often the case, Juanito began talking about his passion for the people's union and the liberty of the working class. "Come, I want to show you something."

Juanito led Diego to his small bedroom and a reproduction of a painting by Francisco de Goya mounted in a narrow oak frame.

"This painting is called *The Third of May 1808*."

Diego had never seen the painting, and he was struck by its drama. It was a night scene; the ghostly skyline of Madrid could be seen in the background. The focal point of the painting was a peasant in white shirt and ochre pants the color of the earth, kneeling before a broad stain of blood. The Spaniard's arms were outstretched above his head, his face illuminated by the light of a large lantern. The heroic man, surrounded by terrified villagers pleading for their lives, was about to be shot by a Napoleon firing squad. Diego thought the man's face, dark with a thin mustache and a mat of curly hair, looked like Juanito.

Diego noticed one other thing: The white shirt of the defender of Madrid was open at the neck and chest. Perhaps the Spanish hero had torn open his shirt, giving the invaders a clear target of his heart.

"The man in the painting reminds me of you, Juanito."

"No. That is too great an honor, Diego. I would like to have his nobility; it would be a heroic way to die. But I am just a simple man with too many books and an incurable addiction to breathing."

"I think it is the saddest thing I have ever seen."

"It is a picture of courage in the face of brutality."

"How can such things happen?"

"That is the world we live in. The French soldiers were no doubt duped by their commanders—convinced that they were liberating Spain. But never forget this, Diego: When tyrants talk about going to war for freedom, the real reason is power."

"It is strange to me. When I look at his face—the man before the firing squad—he looks both terrified and courageous."

"He is a man. Naturally, he wants to live. But he is also willing to die for his principles. In the end, I see him as a man at peace."

That began a new conversation. Diego had an entire theory about the state of peace. The two men returned to the kitchen, and Juanito searched for a book.

"Ah, here it is," he said, pulling out a leather-bound book from a precarious stack of volumes. "This is the first book that I ever owned and, forty-five years later, it is still my favorite. It was a gift from my father, who was a very learned man. Have I told you about him?"

"No, you have not. What did he do?"

"He was a professor of philosophy at the University of Granada. I did not follow his profession, but I did inherit his passion for books; most of these belonged to him."

"Is he still living?"

"No, he is gone now, which is probably just as well; he could never tolerate the kind of political and religious hypocrisy that permeates our Republic today." He opened the book's cover. "Would you like to hear my father's inscription?"

"Yes, of course."

Juanito read his father's dedication very slowly with a kind of reverence that touched Diego.

My Dear Juanito:

Think deeply,
Love profoundly,
Serve completely,
And peace will be
Your recompense.

Your Loving Father
December, 1896

"Your father sounds like he was a great man."

"With the possible exception of you, my friend, he was the most virtuous man I ever knew. He was greatly influenced by this tome," he said, patting the cover of the treasured book.

"What is it called?"

"It is entitled *Pencées* by Blaise Pascal. Have you heard of it?"

Diego was beginning to feel as ignorant as a stone. "I am ashamed to say that I have not."

"Ah, then you will have the exquisite joy of hearing his words for the first time. He was a French philosopher who lived three hundred years ago and talked a great deal about faith and human suffering. There is something that I want you to hear; it addresses my father's dedication." Juanito thumbed through the book. "Yes, here it is. Listen to this: 'All the unhappiness of man stems from one thing only: He is incapable of staying quietly in his room.'"

Diego shook his head. "What does it mean?"

"Ask yourself this, Diego: What would happen if you sat quietly in your room? What would you think about?"

Diego pondered a moment and then smiled. "I would think about Lupe. I would think about my father. I would think about the things that are good."

"Precisely. You would think about the things that are good. You asked me about peace. That is the first step to peace: to be silent. When we are silent, we hear the voice of wisdom that lives in us all."

"And when you hear that voice, what happens?"

"Silence always leads to love, and love leads to charity, and charity leads to peace. That is what I wanted to tell you. For me nothing is more important. It is everything: The essence of transcendence."

Diego repeated the words. "Silence, love, charity, peace." He puzzled for a moment. "I am a poor man, Juanito; I can barely eke out a living as it is. How can I afford to be charitable? I have nothing to give."

"Charity is not surrendering a few pesetas to a beggar and then dusting your hands with self-satisfaction. That is not charity; that is dishonesty. Charity is giving yourself—your talents, your knowledge, your love—to another human being. My father used the word 'service.' That is the charity that summons peace."

That year in Granada was not easy. Many times, the lovers ate only one meal a day. Sometimes, usually on Sunday, Lupe would fry a skillet of paella flavored with a little salt and perhaps a few diced wild asparagus or, after a hard rain, a dozen snails that Diego found on his walk back from work.

More often, their meal for the evening was a simple soup. Lupe would slice and toast a section of French bread. Then she would rub a little garlic over the slices and place the morsels in soup bowls. Over the bread she would pour hot water seasoned with thyme and salt. Finally, she would top each bowl with a lacing of olive oil.

After dinner, Diego invariably thanked his wife and said that she could do wonders with nothing.

After six months, Lupe found work as a seamstress, working from dawn to dusk for thirty-five cents a day. Her work eased the burden of expenses, but the days were long, and Diego thought he saw the brightness in her eyes dim just a little, and that was harder to bear than any number of sacks of grain hoisted on his back and hauled from loading dock to warehouse.

The lovers lived for Sundays. The day was theirs to do as they pleased, and it was heaven. They would sleep in late, but not too late, for if they were asleep, they could not lie in each other's arms and declare their love. Then, too, there was much to be done. The apartment needed to be painted and the loose boards renailed.

They purchased a second-hand oil lantern that, when ignited, drove the shadows to the ceiling, giving the room a domed luminosity. Sometimes, they sat at the table in the lantern glow and talked quietly about their dreams and ambitions. But more often, they preferred to leave the apartment after dinner and go for a long, leisurely walk, looking in shop windows and exclaiming their preferences for this dress or that armchair. Sometimes, just for fun, they called the display mannequins by name, commenting how "Maria was looking a little stiff this evening."

Often, their nightly stroll took them past the Granada cathedral. They no longer attended mass—partly because Sunday was too precious to squander within the cold walls, but mostly because Diego had a stomach full of rancor for the church and its clergy.

On one of their outings, Francisco stepped out of the church as the couple walked past the cathedral. The brothers exchanged glances; then Diego took Lupe's arm and reversed their course.

Lupe's eighteenth birthday was on January 5, 1936, and Diego wanted to make it a very special day. He thought it appropriate that Lupe's birthdate fell on the eve of the Festival of the Three Kings. Lupe was God's gift to him; he wanted to celebrate the day with a wonderful gift for her.

As luck would have it, Lupe's birthday arrived on a Sunday, so they would have the entire day together. Diego had a plan. In fact, he and Juanito had been working on the scheme for over three months. But, to put his surprise into place, he had to get Lupe out of the house; he had an idea for that as well.

All day Sunday, Diego pretended that he had forgotten his wife's birthday. In the late morning after breakfast, he noticed that Lupe was pouting just a little, and he almost gave away the surprise.

Finally, in the evening, Diego suggested the two go for a walk. As usual, they passed by the cathedral—this time just as the bells were calling the people to mass.

Diego stopped. "Lupe, do you miss going to mass?" he asked.

Lupe looked carefully at Diego. She knew how her husband felt about the church, so the question seemed odd. "Yes," she said truthfully, "sometimes I do. Sometimes I miss it very much."

"Why do you not go to mass tonight?"

"Really? Will you come?"

"You know I cannot."

"Then I do not want to go either."

Diego insisted. "I want you to go. It will be good for you. Please."

"All right, I will then. I will see you at the apartment in an hour." Lupe licked the tips of her fingers and tamped them across the cowlick on the crown of Diego's head. It was useless; the hair sprung back like a green olive branch. "I love that tuft of hair."

"See you soon."

Diego kissed Lupe and watched her walk up the dozen steps and through the grand arched door. Then he turned and ran as fast as he could back to the apartment. Juanito was already waiting for him with the precious load protected under a tarp in the back of his livestock truck.

"I am so glad to see you."

"I am glad to be seen," Juanito said with an exaggerated bow, seizing his fedora from the back of the brim and flipping it down below his knees in a courtly flourish. "Do you have the mettle, my beaming lad, to put your shoulder to the task?"

"Huh?"

"Are you ready to go to work?"

"Absolutely."

When the two had finished the job, Diego embraced his friend. "Juanito, you have rescued me again. How can I ever thank you?"

"You do not need to thank me. You only need 'grapple my friendship unto thy soul with hoops of steel.'"

"You mean be your friend."

"I do indeed."

"That you have forever."

Diego quickly put the final touches on the room and then rushed down the three flights of stairs. He sat down on the front stoop and caught his breath. Then, seeing Lupe turn the corner on their narrow street, he leaned back and cupped both hands over one knee.

"How was mass?" Diego asked, trying to sound as nonchalant as possible.

"Very lovely. It felt good to be in God's house again."

"Good. Are you ready to go to *our* house?"

"Oh, I do not know. Why do we not walk a bit?"

Diego could not possibly contain his excitement throughout a long, meandering stroll. "No, not tonight. I am feeling a little tired. Would you like to go upstairs and make love?"

Lupe swatted Diego's knee, and he pretended to be knocked off balance by the blow. "I thought you said you were feeling tired."

"I am, but not *that* tired."

The two walked hand in hand up the two flights of stairs, Diego's heart beating with excitement. When they got to the front door, Diego unlocked the door and then turned to Lupe. "Now, I want you to close your eyes."

"Why? What is it?" she said, smiling an irrepressible smile.

"No questions, please. Just do as I tell you."

Lupe placed her hands over her eyes, as Diego opened the door and led her into the center of the room.

"Okay. You can open your eyes now."

Lupe took her hands from her eyes and gasped. The room was ablaze with candles of every description along the windowsill, around the table, and in every crevice of the room. And there, before her, was the most beautiful oak bed frame that she had ever seen. The arched headboard was over four-feet high with raised molding and a hand-rubbed oil finish. Lupe ran her hand along the rounded ridge of the footboard that featured a hand-carved bouquet of flowers centered on the outside surface. She followed the curve of the raised petals with her fingertips.

"These are lilies," she said, her voice quivering with emotion. "They are my favorite."

"I know that, silly."

Lupe turned and embraced her husband, not just with her arms, but with her whole being. "I love you."

"Happy birthday, Lupe."

"Oh, I love you; I love you; I love you."

Husband and wife stood there in the middle of the room, enlaced in each other's arms, the flickering candlelights prancing over their bodies and across the ceiling. Then Lupe broke the embrace and turned to stroke the footboard again. "But how did you pay for it?"

"I did not pay for it. I made it."

Lupe placed her hand over her mouth. "You made it! How did you do that?"

"With the help of Juanito. He knew of a mill in Seville with discarded rough-hewn lumber. Juanito and I made the lumber work. We planed and sanded every board. Then I carved the lilies. That is why I have been coming home so late for the last three months."

Lupe again fell into her husband's arms. "You are amazing. I love you so much." Lupe took Diego's hand and led him to the side of the bed where they both sat down. "Now, I have a surprise for you."

Perfectly silent, Lupe placed her husband's hand on her stomach and looked into his eyes.

"What?" Diego said, not quite getting it, but filled with curiosity.

She patted his hand over her stomach. "Can you not guess?"

The light dawned. "No, I cannot believe it."

Lupe nodded.

"It is not true."

"Yes, it is true," Lupe said. "Are you happy?"

Diego enfolded his arms around Lupe. "I am not happy. I am overjoyed. It is the most wonderful thing that has ever happened to me."

"Really? And all this time, I thought I was the most wonderful thing in your life."

"You are. And he is too," Diego said, placing his hands on the sides of Lupe's stomach and kissing her belly again and again. "*Buenas noches,* my son."

"How can you be sure it is a boy?"

"I can tell—just in the way you carry him. He is a boy."

Lupe laughed. "Right now, he is only a seed."

"And when will this seed be born?"

"In late September."

"You know that?"

"Yes"

"How do you know that?"

"Just as you know he is a boy: I can tell."

That night, lying in each other's arms, Diego thought about his son and all that he would teach him—about olive trees and how to harness a mule and when to plant tomatoes and how to fall in love—and then, just before he drifted off to sleep, he began to worry about all the things that could go wrong when a child is born.

He was suddenly struck by the weight of his ignorance. What did he know about pregnancies? What did he know about raising a child and protecting him from harm's way? And how does a child learn to walk and talk? How does he become a man? In the darkened room, he was overtaken by self-doubt. What arrogance to think that he was ready to introduce his son to the world—a world that was hard and unforgiving.

Then Diego looked down at Lupe, who was sleeping soundly on his shoulder. And there in her beautiful face were all the answers: All the strength, all the wisdom he needed would rise up from their united, undying love.

Diego was sure that love was the answer. And still, perhaps out of fear, perhaps out of tradition, he whispered a small prayer of supplication.

"Please, God. Let everything be all right."

On Sunday, February 16, 1936, Spain went to the polls. It was a close election, the liberal Popular Front eking out a narrow victory over the conservative National Front. But in Granada the local papers announced the opposite results: the National Front was the victor over the party of the working class.

The people were outraged, certain that the lopsided results were due to threats and manipulation by the conservative political bosses. There were confirmed accounts of people in the rural areas of the province being held off at gunpoint from the polling stations. The working class in Granada voiced their resentment loudly, organizing a protest for Sunday, March 8. Diego was part of that rally.

The demonstration began at Granada's Cármenes sports stadium. Diego had never seen anything like it. Some say there were 100,000 people at the protest, all outraged about the injustices of the ruling class. There were many speakers, but Diego was most impressed with the socialist minister of education, Fernando de los Ríos, who was a popular professor of political law at the University of Granada; Diego had never heard anyone speak so eloquently about the rights of man.

When Diego left the stadium, he walked briskly to a square that Juanito had designated as a meeting place for the loading-dock workers. His friend was already there, along with a dozen men from the stockyard, all of them talking animatedly—pointing fingers at each other and shaking their fists in the air.

Juanito was the loudest of the group, immediately taking command of the small group. He expanded his chest, suddenly assuming the bearing of a man captured by a calling.

"Marx was right," Juanito proclaimed. "It is time for a classless society, a society that tends to the needs of the people. It is by the grace of our blood that the people are fed; it is by the mercy of our sweat that the nation is sheltered; it is by the compassion of our tears that the Republic survives. Our blood, our sweat, our tears. And yet, my brothers, we are treated like common slaves."

At this point, Juanito drew a red bandanna from his pocket and snapped it open. "This bandanna represents the blood, sweat, and tears of our struggle against oppression." He held the scarf by opposing corners, gave it a whirl, and tied it around his neck. "I make this pledge: As long as greed denies our brothers a fair wage, as long as political power undermines our pursuit of happiness, as long as tyranny reigns from the Pyrenees to the Atlantic to the Mediterranean, I will wear this bandanna in protest."

The men cheered and slapped each other on the back.

"Today, you have seen with your own eyes how the workers of Spain can unite. Today is an honorable day. We will march in the streets of Granada. We will rally the people. And we will win!"

There was a war cry of approval, and Juanito swept his arm in the air, urging the men to follow him.

There were tens of thousands who marched from the stadium to the center of town that morning. Juanito was at the front, bigger than life, with Diego marching proudly at his side.

"Are you with us, little brother?" Juanito said, wrapping his arm around his friend.

"I am with you." Diego pulled his shoulders back and marched step for step with the union leader.

Juanito's head was raised high, his eyes ablaze, and what he shouted was what the men shouted: "Equal rights, equal share!"

Diego looked intently at Juanito; his friend amazed him. He knew about his kindness, his fondness for a good laugh, and his agility at turning a clever phrase, but this was something new. He was a man possessed with a vision. Although Diego did not fully understand his friend's passion, he was willingly swept up by its momentum.

Diego shouted as loudly as any man. And when the proud, angry men filed past the cathedral, and Diego saw his brother Francisco at the top of the stairs, he bellowed even louder and poked his fist toward heaven.

At the end of the day, Diego pulled Juanito aside and asked his friend to explain the meaning of the day.

"You know that the Popular Front won the election in February."

"Yes."

"What you may not know is that there is division within the party. And where there is division, there is weakness. There are forces that do not want the Republic to succeed."

"What forces?"

"Forces like the church, the landowners, and factions of the military. These are difficult days, Diego, and if we do not stand up for the Republic, we will be crushed like grapes.

"There is a Kenyan proverb that teaches 'Sticks in a bundle are unbreakable.' That is why we marched today—the farmers, the factory workers, the street cleaners, the shop clerks; we are all part of that bundle of solidarity. We must never give up the fight."

A little more than four months later, Juanito's impassioned words were silenced by the military strength of Franco's rebels. On Monday, July 20, the Nationalist military, as they called themselves—bolstered by the soldiers of the Granada garrison, most of whom sided with the fascist leader—marched into Granada, overtaking the city hall and arresting the civil governor and staff without opposition.

By nightfall, the entire center of the city was captured. After that, if there was to be any resistance, it would be left to the working-class men within the steep and narrow streets of the Arab Quarter who had already dug ditches or built barricades across the roads to stop the encroachment of armored vehicles.

The battle began on July 21. The Republican civilians positioned themselves at the windows and balconies of their tightly packed houses, but they were poorly armed. By the end of the day, many had either been killed or surrendered, which in most cases meant a summary judgment and execution.

Diego and Lupe stayed huddled in their apartment during the shooting. Diego had no weapon and would not have known how to use it if he had.

He had only one interest: Protecting the life of his wife and his unborn child.

Then, on the early morning of July 22, Radio Granada announced an ultimatum. The women and children were to leave the quarter and gather at specified assembly points. The men were to attach a white flag of surrender to their windows or balconies, throw down their arms in the center of the street, and stand in the doorways of their homes. In the event of non-compliance, the quarter would be unmercifully bombed.

"What do we do?" Lupe asked, her round eyes charged with fear.

"I do not know."

Diego crawled to a window and stole a glance at their narrow street below. The women and children were filing out of the quarter. However, there was not a single man in the doorways; they would give it a fight.

"What is happening?"

"The women and children are leaving."

"Should I go?"

Diego paused. It was the most difficult question of his life. "I do not think so. I think you are safer here than in the hands of the Black Squads."

"What are the Black Squads?"

"Juanito has told me about them. They are savages who take obscene pleasure in killing. Their sole purpose is to create fear in the city. They have no conscience. No, I cannot place you in their hands. Forgive me, Lupe; I cannot be sure it is the right decision, but it is what I think."

"Then that is what we will do."

At 2:30 p.m., the bombing began. Supplied by the Nazi Luftwaffe, Heinkel He 112 fighter planes buzzed the quarter and machine-gunned the pockets of Republican resistance. The Heinkels were single-winged fighters with retractable running gear and a bubble canopy. They were sleek, fast, and horrifying. They strafed the streets and squares with bolts of thunderous lead.

The couple could hear grenades exploding throughout the night and even more fiercely the next morning. Finally, just before noon, the shooting subsided, and Diego could see white flags appearing in the windows of the surrounding houses.

"I think it is over," Diego said from the window. Then a moment later: "Oh, God, here they come."

"Who?"

"The Black Squads. They are searching all the houses."

"Maybe they will not come here."

"We cannot be sure of that."

Diego was terrified, and he was not at all sure that he was thinking clearly. They had to hide, but where? With the exception of the bed, there was practically nothing in the room. "Under the bed."

"What?"

"I want you to hide under the bed. They are not going to take a lot of time; there are too many houses to search."

"But if they find me?"

"We have no other choice," Diego said, embracing his wife, who was now trembling with fear.

"Diego, I am frightened."

"I am frightened too, sweetheart, but we will get through this."

"Where will you hide?"

"Do not worry about me."

Diego lifted the sideboard, giving Lupe space to slide on her back under the bed. It was a tight fit, the slats pressing against her rounded stomach. Then, Diego raced to the half-panel door that opened into an unfinished storage space and retrieved their two small suitcases. He stuffed the suitcases and random pieces of clothing under the sideboard of the bed; the camouflage was makeshift, but it was all he had.

Diego crouched at the window. The squad was coming. He unlocked the door and set it ajar, reasoning that the soldiers might conclude that the apartment was already abandoned.

Heavy feet were moving up the stairs.

Diego raced to the balcony opposite the front door, climbed over the railing, and choosing a spot where his hands were shielded by a large terracotta pot, hung like a marionette from the balcony edge.

A man crashed into the house, his bayoneted rifle swinging full circle. He kicked open the door to the bathroom. Finding nothing, he turned to the bed. Then, as if preparing to dig a posthole, he lifted his rifle overhead with both hands. With an angry grunt, he thrust his bayonet into the center of the mattress once, twice, three times. Diego could hear the sound from the balcony ledge, and he was filled with horror.

The first bayonet puncture streaked past Lupe's side, piercing a fold in her dress. She sealed herself to the wall. The second stab hit a slat directly above Lupe's face, and the third sliced just over her shoulder.

For a moment, Lupe thought that she might be safe, but it was not over yet. In the solitude of the storage room, a scrawny grey rat had gnawed his way into one of the cardboard suitcases and nested there. Now, the rat peered out from his disturbed shelter, crawled over Lupe's legs, and scurried along the wedge between the wall and the length of her body. The rodent inched his way over Lupe's neck, stopping to look into her eyes. Lupe's face shriveled in horror; she sealed her hand over her mouth, but could not hold back a gagged cry.

The soldier cocked his head.

Lupe backhanded the rat, and it scuttled out from under the bed and across the soldier's boot. "Shit!" The man jumped back and stabbed at the rodent, ultimately hitting the squealing target. He held the skewered rat above his head and then flung it out the balcony door.

Diego saw the bloodied rat sail through the air and strike the stone wall on the opposite side of the alley. He squeezed his eyes shut and silently repeated Lupe's name.

"I have found one! I have found one!"

At first, Diego thought it was the voice of the man hovering over Lupe. It was not. Another soldier on the second floor was calling out from the landing, and the soldier left Lupe's hiding place and scrambled down the stairs.

Diego continued to hold on to the balcony ledge, but his arms were quickly giving out, and he was afraid that other soldiers would see him from the backside of his apartment. He managed to lift one foot onto the balcony lip and, then, with a last surge of effort, grabbed for the iron railing. His grip held, and he pulled himself onto the ledge and over the railing.

Diego stood sideways behind the open door and heard the soldiers dragging a screaming man into the street. Meanwhile, he peered into the room, making out the pool of rat blood and the sliced mattress, the down rising off the bed from the cross draft.

A moment later, there was a report and a round of laughter from the street.

Diego charged into the room and tore back the mattress. He could see Lupe through the slats, pinned against the wall. Although she was silently sobbing, there was no sign of blood. He reached through the slats and caressed her face.

"Are you all right?"

Lupe nodded, too afraid to speak.

"They are gone."

Diego lifted the bed frame and helped Lupe to her feet. They cried in each other's arms, emotion bursting with both terror and relief.

"I hate rats," Lupe said, her voice quivering. "I really hate rats."

Diego had made the right decision. The men and women who were captured were either imprisoned or placed in internment camps outside the city. In the months to follow, hundreds of them were trucked in the early morning to the municipal cemetery southwest of the Alhambra—a vantage point that offers a commanding view of the Sierra Nevada Mountains and the city of Granada. It would be the defenders' last glimpse of Spain.

The executions were quickly carried out. The Republicans were lined up with their faces to the cemetery wall. The firing squad was two-deep, the first line kneeling. The officer would raise his saber overhead and then, as a command to fire, slash the sword down at his side. Finally, each defender of Granada was shot in the head at close range to ensure his or her death—a mercy since many were not killed by the first volley. Diego and Lupe heard those early morning shots, and they were sickened.

The Albaicín, with its maze of narrow cobblestoned streets and small squares, had become a ghost town. For days, Diego and Lupe dared not move from the apartment. The heat was stifling; Diego stripped to the waist, and Lupe took to wearing one of her husband's ribbed tank-top undershirts. When the heat was the most unbearable, Lupe would dampen a washcloth and pass it across her chest and the back of her neck, repeating the process for her husband.

When they had eaten everything they had, Diego crept down the stairs to the second-floor apartment and took whatever food he could find.

It was an eerie existence: waiting for time to pass in the half-hearted hope that another dawn might dispel the nightmare. The hours of darkness were hellish, their sleep interrupted by the oppressive heat and the echoes of gunshots, sometimes at a distance, sometimes terrifyingly close. The couple measured time, not by the slow steeple tolls, but by reports in the night.

At last, the nights quieted—not all at once, but gradually, like a music box winding down and giving up its tune. Diego became restless. He was haunted by images of his friend, Juanito—a heavy feeling of dread that he could not shake. He had to see him.

"I am sure he is in danger," he said to Lupe.

"And we are in danger."

"Yes, but we are alive. What if he is wounded?"

Lupe could see that her husband would not be dissuaded. "Do what you must do, but please come back to me."

"I will, Lupe. I promise."

"Say it again."

"I promise."

Despite a citywide curfew, Diego left the house at 2:00 a.m. He estimated that he could make it to Juanito's apartment in fifteen minutes. At midpoint, he spotted a Nationalist soldier and backed into a doorway. He held his breath, but his heart was pounding like a bass drum, and he was sure that if the soldier passed, he would be discovered.

Then the rebel stopped and inclined his head, as if trying to remember a detail or listen to a strange sound. He spun around, spotted another soldier, and called out to him the way friends greet each other across a crowded room. He reset his rifle shoulder strap and hurried down a side street.

Diego held his position. Suddenly, he realized that his plan was lunacy and decided to steal back to his apartment. Then, he heard a noise behind him, a footstep he thought, and, looking over his shoulder as he rounded a corner, he collided into the chest of one of three Black Squad soldiers.

"Hey!" the rebel blustered, waving an uncorked bottle of wine. "What are you doing here, you Republican hyena?"

Diego seized the first answer that came to his head. "I am . . . I am trying to get to my mother's house. She is terribly sick."

"No one is in the Albaicín."

"But I am afraid my mother is still here. I am afraid she was too sick to leave when ordered."

"And where does she live?" another soldier asked, his speech slurred from too much alcohol.

"Not far from here."

"Then take us to her. I would like to meet this sick mother of yours. Maybe we can help her."

The third soldier was distinguished by a fresh and badly stitched scar that ran from the outside corner of his sightless right eye, down his cheek, and along the ridge of his jaw. When he spoke, his words were pure sarcasm. "Yes, perhaps she needs someone to hold her hand. Or spread her legs."

All three men laughed and backhanded each other on the chest.

"All right," Diego said, pointing down a long and dark side street. "It is this way."

Diego pretended to take the first step forward, then, whipping around on the rebels, he hooked his foot behind the boot of the scarred-face man and shoved him into the two other soldiers. The man toppled over like a domino, and Diego bolted down the familiar street toward Juanito's apartment.

"Halt!"

A bullet zinged past Diego's head. He started to zigzag, bouncing off one side of the narrow street to the other.

The soldiers were drunk and much slower than Diego, but he still needed an advantage. Running frantically in and out of the shadows, he spotted a loose brick at a doorway and hurled it through a window, hoping that it might serve as a momentary diversion.

Again, he lunged forward, when, almost knocking him off his feet, someone hooked his arm and yanked him through an open doorway.

Diego fought back wildly, swinging both arms at the shadowy man.

The man locked his arms around Diego in a bear hug. "Diego. It is me," he whispered.

It was Juanito.

"Follow me," Juanito said, swiftly closing and latching the street door.

The two men bounded up the two flights of stairs and lunged into Juanito's apartment, quickly easing the door shut behind them. They stood with their backs to the door, gasping for breath.

"You are alive," Diego said.

"Yes."

"But how?"

Juanito shook off the question and pressed his ear against the door, straining to hear the sounds from the street.

"Are they gone?" Diego whispered.

Juanito held his finger across Diego's lips. First, there was silence and then the unmistakable sound of a gunstock pounding against the ground-level door. "Damn. We have to get out of here."

"But . . ."

"Now, Diego!"

Juanito ran headlong to the facing side of the studio apartment. He quickly opened the doors and shutters that swung onto a small balcony. Attached to the balcony railing was a coil of rope that Juanito threw over the side to the street below.

Seeing the rope, Diego looked questioningly at his friend.

Juanito pointed to a bombed-out hovel directly opposite his apartment. "Run to that house! Jump the barricade and hide in the cellar. It is open."

The men heard the soldiers breach the street door and scramble up the stairs.

"Hurry," Juanito said. "You first."

"No . . ."

"Listen to me, Diego! I have to collect some papers. Now go!"

The soldiers were now pummeling the front door. Diego swung over the railing and quickly let himself down, while Juanito rushed to his desk and furiously stuffed papers into his shirt. He then charged for the balcony. He had one leg over the railing when the soldiers broke through the door.

"Halt!"

Juanito froze, knowing that if he moved a muscle, he was dead. Diego, who was now on the ground, signaled for his friend to come, but it was too late. Using his leg as a shield, Juanito flicked his outside hand, motioning Diego to take flight. But Diego did not run—not until the soldiers rushed to the balcony and, seeing Diego, opened fire. Diego dove over a six-foot barricade, a bullet blasting into the wall under his leg. He ran along the backside of the wall, working his way to the street corner, and then circled back to the front of Juanito's building. He hid in a darkened doorway two doors down on the opposite side of the street. Then he waited.

A few minutes later, the three soldiers came out of the apartment, the scarred-face man carrying a lantern, another sporting Juanito's black fedora. Juanito was surrounded by the rebels, being shoved along at gunpoint. His head was bleeding from his scalp and trickling down his face. Watching this, Diego felt helpless and, for the first time in his life, wished he had a gun.

Juanito asked the Black Squad where they were taking him, and the man with the fedora responded by planting the butt of his rifle in the middle of his lower back, which dropped Juanito to his knees and made Diego groan in sympathy. Both Juanito and the scarred-face soldier heard the sound, but it was Juanito who actually spotted Diego in the darkened doorway.

The scarred rebel slowly lowered the lantern to the ground where Juanito was kneeling and snapped his rifle into position. He tilted his head left and right, cracking the vertebras in his neck, and then edged forward by half steps toward Diego's hiding place. Diego pressed his back hard against the door.

Juanito saw that his friend was trapped. "Hey, scar face! Did your mother give you that when you raped her?"

The soldier spun around and trained his rifle on Juanito's head. His finger was on the trigger ready to shoot, and then, thinking twice, he relaxed and lowered his weapon. "You must really want to die, you filthy communist pig."

The soldier spit into Juanito's face and then, intent on flushing out his prey, turned again, moving slowly toward Diego.

"I may be a communist," Juanito jeered, "but your mother loved it when I humped her like a dog."

The eyes and mouth of the scarred soldier narrowed, and in one movement he recircled and belted Juanito under the jaw with the stock of his rifle. Juanito's jaw was broken, but he was not unconscious. The soldier pointed his gun at the heart of his prisoner.

Diego was overtaken by the horror of the scene, his mouth open in a silent scream. At the same time, his brain was spinning. Should he rush out of his hiding place and plow into the soldiers? Could he seize one of the rifles and turn it on the Black Squad? Or should he stay where he was and live another day for Lupe and his unborn son? In the end, he remained motionless and undecided.

"You are going to die, you piece of cow dung," the soldier said, again popping his neck vertebras. "Would you like to say something else before I send you to hell?"

Juanito spat out a mouthful of blood. He tore open his white shirt, exposing his chest, and raised his hands over his head. The lantern light cast a yellow, shadowy glow across his body. There, kneeling before his own blood, Juanito recreated Goya's painting of the 1808 Madrid execution. Diego saw this, and tears pooled in his eyes and streaked down his cheeks.

When Juanito spoke, each word was agony. "Silence, love, charity, peace. Silence, love, charity, peace. Silence, love—"

"Shut up! Enough of your communist propaganda!" The scarred rebel aimed and shot a round into Juanito's heart. He reloaded the bolt-action rifle and shot a second time and, then, a third time. He reloaded a fourth time, but the other soldiers stopped him from firing.

"That is enough, Cecilio," one of them said to the scar-faced man. "Leave him for the crows to peck out his eyes."

In his rage, Cecilio forgot about the muffled sound in the shadows. He shouldered his rifle and hooked his arms around the necks of his drunken comrades. The three retraced their steps, moving away from Diego's lair, the voice of the scarred soldier echoing in the ghostly corridor: "He had it coming, the son-of-a-bitch."

Diego was frozen with fear and shame. His tears were streaming as he stared at Juanito's crumpled body in the lantern's light. "Silence, love, charity, peace," he whispered to himself.

When the Black Squad was out of sight, Diego ran to his friend, dropped to his knees, and cradled him in his arms. He cried in torment: "My God, my God, what have I done? I am sorry, my brother. Please forgive me."

Diego slowly unknotted the red bandanna from Juanito's neck, opened it, and pressed the scarf against his friend's bloodied chest. Then, saturated with the patriot's blood, he tied the bandanna around his own neck. "Now I will fight the fight against tyranny."

Diego heard the clacking of approaching footsteps, and he knew he must leave his friend. He gently laid him down in the lantern light. Then, more by raw luck than stealth, he made his way back to the safety of his apartment and Lupe's arms—all the time repeating to himself, "It is my fault. It is my fault."

Diego was racked with grief. How was it possible that in the same moment one man could be so courageous and giving and another so unspeakably cruel? It was a question that would haunt Diego's dreams for years to come. One thing was certain: From that day forward, he wanted no part of soldiers or tyrants or politicians or, for that matter, any other icons of authority.

Two weeks after the execution, a few citizens began to drift back into the Albaicín. Although curfew was still enforced, life began to regain a guarded sense of normalcy.

Again, Diego felt compelled to return to Juanito's apartment. He chose Sunday afternoon, well within the hours of curfew, and reached his friend's studio without incident.

Juanito's body was, of course, gone, but his blood still stained the cobblestoned street. Diego knelt at the mark of his friend's execution, placed his hand over the dark blot, and then over his heart. He did not stay long in that position; it was too dangerous.

He climbed the stairs to Juanito's studio and knocked on the door, thinking that the Nationalists might have confiscated the apartment. There was no answer, which was a mercy, for Diego had no plan for appeasing marauding soldiers. He turned the doorknob; incredibly, it was unlocked.

Inside, the apartment had been ransacked. Juanito's books—all the wisdom of the ages—did not interest the soldiers; they would have been content with a few pesetas and a bottle of wine.

Diego reasoned that the drunken soldiers had forgotten about the room and never returned. That was fortunate. Normally, such intellectual wealth was considered dangerous to a fascist state and was immediately burned; after all, grand ideas can foment discontent and disloyalty to the regime.

The Black Squad had missed more than classical literature. The condemning evidence that Juanito had tried to hide at the last minute was still scattered on the kitchen table: Republican pamphlets that exalted human rights and denounced the Franco junta as a blasphemy against the people of Spain.

Diego walked into the bedroom. Goya's masterwork was still hanging. Now, more than ever, the painting had special meaning for Diego. He unhooked the reproduction from the wall and wrapped it in a bed sheet. Then he searched the room for one special book, Pascal's *Pensées*, and when he found it, he tucked it under his jacket.

Diego went to the front door and listened. There was nothing. He looked at the room one last time and said, "Thank you, my brother." Then he was out the door, down the stairs, and on his way back to his apartment.

Now it was Diego's time for a nap. "I am tired," he said, his eyes slowly closing.

Miguel was silent for ten seconds, looking first at Lupita, then Diego, then back at Lupita. "Is he asleep? Do not tell me he just fell asleep."

Lupita smiled. "Oh, yes."

"That is not possible. He still has not told us about the stranger."

"That will come. He likes to do things in his own time."

"But when?"

"Do not be so anxious, Miguel. He will wake up in ten or fifteen minutes. What is fair is fair. You had your little siesta; now it is Tito's turn."

Miguel sighed heavily. "I could use a refill, if it is not asking too much," he said, tapping the side of the mug with his ring.

The two walked into the kitchen, Miguel sitting down at the table. Lupita served a round of coffee and leaned back against the sink, cupping her elbow in her hand. When Miguel pulled out a fresh pack of cigarettes from his shirt pocket, Lupita glared at him. Miquel wagged his head, breathed a long-suffering sigh, and returned the pack with a single tap into his pocket.

"You are more like your father every day," Miguel said.

"In what way?"

"He was hard too."

"No, he was like his namesake: happy, passionate, fiercely loyal."

"It is true. Your father was a good man."

"And my mother a good woman."

Lupita stared at the coffee cup and pictured her parents sixteen years earlier, leaving the house to pick up supplies in Córdoba. "Bring me back a surprise," Lupita had called out to them as they drove away.

She never saw her parents alive again.

The tragic scenario that she pieced together from the police report was not far from reality:

It was near midnight. Lupita's parents were on the return leg of their trip. They were lighthearted, chattering about their purchases and the chances for a good harvest. Then, straight ahead, they saw the oncoming lights of a semi-trailer truck fishtailing across two lanes.

"Slow down," Lupita's mother said. "He is out of control."

"I see him."

Lupita's father reduced his speed, but just as they were about to pass, the semi jackknifed and plowed directly into their small passenger car. They were both killed instantly. Ironically, the truck driver, who was drunk and had fallen asleep at the wheel, survived unscathed.

Lupita's father was only thirty-eight years old and her mother thirty-six.

In the wreckage was a package with a small charm of an olive tree on a long silver chain. The words "For Lupita" were scrawled on the little box in her mother's script. At first Lupita could not wear the necklace, feeling that her offhanded plea for a surprise was somehow linked to her parents' death. A year later, on the anniversary of the accident, she released her guilt and placed the chain over her head. From that day on, she wore the necklace in memory of her parents.

While Lupita and Miguel conversed quietly in the kitchen, the stranger was deep asleep and reliving a teenage experience that would become a metaphor for his personal world view.

It was one o'clock in the morning, the second day of a two-day climb to the 14,410-foot summit of Mount Rainier. Tony was only sixteen years old, and he was climbing with his third foster father, Michael, who was a vigorous forty-eight.

On the first day, they had climbed nine miles to Camp Muir and set up their tent for the night. Tony did not think the day's climb was too tough.

It was true, his thirty-pound pack had cut into his shoulders, but he could manage; the day had been little more than a slow slog up the snowfield. The second day, however, would be altogether different.

At the 10,000-foot-elevation base camp, Tony was already feeling a little queasy. He hadn't slept well that night, and he didn't feel much like eating.

Michael, on the other hand, was in top form. He was tall and lean and perfectly straight. He could still outclimb most men half his age, and he was proud of it. It delighted him every time he passed a younger climber on the trail.

The two stepped into their crampons and roped up, Michael taking the lead. After an hour, they were on Ingram Flats, which was considered the beginning of the real climb. At that point they had a choice: To climb the standard route, which skirted an extended rock buttress, or to take the more direct and more dangerous glacier route, which was a mass of ice blocks and crevasses.

"What do you say, Tony? Feel like a man?"

"Fuck you," Tony whispered under his breath.

If Michael heard the slur, he ignored it. He did what Tony knew he would do: He took the more difficult glacier route.

The two trudged up the mountainside, sometimes taking long switchbacks, sometimes challenging exposed ledges. Then, at 13,000 feet, with the wind beginning to kick up, the two prepared to cross a three-foot-wide snow bridge. Michael went first and set an anchor and belayed. Tony followed, easing his way forward. When he was halfway across the bridge, he looked down the side of the ice-blue crevasse; he could not see bottom, and it made him dizzy.

"Keep moving!" Michael boomed.

The boy took another step too far to one side and a chunk of the bridge fell away under his foot. He fell to his stomach and punched his ice axe into the snow and ice.

"I've got you," Michael shouted. "Get up and get the hell across."

Tony pulled himself to his knees, and then his feet, and lunged forward to the other side, but he was done in. He was utterly sick now.

"I'm going to throw up," he said.

"Then do it."

The boy's stomach convulsed, but offered only dry heaves. "I don't think I can make it," he said, his eyes tearing up, not out of suffering, but out of rancor.

"Oh, no, you're not going to cry on me! You've got a little altitude sickness. That's all. It's no big thing; a lot of people get it."

"My head really hurts, Mike."

"So what? You want to give up now? We're just 1,000 feet from the summit." Then he added, with a face of stone, "You pathetic pussy."

The boy shot his foster father a look of contempt, which went unheeded. Tony was motionless.

"For God's sake!" Michael bellowed, slapping Tony's helmet with such brute impact that the boy thought his head would explode. "Get up before we both freeze to death. We are climbing this mountain, if I have to drag your lazy ass all the way to the top."

The boy struggled to his feet, and the two climbers faced the mountain and plodded up the glacier. With each step the boy cursed his foster father: "He will not beat me, the son-of-a-bitch. He will not beat me."

When Tony reached the summit, it was not a victory over the mountain, but a victory over Michael. He unhooked the rope from his climbing harness, fell to his knees, and then to his back. Overhead, he watched the clouds drift across the August sky, and he wished he could be there—sailing, far away from the grasp of his guardian's loveless demands. Then he thought about the descent. He imagined Michael breaking through a snow bridge and dangling helplessly above the deepest crevasse. Tony would fall to his face and bury his axe into the ice. Michael would call out to him. "Help me, Son!" And he, Tony Rossi, who was not his son, who was no one's son, would fumble for his Swiss army knife, open the razor-sharp blade . . . and slice the rope in two.

When the conversation came to a lull, Lupita begged Miguel's pardon and walked to her bedroom to check in on her patient. The stranger was sweating. Lupita looked into the man's face, as if trying to solve the mystery of his life. She watched his closed eyelids quiver and wondered what torment he was reliving.

Lupita took a washcloth from the bedside table, dipped it in a basin of water, rung out the cloth, and dabbed it across the stranger's face. She was shaking her head, when Miguel followed her into the room.

"What is it?" Miguel asked.

"I do not know," she said. "That is the problem; I just do not know. What secrets does he hold? What sadness does he harbor?" Then, looking at Miguel, she added. "I do not know, Miguel, but I do know this. I will not abandon him now."

Miguel started to speak and then, realizing there was no arguing with Lupita, censored himself and held his peace.

Lupita and Miguel returned to the terrace and found that Diego had already awakened from his nap.

"Well, do you want to hear this story or not?" Diego asked with feigned irritation.

"That depends," Miguel said. "Are we going to hear about the stranger?"

Diego widened his eyes. "Yes, *Señor* Chief of Police, but all in good time."

The date was September 10, 1936. In the opening weeks of the civil war, hundreds of Granada's Republican sympathizers—union workers and intellectuals, mostly—had been executed or imprisoned. Cemetery records showed 572 executions for the month of August alone. It did not require much to be found guilty of treason against the Franco regime: failure to attend mass could do it, as could affiliation with a workers' syndicate or communist association. Diego was guilty on all counts, and it frightened him.

He returned to work, but it was not the same without Juanito. His heart was out of it, and he began thinking that once his son was born (he was still sure he would have a son), he would take his family back to Espejo.

One night after work, Diego returned to the apartment and found Lupe lying in a cold sweat on the bed. He rushed to her side and turned pale; her white cotton dress and bed sheet were stained with blood.

"Something is wrong," Lupe cried, her face distorted with fear and pain.

Diego tried to control the terror that was turning inside his gut. He leaned over his wife, brushing the tangled hair from her face. "What should I do?"

"The baby is coming. We have to get to the hospital."

"Can you move?"

"I have to."

Leaning heavily on Diego, Lupe managed to right herself on the edge of the bed. She lifted herself to her feet and, with both hands cupped under her stomach, shuffled slowly across the room to the door. She was shoeless, and Diego remembered the first day he saw her working barefoot in the olive orchard. Those carefree days seemed so far away now.

At the door, Diego slipped Lupe's feet into her sandals.

It was too painful to see his wife descend the stairs, so he picked her up in his arms and carried her to the street. "Can you walk?"

"I think so."

The streets were deserted, as they had been every night since the beginning of the war; it was just too dangerous to be outside after dusk. But the couple had no choice. Slowly, they made their way to the hospital, which was almost two kilometers away.

At the hospital's main entrance, Diego swept his wife into his arms and carried her up the steps and through the door to the front desk.

"Help us! Please, help us!"

Behind the desk was a nurse who flushed when she saw the man and wife. She started to stand, but was forcefully shoved back into her seat with the weight of a man's hand on her shoulder.

That hand belonged to Francisco. "These people are communists," the priest snapped. "There is no room for their kind here."

"But, Father . . ."

"You heard me, nurse. Get them out of here."

"Francisco, I am your brother!" Diego cried, straining under the load of his wife, who was now in and out of consciousness.

"You once said that I was dead to you. Now I say to you: 'If thy brother trespass against thee, rebuke him.' Get them out!"

Diego looked left and right and saw the swinging doors that led to the emergency unit. He moved as quickly as he could in that direction, but Francisco cut him off and called for orderlies who immediately answered his call.

"Escort these communists out of here."

Two burly men in hospital whites grabbed Diego by shoulder and elbow and forced the couple to the entrance. One orderly opened the door; the other gave Diego a shove in the middle of his back that sent him lurching forward. He lost his balance and fell to one knee, but still managed to cradle Lupe.

His mind was muddled. "Darling, what do I do?"

"We have to go back to the apartment," Lupe said, barely able to vocalize the words.

"Yes." With his wife in his arms, Diego lumbered down the hospital steps and threaded his way from one street to the next. "God, give me strength."

Finally, in their apartment again, Diego laid his wife on the oak-framed bed. "I am going for help."

He ran down the stairs and hammered on one door and then the other. "Help me! Help me!"

A woman with no evidence of upper teeth came to her door, took one look at Diego's bloodstained hands and slammed the door shut. Diego ran back up the stairs to his wife.

"We will have this baby ourselves. You can do it, sweetheart. You are strong."

"*Bueno*. All right, then."

Lupe had one contraction after the other; Diego lost count of how many. And with every contraction she seemed to get weaker. One hour slipped into the next and then the next. Between contractions, Diego patted his wife's face with a wet compress, not knowing what else to do. He was panic-stricken; Lupe's eyes vacillated between terror and total exhaustion.

Finally, Diego cried out, "I can see the head. My, God, I can see the head. Just a little more, sweetheart."

Lupe screamed one last shattering cry, and the child was born.

"It is a boy! Oh, my God, it is a boy!" He held the baby in his hands for Lupe to see, but her eyes looked nearly lifeless. Then, cradling the baby in his right arm, he sat down at his wife's side.

"We have a son, Lupe, a beautiful son," he said, kissing her forehead.

Lupe reached out and caressed her baby's chest and stomach. Then, turning to Diego, she smiled and smoothed his unruly cowlick. "I love . . . I love that tuft of hair." Slowly, her hand slipped to Diego's face, his chest, and then to her side.

Diego looked down at her and suddenly realized the light was gone from her eyes. He swept her up with his left arm and pressed her body against his chest. Like a prayer, he whispered into her ear, "Breathe, breathe," but she did not move and then, in a slow revelation, he knew her spirit had vanished. He laid her down, fell across her body, and wept.

They stayed that way for a long time: mother, father, and son. Then, as the shadows grew longer and darker in their little apartment, the baby cried, and Diego knew it was time. Forty days alone in a shed had taught him about endurance: There comes a time when the crying must stop, and the work must begin. It was now time.

That first night, Diego sat beside Lupe, their baby in his arms, and spoke softly to his wife: "We will call him Juanito. He will be a great man, Lupe. He will have Juanito's courage and your tenderness of heart."

On that darkest and most sorrowful of nights, Diego decided that he would never love another woman. In Lupe's place he now had a son, and he would live for him. It was a cruel bargain, but even in his unspeakable grief, Diego could see that the child was beautiful: sturdy and handsome with the breath of Lupe's spirit in his soul.

Diego was numb, sleepwalking through the activities of the following days: the funeral, the feeding and bathing of Juanito, the preparations for his return home. But first, before leaving Granada, he had some unfinished business.

In the two weeks that followed, Diego began rehearsing the job to be done in his mind's eye. He trained for it. Every day, he pumped out a hundred pushups and two hundred situps at a time. Then, he would hang over the balcony ledge and chin himself—twenty, fifteen, ten repetitions in a set. He was getting stronger and stronger in body and mind. Finally, on the morning of the fourteenth day, he knew he was ready.

Diego left baby Juanito in the care of a co-worker's wife. Then, he walked directly to the hospital, through the front door and past the reception desk to his brother's office.

"You cannot go in there," a nurse protested.

Diego ignored her. He crashed into the office and found no one. He spun out of the room and pressed down on the nurse who pinned herself against a bank of file cabinets.

"Where is he?" he asked, his voice so quietly and horribly seething that the nurse shook with fear.

"He is not here."

"Where then?" Diego demanded, glowering over her.

"At the cathedral. He must be at the cathedral."

Diego stormed out of the hospital and set out in the direction of the church. At the same moment, the nurse telephoned the police and reported the incident in detail.

Diego climbed the steps of the church two at a time. As he walked into the sanctuary, he saw a squat, elderly woman enter a confessional. Moving quickly in that direction, he took a folding knife out of his pocket and opened the blade. At the confessional, he pulled back the heavy red cloth and faced his brother. Diego put his knee between the priest's legs and his hand on his throat. He pulled back the knife, ready to plunge the blade into his heart.

Diego's face was stone cold. "You killed my wife," he said, his voice trembling like a death rattle, "you self-righteous hypocrite."

An old woman pressed her nose against the confessional grill and emitted a crescendoing burst of staccato yelps: "Oh, oh, oh, oh."

"Shut up and say ten Hail Mary's," Diego barked.

The old woman straightened up, shut her mouth, and showed the whites of her eyes. Then, the blood drained out of her head, and she slid down onto the floor of the confessional, her chin dropping to her chest and her legs sticking out from behind the curtain like a pair of grotesque link sausages.

Diego tightened the grip around his brother's neck.

The priest was gasping. "Would your wife . . . want you . . . to kill me?"

"Do not dare talk about my wife," he said, his jaw twitching in fury.

"God then . . . Is this God's will?"

Diego recoiled his arm and held fast, the knife quivering in his hand. "I do not know. Maybe you can ask him at your judgment."

Diego froze. A flood of images of Lupe flashed through his mind. He could see her smoothing his hair, swatting the olive branches, stirring the evening soup, sitting at the windowsill, the light on her beautiful face. He held his breath. Then, with lightening speed, he drove the blade past the priest's head, just nicking his ear and sticking into the back wall of the confessional.

"You are not worthy of bloodying my knife," he said, releasing his grip from his brother's throat.

Diego stood over the priest, pulled the blade out of the wall, folded it, and crammed it into his pocket. When he left the confessional, he saw two policemen cautiously approaching him. He stood still a moment.

Francisco lurched out of the confessional, massaging his throat, and seeing the policemen, pointed his finger at Diego and shouted hoarsely, "Arrest him!"

The policemen dashed forward.

Diego turned on this brother and snarled—the priest responding by blinking his eyes, drawing back his neck, and retreating into the red drapery.

Diego leapt onto a pew, ran the full distance of the bench, and hurdled to the center aisle, overturning the pew in the process.

"Stop!"

Both policemen drew out their weapons and aimed.

"No! Not in the house of God," the priest shouted.

The policemen shot a look of disdain at the priest, lowered their arms, and again broke into a sprint. It was too late. Diego had already escaped by a side door and was well on his way into the labyrinth of the Albaicín.

As Diego approached his apartment, he was confident that he had ditched the police and, not wanting to bring attention to himself, slowed down to a fast walk. He smiled, feeling cleansed by the ordeal. "It is always good to go to confession," he said to himself.

Before closing the door of the apartment for the last time, Diego completed one last task. He built a small recessed ledge above the cornice of the street door and on the ledge placed a vase with a single lily. When his work was done, he offered a final kiss from his lips to his fingers to the cornice. Then, with a suitcase in hand and little Juanito bundled in the crevice of his arm, he took the first step of his journey home to Espejo.

Diego sighed and folded his hands in his lap. "And that is my story."

Miguel spoke quietly, as if in church. "Yes, Diego, that is a beautiful story. I am honored to hear it. But you still have not told us about the stranger."

"You want to know about the stranger?"

Miguel mopped his face with his big hand.

Diego turned to his granddaughter: "He wants to know about the stranger, Lupita." Then returning to the police chief: "Why did you not tell me, Miguel?"

Miguel's feet started tapping.

"Tell him about the stranger," Lupita said, taking pity on Miguel.

"Yes, of course. I was going to tell him. I do not know why he is always in such a big hurry. It is not good for a man to be so hurried all the time. It is bad for the heart. Do you not realize it is bad for the heart, Miguel?"

"Yes, Diego," the policeman said with slow exasperation.

"Good. It is important that you know that. All right, where was I?"

"The stranger, Tito."

"Yes, the stranger." Diego rolled his shoulders, and his back crackled. "Did you hear that? It is a strange thing when you get old. Everything snaps and pops. It did not used to be like that. Now, when I pick up a toothbrush, my elbow sputters. Really. I do not think an elbow should sputter. I think it should bend; it should twist, but it should not sputter."

"Tito."

Diego smiled at his granddaughter. "Right. The stranger. Well, as you know, Lupita, September 8 is the anniversary of Lupe's death. Every year on that date, I go back to Granada. I like the long drive; it gives me time to think about Lupe. And, when I arrive at our old apartment, I put a fresh white lily in the vase above the entry door. You know I do that?"

"Yes, Tito."

"Did you know I do that, Miguel?"

"I did not know that, Diego."

"Well, I do. But this year was different. This year, after replacing the flower, I started to walk back to my van. I park it on the sidewalk about a hundred meters from the apartment. It is illegal to do that, but I am an old man, and I do it anyway." He squinted at the chief of police. "You are not going to arrest me, are you, Miguel?"

Miguel did not bother to respond.

"Well, anyway . . . where was I?"

"You were parked illegally," Miguel groaned.

"Yes, I was parked illegally." Diego shook his head. "In the name of heaven, why are you harping on that, Miguel?" Diego clucked his tongue. "It is such a little thing and has nothing to do with the story."

"Tito," Lupita said, lengthening the word into a caution.

"All right, all right. I was illegally parked, if you have to know, Miguel, and I was walking back to the van. Then I heard a scream."

"Was it a man's scream?" Miguel asked.

"Yes, it was a man's scream. Why do you keep interrupting me, Miguel? You make me lose my place."

"I am sorry. You heard a man scream."

"Yes, that is what I said." Diego took in a long breath. "It reminded me of Juanito. The Black Squad soldiers. The rifle butt. The execution. I froze that day, but never again. Never again, Lupita."

"Yes, Tito, I know."

"So, I ran back to the apartment, when I heard a second horrifying scream." Diego turned to the police chief. "And, yes, Miguel, it was a *man's* scream. Anyway, this time, I shouted, '*¿Quien es? ¿Que Pasa?*'"

Diego sat back and looked out over the village. He was silent for a long moment.

Miguel bid his time, chewing on his bottom lip.

Then, as if an afterthought, Diego added: "I made my voice as big as possible, you know. I must have scared them, because when I entered the doorway, they were running down the hallway and out the back door."

"Did you get a good look at them?"

"No, Miguel. It was dark. All I know is that there were two of them."

"How big were they? Were they Spanish, African, Arab?"

"I just told you it was dark, Miguel. How am I supposed to know their ancestry? They did not stop for an interview. You heard me say it was dark?"

"Yes, I heard that."

"Well, I was not sure. Sometimes I wonder about your hearing."

"Tito, finish the story."

"You see, Miguel? Now there is a woman who likes to hear a good story. All right. The stranger was my responsibility. Juanito was my responsibility too, but I let him down. I was not going to let this man down. I bent over him. He was bleeding from everywhere. In the dark, the wound that looked the most serious was his throat. I wrapped my bandanna around his neck—firm enough to stop the bleeding, but not so tight to choke him. I do not know if I did the right thing, Lupita."

"You did fine, Tito."

"Anyway, that is what I did. Then I ran back to the van and backed down the street. I lifted the man into the van—well, half-lifted, half-rolled. He was heavy, and I am not as strong as I used to be. Then, I drove as fast as I could back to Espejo—I probably broke the speed limit, Miguel—and you know the rest of the story."

Diego closed his eyes as though he were replaying the scene. All three were silent for a moment.

Lupita thought about the first time she had heard her grandfather's story. It was on the evening of her sixteenth birthday. In fact, it had served as a rite of passage. On that occasion, it was her father who shared the story, just two weeks before the fatal accident. She could still hear the rhythm of his voice, quietly unveiling the narrative like a tragic love ballad. It was one of her last treasured memories of her father.

With Diego's retelling of his story, Lupita felt, as always, proud to be the granddaughter of Diego Garcia and her namesake, Lupe. For her, it was a noble heritage—one that had driven her to become the best physician that her mind and spirit would allow.

Diego continued to sit quietly with his eyes closed, and Miguel wondered if the old man had fallen asleep again.

"And still, there is the mystery of the stranger in Lupita's bed," Miguel said.

Diego opened his eyes and looked directly at Miguel. "There is no mystery. He is a man who needs our help."

"Agreed. But he is also a man with a history. He, too, has a family. And they must be worried about him."

That made good sense to Diego. "That is true, Miguel. What do you suggest?"

This was the first time in Miguel's memory that Diego had asked for his advice. It gave him a sense of satisfaction. He wanted Diego and, especially, Lupita to know that he was a professional. He rehearsed a carefully chosen question in his head before speaking. "Was there any identification on the man?"

"We found nothing," Lupita said. "We imagine that he was robbed of everything."

"That is likely," Miguel said. "Either that or he is a derelict."

"I do not think so," Lupita said.

"Why not?"

"Two things: his haircut and his shoes. His hair is precisely clipped, a two-thousand-pesetas haircut at least. And his shoes are very expensive; Italian leather, I think."

Miguel could not squelch a grimace. He felt a raw twist of irritation; Lupita's detective work had crossed over into his domain. "May I see his clothes?"

"Of course."

Lupita led Miguel into the utility room. The stranger's shoes, shirt, and pants were still in the sink, undisturbed from the night before.

Miguel examined the loafers: brown suede and leather with wingtip detailing. Indeed, they looked like they could be Italian. Then Miguel noticed the inside label. It read:

Shoes by Dominico
Chicago, IL

"The man is American," Miguel said, visibly proud of his investigative prowess.

"How do you know?" Lupita asked.

"Look at the label," Miguel said, showing Lupita the inside of the shoe. "Chicago. He is American."

"How do you figure that?"

"Deductive reasoning."

"No, Miguel," she said gently, "that is not deductive reasoning; that is *inductive* reasoning."

"What?" Miguel could feel his scalp start to itch.

"In *deductive* reasoning, the premise guarantees the conclusion. That is not the case here. The Chicago label only supports the conclusion; it does not guarantee it; that is *inductive* reasoning."

If there was anything about Lupita that got under Miguel's skin, it was her intelligence. He despised being out-maneuvered, particularly by a woman, and Lupita did it all the time—not because she was haughty, but because she was so darned smart.

"So what are you saying?" Miguel asked.

"I am saying that just because the label says 'Chicago, Illinois' does not mean that the man is from Chicago or even from the United States. He could just be a well-traveled businessman. You follow?"

"*Si, si, si.* Of course. But it is a possibility. The man *could* be American."

"Yes, it is a possibility."

"Ah." A small vestige of his pride recovered with that concession, Miguel returned quickly to the contents of the sink. He drew out a ballpoint pen from his shirt pocket, not because he was concerned about contaminating the evidence, but because he had seen the procedure a thousand times on television. He hooked the torn bloodstained shirt with the pen and lifted it straight up from the basin. Then, spotting the breast pocket of the garment, he nudged the pocket open with the tip of his finger.

"Hmm, what is this?" Miguel reached into the pocket with thumb and forefinger and retrieved a small, uneven piece of paper.

The fragment was bloodstained and folded in half. Miguel carefully unfurled the snippet of paper on the utility counter. It was a note, hastily handwritten in English.

As much as Miguel hated to defer to Lupita, he had no choice. "My English is a little rusty, Lupita. Can you translate?"

Lupita leaned over the scrap of paper and read slowly, first in English and then translating into Spanish:

Anthony,
You were unbelievable.
Savannah.

"Then his name is Anthony," Miguel said and then immediately corrected himself. "I mean, his name *could* be Anthony. It is a possibility."

Lupita smiled. "It is a good possibility."

Diego looked at the small piece of evidence. "We will call him Antonio. It is a good strong name."

"Okay," Lupita said. "Antonio he is, at least until we know better."

Miguel completed his examination of the clothing. With the exception of a neatly pressed handkerchief, disappointingly without monogram, there was nothing else.

Apparently satisfied with his investigation for the moment, Miguel wished Lupita and Diego a good day and asked to be contacted as soon as the stranger revived. Lupita walked the police chief to the front door.

Miguel turned to face Lupita. "There is one other thing, now that I think about it."

"Yes?"

"There is a festival in the town square on Sunday. There will be much to eat and drink. Flamenco dancers, too, I think. Would you like to go with me?

"Thank you, Miguel. That is very kind, but I have so much work to do now. I am behind on my rounds, and I know I will be working straight through the weekend."

"All right," Miguel said, rotating the band of his cap with both hands. "But you have to rest sometime."

"I know. And I will. Thank you."

"*Hasta luego*."

"*Hasta luego*."

Lupita closed the door and walked to the kitchen where Diego was reading the regional newspaper at the kitchen table.

"Has he asked you to marry him?" Diego asked without looking up from his paper.

"No, Tito, he has not."

"But he wants to."

"Yes, I am sure he would like to marry me."

"And what will you say when he asks you?"

"I do not know. I hope he does not ask."

"He is a good man."

"Yes, he is a good man, but I do not love him."

"That is important," Diego said, turning the page of his paper.

And during this time, the stranger plunged deeper into the times of his life.

Tony's third foster family was not easy; his foster father, Michael was as demanding and autocratic at home as he was on a glacier mountain top. Still, he was better than the first two foster families.

The first family lasted only a month. They were Isaiah and Millie McAlister, devout Pentecostal Christians, who believed that youthful rebellion was a sign of the devil and needed to be beat out of the child with what his foster parents called "the rod of righteousness and obedience."

Tony received his first and last beating after literally calling "bullshit," when his fifteen-year-old foster brother said he could beat him in arm wrestling. Tony never got the chance to prove his claim.

"You go to your room right now," his foster father said.

"Wh'd I do?" Tony protested.

"It's not what you did," Isaiah said. "It's what you said."

"Wh'd I say?"

"You know very well. I will not have that filth in my house. This is a good Christian home. Just as Jesus cleared the temple of the money lenders, so I will clean my house. Go to your room right now."

Tony obeyed. He walked slowly to his room, sat on the bed, and waited.

In a few moments, Isaiah opened the door. His belt was in his hand. He spoke calmly, "Drop your pants, young man, and grab your ankles."

Tony was just fourteen years old, but already he was not intimidated. He already had a plan.

"I will if you will," he said without losing a beat.

Isaiah was caught off guard. He was the kind of man who was easily unsettled: afraid to walk in tall grass, because there might be snakes; afraid to leave his car unlocked, even for a moment, for fear of thieves; afraid to skip out on Sunday worship, for fear of eternal damnation.

Tony's surly challenge made Isaiah drop his jaw. When he had collected himself, he said, "You've just earned yourself ten more lashes."

"Knock yourself out," Tony said, unzipping his pants and bending over to form a tight surface across his buttocks.

The first whack caught Tony off guard; he winced and uttered a muted grunt: "ehhh." After that he was perfectly silent.

Isaiah had counted off the strokes. At twenty he stopped. "You can pull up your pants now," he said matter-of-factly. "What do you have to say for yourself, young man? What have you learned?"

Tony stared coldly into his foster father's eyes, who was wiping a bead of sweat from his forehead. "I've learned that you are an asshole," Tony said, "and that you get your kicks out of beating helpless children."

Isaiah's face reddened. He raised the belt over his head with the intention of snapping it across Tony's face.

Tony grabbed Isaiah's wrist with one hand and his neck with the other and pinned him against a five-foot-high bureau. "Don't even try it, old man. There will be no more beatin's tonight."

Tony pushed the man to one side and stared him down. Isaiah's eyes were darting like a cowering animal.

Tony knew he was in control. He laughed. "Don't wet your pants, old man," he said. "Jesus wouldn't like that. You know where people go who can't hold their water. Right to hell, Isaiah, right to hell."

There was a leather jacket draped across the bed. Tony picked it up, slipped into it, and snapped the collar up. "See ya, old man."

Tony made his way out of the house, and walked three miles to the police station. He reported that he had been beaten and lowered his pants to the sergeant on duty to prove it. That was the end of his stay with the McAlisters—one month to the day.

Tony stayed almost a year with his second foster family; it took that long to learn the real story.

Their names were Richard and Kathy Madison. They also had a thirteen-year-old daughter, Lizzy, who was strangely sullen. Tony was two years her senior. When he met his foster sister for the first time, he extended his hand. She did not move. She kept her eyes fixed on the floor.

"She's just a little shy," Richard said. "She'll warm up to you."

Tony looked first at Richard, who had a round, smooth face, his lips naturally red, as if he were wearing lipstick. He was at least fifty pounds overweight. Then he looked at Kathy, a plain, mousey woman, who, like her daughter, also looked away. In those first moments, Tony knew that something was wrong. Nine months later, in midsummer, he learned the truth. Lizzy and he were sunbathing on the deck of the public swimming pool. By then, the two felt comfortable with each other. Tony did not challenge Lizzy's silence, and she loved him for that. So, Tony was surprised on that summer day, when Lizzy took a deep breath and made her confession.

"He touches me," she said without warning.

Tony knew instantly what she meant. He spoke softly, almost whispering. "Who touches you?"

"Daddy."

"In a nice way?" Tony asked.

Lizzy shook her head.

That was the end of the conversation. Tony felt the rage turning in his gut, a rage that was familiar to him. And he thought he would not let that happen to Lizzy again . . . and, by god, not to him.

In a few weeks, he would make good on that covenant.

Tony was asleep when Richard entered his room. When he awakened, Richard was sitting on the side of his bed, his left hand slipped into the boy's pajama bottoms. He was fondling Tony.

Tony's eyes opened slowly. He was not startled. In fact, he smiled—almost serenely. "Richard, give me your hand," he said softly.

Richard looked at Tony with mild surprise and then gratitude. He slipped his hand out of Tony's pajamas and offered it to the angelic boy, palm turned up. Tony gently kissed the fingertips of Richard's hand, turned it over, and lay it, palm down, on the mattress at his side. Then, looking lovingly into Richard's eyes, he reached under his pillow, drew out a pin-point sharpened pencil and with all his force drove the weapon into the back of

Richard's hand. The downward thrust was so crushing that the pencil passed through the entire hand and pierced the mattress below.

Richard bellowed in agony, while Tony threw back the blanket, sprang out of bed, and dashed down the hall, colliding with his foster mother, who had rushed out of her bedroom into the hall.

"What are you doing? Where are you going? What has happened?" Kathy screamed all at once.

"I'm leaving," Tony said, breathlessly.

"Leaving where?"

Tony did not answer. Richard had bounded out of Tony's bedroom and staggered down the hallway. He held his mutilated left hand to his chest. In his right hand he grasped the bloody pencil.

Tony turned and ran diagonally across the living room and exploded through the front door. Richard would never catch him. "Help me!" he shouted, as he sprinted to the neighbor's home and slammed on the door. The front porch light snapped on.

The door flew open and Tony pushed past the bewildered neighbor into the safety of their home.

The next three months were a blur of incriminations, litigations, and court hearings. Throughout the proceedings Kathy and Lizzy remained silent. In the end, Richard pleaded his innocence, arguing that Tony was a troubled and severely disturbed boy, as demonstrated by the "unprovoked attack." The court agreed with him, and he was set free. In turn, Tony would again be processed through family social services. It was not long before he met his third and final foster family.

II

ON THE DARK SIDE OF THE MOON

Tuesday, September 11, 1990

On the morning of the third day, Diego awakened to the sound of soft chords played from a Spanish guitar. He looked at the alarm clock at his bedside; it was already 6:30. He had overslept. He had wanted to be up before sunrise to look in on Antonio. Disgusted with himself, he tore the sheet back and bounded out of bed. He wore only striped pajama bottoms. His bare chest, frosted with white like the Sierra Nevada Mountains, was still lean and firm from years of hard work in the orchards. He snatched the bathrobe that was draped across the foot of his bed and cut a straight line to Lupita's bedroom. He stopped at the doorway.

Lupita sat cross-legged on a chair beside Antonio's bed, her back to Diego, her body caressing her guitar. Her fingers passed gently over the strings, a sorrowful current of minor major seventh chords rising and falling from her classical Spanish guitar. If she knew Diego were in the room, she made no sign.

Gradually, she drifted into Diego's beloved song, "*La Violetera*," breathing new life into the melody with her own lyrics. The rendition was so tender that Diego's eyes glistened with tears.

Do not sleep too long, my sweet friend.
Do not linger in this twilight.
Soon the dances will begin,
Leave the night where you have been,
Chase the music to the light.

The music stayed on after the last word was sung, after the last note was played. Lupita sat motionless, her eyes resting on Antonio.

Diego stepped into the room and put his hand on his granddaughter's shoulder, Lupita responding by tilting her head to feel the back of his hand on her cheek.

"He is still asleep, Tito."

"Yes, I know, my dove."

"If I could will him to awaken, I would."

"I know."

Lupita stood, leaning the guitar against the chair, and then took Antonio's hand. "It is time to awaken, Antonio," she said. "Look at him, Tito. He is in torment."

It was true: The stranger was in anguish. Behind his closed eyelids, he was reliving some horrifying nightmare, his eyes flitting in all directions. His face grimaced again and again, unable to escape the demons of his dreams.

"I can do nothing more for him," Lupita said. "He must save himself."

"We can talk to him," Diego said. "We can let him know that he is safe here."

Lupita smiled. "Yes, Tito, that is good. I did not ask for this, but now all has changed. Now, he is our responsibility."

"Yes, Lupita."

Diego sat on the edge of the bed and looked into the stranger's face. "I have seen torment like this before," he whispered.

"Where have you seen this?"

"During the war, Lupita. I saw this torment, this ugliness in the face of the Black Squad soldier who took the life of my friend, Juanito. Do you know the name of that soldier?"

"No, Tito. You have never told me."

"His name was Cecilio." Diego flared his nostrils for just an instant. "It is not a good name. Cecilio means 'blind.' The soldier was true to his name; he was blind to grace, blind to compassion, blind to forgiveness. He was a man of suspicion and revenge."

"Do you think Antonio is that kind of man?"

"I do not know, Lupita. If he is, we must help him. No man should know that kind of hell. If he is blind, we must teach him to see again."

Diego looked again into Antonio's face, deep into his face, like a man searching for light at the end of a black hole of despair: deeper and deeper, beyond the skin, behind the eyes, and into the dark passages of his soul.

Anthony was hunched over his desk, poring over the firm's weekly progress reports. With his left hand he massaged his temple, while marking in red the passages that disturbed him: delays, overruns, material shortages, the kind of setbacks that his managers tried to bury in oblique rhetoric. The ploy was futile; the snags never got past Anthony.

"No, you son-of-a-bitch," he said, slashing his pen under an evasive phrase.

Anthony straightened his back and swiveled his chair around to gaze over the Parisian skyline, accented by the Eiffel Tower to the northwest. It was a spectacular cityscape, viewed from his 52nd-floor corner office atop *La Tour Montparnasse*, but on this night the vista was wasted on him. He neither had the time nor the inclination to be seduced by the city of light. The sun was beginning to set. He looked at his watch. "Damn." It was 7:45. Monique was expecting him in fifteen minutes. He turned back to his desk and gathered the layers of scattered papers.

Then it happened—not all at once, but slowly, listlessly like a reluctant dream. It was the scent of something strange that he noticed first. He sniffed the air. What was it? There was something familiar about it—like an old melody just out of reach—but whatever it was, it was not friendly. The odor—pungent and dank—filled him with dread.

He searched the room: the long bank of floor-to-ceiling windows, the wet bar, the solid oak entry door, the brass coffee table and cluster of over-stuffed chairs. There was nothing out of the ordinary, and yet . . . he held his breath for a moment, listening for something: a clue, a piece of logic, something he could wrap his mind around.

Then his eyes flashed back to his office door. My God, what was that? A thread of black smoke spiraled out from the center of the door. And then the smoke undid itself, passing back through the door. Anthony stared at the oak entry that was now normal again. He felt a dull, indescribable spasm in his gut. Then, with the eerie sense that there was someone lurking over his shoulder, Anthony slowly turned and looked out his window. The city was gone! He lurched for the window and pressed his face to the glass. There was nothing, only blackness.

Anthony turned, rushed to the door, and flung it open. In the next instant, his body convulsed, and a scream leapt from his throat. There, standing before him was a specter of a man in a black, tattered military coat and muddied boots, his face a frightening mass of lines and ridges. A fresh, raised scar ran from his right eye and across his hollowed cheek. His right eye was blind and encrusted with a white, opaque, glistening glaze.

The unwelcome guest was not standing where he should be—in the secretary's adjoining office; that room had disappeared. He was standing at ease in a narrow, smoke-filled, cobble-stoned street, bordered by bombed-out apartments, a fallen beam, and the word "*CERDO*"—pig— scrawled in red letters across an unhinged door.

"Wha . . . what?" Anthony stammered. "What's going on? Who the hell are you?"

The specter moved forward, backing Anthony into the front of his desk. His face hovered over his captive, and when he opened his mouth to speak, Anthony got a strong whiff of his breath. It was, again, that vague odor that now registered in his mind: the scent of dust.

"I am Cecilio," the specter said in a broad Spanish accent. "Who the hell are you?"

"I am Anthony Rossi, the president and CEO of Transnational Management Services, and you are trespassing." His words were haughty, but his voice was trembling. "I'm calling security now," he said, reaching for his phone.

Without taking his eyes off Anthony, the specter slammed the back of his hand into the phone, sending it flying across the room. "*Cállate*, you piece of cow dung. Shut up and sit down."

Anthony edged around the desk and took his seat, sitting slowly, as if the chair were wired to explode. His hands wrapped like claws around the ends of the armrests.

The specter hoisted himself onto Anthony's desk and crouched with his feet set flat and at shoulder's width, his elbows pressed against the inside of his knees. "You are not in command now, cow dung." The phantom soldier unsheathed a bayonet from his belt and pressed the tip of the blade under the chin of his victim, twisting the blade a quarter turn like setting a screw. A single drop of blood suspended from the puncture like a hanging bat and then fell languidly to the desk. The droplet splattered across a ledger of numbers, the dark stain connecting the red underlines from Anthony's pen.

"Okay, listen," Anthony said, very slowly, very methodically, "I can give you whatever you want. I am a very wealthy man."

The specter's face clenched as if he had just caught the stench of something rotting. He leaned over Anthony's face and yawned. A single fly escaped from the soldier's gaping throat, encircled Anthony's head—once, twice—and then flew into the mogul's mouth. Anthony gagged on the fly and swallowed it.

"You think I want your money, cow dung? I do not want your money; I want your soul, pathetic as it is." Then the specter whooped a laugh of scorn, and when he was through, he tilted his head left and right, popping the vertebras in his neck.

"My soul is not for sale," Anthony managed to say, the blade still under his chin.

"Really? I thought you had sold it years ago."

"No, I have not sold my soul. I have not."

The specter sheathed his bayonet. "Well, we will see about that. You and I are going on a little trip."

"What are you talking about?"

"You will see."

In that instant, man and ghost were engulfed in a helix of smoke that rose and vanished, and the office was void.

Anthony was outside his body now, staring down through his own eyes at himself. He—the Anthony he was watching—was sitting at a control panel in a room dimly illuminated by three banks of monitors, dominated by a massive central screen.

"I believe you know where you are," the specter said at his side.

"Yes. That is the security surveillance room."

"Is that what you call it? It is the 'peeping room.' You peep on your own wife, no?"

Anthony was silent, consumed by his own image. He watched the Anthony below, who leaned over the control panel and studied his wife, Penelope, like a lecher ogling a schoolgirl:

Penelope was sitting sprawled in her favorite overstuffed armchair. She was wearing a crimson evening gown that reveled her bare shoulders. She was still seductive, despite her approaching fortieth birthday.

"I thought they would never leave," Penelope said, kicking off her high-heeled shoes and lifting her feet onto the ottoman. Her dress fell to either side, revealing her firm calves and lower thighs. "My feet are killing me," she said.

"Who is she speaking to?" the specter asked.

"Hennessy Duncan."

"And he is?"

Anthony scoffed. "My oldest friend and business partner. He was the best man in my wedding."

"You have known him long?"

Anthony felt strange. Normally, he would not respond to personal questions. But the ghostly intruder was no ordinary inquisitor. Anthony felt obliged—no, *compelled* to respond. "All my life. He has always followed me. When I played baseball, he followed. When I sailed, he followed. When I switched majors from chemical engineering to construction management, he followed. And when I said we should go into business together and open an office in Paris, he trailed along like a puppy. But Hennie is like that: He's soft."

"Maybe not as soft as you think. He also seems to be following after your wife," the specter said, sardonically. "But you had nothing to do with that, of course."

The two night visitors returned to the scene unfolding in the surveillance control room.

Anthony sneered at the screen. He glared at Hennessy, who looked longingly at Penelope, his hands hanging limply at his sides, his rimless glasses tacked to his round face like translucent shutters.

Anthony pointed his finger at the screen. "You bastard."

Hennessy sucked his teeth and sat down on the ottoman. He took Penelope's feet in his hands, placed them on his lap, and began massaging her arches.

Anthony heard something he could not quite make out. He twisted the knob on the master volume control. Hennessy was humming "Singing in the Rain."

Penelope closed her eyes and settled deeper into her easy chair. She had a sensual smile on her lips, as if she were soaking in a hot tub. "Umm, you read my mind."

After a moment, Hennessy moved his hands up Penelope's calves, beginning high and pulling his hands slowly down each calf muscle.

Anthony zoomed in on his wife's face and shoulders. She actually shivered.

"Oh, this is heaven," Penelope moaned. "If you stop, I'll kill you."

"Do we have to watch this?" Anthony asked the specter.

"Are you not enjoying it? Do you not see how much your partner adores your wife?"

"Yes, I do see that, and I can't stand it."

"All right, then. We will watch something else. This is the best part anyway."

The Paris city lights from the window on the far side of the bedroom fell across the old English four-poster bed. The spread and duvet had been thrown back. Penelope was propped up against three or four pillows, the light cascading over her body. She wore a black, lacy corset with garters and textured nylons, the latter replete with a border of frill along the top edge. She had stepped back into her heels, and, with one leg bent and the other fully extended, she looked like the picture of desire. Anthony's face hardened.

In the next moment, Hennessy lunged into Penelope's arms.

"Easy, sailor. Let's not break the merchandise."

Hennessy bolted straight up and smoothed his hair. "No, of course not. I'm sorry. I'm really sorry."

Penelope slipped Hennessy's glasses off his nose and tossed them to the nightstand. "Stop saying you're sorry and kiss me, you big doofus."

Their lips were sealed, and Hennessy blindly began unlacing the front of Penelope's corset, but he was all thumbs and in frustration gave one of the laces a vicious tug, which actually cinched the corset a notch tighter."

"Wrong lace, cowboy," Penelope said from the corner of her mouth, their lips still interlocked.

Hennessy broke the kiss and turned all his attention to the lace, but it was now impossibly knotted. He picked at the jumble of string, then gnawed at it, then in desperation squeezed Penelope's breasts together, thinking they might pop out of the cursed cladding. They did not, and, as the next best thing, Hennessy fell back to his strategy of cluster kissing.

"Please, whoever you are, no more."

"But you enjoy watching them."

"I don't. I don't enjoy watching them at all."

"Do not lie to me, Anthony," the specter said with venom in his tone. "I know you. I know everything about you. You watched them for months. Do you not remember this scene three months later?"

Hennessy and Penelope were sitting side by side in the four-poster, a sheet over their legs and hips, their torsos naked.

"This is crazy," Hennessy said.

"What are you worried about? He's with his mistress; he's always with his mistress."

"You don't know that. You don't even know if he has a mistress." Suddenly, Hennessy sat straight up, cocking his head like a dog on watch. "What was that!" he whispered.

"It's nothing," Penelope said offhandedly.

Hennessy stared quizzically at Penelope. "You act like you want to get caught."

"Would it be so terrible? Wouldn't you like to drop the deception and get on with our lives? Besides, what if he does come? You told me yourself you have a plan if he surprises us. You brought a set of blueprints, remember? You're here to talk about business."

"Yeah, sure, business, but not from his bed. Just how long do you think it would take to jump out of bed and get dressed?"

"Relax, Hennie. It's not going to happen."

The specter clutched Anthony by the shoulder. "Now watch this," he said with a hollow laugh. "This is pure inspiration."

"I've had enough."

"No, no, no. You will see how much you enjoy this."

Anthony picked up the telephone handset at the control panel and dialed his home number. On the first ring Hennessy leapt straight up off the bed. When he came down, his feet were tangled in the sheets, and he tumbled to the floor banging his head on the sideboard. He stifled a cry of pain and bounded toward the side chair where his pants were slung over the back. In his rush he stubbed his big toe into the nightstand, causing him to dance on one foot, again stifling the urge to holler out in agony.

On the second ring, he reached again for his pants. In the process, he bumped the lamp on the nightstand, and the lamp rocked and then ultimately tipped over. Hennessy reached out with one hand to catch the lamp, but his grip was tenuous, so he tossed the lamp into the air to give himself a split second to grab the light with both hands.

On the third ring, the electrical cord came taut and the lamp stopped in midair and reversed directions. Because the perimeter of the bedroom floor was tile and the base of the lamp porcelain, Hennessy had no choice but to cushion the fall of the lamp with his foot. The table lamp came down at an angle and landed squarely on the big toe that Hennessy had stubbed only seconds earlier. With that, the nervous lover was now spinning on one foot and silently cursing.

Penelope was shushing him, as she picked up the receiver. "Hello."

"Hello, sweetheart, it's me."

"Hi, Anthony," Penelope said without a flicker of concern.

Hennessy was holding his head with the heels of his hands.

Penelope reached out to Hennessy, grabbed him by the wrist and pulled him back into her bed.

Hennessy mouthed, "What are you doing?"

Penelope silenced him by kissing him on the lips.

"What was that?" Anthony asked.

"Oh, nothing," Penelope said. "I'm just watching a little TV."

"Really, what are you watching?"

"Oh, it's one of those old French movies I like."

"Which one?"

"I don't remember. Something with Jean Gabin, I think. He kills someone, but he has good reason."

"Le Jour Se Lève?"

"Yes, I think that's it: Le Jour Se Lève.*"*

"Do you think murder is ever justifiable?"

"Maybe. Maybe I do," Penelope said, putting her hands between Hennessy's legs.

Hennessy groaned despite his panic.

"What's happening now?"

"The murder scene. It's wonderful."

"You have a sadistic side to you, Nel."

"Do you think so?" Penelope asked, turning over onto Hennessy, pinning him under her body.

Hennessy's face was transforming from agony to desperation to frenzy.

Penelope was now riding him, one hand holding the phone, the other on Hennessy's chest. For his part, Hennessy was too terrified to be aroused.

"Oh, yes," Anthony said, "there is something very sadistic about you."

"Really. Why would you say that?"

Then, regardless of his fears, Hennessy was beginning to slowly writhe under Anthony's wife. Penelope responded with a gasp and quickly cupped her hand over the telephone mouthpiece.

Suddenly, Anthony no longer wanted to play the game. He whispered into the phone: "You are a bitch."

Penelope stopped moving. "Me? I'm a bitch?" she asked, cool as a street prostitute negotiating a fee.

When Hennessy heard that, his eyes popped open; brutally awakening him from his desire, he rolled out from under Penelope and tumbled to the floor.

"Goodbye, Anthony," Penelope said, hanging up the receiver with a firm click.

Hennessy was already zipping up his pants.

"Where are you going?" Penelope asked. "We have unfinished business."

"I'm sorry, I can't do this. It's driving me crazy."

Penelope smirked. "You big baby. Think about it: You're letting yourself be scared off by a telephone call."

"He knows, Penelope. Can't you see, he knows?"

"He knows nothing. He is too consumed by his own world to know anything about mine."

Hennessy was seated on the side chair lacing up his shoes. "Sorry, Penelope. You can't shame me out of this. I'm calling it a night." He grabbed his suit jacket, pecked Penelope on the lips, and was gone.

Anthony switched cameras, following his partner into the living room. In his haste Hennessy forgot to retrieve the blueprints from the coffee table.

Anthony smiled.

Anthony and the specter were back in Anthony's office. The ghost was looking out the window at pure darkness where Paris should have been. Anthony was again at his desk.

"What is this all about?" Anthony asked.

The specter responded with his own question. "Are you familiar with Goya's painting, *The Third of May 1808*?"

"Yes, of course."

"That painting was the beginning of the end for Goya. He was not a happy man. He was embittered by the war against Napoleon, embittered by the inhumanity of man. The paintings that followed were black and full of terror and death."

"What does that have to do with me?"

"Shut up. You do not have the right to speak. You have no merit. You are the commander of a Napoleon firing squad."

"I do have merit. I am the president of . . ."

The specter opened his mouth and the sound of all the torment of hell exploded into the room. It was horrific and deafening, and Anthony clapped his hands over his ears.

"Look at your hands, Anthony."

Anthony slowly lowered his hands from his ears and held them before his eyes. The knuckles of his hands slowly mutated, becoming cracked and gnarled with blotches of red rashes and brown liver spots creeping like oozing blood across his skin. They were the hands of a man a century old. He tried to stand, but his body was no longer youthful; it was torture to lift himself out of his chair and walk to the window that now reflected his image.

Anthony screamed with horror. The skin of his face hung from his skull like frayed linen. His eyes—streaked with blue and red veins—bulged from their sockets. His teeth were yellow and black with rot.

"Do not tell me who you are, cow dung. You are nothing. You are a sack of garbage. Even less, you are dust in the wind."

And then, before his eyes, Anthony's skin peeled off his face. First there was raw flesh, then bones, then his skull dissolving into dust and maggots. Then there was nothing—nothing but the sound of his scream.

Antonio's piercing cry shattered the silence of Diego's home. It was a scream from another world, so horrific that both Diego and Lupita were, for a moment, paralyzed with terror. For one instant, Lupita stood rigid, staring at Antonio, a man possessed, his legs thrashing, his back arched, his face contorted in unearthly panic.

"Tito, help me," she cried, throwing her body over Antonio's chest. "Hold down his legs."

Diego leapt onto the bed and straddled Antonio's legs.

Lupita began speaking softly to Antonio. "It is all right, Antonio. You are safe. You are with friends. We will take care of you. Hush now. You are home."

Very slowly, Antonio began to relax. His breathing was still heavy, but he was less agitated. The more Lupita spoke to him, the calmer he became.

"If he does that again," Diego said, "he will tear out his stitches."

"It is too late. They are already torn."

It was true. In fact, blood was seeping into the gauze at his neck and shoulder. For the next two hours, Lupita meticulously repaired the damage, Diego serving as his daughter's scrub nurse.

When it was done, Lupita did something that surprised Diego. She leaned over her patient and kissed him on both cheeks. "Rest now, Antonio. And when you awaken, you will be with family."

Diego smiled. "Did you mean that, Lupita? Did you mean it when you said he would be with family?"

Lupita sat down on her grandfather's lap and put her arms around his neck. "Yes, Tito, I meant it. This man is in torment. He is a man who needs a family right now, this very moment. He has chosen us, and now we have chosen him."

"*We* have chosen him?" Diego said with a wry smile.

"Did I not speak the truth?"

"Yes, my dove, you speak the truth."

Lupita kissed her grandfather on his forehead and returned to her patient. "He is calmer, now, but he is still dreaming. He is still battling his demons." Then, slowly, as if tending to a sleeping baby, Lupita bent over Antonio and whispered in his ear. "Do not worry, Antonio; I am here."

Anthony was still standing at the mirrored window, but he was calm now. His head was down, his arms at his sides, his breathing slow and even. He slowly raised his head, afraid of what unspeakable hideousness he might discover reflected in the glass. It was his face, and with trembling hands he passed his fingertips over his mouth and cheeks and eyes to confirm his existence. "Thank God."

"God had nothing to do with it."

Anthony's head and shoulders dropped in despair. It was the voice of the intruder. Anthony turned around and was greeted by the ghost who, as if seated in a chair, but not in a chair, was suspended in midair above his desk.

Anthony was less frightened. He had already become acquainted with the phantom's sorcery. "What do you mean?"

"Your salvation is not an offering of divine intervention. It is not celestial; it is not that complicated. Your salvation is the consequence of a simple gift: human love."

"I don't understand."

"Of course, you don't understand. You are too calloused to understand. Sit down, cow dung."

Anthony returned to his desk chair, while the specter floated down, crouching again on the desktop like a vulture waiting for the slow death of an animal to scavenge.

"Shall we talk about Monique Ducros?"

Anthony went silent.

"I said, shall we talk about Monique?"

"I have nothing to say."

The specter offered a simpering smile. "Really? Well, it does not matter. You need not say anything. I know it all anyway: She is a beautiful French woman, only twenty-seven years old. How old are you, cow dung?"

Anthony mumbled something incomprehensible.

"I do not hear you. Speak up."

"I am forty-five."

"Yes. You are forty-five. And you have made this sweet child your mistress."

"She's of age."

The specter roared: "Shut up, maggot!"

Anthony cowered into his chair.

"I think I prefer your silence. Whenever you speak, it hurts my ears. No, I am bored with you. We will pay Monique a visit instead."

The journey in time began again. This time Anthony and the specter were transported in a funnel of fog to Monique's apartment, looking down on it through an open ceiling like crows on a wire.

The room was dimly lit. The dining table was exquisitely set with white tablecloth, long-stem candles, and salad plates centered perfectly over dinner plates.

Monique sat morosely in the darkened room, embracing a cushion pressed to her stomach. Even in her misery, she was an extraordinary beauty. Her long blond hair was held back away from her face to accent her high cheekbones. She wore a gypsy skirt and a belted chocolate-brown blouse slit provocatively to her sternum.

Monique looked at the wall clock. It was eleven o-clock.

The doorbell rang.

She waited a moment and then stood, smoothed her dress, and strode to the front door. Before she had reached the entryway, the doorbell sounded again.

"Oh là, qui est pressé maintenant? *Who's in a hurry now?" she said to herself.*

Monique opened the door. Anthony Rossi was leaning against the door jam, his legs crossed, and a bottle of red wine tucked under one arm. In his dark navy suit and solid silver tie, he cut a handsome figure, and he knew it.

"You are so full of yourself," the specter said.

The prisoner said nothing. He stared sadly at the scene, knowing what was to come.

Anthony leaned forward, intending to kiss his mistress on the mouth.

Monique countered by welcoming Antonio, not as a lover, but as a friend: In Parisian fashion, she offered four polite, cheek-to-cheek kisses, making the kissing sound, but never allowing her lips to touch his cheeks. Anthony despised the custom—"air kisses," he called them; at a French cocktail party it could take ten minutes to greet a half-dozen women.

Although unamused, Anthony ignored the rebuke for the time being. "Would you like some company, little girl?" he asked, still standing at the threshold.

"Absolutely not," Monique said, her warm eyes belying the disdain in her voice. She lightly swung the door closed and walked back into the apartment.

Anthony stopped the door with his shoulder. "Well, that's okay," he said, "because I want your company, and what is good for me is, by definition, good for you."

"I know that is what you are thinking, but thinking it does not making it so," she said, straining her English syntax.

Monique sat on the couch and patted the cushion next to her, an invitation to Anthony to sit down beside her.

"Look at that," the specter said. "She should be furious, and, yet, she still welcomes you. How does that make you feel, cow dung?"

Anthony spoke coldly. "It disgusts me."

"What disgusts you?"

Anthony turned to the specter. "Her sweetness, her long-sufferance, her compliance. It all disgusts me."

"I see. Let me show you what disgusts *me*."

The specter took Anthony's head in his hands and directed his face to the scene playing out below them.

"Let's put some light on the subject," Anthony said, switching on a table lamp. Then, he swaggered into the kitchen, found a corkscrew, and uncorked the bottle of wine. In a moment, he returned with two goblets of Bordeaux. He sat down beside Monique, offering her a glass.

"I offer a toast," he said, lifting his glass. "To the most beautiful woman in the world."

Suddenly, Monique was *angry. "Beautiful," she said, "but not important enough for you to be here* à l'heure*—on time."*

"I'm sorry, Monique; it could not be helped."

"Ça va pas. *That's not good enough, Anthony."*

Anthony was surprised by this display of defiance, and he didn't like it. He pulled on his jaw, his eyes unfocused in space. "Don't do this, Monique."

His voice was menacing, the tone saying that there would be a hard price to pay if she continued.

She ignored the warning. "Do not make what?" she questioned, translating straight from the French.

"Do not be makING zee trouble," he said, mocking her French accent.

"What are you saying? Que veux-tu dire? *Do not be irritated that you are three hours late and did not bother to call? Or do not be upsetting about a dinner I spent hours to prepare, a dinner that is now garbage? Or maybe you mean I should not be angry when you treat me like a 100-franc* prostituée.*"*

"Is that what I'm paying you?" Anthony said remotely, settling back into the couch. "Oh, that's not right. How could I be so stupid?" He leaned forward now, with one hand on his hip, the opposite forearm across his knee, staring her down like a boxer before the opening bell. "That's not good business. You know why, angel? You are way overpriced."

In a split second, Monique flung her wine glass at Anthony, the red droplets drenching his face and splattering across his suit.

Anthony hardly moved. He slowly withdrew a handkerchief from his inside suit pocket and sopped up the wine from his face and neck. For a long moment, he considered backhanding the woman and then gave in to another thought. He examined the red-stained handkerchief in the palm of his hand and with a half twist shoved the cloth into Monique's face like pressing an orange into a strainer.

Monique leapt to her feet. "Fous-moi le camp!" *she screamed. "Get out, you arrogant . . . !"*

Anthony rose slowly and edged toward Monique. "What's the matter, Monique, can't think of the right word? English vocabulary was never your strong suit, was it? Let me help you. How about 'you arrogant bore.' Or perhaps 'you obnoxious brute.' Or, for a more literary nuance, why not try 'cretin' or 'prig' or 'swine' or 'ogre' or 'fiend'? You see, ma petite, *there is a plethora of words to choose from. Oh, I'm sorry; you don't know the word 'plethora,' do you?"*

"Salaud, fils de pute! *You son-of-a-bitch!"*

"Oh, that will never do, angel; that's much too crude coming from lips as lovely as yours." Anthony grasped Monique by the shoulders.

"Do not be touching me," she said through her teeth.

"Or what?" Anthony said, pulling her body into him.

Anthony kissed her hard on the mouth, and Monique bit down on his lower lip. Anthony jerked his head back and wiped the back of his hand across his mouth, revealing a smear of blood.

"I don't have to see this," Anthony said.

"Oh, I know that, but grant an old soldier his indulgences. You have created a work of art, and now it is time to admire your masterpiece."

"What are you trying to prove? There is no beauty here. It is ugly."

"Are you sure?"

"Yes, yes, I'm sure."

The specter cocked his head and stared for a moment at his begrudging student. "No," he finally said, drawing out the word, "I am sorry, cow dung, I do not believe you. I think we need to continue."

Anthony glared at Monique, who stood erect, her arms trembling at her side, her eyes livid.

"Get out," she said again, this time in a seething whisper.

"Sure, Angel." With that, Anthony turned toward the door. Monique relaxed her shoulders a moment and breathed a long, uneven sigh. Then Anthony swung back again, grabbing Monique by the waist and forcing her back against the dining table. With one sweep of his arm, he cleared one-half of the table, sending plates and goblets flying and crashing to the floor. Anthony reached under her skirt and tore off her panties with a single jerk.

Monique's face erupted with rage. "Non, non, non!" *she screamed. She pushed the heels of her hands against Anthony's shoulders, but he was impossible to budge. She was helplessly pinned to the dining table, a rag doll in his hands, and so she suddenly stopped struggling. Her body went limp; she was a lifeless body of meat under him.*

Monique's strategy rattled Anthony to the core. He stopped cold.

"You did not like that, did you?" the specter said.

"No."

"And why not?"

Anthony spoke matter-of-factly. "Because she was in control."

"That is right. Submission angers you, but dominance terrifies you, cow dung. You were going to rape her, but suddenly she had the upper hand. You would not have your way with a corpse; that would make Monique the victor. And we both know that you cannot bear losing—not anything. Do you remember what you did next?"

"Yes."

"Good. We will both enjoy seeing it again."

Anthony's hips were wedged between her legs. He propped himself up, his arms locked on either side of Monique's shoulders. He glared silently at her, while she stared stoically at the ceiling, her chest heaving with tempered fury.

Anthony reached across her body. Monique stiffened.

"Relax, ma petite. *I only want to season the salad."*

He stretched farther, his face brushing her cheek. Then he had it: a crystal vinegar and oil cruet. He flicked off the stopper with his thumb and slowly, systematically, emptied the vessel over her face and down the length of her body. Monique cringed, but still lay motionless on the dining table, not even lifting her hand to wipe the oil from her eyes—eyes that were now silent pools of dark defiance.

Anthony polished his hands on the hem of her dress and walked to the door. Then, as a mere afterthought, he said with his back to Monique, "You have forty-eight hours to get the hell out of this apartment."

He opened the front door and then turned for one last look. Monique lay perfectly still, her legs dangling from the end of the table. She stared blankly at the ceiling.

The two visitors silently contemplated the long slack body.

Finally, the specter asked: "Do you know what she is staring at?"

"No."

"Follow her eyes. She is fixed on the kitchen globe light overhead. She sees the sprinkling of dead gnats at the bottom of the bowl that surrendered to the temptation of the light and ultimately gave in to the heat."

The picture of Monique on the kitchen table faded to black, and the two travelers were suspended in a void of black.

"Yes," Anthony said blankly.

"You are the source of that heat."

"I don't want to be."

"And, yet, you are."

"Can I not change?"

"I don't think so, at least not by your own pathetic efforts. If you are to change, it will be by the grace of someone who loves you."

"Who would do that for me?"

The specter shook his head. "No, it is too soon to speak of that. It is too sacred, and you are not ready. You still have much to learn."

Anthony was exhausted. "What more can I learn?"

"Look at these men."

A new scene sprang to life. Fifteen men and one woman sat around a long, ornate teak table. A long bank of windows overlooked Paris.

"You know these men?" the specter asked.

"They are my executive staff: half French, half Americans."

"Do you enjoy working with the French?"

"The French don't work; for them work is a bothersome interruption between vacations. I use them mostly as administrators—it's what they do best."

"And the Americans?"

"The Americans are my construction project managers; they know how to get the work done."

"There is one exception, of course: Jean-Pierre. He is a French project manager."

Anthony nearly snarled. "Yes."

"And the woman?"

"Her name is Lucy. She is my office manager."

The French administrators sat like manikins in their crisp white shirts, waiting in silence for the meeting to begin. In contrast, the American project managers looked ill at ease in their ill-fitted suit jackets and cinched ties, several of the men straining at their collars. One paunchy American with unkempt hair patted a pack of cigarettes in his shirt pocket and, savoring the memory of nicotine, wished for all the world he could light up; he could not, of course.

Anthony crossed his legs in the high-back captain's chair at the head of the table, his back to the Tour Eiffel *and the* Arc de Triomphe *beyond. In contrast to the president's carefree demeanor, his staff leaned forward around the table, ready to respond to the commander's most offhanded directive. Chief among them was the vice president, Hennessy, who was seated at the opposite end of the boardroom table with his back to the door, his eyes darting about the room.*

"You recognize the setting?" the specter asked

"Yes, it's my conference room—the Monday morning staff meeting."

"I must say you are looking particularly fresh and self-confident in your custom-made suit."

Anthony did not respond.

"Tell me, cow dung, where is your agenda?"

"I don't use an agenda."

"Oh?"

"The agenda is whatever is on my mind at the time."

"That must be convenient."

"It's the way it is."

The specter shook his head at the depth of Anthony's self-importance. "Shall we watch, cow dung?"

"Do I have a choice?"

The specter laughed one of his hollow laughs. "No, you do not."

The room was hushed, everyone's eyes riveted to the president.

"Good morning, gentlemen," Anthony said.

A chorus of morning greetings rolled out like a wave across the table.

"I hope you had a pleasant weekend," Anthony continued.

The band of men waggled their heads. "Oh, yeah." "You bet." "Absolument." *And then there was silence, as all heads turned to the president again.*

"Good. I'm happy to hear that. It's important to relax over the weekend, because on this Monday morning, we've got our work cut out for us."

The staff straightened up in their chairs.

"How was your weekend?" Anthony asked, speaking to Jean-Pierre Badeau, a thirty-eight-year-old project manager with thinning brown hair and a neck that seemed a little too long for the rest of his body.

The specter interrupted the scene. "Now, *Señor* Badeau is an interesting fellow, is he not?"

"He is a French fuckup."

"That is harsh. True, he is a fidgety man, but he is also very kind."

"I don't care about kindness. Watch him. He has a nervous stomach. Whenever he's stressed, which is most of the time, he has the disgusting habit of leaning to his left and farting."

"That seems a small price to pay for a good manager."

"It is more than that. Hennessy hired him five years ago, and he has been a disaster from the start. He's too nervous, too unstable. He's in charge of the construction of a seven-story parking lot in the tenth *arronndissement*, and the job is a complete screw-up."

When the president had targeted Badeau, a collective sigh of relief wafted from the other managers. Their shoulders relaxed, a few falling back into their chairs, gently rocking away whatever anxiety remained in their craws. All eyes were now on the president's victim. Only Lucy looked at Jean-Pierre with compassion—truly distraught that she could do nothing to protect her friend.

Fully focused on Anthony, Badeau raised his eyebrows and pointed to himself, as if to say, "Moi?"

Anthony tipped his head in one sweeping diagonal motion.

Looking decidedly queasy, Badeau pressed his fingers into the side of his stomach. He tried to moisten the inside of his mouth with his tongue. "Très bien, merci," *he said softly.*

"I'm sorry, Badeau, I didn't quite get that."

"Very nice, thank you," Badeau repeated in English, scarcely louder.

"Ah, 'very nice.'"

Badeau nodded.

"What was 'very nice' about it?"

"Pas grand-chose," *Badeau said. "Just a weekend* typique.*"*

"No, no, I'd really like to know. You said it was 'very nice.' I believe you; it must have been nice." And then slowly, with space between each word: "Just how was it very nice?"

Badeau's jaw tightened. He leaned over the left side of his chair and raised his cheek; the fourteen managers pulled back and turned their heads away from Badeau; it was a false alarm, and Badeau rested back in his seat. "My wife and I went sailing on the Mediterranean."

"Ah, you went sailing. Splendid." Anthony paused a beat. "Your boat is ten meters, right?"

"Eleven meters."

"Ah, eleven meters. Tell me, Badeau, is it paid for?"

"Non. Pas encore."

"Would you like to pay for it?"

Silence. Badeau stared into empty space. He leaned to the left again, and the managers prepared themselves for the inevitable, to which Badeau did not disappoint.

"I said 'would you like to pay for it'?"

*Badeau woke up from what was a near-death trance. "*Oui, bien sûr, *I would like to pay for it."*

"Of course you would. And so would I. And so would the company. It's simple: You make money for us, and we make money for you. You see how that works now?"

"Oui, monsieur."

"Don't 'oui-monsieur' *me. Just get the goddamn work done. Your job is three weeks over schedule, Badeau. Do you know what that is costing this company daily?"*

"I . . . eh bien, je ne sais pas; *I do not know exactly."*

"Well, I do know exactly: It's 12,000 francs a day, and it's killing me." Anthony readjusted himself in his chair and then sat back and brushed imaginary dust off his pant leg. "Now, you tell me what the hell the problem is, and I don't want to hear 'je ne sais pas.'*"*

"Non, monsieur. C'est à dire, oui, monsieur. *I mean the problem is testing the tensile strength of the support pillars. We send that work out to a subcontractor. And their* temps d'exécution*—how do you say, their 'turnaround time' is slow, very slow. I have been waiting ten days for a report on the last order. And without those numbers we cannot move ahead."*

"And that is—how do you say in French—bullshit! Who's the subcontractor?"

"Dupré Ingénieurs."

Anthony looked up at the ceiling, closed his eyes, and exhaled. "Do you know how much business we give Roland Dupré each year, Badeau?"

Badeau haltingly hunched his shoulders.

"No, of course you don't." Anthony turned to the CFO sitting to his left. "Ferrand, how much did we pay Dupré Ingénieurs in '89?"

Ferrand straightened himself. "It has been un bon moment *since I have looked at the numbers, but, if my memory is correct, I would say* environ*—approximately—3.8 million francs."*

"And would you say we are their most important client."

"Sans aucun doute—*without a doubt."*

"That's my assessment, too." Anthony turned to his office manager who was taking meeting notes. "Lucy, get Dupré on the line for me, and put him on the speakerphone."

Lucy rushed to her desk and retrieved Dupré's private phone number. In the next moment, she was dialing the number on the conference speakerphone placed in the middle of the table.

"Take notes, Badeau. You're going to learn something."

The phone rang and was picked up on the fourth ring. A sandpaper voice answered: "Allô. Je vous écoute." *His words were impatient and clipped.*

"Good morning, Roland. This is Anthony Rossi."

"Good morning, Monsieur *Rossi," Dupré said, his tone of voice suddenly softening.*

"I've got Jean-Pierre Badeau on the line with me."

"Bonjour, Monsieur *Badeau."*

"Bonjour, Monsieur *Dupré."*

"It seems we have a little problem," Anthony continued. "We're behind schedule on that parking garage job, and you are the cause of that delay."

"Attendez un petit moment, Monsieur Rossi . . ."

"No, you wait a minute. We're losing 12,000 francs a day on this job. As of today, that adds up to 252,000 francs in lost revenue. That's money out of my pocket, and, believe me, I will not let that continue for long. Are you getting my drift? Tu comprends?*"*

"Je vous en prie, Monsieur Rossi; we are very busy . . ."

"Écoute moi! *You think I care about your pissant problems? I don't give a shit about your problems.* Tu me fais chier—*you piss me off."*

The French administrators gasped.

"Now, wait a moment. Ça va pas, quoi.*"*

"This is very simple, Roland. We do nearly four million francs of business with you every year. Look it up. If you want that to continue, you absolutely must deliver, and deliver now. Are you getting this? Tu comprends?*"*

"Oui." *Roland's voice was not happy, but it was compliant.*

"Now, you have some of our samples that have been sitting in your warehouse for ten days."

"Je ne le savais pas. *I did not know that."*

"Well, now you do. And here's the bottom line: I want the tensile strengths of those samples by closing time tonight. Got it? D'accord?*"*

"That will be very difficile . . .*"*

"Roland?"

"Oui.*"*

"La ferme! *Shut the hell up."*

The French administrators looked at each other with gaping eyes.

There was silence on the line. Anthony waited calmly with folded arms, a tight-lip smile drawn across his face. Then, he raised a single index finger to the managers in the room, indicating both silence and patience, as ten seconds ticked off the clock. Then, finally:

"Monsieur *Rossi?"*

"Yes. I'm here"

"D'accord. *We have an understanding."*

"That's good, Roland. Have a nice day."

"Ouais.*"*

Anthony pointed a finger at Lucy to terminate the connection.

"And that, Badeau, is how the big boys play hardball."

"Oui, monsieur,*" Badeau said.*

Anthony glowered at the French project manager. "Ah, one other thing, Badeau," he said offhandedly. "You let this kind of thing happen again, and your foul-smelling ass will be on the street."

Badeau did not understand the expression "foul-smelling ass," but he knew it wasn't a compliment. He started to lean to the left.

"Badeau."

Badeau was in mid air. "Oui, monsieur?"

"Don't even think about it."

Badeau sat back down squarely in his seat, his face pinched around the mouth and eyes. "Yes, sir," Badeau mumbled, speaking to a spot on the conference table.

"Well, you certainly took care of that problem," the specter said.

Anthony could find no words to say. The color drained from his face, while he blinked away a tear.

"Wait a minute. You are not crying? Tell me those are not tears of compassion."

"Am I that much of a monster?"

"You tell me. Remember when you were peeping on your wife? Hennessy left a blueprint at your home. It was condemning evidence of your partner's treachery and your wife's unfaithfulness. Why don't we see how you leveraged that piece of information?"

Anthony reached down into his top-loading leather briefcase and pulled out the folded blueprint; he placed it before him like a dinner plate, making certain that it was square with the table. Then, he fished out a pair of standard office scissors and, with equal precision, placed them perfectly parallel on the right side of the blueprint.

"Now, we've got a second problem, and this one is more serious."

On cue, the shoulders of the men around the room contracted, their faces morphing into wads of tension.

"And the problem is the lycée *remodel job," Anthony pronounced, placing his right hand on the blueprints. "These are the prints."*

With that, Anthony slid the drawings the full length of the table, skimming the speakerphone and coming to a stop at Hennessy's water glass. It was a perfectly placed shuffleboard stroke. Hennessy visibly blushed, unconsciously loosening his tie and undoing the top button at his collar.

Anthony took the scissors in hand, stood up, and started walking slowly around the room. All the managers watched in silence, as Anthony patted the blades of the scissors in the palm of his hand. He walked counterclockwise around the executive table, passed Hennessy and then returned, settling in directly behind him.

"We were low bid on the lycée *project. In fact, we left 350,000 francs on the table to the next lowest bidder. I don't like that. I don't like leaving money on the table." Anthony punctuated each word of his last sentence by lightly tapping the jaws of the scissors on Hennessy's right shoulder.*

"So, tell me, Hennie, what do we have to do?"

Hennessy started to speak, but his throat was dry and as a result squawked out an indecipherable syllable. He took a drink of water and then a second gulp. Finally, looking over his shoulder to glance at Anthony, but catching only the outline of his suit, he said, "We'll have to come in under budget."

"That's right," Anthony said. "We'll have to come in under budget. That means snipping the overruns and waste wherever we can." Anthony dropped his left hand over Hennessy's left shoulder and lifted the midsection of the vice president's tie. With his right hand he inserted the scissors' jaws across the bottom

three inches of the necktie. "We'll have to snip the material costs," Anthony said, slicing off Hennessy's $100-designer tie.

The eyes of the executives rounded. One American undid a tentative smile, while a French counterpart mouthed, "Oh là là."

"And then we need to snip labor costs," Anthony continued, slicing off the next three inches of his partner's necktie. "And, just to be on the safe side, we will snip nonreimbursable overhead costs." As Anthony drew out the word "s-n-i-p," he slashed off another section of silk, leaving a pile of material on Hennessy's lap and a ridiculous chopped flag at his neck.

The vice president was mute. He undid what remained of his severed tie, balled it up, and tried to stuff it into his suit pocket. But his pocket was sewn shut to protect the drape of the suit, and, out of pure frustration, Hennessy ripped the side pocket open and crammed the tie remnant into the new cavity. Anthony saw all this and huffed a small laugh of satisfaction.

The company president returned to his chair and sat down, placing the scissors on the table to his right. "This meeting is over," he said without fanfare.

The men began to get up and leave, and then Anthony spoke again. The men froze.

"One other thing, Hennessy. Don't ever loosen your tie in an executive staff meeting again. It shows weakness. And we all know you're not a weak man."

The managers stood immobile, not knowing if they were excused.

"That's all."

The men quickly filed out of the room, most taking a long draw of air outside of the boardroom, visibly thankful that they had been granted a temporary reprieve.

"I know what is next. You've made your point."

"What is my point?" the specter asked.

"The point is I'm a contemptible human being."

"Is that how you would put it?" the ghost asked with a patronizing tone. "My language would be much more vulgar than that."

"You know, I don't care about your language. There is nothing that you can show me that I don't already know about myself."

"And still you are—how did you put it—oh, yes, 'a contemptible human being.' Shall we see just how contemptible?"

Hennessy was at the door when Anthony stopped him. "Hold on, Hennie."

The vice president turned and faced Anthony, who was still seated, kicked back in the captain's chair. Hennessy took his seat at the opposite end of the table, separating the two men by twenty feet.

Anthony stared at Hennessy, whose forehead was glistening with small beads of sweat. "You don't look well, Hennie," Anthony said.

"Yeah, I think I have a cold coming on," Hennessy said, pulling a handkerchief from his back pocket and patting the back of his neck.

"Hum. Well, keep hydrated and get a good night's sleep." Anthony paused. "Are you sleeping well these days, Hennie?"

Hennessy's right thumb started twitching uncontrollably. He took his hands off the table and placed them on his lap.

"Look, Anthony, I'm sorry."

"Sorry?" Anthony said innocently. "What are you sorry about?"

"You know what I mean."

"Hennie, you have something to say to me?"

Hennessy took in a deep breath. His eyes fashioned a slow blink. "Penelope and me."

"What about Penelope and you?" he asked without mercy, reverting to tapping the scissors in his hand.

"Well, you know, I'm . . . she . . . I mean, we're . . . you know."

"What are you jabbering about, Hennie?"

"We're sleeping together." Hennessy sopped up the sweat on his forehead. "You knew that, of course."

"Not until just now," Anthony said calmly, reveling in the lie.

"Damn." Hennessy looked woefully out the office window. "I'm sorry, Anthony. I'm really sorry."

"You said that, Hennie."

"Well, I mean it."

"Uh-huh. So, tell me, is she a good lay?"

"Damn it, Anthony."

"No really, I'd like to know. Does she do that swishing thing with her ass, when she wants you to mount her?"

"Please, Anthony."

"Isn't that the best? Don't you just love that? Damn, I love it when she does that."

"Okay, Anthony, what do you want? What do you want me to do? You want me to sell out? You want me to go back to the States? You want me to . . . what do you want from me?"

"No, no, no, no, no. It's not what I want, brother. It's what you want. Do you want my wife?"

Hennessy looked questioningly at the president.

"That's not a trick question, Hennie. Do you want my wife?" After a pause, he added, "Understand that although she can be very seductive—and she does do that swishing thing with her ass—she can also be manipulative and pouty and completely self-centered. So, what's it going to be, Hennie? Do you want my wife?"

Hennessy was dead still, as if in a trance. Finally, he muttered, "I don't know."

Anthony pursed his lips and ran his knuckles across his jaw line. "You don't know. Okay, I'll tell you what: Tuesday of next week, I'm going to Spain on the Águilas project. I'll be gone for five days. During that time, I want you to think very hard about your role in the company and your future with Penelope. And when I get back, we will sort this thing out."

Anthony's speech was delivered with cool, almost calming, reserve. What was menacing was the sound of metal slicing across metal, as the president snapped the blades of the scissors again and again: swish, click . . . swish, click.

"Okay," Hennessy said. He opened his mouth as if to apologize, but changed his mind and only said again, "Okay, okay then." He stood up to leave, turning his back on Anthony as he moved toward the door.

"One other thing, Hennie."

Anthony didn't bother to turn around. "Yes?"

"As long as I'm in town, keep your swinging dick away from my wife."

Hennessy said nothing. His back still to Anthony, he simply nodded and walked out.

In the next instant, Lucy stepped into the room, shutting the door behind her. "Miss Monique Ducros is on the line. She seems quite upset."

"Tell her I'm not in," Anthony said blankly.

"Yes, sir."

Lucy opened the door to leave.

"And, Lucy, don't take her calls again—ever."

"Yes, Mr. Rossi."

The scene went to black. The president and specter were back in Anthony's office. The windows were still opaque—black reflections of the players. Suddenly, the room was cold, very cold.

"Lucy is an interesting character in this morality play."

"She is indispensable to me. She understands the organization inside-out."

"She is American, is she not?"

"Yes. She's been with me since the early days in Seattle."

"She is also a little in love with you."

"I know that, but I've never touched her; she's too valuable to me. She went through a messy divorce, and I think I became her substitute husband."

"And you so enjoy her adoration; after all, it gives you so much leverage."

"I know I can trust her," he said without expression.

Anthony stood before the mirrored windows. He could see himself; he could not see the phantom. Except for the voice of the specter, he was alone in the darkened room. He examined his reflection. His face was drawn and sallow; he hardly recognized himself. He shook off a shiver.

"What do you see in the glass?" the specter asked, his voice echoing, as if from a dark abyss.

"I don't know anymore. What do you see?"

"I see a man at the crossroads of his life."

"What road do I take?"

"That depends on you."

Anthony turned to face the phantom. "I beg of you: Who are you? Please tell me."

"I was a man who confused power with virtue. I believed that savagery was the only redeeming force in life. I was like you, Anthony."

"Why do you haunt the earth? Why have you not found peace?"

"Who are you to talk of peace?"

"It's what I want."

"There is only one pathway to peace."

Anthony's eyes were yearning. "Please tell me."

The specter became visible again, standing just behind the president's shoulder. He leaned into Anthony's ear. "Charity," he whispered, pronouncing the word as if it were the holiest of benedictions.

Anthony pondered the specter's words. For a moment, it appeared that he understood everything. Then, slowly, like an unexpected storm, his expression changed from humility to arrogance. When Anthony asked the next question, his voice was not pleading, not even remorseful; it was defiant and marinated in pride. "What do you want from me?"

The phantom bristled. "You have the audacity to speak to me in that tone? Have you learned nothing, cow dung?"

The specter gripped Anthony's shoulder with his boney fingers and squeezed. Anthony buckled and fell to his knees.

"You are a cold fish," the specter said, "but not nearly cold enough."

A piercing chill stabbed the flesh and bones of Anthony's shoulder. Then, veins of ice splintered from the phantoms grip, cutting up and around Anthony's neck and across his chest. Anthony opened his mouth in agony, and his breath, a thin white vapor, crystallized and fell to the ground like shattered glass. The rivulets of ice traversed crisscross over his body. His nose turned pale, then blue, cracked at the seams, and separated from his face. When the phantom finally released his grip, Anthony toppled to the floor, a solid block of ice.

San Bartolomé, the sixteenth-century church on the hill, was only a few steps up a winding passageway from the Garcias' home. The sanctuary was deserted with the exception of one sole figure, Lupita, who knelt at a front pew near the center aisle, her head covered with a white cotton scarf that draped around her neck and down her back.

Usually, she came to pray for her parents. No, that was not right: She came to pray *to* her parents. They had been gone for sixteen years, but for Lupita their memory had never dimmed. She remembered her mother, how she would brush out her long black hair at night. "You have such beautiful hair," she would say. "You will drive the boys crazy with desire."

It was a nonsensical thing to say, and her mother knew it, because Lupita had no interest in turning the heads of young boys. She was more preoccupied with climbing trees or playing hide-and-seek with her school friends in the narrow and crooked side streets of Espejo. And so Lupita would laugh and say, "Oh, Mama, you are so silly," which would make her mother laugh, and they would fall into each other's arms, until her mother raked her fingers across her daughter's ribs, which straightened Lupita's back in a hurry.

Lupita loved her mother more than her own life, but her father, Juanito, commanded a special place in her heart. Juanito was like Diego: courageous and strong. But there was something more: He was funny. Everything about him made Lupita laugh.

Juanito loved to dance. When he heard a favorite song on the radio, he often invited little Lupita to dance with him. "May I have the pleasure of this dance, *señorita?*" he would ask with the deepest of bows.

"Oh, yes, my prince charming," Lupita would say.

Then the little girl would put her bare feet on her father's shoes, and Juanito would waltz or tango his daughter around the living room, spinning her left and right, and invariably ending the romp with a grand dip, which would make Lupita giggle.

Juanito was like that: full of good humor and unrelenting mischief. One of Lupita's last memories of her father immortalized that sense of impish playfulness.

It was only a few days before the accident. Mother and daughter cleaned up the dinner dishes, and Lupita returned to the dining table to finish her homework, as was her custom. She was intent on deciphering a stubborn algebra problem, when her father crept up behind her and laid his hands over her eyes.

"Guess who, my sweet and lovely maiden."

"Oh, Papa, I am studying," Lupita said without looking up.

"But I want a bite of you," her father said in his best Dracula voice.

Lupita turned to look at her father, who had the devil in his eyes and two raw string beans wedged under his upper lip. He brushed away Lupita's hair and plunged the green fangs into his daughter's neck, growling like a pit bull over a disputed shank of meat.

Naturally, Lupita laughed and then leapt from her chair and tackled her father, sending him tumbling to the ground. The wrestling match ended as they always ended: Lupita plunked triumphantly on her father's chest, her hands pinning his hands to his ears, and her hair swishing across his face until he cried for mercy.

"You give up?" she warned, implying there was more torture to come if he did not relent.

"I give, I give," he yelped through tears of laughter. "You are still the undefeated champion of the world."

"Good. Let that be a lesson to you," she said, kissing her papa on the cheek.

Those memories always washed over Lupita when she prayed in the church. But this day, she was not thinking so much of her parents; she was praying for Antonio. It was curious how the stranger had crept into her heart. They had not shared a single word; they had not even looked into each other's eyes, and yet she cared deeply for the mysterious man.

Lupita's plea was simple: "God in heaven, hear my prayer. Let Antonio awaken. Let him come back to us."

Lupita crossed herself. As she slowly came to her feet, she heard her name called in a whispered but frantic voice. At first she looked to the crucifix, then she realized the voice was coming from behind her. It was Diego standing silhouetted at the church entry, his hands propping the doors open.

"Lupita! Come, come, come!"

Lupita ran to her grandfather. "What is it? Is he all right?"

"No, something is wrong. Something is very wrong. Please hurry."

The two dashed out of the church, onto the church square, and down the twisted steps to their home, Lupita leading the way. Lupita slammed through the front door, crossed the living room, and charged into her bedroom. The sight of Antonio took her breath away.

Antonio's face was swollen and blue-gray in color. She touched his cheek with the back of her hand; he was freezing. She placed her thumbs over his eyes and pulled back the lids; his eyes were dilated.

Diego was now at her side. "What is it? What is happening?" he said out of breath.

"He is in profound hypothermia," Lupita said, pulling back the bed sheet.

Antonio's entire body was shaking. His chest, arms, and legs were pale, almost white, with an irregular patch of blue shrouding his stomach. She gently lifted his arm; it was stiff.

"How could this happen?" Diego asked.

"I do not know. I have never seen anything like it, but we have to warm his body core immediately, or he will die."

"Should I get hot water?"

"No, that will not work. Find a stocking cap and a wool scarf."

Diego stood immobile for an instant, staring blankly at Antonio.

"Now!" Lupita shouted.

Diego came to his senses and rushed from the room.

Lupita placed a thermometer under Antonio's tongue, waited a moment, and then quickly withdrew the glass tube. She looked at the thermometer calibration. Impossible. She looked at it again: 26.6 Celsius. She checked his pulse at his wrist; it was weak, very weak, pulsing at only thirty-two beats a minute. "God in heaven help us."

Diego was back with the cap and scarf in hand.

"Put the cap on his head and the scarf around his neck," Lupita ordered. "When you have done that, get blankets, as many blankets as you can find."

Lupita began to undress.

"What are you doing?" Diego asked.

"We have to raise his body heat. Get those blankets now!"

Lupita stripped naked, flinging her dress toward a chair near the door, and slipped under the bed sheet, gently pressing the length of her body against Antonio. She tucked her arm under his back and pulled him into her. The cold made her shiver.

Diego rushed back into the room and snapped four wool blankets over the bed, one after the other. Diego watched his granddaughter enfolding Antonio in her arms. She looked cold.

After a few minutes, Lupita called out to Diego. "It is not enough, Tito. Get undressed."

Diego did not even blink. He kicked off his shoes, lowered his pants, and tore off the work shirt over his head. He stood for a moment in boxer shorts and singlet.

"Everything," Lupita said.

Diego pealed off his underwear and eased under the mountain of blankets, his chest and stomach sealed against Antonio's back and rump.

The three lay there in silence for just over an hour. Gradually, Antonio stopped shivering, and his body heat began to rise. As for Lupita and Diego, they were drenched in sweat, their hair flattened by the moisture. Lupita was beginning to think it was safe to leave the bed.

Just then there was a knock at the front door.

"Lupita. Diego. Anybody home?"

"It's Miguel," Diego whispered to Lupita.

"This could be hard to explain," Lupita whispered back, a pixilated smile on her lips.

"Even harder for me to explain," Diego said, suppressing a giggle. "What do we do?"

Lupita put her finger to her lips. "Shh. Get out and close the door," she mouthed, as she began to slip her arm out from under Antonio's neck.

"Lupita. Diego. The door's open. I'm coming in."

"Oh, my God," Diego said, moving to the bedroom door, dressed only in a thin coat of perspiration.

"Lupi . . ." Miguel rounded the corner into the bedroom and collided with Diego at the door. In the scuffle, he caught sight of Lupita, as she peeled back the load of blankets and emerged naked from Antonio's bed. The police chief stood gaping. "*Caramba*!" he said. Then, after a moment—after the shock had turned to revulsion—he added, "That is the most disgusting thing I have ever seen."

Lupita's dress was pooled on the chair next to Miguel. She spotted the dress and looked beseechingly at Miguel. Without a word, the police chief lifted the dress with one hand as if lifting the tail of a snake and held it out to Lupita with a straight arm, finally remembering to divert his eyes as Lupita plucked the dress from his hand and held it against her body.

"*Caramba*," Miguel repeated, his face squashed like a prune. "What in the hell is going on here?"

Diego scrambled to the far side of the bed to recover his clothes.

"I can explain," Lupita said.

Miguel held his ground, waiting for the explanation, something that Lupita had no intention of starting in her state of undress. She looked at Miguel with imploring eyes, pointing the way to the door with her eyes. Miguel did not get the hint.

"Could you give us a minute?" Lupita finally asked in exasperation.

"Huh?" Miguel said, taking a moment to catch on. "*Si, si,* I will be in the living room," he said, closing the door to the bedroom.

A moment later, Lupita and Diego stepped out of the bedroom fully dressed. Miguel stood up and faced the accused. There was a long, awkward pause.

"Well?" Miguel asked.

"Well what?" Diego quipped, slicing his shirttail into his pants.

"I am talking to Lupita," Miguel said, firing a threatening squint at Diego, who responded with a shrug. "Lupita, you said you had an explanation."

"I do," she said in a professional tone. "Hypothermia."

Miguel could not believe his ears. "What?"

"Abnormally low body temperature, Miguel."

"I know what hypothermia is."

"Good. Then you probably know that skin-to-skin contact is the best way to transfer heat."

Miguel ran his fingers through his hair in frustration. "Lupita, what are you talking about? This is not the Antarctica. This is Spain. Today's temperature is twenty-nine degrees Celsius. How in the world can he have hypothermia?"

"I do not know. I just know it happened."

Miguel's head bobbed—propelled by pure skepticism. He stared at Lupita like she was out of her mind.

"Do not look at me that way," she said. "I am not on trial here."

"Of course not, but you have to admit, it sounds very strange."

"I do not care what it sounds like. It is the truth."

"I believe you, Lupita," he said, not sounding altogether convinced. "May I see him?"

"Of course," Lupita said, leading Miguel back into the bedroom.

Lupita checked Antonio's pulse. It was normal. More importantly, his skin was warm to the touch. There was color in his face. "He is all right now," she said.

"Uh-huh, I can see that," Miguel said.

"Stop that, Miguel. There is nothing depraved happening here."

"Uh-huh," he repeated.

At that moment, Miguel hated the stranger. He had no right to lie in Lupita's bed; he certainly had no right to be caressed in her arms. Suddenly, the image of Lupita slipping naked out of Antonio's sickbed twisted in his gut—not with jealousy or disgust, but with craving. The curve of her breasts and hips replayed in his mind. He wanted her. He was sure that he must act now, this very instant, or lose her forever to the stranger.

Miguel took Lupita by the shoulders and turned her around. They were standing face-to-face.

"Miguel?" Lupita asked in confusion.

"Lupita, I love you. I have always loved you. I want you to be my wife. I want you to have my babies." With that, Miguel pulled Lupita into his body and kissed her on the mouth.

Lupita struggled to be released, and Miguel held her more firmly.

"No," Lupita said, twisting her head away from Miguel. "I am sorry, Miguel," she said breaking loose from his grip. "I do not think of you in that way."

"But why not?" Miguel was pleading. "We have known each other our entire lives. We belong to each other."

Lupita smiled sadly, sympathetically. "No, Miguel, we do not belong to each other."

"Then who do you belong to?" He waved his hand over Antonio. "This stranger, this gutter rat?"

"That is enough, Miguel. I want you out of our house."

The police chief did not move. He stared at Lupita, his chest heaving.

Diego was now standing at the bedroom door. "I think my granddaughter asked you to leave, Miguel."

The policeman turned, his eyes blazing, and faced Diego. "Do not worry; I am leaving," he said, brushing past Diego and plodding out of the house.

Diego went to Lupita and softly patted her back. "Are you all right, my dove?"

Lupita's jaw was trembling. "I think so, Tito. Yes, I am fine."

Diego took his granddaughter in his arms, while Lupita quietly sobbed.

That surprised Diego. His granddaughter was not easily shaken and not easily brought to tears. After her parents' death, she added a veneer of toughness to her personality. It was not that she became calloused or cynical; no, what she became was undaunted.

For example, in medical school she was the only female surgeon in her class—a courageous act in itself—but some of her male classmates treated her, not as a serious student, but as an object of their sexual fantasies.

Once, at the end of a grueling term, Lupita went to a bar to celebrate with three other medical students, including Gabino, the most brazen of the three, who flirted with her most of the night. At the end of the evening, Lupita was the first to leave. She kissed her companions goodnight and made her way home, stopping briefly at a small all-night grocer for a can of coffee.

By the time she reached her home, she was no longer alone. She climbed the front steps and inserted her key into the lock at the front door when Gabino crept up behind her from the shadows. He hooked his arms around her and groped at her breasts. “Good evening, doctor,” he said, half drunk.

Lupita’s body jerked, and the coffee slipped from her hand and rolled down the stoop, one step at a time. In the next instant, she took control. She recognized Gabino’s voice and slowly turned to face him. “Gabino, you scared the wits out of me, but I am so glad you came.” Then, seductively, she added: “I have something I have been wanting to give you for a very long time.”

“And I have something for you,” he said, adjusting the package between his legs.

“Me first. This is my gift for you.” She took his hand from his crotch and placed it on her breast.

“Oh, yes,” he said with a long sigh.

With her other hand she reached down and gently squeezed his genitals, and Gabino spread his legs to accommodate her.

“Does that feel good?” she purred.

“Yes, yes,” he moaned.

“Good. And how does this feel?”

Lupita moved her hands to his shoulders and with all her might swung her knee into his groin, perfectly hitting her mark. Gabino crumbled to his knees and toppled to one side.

“Do not ever touch me again,” she said between clenched teeth, standing over her victim like a fighter who had just landed a knockout punch.

That was the last of her trouble with Gabino. He never spoke to her again, nor did he ever admit the defeat to his colleagues; that would have been too damaging to his Latin pride, and Lupita knew it.

So Diego was somewhat astonished when Lupita cried in his arms. He lifted Lupita’s chin with one finger and looked into her eyes. “All is fine,” he reassured. “Do not worry about Miguel.”

Lupita gave up a little laugh through the tears. “I am not worried about Miguel; I can handle Miguel. Besides, I can never stay angry with him; we have been friends for too long. I have already forgiven him.”

“What then?”

“I am worried about Antonio. His body temperature is normal again, but he is still showing no signs of reviving.”

They turned and moved to Antonio, whose voiceless lips were moving. "Look at him, Tito. He is still fighting to come out."

Then, Lupita saw something curious in Antonio's face. She sat down on the edge of the bed and studied her patient, holding her fingers lightly over his mouth. "This is crazy, Tito."

"What is it? What do you see?"

"I cannot read lips," she said, smiling softly, "but I could swear he is calling my name."

"Lupita! Lupita!"

Anthony looked into the doctor's eyes when she bent over him and passed her fingertips across his lips. Her eyes were angelic, and her touch divine.

"My God, why doesn't she answer me?"

"What do you want from her?" the specter asked.

"I want to thank her . . . to know her. I want . . ." Then he knew what it was: "I want to love her." Again, he called to her—longingly, pleading—this time pronouncing her name like a prayer: "Lupita."

"You are wasting your time. She hears nothing."

Anthony looked at the ghost, a small head in the distance, outlined in a vat of darkness. "But why?"

"She is in her world; you are in mine."

"How long must I stay in your world?"

"Until you have learned something."

"God damn it to hell. What is there left to learn?"

The specter stiffened. "Watch your words with me. You know what I am capable of doing."

Anthony waved his hand in surrender. "I'm sorry; I apologize. Please help me."

"That is better." The face of the ghost swooped in from the black and landed silently before Anthony. "You remember what you did in Águilas, Spain?"

"I am so tired," Anthony said, his head dropping to his chest.

"I did not ask you if you were tired, cow dung. I asked if you remembered what you did."

Anthony slowly lifted his head like a man with a knotted, arthritic spine. "I cut a business deal there."

"That is right. Do you remember the man you made the deal with?"

"Harry Tubbs: An American fat slob—a real-estate developer from Seattle with a second office in Paris. I met him in Águilas to seal the transaction."

The specter waved his arm, splitting obscurity and revealing *La Glorieta*, the principle town square in the Mediterranean seaport of Águilas.

"Look," the ghost said, "He is waiting for you."

Tubbs was seated at an outdoor café under a four-story rubber tree with a trunk like a bundle of elephant legs. He was morbidly obese, looking more like a kumquat than a man, the end of his chin and the beginning of his neck nearly indistinguishable. He was sweating under a white, short-sleeve shirt with an open collar that was three sizes too small for his massive neck.

Despite the titanic effort, Tubbs stood up when Anthony approached from across the park. The two men shook hands and sat down.

"What'll you have?" Tubbs asked.

"A cup of black coffee and a croissant."

"Good." Tubbs signaled for the waiter and ordered Anthony's breakfast in English.

"I see you haven't improved on your Spanish," Anthony said.

"Hell, no. I'm too old for that shit. I figure if they can't speaky-z-English, I shouldn't be doing business with them. Screw 'em, the goddamn spics."

"You know, of course that the term 'spic' is a pejorative reference to Latin Americans; it doesn't apply to the people of Spain. The word that you're searching for is, from the Mexican vocabulary, 'gachupin,' or, from the French, 'metèque.'"

"Really? Well, la-di-da," Tubbs said, folding his arms over his stomach like it was a lunch counter. "They're still all spics to me. And if you think I care about what's politically correct, you can call 1-800-FAT-CHANCE."

Anthony sat back in his chair and crossed his legs.

"I never did like him," Anthony said to the specter.

"Why is that?" asked the phantom.

"He's a pig. But he has a gift for making money. He's a cutthroat negotiator, lacking in both subtlety and compassion."

"In other words, just the kind of man you respect in business."

Anthony sucked in air. "That's right."

The coffee was served and Anthony took a long sip, appreciating the strong black espresso. It was early September, and the morning air was already pleasantly warm.

He looked past Tubbs at a tall, young woman walking briskly across the square. She wore high heels with straps that crisscrossed around the ankles. Her leather skirt was short, only marginally covering her buttocks, and her black angora sweater was pulled down over both shoulders.

"Oh, my," Anthony said.

Tubbs looked over his shoulder and caught sight of the beauty. "Whoa, mama, and la-di-da. Gimme some of that for Christmas."

For one timeless instant, the young woman caught the admiration of the two men and in her eyes flashed the entire history of Latin conquests: "If you're man enough and leave me satisfied afterwards, then just maybe I won't rip your heart out." Then she tossed her long hair over her shoulder with a flick of her head and strutted away, her heels clicking like castanets.

"If there was a God in heaven, he'd give me fifteen minutes alone with that skirt," Tubbs said.

"You wouldn't know what to do with fifteen minutes."

"OK, five minutes, plus ten to tie me up."

Tubbs laughed heartily, causing his huge belly to heave, which jostled the small plastic table that was pressed against his stomach. Luckily, Anthony had his coffee cup in hand. But Tubbs' demitasse, which was posed half full on the tabletop, flipped over and landed in his lap.

"Goddamn it!" the fat man howled, brushing the cup off his lap with a single swat, which rocketed the vessel into the chair at the next table, a chair that was occupied by an impeccably dressed Spanish businessman.

"Señor!" the Spaniard protested.

Tubbs ignored the man.

"Señor!"

This time, Tubbs briefly squinted at the man and said, "Well, La-di-da. If you don't like it, spic, you can kiss my Yankee doodly-dum."

Tubbs turned back to Anthony. He hoisted his bulbous buttocks, wrangled out a soiled handkerchief from his back pocket, and made a half-hearted effort to pat himself dry. Meanwhile, the Spaniard turned his back on the Americans, muttering something profane about the rudeness of foreigners.

After a moment, Anthony said, "Let's talk business."

"That's what I'm here for, kemosabe."

"I've seen the photos of the property. It looks impressive."

"You're damn right. Get this. It's a twenty-five-acre piece of coastline south of Águilas that belongs to—I love this—a frickin' fisherman."

"What's the going price per acre?"

"In today's market, $128,000 an acre, and that's on the low side."

Anthony quickly did the math in his head. "That's over three million for the twenty-five acres."

"Three million two, to be exact."

"That's a bundle of money."

"Tell me something I don't know. It's a bitch. Blame it on Franco. When he died, the whole goddamn market went to pot."

"Meaning, you can't buy the land for a few pesetas and a bottle of wine anymore."

"Exactly."

"Are you sure about that?"

"About what?"

"About buying the land for a few pesetas."

"What do you mean?"

Anthony leaned across the table. "What do you know about this fisherman?"

"I know he's broke, but I also know he ain't stupid. He's hired himself a spic lawyer."

"Fine. We've got lawyers too," Anthony said. "Here's what I want you to do. Write up a contract for two million dollars and give him $75,000 in earnest money—it's probably more money than he's seen in his entire life. Add a clause that twenty percent of the remaining payment will be paid each year upon completion of the construction project."

"That's still a lot of money," Tubbs protested.

"I'm not through," Anthony said, annoyed by the interruption. "Then, we start building our resort. And we build, and we build. And we never finish building—at least not for twenty years."

"I'm way ahead of you. And if we never finish, we never start payments."

Anthony turned over both palms of his hands, as if to say, "And it's that simple."

"Well, drop my pants and slap me silly."

Anthony finished the last of his coffee. "Listen, you've got your work cut out for you. Get that contract written up. I'm going to drive up to Granada for three days. When I get back, we'll go over the contract."

"It might take a little longer than three days."

Anthony turned slowly and held a searing gaze. "Three days, Tubbs. If my lawyers can do it, your lawyers can do it."

"You're right. I'll get on it."

Anthony stood up and threw a 1,000-peseta bill on the table. He did not offer his hand. Tubbs took a moment to lift his girth from the chair. A dark spot lay like a lily pad over a tube of material stretched to the breaking point below Tubbs' beltline. He started to extend his hand and then, sensing Anthony's reserve, withdrew his mitt and, feeling awkward, hitched up his belt with both hands. The buckle of that belt was on the last notch, and the tag was too short to tuck under the leather loop and so stuck out like a dog tongue, pointing the direction to Tubbs' next meal.

Anthony began to walk away, but then suddenly circled back. "How many rooms do we have in this complex?" he asked.

"Three hundred and twenty."

He stepped toward Tubbs. "If the fisherman gives you any opposition, offer him a room free of charge for the rest of his life. How old is the guy anyway?"

"Seventy-nine."

"Perfect."

Tubbs shook his head in admiration of Anthony's brutal business sense. "In-fucking-credible," he said with a grand guffaw, plopping back down into his chair, the plastic legs bowing under the strain.

"You are very good," the specter said mockingly from the black.

"It is what I do."

"Oh, you are too modest. It is not all that you do. Your stay in Spain did not end there."

"No, I visited the Alhambra in Granada."

"But not alone."

"You know about her?"

"I told you, cow dung; I know everything."

The specter cupped his hands and held them under Anthony's eyes. Then, he opened his hands . . .

. . . and a sparrow flew out and up and into the Andalusian sunshine, looping over the head of a hitchhiker with a small daypack at her feet and a cardboard sign marking her destination in capital letters: GRANADA.

The road traveler was a tall, slender woman with short auburn hair, combed back wet like she had just stepped out of the shower. She was wearing skintight jeans and a sheer black camisole top that had been chopped just above her navel to reveal a perfectly flat stomach.

Anthony rolled slowly past the girl and then stopped twenty yards beyond the point where she was standing. She turned and bent over at the waist to pick up her daypack; her jeans had a frayed two-inch-wide tear, strategically placed under the full curve of her right cheek. She did not run to the car; she strolled, not like a fashion model, but sashaying like a streetwise city chick who knew the guys were watching, as was Anthony in his rearview mirror.

"¿A donde va usted?" Anthony asked.

"Like the sign says, to Granada." Although her response was in Spanish, her accent belied her American roots.

"Hop in," Anthony said in English.

The girl swung her backpack off her shoulder and stuffed it behind the car seat.

"You're American," Anthony said.

"Born and raised," the girl said, smiling coyly, revealing a perfect set of white teeth. "I take it you're American too.

"Sure enough. Born and raised in Seattle, but work mostly in Paris these days . . ."

"Seattle, huh? Never been. Me, I'm from Savannah." The girl buckled in, and they were on the road. "What's your name?"

"Anthony."

"Like Anthony Perkins."

"Exactly."

"But not the slasher, I hope."

"I don't follow."

"You know, Anthony Perkins, as in Psycho.*"*

"Ah, of course. No, I'm a pretty mild fellow."

"You liked the girl, no?" the specter asked.

"I liked her free spirit. She seemed ready for anything."

"What was her name?"

"I don't know. I never asked. I just called her Savannah."

"Tell me, what are you looking for in Europe?" Anthony asked.

"A lover, of course," she said with a laugh.

Anthony shot a glance at the girl. She did not look like she was kidding. "Really?"

The girl looked out the window over her right shoulder at the lunar Andalusian landscape. "It's a long story."

"We've got the time."

The girl was silent for a moment. "How 'bout a piss break first?"

"Sure. We're coming up on Baza. We should be able to find a café in the main square."

It was market day in Baza, the traffic heavier than usual in the ancient town. Anthony wound his way to the center of town and found a parking space near the cathedral with its mix of Roman and Moorish influences. The two strolled to a nearby outdoor café. The girl asked Anthony to order sherry—"It's famous," she said—and scooted off to find the bathroom.

Anthony sat down at a table and placed an order for two Andalusian sherries. He sat back and watched the townspeople meander to and from the market.

"What are you thinking right now?" the phantom asked.

Anthony muttered something too muted to make out.

"What was that?"

"I wondered if I was going to get lucky."

"Exactly."

The girl was back and sitting at the table across from Anthony.

"Savannah, I'd like to pick up where we left off. You mentioned that you were looking for a lover. Were you kidding?"

The girl stared into her glass of sherry and sighed. "No, I wasn't kidding," she said deliberately and somewhat sadly.

Anthony was silent.

"How old do you think I am?" she asked.

Anthony always hated that question, but he responded as he always did, guessing low. "You look like a kid to me. I'd say twenty-one."

"That's what everyone says. I must have good genes."

Anthony explored Savannah's face. Other than a few faint freckles, her complexion was creamy and the corners of her eyes perfectly smooth.

"So how old are you?"

"Twenty-nine."

Anthony repeated the numbers out loud. "You surprise me."

"I know. I'm lucky that way. But the fact is the clock is ticking, and I don't have the one thing I want more than anything else in the world."

"That being?"

"That being . . . a baby."

"Really? Tell me more about that."

The specter scoffed. "You are so deceitful."

"What do you mean?"

"You appear genuinely interested in the girl. But you were not interested at all, were you?"

"Of course, I was."

"No, you only listened to gain her confidences, to take advantage of her."

"Have it your way."

"It is not my way. It is your way."

"I've wanted a family of my own for as long as I can remember," Savannah said. "I want to see a tiny human being grow into a young man or woman."

"Are you married?"

"No. I was close once, but it didn't work out."

"What happened?"

"Oh, I don't know. I guess I was too bitchy or too particular or too . . . something."

"And now?"

"And now I'm looking for another way. I've thought about adoption, but I really want the kid to be mine from the moment of conception. I want to carry him. I want to give birth." Savannah screwed her finger into her temple. "I know; I'm loony tunes."

"Why would you say that?"

"It's what everyone says. They all laugh at me."

"I'm not laughing. I think you have a perfect right to follow your dreams." Anthony took a sip of his sherry. "What about artificial insemination?"

"I've thought about that too. But it's just too antiseptic. I want a child that is conceived in love with a partner who is a good man."

"And that's what you are looking for now: One good man."

Savannah smiled. "Yep, just one good man. Of course, it wouldn't hurt if he was buff."

"Well, he has to be out there somewhere."

"That's what I keep thinking."

The two were silent for a moment.

"What about a close friend—someone you really admire?" Anthony offered.

"Yeah, I've thought of that. In fact, I once made a list. It was a short list: Only three names. The first candidate was my ex-boyfriend. Every time I saw him, I begged him to give me a baby."

"And what did he say?"

"He said I was crazy. Why in God's name would I want to raise a kid alone?"

"So he refused."

"Big time."

"Who else was on your list?"

"A friend of the family. He's single and bright and not bad looking."

"Uh-huh."

"But then I saw him badmouth a really sweet girl like she was some kind of idiot. He was so disgusting; I immediately scratched him from my list."

"And the third candidate?"

Savannah smiled.

"Judging from your expression, he must be something special."

"Oh, yeah, he's a sweetheart. But he's barely twenty and hot to trot."

"So?"

"So, I want more than that. He just wants to get into my pants, and, frankly, I think I would enjoy the hell out of it, but it's not enough. Sure, I'd get off on someone who wants my body, but is that all there is?"

"I think I'm getting the picture. You want a soul mate, a kindred spirit. Anyone can make a baby; what you want is a spiritual child."

That stopped Savannah cold. She studied Anthony's face like a blind person touches the mouth and nose and eyes of a loved one, tenderly exploring every curve and crevice.

"End of story. You knew you had her."

"Yes. It was easy."

"You are so transparent, cow dung. Your heart is beating. You can already see the girl naked, your arms wrapped around her slender body."

"Yes, yes," Anthony said, irritated at how easily the specter read his mind.

"That's exactly what I want," she said softly, "a spiritual child."

Anthony silently took in a breath and let it escape slowly. "Would I do?" he asked in a whisper.

Savannah was again stunned. Her eyes widened, and she did not move a muscle for a long moment. And then she smiled and lowered her eyes.

Anthony reached his hand across the table and caressed the girl's cheek. And with that touch, Savannah closed her eyes and leaned her face into his hand, covering his hand with her own. Then, still holding his hand and looking directly into his eyes, she said, "Are you the one?"

Anthony paused dramatically. "I would like to be."

"But I don't know anything about you."

"What would you like to know?" he said, fingering a staggering diamond ring on his right hand.

Noticing the ring, the girl reached over and took his right hand to get a closer look. "That's an amazing rock. Is it real?"

Anthony smiled. "It's a five-carat canary diamond I bought in South Africa about three years ago." With a heavy tug he twisted the snug-fitting ring off his finger and handed it to Savannah.

"You must be loaded," the girl said with a long whistle.

"I'm not the richest man in the world, but I am very comfortable."

The girl returned the ring. Then she hesitated for a moment, as if frightened to ask the next question: "Are you married?"

"I am a widow," he lied.

"Oh, I'm so sorry."

Anthony waved his hand, as if to say it was not important. "It was a long time ago. We were married only two years. We were just about ready to start a family when she contracted ovarian cancer."

"Oh, my God."

"It's called the silent killer, because it is so hard to detect." He huffed a self-mocking half laugh. "At least we didn't detect it."

"What a bitch."

Anthony affected a hitch in his voice and looked down at his hands. "Isn't it ironic . . . that I could not give to my wife . . . what I can give to you?"

"You are pathetic," the specter said.

"Wow!" Savannah said, shaking her head. "You just blew me away."

A moment passed.

"Where are you staying in Granada?" the girl asked.

"At the Franciscan Hotel," he said, still looking down, rubbing his thumb across the palm of his hand.

"Would you like company?"

Anthony looked into Savannah's eyes. It was the first time he noticed the color of her eyes; they were golden, almost cat-like. "Yes. I would like that very much."

The ghost ended the scene. "You could not get to the hotel room fast enough."

"I admit it. But I was not alone. It was what we both wanted."

"I wonder."

The next act opened on the Franciscan Hotel.

*Although the hotel had been a convent in the 15*th *century, there was nothing grim about their room. It was beautifully decorated in warm yellow and gold tones with ornate chandeliers and Renaissance landscape paintings. The floor was covered with a lush Moroccan carpet in the living room and terracotta tile in the bedroom.*

"I could crash here," Savannah said with cool restraint.

She bolted from room to room. "Hey, they even have a telephone in the can!" she said, calling out from the bathroom. Finally, she skipped back into the bedroom, threw her backpack on the floor, kicked off her shoes, and fell backward onto the bed.

After tipping the bellboy, Anthony followed Savannah into the bedroom and leaned against the door jam.

"You like?"

"I like," Savannah said.

She rolled out of the bed and, with her head tipped down, glided seductively to Anthony, one foot in front of the other, her hands tucked palms out behind the curve of her buttocks. When she stood before him, she raised her eyes and put one hand behind his head. She stood on tiptoe and brought her lips close to his, and when he pressed in to caress her mouth, she backed away, prolonging the moment. She licked her lips. Then, she again mirrored his mouth. Anthony did not move this time, and she slowly stroked the length of his lower lip three times with the moist tip of her tongue.

Anthony placed his hand firmly against the small of her back, brought her in closer to him, and kissed her for the first time.

Savannah brought her hand between their lips. "Wait, Anthony," she said, leaning back against his hand. "I've been waiting for this moment for so long; I want it to be perfect. Right now, I'm starving. I know my timing is lousy, but could we have dinner first?"

Anthony scowled and then, catching himself, softened his expression. "You're hungry now?"

"Famished."

A slow smile. "Okay. Would you like to freshen up first?"

"No, I don't want to freshen up; I want to get sexy," she said with a flirtatious smile. She snatched her backpack and popped into the bathroom.

Meanwhile, Anthony pulled a navy patch-pocket blazer out of his gym bag; it would do just fine for dinner. He heard the shower kick on.

He settled into an armchair and flipped through a tourist magazine. After a moment, he walked to the bathroom and was about to rap on the door when he heard her voice. He could not make out the words.

Finally, he tapped on the door. "How's it going?"

"Don't tell me you're getting impatient out there?" And, then, after a beat, "I'll be worth it."

Anthony returned to his chair, again blindly thumbing through a magazine.

"Cover your eyes," Savannah said from behind the bathroom door.

Anthony complied, and Savannah found her mark six feet in front of his chair.

"OK, you can open them now."

Anthony uncovered his eyes and there before him stood Savannah, one hand on her hip, dressed in a simple black-cotton spaghetti-strap dress, cut at an angle at the hem. Her face was made up with a touch of sparkle in her eye shadow and a splash of red on her pursed lips. With the advantage of open-toed black heels, she looked lean and statuesque.

"Tu es une merveille,*" he said in French.*

"That's good, I hope."

"That's very good. Are you sure you want to go to dinner?"

"Oh, yes," she said, taking him by both hands. "You're not getting off that easy."

As they left the room, Anthony said, "Look at you. I just can't believe you did all that from a daypack."

"You ain't seen nothin' yet, bunkie."

The specter clapped his hands, and the scene jumped forward. Savannah was finishing a layered chocolate-and-cream cake, pressing her fork into the remaining crumbs and, with eyes closed, slowly sucking the fork clean.

"Would you like another piece?" Anthony asked with a chuckle.

"Oh, no," she sighed, "but wasn't that to die for?"

Savannah crooked her finger at Anthony. He leaned forward. "Closer," she said, "I want to whisper something in your ear." He leaned in over the table, and she put her lips to his ear and whispered, "Let's fuck."

Anthony sat back and took in the full measure of Savannah's sex appeal. "I thought you would never ask." Pausing only an instant, he motioned to the waiter and mimed the signing of the bill.

He looked at Savannah. "Are you ready?"

"Ready?"

"Ready to go to our room."

Savannah pouted coyly. "Hmm, no."

"No?" Then, in a whisper: "I thought you wanted . . ."

"Uh-huh."

"Well then."

"Well, I want to get it on; I just don't want to do it in a hotel room." Savannah smiled, peering at Anthony from under her eyebrows.

"Just what did you have in mind?"

Savannah leaned across the table and mouthed the words, "The palace."

Anthony smirked, thinking Savannah was joking, and then, reading her eyes, realized she was serious. "You want to make love in the Nasrid Palace?"

Savannah pouted like a child finagling for one more chocolate.

"Are you crazy?"

"Don't you see how perfect it is? To make love in a palace that was made for kings. It'd be like doing it in the Taj Mahal. It's a hotbed of dreams and desires." She looked at Anthony, licked her lips, and with the tips of her fingers slowly traced the line from the base of her throat to the "V" in the neckline of her dress, pulling down on the fabric to expose her breasts. "Anthony, our first time has to be there; it just has to be."

"Okay," and again, "okay. Let me see what I can do. I think you need to come with me."

Anthony quickly signed the bill. They left the restaurant hand in hand and walked to the front desk. An English couple in their sixties, accompanied by a small sandy-haired boy, certainly their grandson, was checking in. Anthony and Savannah waited to the side. Savannah stood in front of Anthony and, reaching behind her, put her hand between his legs. When Anthony groaned, the English couple turned and looked at Savannah, who smiled back innocently.

When the family had registered, they turned to go to their room, smiling at Savannah and Anthony as they passed. The English gentleman did not tip his tweed walking hat; he pinched it at the crown and boosted it six inches straight up and back down again like lifting the lid of a soup tureen. Savannah, who still had Anthony's sex in hand, returned the smile and, just to be sassy, added a little curtsy.

The lovers moved to the counter.

"We'd like to see the Nasrid Palace," Anthony said directly.

"I'm sorry, sir. It closed at 8 o'clock."

Anthony looked at his watch. It was now 10:30.

"But, of course, we can arrange tickets for a morning viewing."

"I understand," Anthony said, pulling out a roll of 10,000-peseta bills, "but you see, we would like to see it now." Anthony pealed off 30,000 pesetas and placed them on the counter in front of the desk clerk.

"Sir, I could lose my job."

Anthony placed another 10,000-peseta bill on the stack.

"I cannot afford to lose my job. I have a wife."

Anthony snapped a fifth bill on the counter.

"And two children."

"You better not have any cousins," Anthony said, placing another bill before the desk clerk.

"I will have to pay a security guard."

Anthony placed two more bills on the counter. He tapped the bills and said, "Pick a guard with no family."

The desk clerk deftly placed a newspaper over the bills and looked at his watch. "The gate to the Nasrid Palace will be open at 11 o'clock. It will be locked again at midnight with you either inside or outside the palace. That's the best I can do."

Anthony looked at Savannah, who smiled approvingly.

"That will work," Anthony said to the desk clerk.

"Do you know where the entrance is?"

"Yes."

"Now, if you will excuse me," the desk clerk said, reaching for the phone.

Anthony and Savannah walked slowly through the Alhambra gardens toward the fourteenth-century Moorish palace. The September night air was warm and the moon was full. The two were quiet, as if visiting a cathedral. When they reached the gate to the palace, it was precisely eleven o'clock. Anthony pushed the wrought-iron gate, and it silently swung open.

"Yes," Savannah said softly.

Anthony invited Savannah to enter and then shut the gate behind them. The first room they entered was the Mexuar. *The multiple pillared arches with their intricate plaster scrollwork were astonishing. Each arch was meticulously inscribed with ornate Arabic patterns like a miniaturized version of the French gardens of Versailles.*

"Incredible," he said.

Savannah was less interested in admiring Moorish architecture. She pulled away from Anthony's hand and scampered off to the Patio de los Arrayanes, *the Myrtle Courtyard. It was an open patio, approximately fifty-yards long and twenty-five-yards wide. Running the length of the courtyard was a shallow pool, banked on each side by solid three-foot-high walls of myrtle shrubs. Savannah was running so quickly that she almost plunged into the pool, saving herself at the last moment by grabbing and swinging full circle around a pillar that stood two feet from the pool's edge. And there she stood stock-still, dazzled by the reflection of the moon in the pool. Anthony came up from behind her and placed both arms around her waist. Savannah backed into him, slowly undulating into his loins.*

"It's so beautiful," Savannah said.

Anthony breathed in the scent of Savannah's hair.

On the opposite side of the pool were seven arches; at the side of the arches there was a doorway, and it beckoned to Savannah. Again, she pulled away from Anthony and rushed around the pool and through the doorway. Anthony stood still and watched the graceful nymph disappear.

"You look almost delirious," the specter said.

"I was. She made me dizzy. In spite of myself, I was incredibly happy."

"And also afraid."

"I knew if I allowed it, she could easily consume me."

"So you left her."

"I suddenly thought it was madness. I retraced my steps, getting as far as the entryway to the *Mexuar*. And then I thought, 'Why not take it for what it was'?"

"That being?"

"That being a night of passion."

"No, you are too easy on yourself. Call it what it is: A night of depravity. You lied to her, and then you took advantage of her."

Anthony whirled around and ran full speed back to Savannah, crashing into a passage wall as he rounded the corner into the Myrtle Courtyard. He sprinted alongside the length of the pool and lunged through the open doorway into total darkness. By fully extending both arms, he could feel that he was in a corridor, but nothing more. He turned one way and was met with a solid wall. Quickly, he retraced his steps and then stopped dead in the dark and listened.

Silence.

"Savannah," he called in a stage whisper.

He listened. He heard nothing.

"Savannah," he called again, this time in full voice.

He closed his eyes and listened intently, and, more like a thought than a sound, he heard his name called.

"Anthony. I'm here."

"Where?"

"Here."

Anthony followed the sound of her voice, threading through the maze by feel. Finally, he broke into the open Lion's Courtyard, the Patio de los Leones. *Only a bit smaller than the Myrtle Courtyard, this rectangular patio was an exquisite masterpiece of Arabic architecture, the perimeter arches supported by a hundred pillars.*

Anthony was welcomed by some twenty marble columns, topped with filigree arches placed in mirror perfection around a small ground-level fountain with a slender trough, which led to the center of the square. And at the center was a waist-high alabaster basin, perhaps seven feet in diameter, with a small spring of water spouting from its center. But, most stunningly, the basin was supported on the haunches of twelve rough-stone lions, placed symmetrically around the basin, as if indicating the hour of the day. From the mouth of each lion spouted a stream of water, which poured into a shallow channel before the lions' front paws.

Anthony could make out the figure of Savannah standing with her back to him at the side of the six-o'clock lion. He walked toward her and then stopped midway, a few paces from where she was standing. He could see the curve of her figure in the moonlight, and it took his breath away.

Three times Savannah sliced her hands into the basin. Three times she raised the water to her face and, from her temples to the back of her neck, dispersed the water across her hair. Then she turned around and faced Anthony. Without hesitation, without the slightest hint of self-consciousness, she laid her arms across her chest, lifted the straps of her dress off her shoulders, and let the dress slip silently off her body and pool at her feet. She then stepped out of the dress and, with one graceful sweep of her foot, brushed the dress under the feet of the adjacent lion. Then, with her back to the basin, she reached behind her, cupped her hands in the water, and poured the water over the front of her body.

Meanwhile, Anthony stood in perfect silence, clearly overwhelmed by the exquisite rite of seduction. He was mesmerized by Savannah's beauty, her wet body glistening in the moonlight, the shadows and light dappling her shoulders, breasts, and hips.

Neither said a word. Savannah straddled the six-o'clock lion and reached out her arms toward Anthony, like a siren calling him into the rocky shore. In turn, Anthony slipped his shirt over his head and flung it to the side. He walked to Savannah. With one firm tug, she unbuckled his belt. He kicked out of his loafers and pants, sat backward on the lion's withers, and Savannah eased down on his lap, her legs hooked around Anthony's waist and the neck of the stone lion. She reached in the basin for a handful of water and spread it across his body, admiring how the warm water coursed over his chest and stomach.

They embraced and kissed as though discovering desire for the first time. Anthony devoured her, kissing her mouth and neck. He gently cupped her breasts and filled his mouth with one nipple, then the other, while Savannah arched her back, the nape of her hair swishing in the basin water. When he entered Savannah, she interrupted the silence of the night, whispering in his ear, "Our son will be a king."

Black.

Anthony turned to the specter. They were both silent for a moment.

"I understand," Anthony said quietly.

"Do you? Do you truly understand?"

"Yes. I understand that I am a bully. I understand that I use people." He paused. "I understand . . . that I am despicable."

For the first time, the specter broke into a genuine smile. "Good. Very good, Anthony. You have finally arrived at the first step of transformation."

Anthony looked again at the specter. Then, before his eyes, the ghost slowly transfigured. Age evaporated from his face. The scar that ran from his eye to his jaw melded into his skin and disappeared. His blind eye was suddenly healed, sparkling with life. His hair darkened and thickened. And in the next moment, the specter was young—not much older than a schoolboy—with a spirit that was warm and engaging and full of innocence; he looked like a youngster without a care in the world.

"What is happening?" Anthony asked.

"My work is done," Cecilio said. "The rest is up to you."

"But what is up to me? What must I do?"

"You must awaken. You must come to learn what a real family can do."

"Will I see you again?"

Cecilio smiled. "You may, if you need a nudge in the right direction."

Anthony looked sideways at his teacher. "Tell me you are not going to freeze me again; I hate being frozen."

Cecilio laughed a gentle laugh. "Not unless you really need it."

"Will I remember you?"

"I am afraid not."

"Will I remember what you have taught me?"

"I hope so."

Anthony looked hard at his young guide, trying to memorize his features. Then the two men embraced. Cecilio felt warm against Anthony's chest; in fact, he thought he could feel the Spaniard's heartbeat. Cecilio held Anthony tightly in his arms like a dear friend who was thought to be lost and was now found. He spoke softly into Anthony's ear. "It is all right. You can awaken now; you are expected."

III

EPIPHANY

Wednesday, September 12, 1990

It was the afternoon of the fourth day, and Antonio still lay in a coma. His physical wounds—the severe abrasion to his forehead, the puncture to his left shoulder, the massive contusions behind his knees—were healing as hoped, despite an extraordinary third day of agitation. The most troubling injury was the clean slit across the stranger's larynx, the damage to his vocal folds impossible to determine until he revived.

Lupita redressed Antonio's wounds and bathed his face and torso. She also verified that the chest catheter supplying nutrition and the arm catheter providing hydration were free of inflammation. These were routine acts of medical maintenance, but for Lupita, they were more than that: They were acts of love.

Then it happened: Antonio awakened. Lupita was at his side, checking his vital signs, when she heard a weak groan. She sat on the side of the bed and took her patient's hand.

"Are you awake now?" her voice trembling with excitement.

Antonio opened his eyes slowly for two or three seconds without focusing and then closed them again. He briefly panted and then swallowed with effort, trying to bring moisture to his throat. Then he was asleep again.

Lupita wanted her patient to come around, and so she gently patted Antonio's hand. "Antonio. It is time to wake up now."

Again, Antonio's eyes fluttered and then opened. For the first time, he focused on Lupita, and then beyond the doctor to the open window. A ray of sunlight streamed through the white, wispy drapes and danced on the wall.

Antonio opened his mouth to speak, but no word was spoken. He furrowed his brow in confusion. Lupita placed her fingertips lightly across his lips.

"Shh. *¿Habla usted español?*"

Antonio nodded.

"You have been in an accident, and there may have been some damage to your vocal chords," she said in Spanish.

This news prompted Antonio to attempt to speak again, which was exactly what Lupita did not want. Again, she touched his lips. "No, you must not try to speak—not yet. Your vocal chords need time to heal. If you try to force it, you will only delay that process. Do you understand me?"

He nodded.

"My name is Lupita Garcia. I am a doctor. You are in my home and the home of my grandfather. His name is Diego. You will meet him later. We live in a village near Córdoba called Espejo."

Antonio became agitated and made an effort to get up. He was stopped cold by the shooting pain in his shoulder. Lupita moved quickly, slipping her hands behind his back and easing his body down. "*Por favor*, your shoulder has been seriously injured. You must give it time."

Antonio motioned for a pencil and paper.

"All right," Lupita said, placing her hand lightly on Antonio's chest. "Do not try to move. I will be right back."

While Lupita was gone, Antonio looked at his surroundings. Everything—the window casing, the wall radiator, the light switch—told him that he was in Europe. If the woman were not lying (why should she lie?), he could indeed be in Spain.

The walls of the room were sculpted white plaster. The bed headboard and seven-foot-high armoire were oak. On one wall was a painting of a white house in an olive orchard. On the opposite wall was a reprint of Goya's *The Third of May 1808* in a simple oak frame.

For a moment, Antonio identified with Goya's central figure, his arms uplifted, waiting for his death. He felt as if *he* were kneeling before a firing squad. Had someone tried to kill him? Where was he? Who were these people? His head was reeling with questions.

Lupita returned and placed on her patient's lap a small notepad and pencil. Diego walked in behind her, and they both sat down on chairs at the bedside.

"This is my grandfather. He was very anxious to meet you. His name is Diego, but I call him Tito."

Diego, his eyes warm and shining, looked down on Antonio. He pressed the man's hand between his own callused hands and smiled. "*Buenos días*, my son. Welcome to our humble home."

Antonio had wanted to write a thousand questions, but suddenly he was inescapably sleepy. His eyes began to close.

"Yes, that is right, you get some sleep now. We will talk some more later. I am going to take out the catheters; you will sleep more peacefully." Then, with Antonio already asleep, the doctor gently withdrew the needles from her patient's arm and chest.

Antonio slept until the next morning, but it was not a peaceful sleep. Disconnected voices and images whirled in his head, hurling from every direction without meaning: a black tattered sleeve, a hollow laugh, a lion's head, a basin of water. It was all random, and when he awoke the following morning, he remembered none of it.

He recognized the room from the day before, but beyond that, all remained a mystery. He heard Lupita and Diego talking in the kitchen and tried to call out and then, with a spasm of piercing pain to his throat, remembered that he was mute. Seeing a glass of water on the nightstand, he instinctively tried reaching for it with his left hand and jerked back with pain. He looked down his torso and frowned; his left arm was taped to his chest. He pressed lightly against the compress over his shoulder wound, which instantly made him feel woozy. He lay back and rested a moment, then, rolling slightly to his side, reached over his body with his right arm and pawed at the glass, which tipped over and rolled beyond his fingertips off the table, exploding on the tile floor.

Lupita and Diego came into the room. Antonio gestured to the broken glass, expressing his apologies with his eyes.

"It is nothing," Lupita said.

"I will take care of it," Diego announced, leaving the room.

Lupita sat down on the side of the bed and took Antonio's pulse and blood pressure. "Your vitals are strong this morning, and your eyes look brighter. Are you feeling better?"

Antonio nodded and smiled at the woman, registering her features for the first time. She was tall—much taller than most Spanish women—and slender at the waist. Her skin was the color of cocoa butter and her long hair, twists of jet black, was held back away from her face, cascading midway down her back. But, most of all, Antonio, like everyone who knew Lupita, was taken in by her almond-shaped eyes; they were the darkest brown, almost black, with long, thick lashes—eyes you could not escape, nor would ever want to.

"Are you hungry?"

Antonio's face brightened.

"All right, then," Lupita said with a chuckle. "Let us see what we can find for you. I am going to suggest something very light to begin with." Lupita turned to Diego, who had already swept up the broken glass and sopped up the water. "Tito, would you help me lift Antonio? I would like him sitting upright."

"*Si.*" Diego moved to the opposite side of the bed.

"Place your hand below his buttocks, and we will lift together—gently and slowly. On three. Ready? One, two, three." With Lupita's and Diego's hands against his bare skin, Antonio realized for the first time that he was completely naked, and he flushed with embarrassment. The move triggered a surge of pain in his legs and shoulder, but ultimately it felt good to be sitting up.

Lupita prepared a bowl of rice with bits of parsley and mushrooms, a small dish of applesauce, and a cup of hot tea. She placed everything on a tray and returned to Antonio's room. "Do you think you can handle it yourself or would you like me to feed you?" Lupita said.

Antonio pointed at Lupita, not because he thought he could not manage, but because he wanted to look more deeply into the doctor's eyes.

"All right," Lupita said, with a smile, "but just this once."

As Lupita slowly spooned the rice into her patient's mouth, pausing between each morsel, Antonio did, indeed, explore her eyes. Without a trace of makeup, Lupita was amazingly beautiful. She had a clean and natural luminescence that immediately captivated him. He swallowed slowly, savoring each bite, extending the intimacy of the moment with the exquisite brown-skinned woman.

When they had finished, Lupita asked Antonio if he would like to ask any questions. He nodded "yes," and Lupita drew the notepad from the nightstand and handed it to her patient.

He thought for a moment and then wrote in Spanish, "Where did you find me?"

Lupita read the question. "I think that Tito should answer that."

She called for Diego, who came into the room and sat down next to Antonio. When Lupita showed him the question, Diego looked questioningly at Lupita. She motioned for him to respond.

"I found you in Granada—in the Arab Quarter. Do you remember?"

Antonio shook his head no.

"You were badly beaten. You were dying, Antonio. I brought you home to Lupita to heal you."

Antonio looked at Lupita and mouthed the word, "*Gracias.*"

"*De nada,*" Lupita said, patting her patient's hand. "Perhaps what Tito did was more important: He gave you his blood." She did not mention that both Diego and she had lay naked in his bed for over an hour; despite her normally detached professionalism, that piece of information seemed too intimate. Besides, there was nothing normal about this case.

Antonio looked at the old man. His face was creased and weathered, his hair thinning and perfectly white. His eyes were sparkling—joyful, Antonio thought—and his smile was pure compassion, somehow made all the more brilliant by a frayed red bandanna tied at his neck. Antonio instantly liked the old Spaniard. He gingerly lifted his right hand to him.

Diego reached out with both hands and kissed the back of Antonio's hand. The simple act was so tender and loving that Antonio wondered what it meant. In some strange way, he felt that he knew the kind old man from another time and that their lives were inexplicably intermingled. Instinctively, he knew that Diego was a man he could trust.

Motioning for the notepad, the stranger wrote, "Why do you call me 'Antonio'?"

Lupita read the scrawled words upside-down as Antonio composed each word, again smiling at her patient's natural struggle to unravel the mystery.

She withdrew the bloodstained slip of paper from a pocket in her skirt. "We found this note in your shirt," she said, passing the fragment to Antonio.

Antonio read the note, pondered a moment, and then reread:

Anthony,
You were unbelievable.
Savannah

Antonio quickly scribbled a few words. "What does it mean?" he wrote. He held the notebook in front of Lupita's eyes.

"We were hoping that you could tell us," she said.

"I like the name 'Anthony,'" Diego said, "but I prefer 'Antonio.' May I call you Antonio?"

Antonio smiled and nodded at the old man.

Lupita was touched by her grandfather's need to be on a first-name basis with their guest, but she knew there was a more basic question. "Is that your name: Anthony?" she asked.

Antonio posed the pencil on the notebook, but did not write. He looked at the notebook, looked at Lupita, and then at the pad again. Then he wrote, "I do not know."

"Do you know where you are from?"

Antonio pointed at the last line in the notebook.

"Who is Savannah?"

This time he stabbed at the line in the notebook, underlining again and again the words, "I do not know." He shook his head vigorously and threw the pad and pencil against the wall across the room—a motion that tore at the stitches in his shoulder.

"*Calmaté, Calmaté,*" Lupita said, taking Antonio by both shoulders. "Shh. I am sorry. It is my fault; I went too fast."

Antonio looked into Lupita eyes, his own eyes whelming with tears. Lupita felt his torment and said, simply, "Oh, oh."

The patient fell into Lupita's arms and suddenly began sobbing. Lupita held him tenderly and lightly rocked him. She looked at her grandfather. Diego's mouth was trembling, and he turned and left the room. "Easy, easy now," Lupita whispered to Antonio. "It will be all right."

She held him for a long time, until Antonio's sobbing subsided, and then she gently laid him down. Antonio could not look at Lupita.

He began to write. "Sorry. That is not like me."

"How do you know what you are like?"

"I am not like *that*," he wrote, underlining the word "that."

"Maybe it would be better if you were."

Antonio looked again at Lupita and, touched by her tenderness, conceded her point by placing his hand over his heart. He wanted to talk more with the beautiful doctor, but suddenly his eyes were incredibly heavy.

"You look like you could use some rest."

Antonio nodded, closed his eyes, and instantly fell asleep.

When Antonio awoke again, it was midday. He could overhear Lupita speaking to someone in the living room outside his room. "It cannot be rushed," she was saying.

"How long will it take?" a man's voice said.

"That depends."

"On what?"

"That depends on the type of amnesia. It could be transient global amnesia or limited amnesia. In any case, I think it is safe to say that it is trauma-induced. The connection between repressed memories and the unconscious mind is very complicated. It may take a day or two or . . ."

"Or what?"

"Or it could be much longer."

Antonio tapped his headboard with his knuckles. Lupita appeared at the door, Miguel standing behind her. She entered. "Antonio, I would like you to meet a good friend of the family. His name is Miguel."

Miguel looked at Lupita. After his clash with her, he had wondered if he would ever be called "friend" again. Was it possible that she had already forgiven him? He was touched by the simple word of kindness: "friend." The word felt like a blessing, and his devotion to Lupita grew all the more.

Antonio tipped his head.

"*Mucho gusto*," Miguel said, moving into the room and taking a chair.

Lupita stood behind Miguel.

"Miguel is not only a friend, but he is also the chief of police for Espejo. He would like to talk to you for a moment. Not because you are accused of anything, of course, but because he would like to help you find your family."

Antonio indicated his consent.

"Lupita has told me that you have a form of amnesia."

Antonio's eyes darted to Lupita.

"We do not know what kind, of course," Lupita said quickly. "It could be something very transient, which is probably most likely."

"You may not be able to tell me much," Miguel continued, "but anything would help. Any scrap of information."

Antonio crossed two fingers across his palm: a call for the notebook. He wrote a sentence and showed it to Miguel. It read, "What kind of information?"

"Anything. Your nationality, your profession, the name of a loved one. Anything."

Antonio lowered his head and massaged his temple. He then looked up and hunched his shoulders, indicating that he had nothing.

"You cannot think of a thing?" Miguel asked. There was a chill in the police chief's tone. Despite his affection for Lupita—or perhaps because of it—it was clear he held no fondness for the stranger.

"No," Antonio mouthed.

"I think that is enough," Lupita said, directing Miguel out of the room.

Miguel turned around at the door and said, "We will talk more later," which to Antonio sounded more like a threat than a friendly goodbye.

Outside the door, Antonio could hear Miguel talking. "I do not trust him. There is something that does not smell right."

"There is nothing," Lupita said. "How can you condemn him, when you know nothing about him?"

"He is hiding something."

"*Hasta luego*, Miguel."

"All right. *Hasta luego.*"

Lupita returned to Antonio's room. "Do not worry about Miguel. He is sometimes just a little over-protective."

Antonio wrote in his notebook. "I think he loves you."

Lupita crinkled her brow and then broke into a smile. "Perhaps."

"Do you love him?" he wrote.

"Not that it is any of your business, but no, I do not."

"Good."

In the middle of the night, Antonio had the urge to go to the bathroom. Although his left arm was still anchored to his chest, he managed, despite a jolt of pain, to swing his legs around and haltingly lift himself out of bed. He was naked, and there was no sign of a pair of pants, so he took a pillow from his bed and held it below his waist.

He was in that state of half-sleep, half-wakefulness, when a side chair can become a mad dog or a shadow a malicious intruder. His eyes were mere slits. When he arrived at the bathroom door, his head was lowered, his chin nearly resting on his chest. He reached for the door handle. At that instant the door sprung open, startled him, and clipped him hard on the upper ridge of his forehead. He moaned in pain and dropped the pillow to rub his head and then found himself face-to-face with Lupita who was also half asleep, though looking comfortable in a man's white, long-sleeve dress shirt rolled up at the cuffs.

"Oh, I am so sorry," she said, taking Antonio by the shoulders and lowering her head to look into his eyes to see what damage she had done.

Suddenly, Antonio realized that he was stark naked and quickly bent over to pick up the pillow, clunking heads with Lupita in the process, who groaned even louder than Antonio.

The pair of yelps was sufficient to rouse Diego from his sleep, who was now standing at his bedroom door watching with delight as Antonio and his granddaughter negotiated the midnight rendezvous.

Antonio sympathized with the injured doctor. He reached up to massage her head, forgetting for the moment that he was still stark naked.

Reviving from her half-sleep, Lupita looked into Antonio's eyes and then glanced below his hips, not to goggle what she had already seen when she first stripped her patient and put him to bed, but to delicately indicate to Antonio his state of undress.

Lupita's signal slowly penetrated Antonio's consciousness, and again he swept up the pillow that was resting at his feet and jammed it against his loins.

"Tomorrow I will go into Córdoba and get you some clothes," Lupita whispered, her face registering an apology.

"Right."

"Goodnight, Antonio."

"Goodnight, Lupita,"

Lupita rounded Antonio and then, out of sheer mischief, looked over her shoulder as he entered the bathroom to sneak a glimpse at her patient's backside. She smiled impish smile, just as Antonio turned to close the door and caught her looking.

She quickly undid her smile, looked away, and reached up to twirl her hair into a pile at the top of her head. The fiddling with her hair was a mindless act, because she really didn't want her hair up at all, and even if she did, she didn't have a hairpin to stake it, and so she let her long, black hair fall.

Antonio saw all this and smiled.

On the way to her bedroom, Lupita passed Diego who was still standing at his door, grinning like a boy remembering his first kiss. She furrowed her brow as if to say, "And what is on *your* wicked mind?"

Diego raised both palms in defense of his innocence. "Goodnight, Lupita." he said singsong.

"Goodnight, Tito," Lupita mumbled, escaping into her room.

"Goodnight, Antonio," Diego called out, shaking his head as he circled and returned to his bed.

Antonio heard Diego's goodnight wishes. It made him smile, and he silently returned the greeting: "Goodnight, Diego."

When Antonio slept, he journeyed again—deeper, deeper into the roots of his life. They were night visions that he would not remember, could not remember and survive.

Although Tony Rossi was seven years old, he still had not learned to tie his shoes. So he made a square knot and forced his feet in and out of his worn and crusty tennis shoes with a grunt. They did not slide easily; he did not wear socks; he did not own socks.

On this hot East Harlem night, he tugged the canvas shoes off his feet, tossed them under the bed, and because there was nothing else to do, he cradled his right foot and drew it to his face for closer inspection. There was an angry blister on the curve of the foot below the big toe. Tony poked at the milky center of the blister and winced, but did not whimper. Then he pressed his finger into the wound again, intrigued by how the pus oozed in all directions.

Tony examined his toes with interest. He did not know them by name; they were not "little piggies" who "went to market" or "had roast beef." Nor were they soft and white. They looked more like the toes of an old man: scuffed and bruised and calloused, the consequence of running barefoot more often than not in and out of the backstreets and alleys of East Harlem.

Tony was still peering at his toes, when the urge to sleep swept over him. He rolled his body to all fours on the hardwood floor and lifted himself onto the bed, a rat's nest of clothing, stained bed sheets, whiskey bottles, and the smell of alcohol and piss. Tony was hungry, but he was already half asleep. He lay on his side, his skeletal back curling around his knees in the depression in the middle of the bed.

Once again, the boy dreamt about stickball, which was truly a dream, for most of the big kids would not let the scrawny Dago play any of their street games.

"He's too little," one of the older boys would complain.

"And too stupid," another would add.

Then everyone looked to the self-appointed, twelve-year-old leader of the block. His name was John Mancini, but no one knew him by his real name. Everyone called him Jackoff, a name he neither denied nor despised. His unquestioned authority was based on one facility: he knew more about the dark side of Pleasant Avenue than any other kid in the neighborhood, and he used that information like a weapon. If another boy challenged his right to command, Jackoff would counter with a deadly retort: "Oh, yeah. Well, maybe you'd like a visit from Louie De Luca." And that was all it took. Most kids didn't even know Louie De Luca, but that didn't matter. The way Jackoff said the name, like a forbidden curse word, was enough to change the attitude of any would-be rival. Discussion over.

So whenever Tony wanted to play stickball, Jackoff always had the same response, offered in a sickly sweet tone of voice. "Hey, don't be messin' with the kid," he would say. "He's not all bad. Are youse kid? After all, Louie De Luca says your mama's the best fuck on the block—and cheap too. Ain't that right kid?"

At seven, Tony did not know what it meant to be the "best fuck," but he knew it was not good. He knew it was dirty: something vile and unimaginable.

One day, after Jackoff had spoken the dirty words, Tony's eyes turned hard. He lowered his head, converting it into a battering ram, and launched himself into the crotch of the block leader. It was a direct hit. Jackoff fell to the ground as if every muscle in his body had gone to mush. He rolled in agony for a long time in the middle of the street, until a beautiful woman with pitch-black hair strutted out to the boy, cupped her hands under his armpits and lifted the groaning bully to his feet. It was his mother, Mrs. Mancini. "You get-a you skinny *culo* back-a home," she pronounced in a husky Sicilian accent.

As the two marched to the brown-brick tenement house, Mrs. Mancini backhanded her son's backside, but Jackoff saw the blow coming and he tucked in his butt just in time. Having just missed her mark, Mrs. Mancini took an extra step and pinched her son's ear between thumb and forefinger. She led him that way across the street, like a dog owner escorting a reluctant hound into the dreaded kennel. Every boy in the street knew that the pain of being tugged by the ear was short lived; the public humiliation was eternal.

In all of that, Mrs. Mancini asked no questions. She seemed to know instinctively that whatever pain her son endured, it was something he fully deserved. "Why you do dis to you mama, Mist'r Jackoff?" she scolded, having long ago picked up on the neighborhood nickname. "Why you do dis bad thing?"

But on this night in Tony's dream, there was no Jackoff. There was only he, Little Tony, tapping the manhole cover that served as home plate with the tip of his broomstick and swatting the handball into the heart of Manhattan. SMACK.

Tony was awakened with a rude whack to his butt. He opened his eyes and stared into the round, ruddy face of a redheaded stranger.

"You'll be gettin' your bum out of bed," the stranger said, more of a command than a request.

Tony looked past the man at his mother, who was propped against the bathroom door. Her head fell forward and lifted, again and again, as if she were fighting sleep and losing. Her arm lay limp at her side, an uncorked bottle of whiskey in her hand. She loosened her grip, and the bottle fell to the ground and poured through the cracks in the wood floor.

The stranger turned and strode directly to the overturned bottle, moving sideways with his shoulder pointing at the target. He swept up the bottle by the neck.

"'Tis enough o' that," the man said. He leaned over Tony's mother, bracing himself on his forearm and pushed the tip of the bottle neck under her jaw. "God help me, I was payin' good money for that whiskey. You'll not be servin' it to the rats. Are you hearin' me?" he said, pressing the bottle spout deeper into her neck.

Tony's mother did not move nor protest.

Tony felt a surge of anger in his throat: the same feeling he had when he head-butted Jackoff in the balls. He bounded out of bed and at full speed tackled the legs of the stranger. The blow made the man stumble a step, but no more. He turned and slapped the boy across the face with his opened hand.

Tony did not cry, but the smack made him dizzy for a moment, and he did not know what to do.

Tony's mother raised her head. Her eyes focused for the first time that night. She went to the boy and held him by both shoulders. In Italian, she said, "Go out and play, Tony. We no be long. You come-a-back when he-a be gone."

"But it's the middle of the night," Tony protested.

"I know what-a time it is. That no matter. You-a listen to you mama. I be the only mama you-a got. Now you-a go."

Tony crossed the room to retrieve his shoes from under the bed.

"No," his mother said. "You-a go now."

"But my shoes."

"You no need you shoes," she said. "You no need anything."

Tony turned and glared at the redheaded stranger. If he were only bigger, he would kill him and not think twice about it. Then he left the room. He walked down the three flights of stairs, punching the handrail with the side of his fist at each step. He opened the front door and sat in the middle of the stoop, his hands supporting his face. Once again, he stared at his toes: toes that did not belong to him, that belonged to some old man, to someone else—but not to him.

"Momma's right," he said to himself. "I no need anything." And then, with the anger and the shame and the hunger raging in his gut, he added, "I no need *nobody*—not now, not ever."

Two weeks passed. It had not been easy for Lupita. Since the stranger's arrival, she had scrambled from the house to clinic to the house again. For a physician with less vigor, it would have been impossible; for Lupita it was merely exhausting. But at the end of each day, Lupita welcomed her weariness with a kind of satisfaction. Yes, she had worked hard, but she was making a difference.

Happily, Antonio's medical condition improved with every new day. His left arm was no longer taped to his body, but rather comfortably supported in a sling. The piercing pain that had stabbed him with every false move had thankfully diminished in number and intensity. As for the bruises on the back of his legs, they had almost entirely disappeared.

The best news regarding his recuperation was that his voice had returned. Granted, it was a bit soft and raspy and could not be overused, but he could speak. The notepad was discarded.

Antonio had free run of the house, which was a simple all-white, single-level home cut into the hillside. He was particularly fond of the view from the terrace, where he enjoyed reading in the late afternoon.

In fact, reading was his primary pastime. The living room was conspicuous in its absence of a television. In its place, against a twelve-foot length of wall, was a floor-to-ceiling bookcase, stocked with world classics. Although there was a fine collection of European, American, and Russian novels, the heart of the library focused on philosophy, theology, and history, including both ancient and modern masters. Finally, there was a section reserved for Lupita's medical books. In brief, it was not a library for someone looking for a breezy diversion.

What was more, the library was heavily used. When Antonio opened a book, he invariably found comments penciled in the margins. It was not unusual for Lupita and Diego to spend two or three hours a night poring over works ranging from ancient history to modern ethics. This was a family that put a high premium on knowledge.

With the return of Antonio's voice, one thing was clear: He was not Spanish—not with his accent. The Garcias discovered that he was not only fluent in Spanish, but also French and English, the latter appearing to be his mother tongue. Although nothing was certain, Lupita reasoned that he was most likely British or American. Beyond that, they still had no other clues about his identity.

Antonio was still without personal memory. He could comment on world affairs and decipher mathematical equations, but he had no recollection of his personal life. That was frustrating, sometimes agonizing, for him. And yet, Diego and Lupita were so kind and really so much like family that he was not altogether sure he wanted another home. He had not admitted this to Lupita and her grandfather, but it was on his mind.

Antonio had been moved to a smaller room in the home, allowing Lupita to recover her own bedroom. Antonio was happy for that. The family had given so much to him that he no longer wanted to be an imposition; he hoped that he might find some way soon of repaying their generosity.

"How would you like some fresh air?" Lupita asked at breakfast.

"That would be wonderful."

It was the first time that Antonio had left the house. The front door opened to a narrow cobblestone street. Antonio looked across the road and up the hill at the village church. Just then, the bells rang out announcing morning mass, which rousted the pigeons from the belfry and sent them zigzagging in formation across the sky.

Lupita backed her small car into the street and drove slowly down the hillside. The lane was lined with houses, all painted white and attached to the next house, an ancient construction method that preserved both energy and space.

Antonio noticed a woman standing at her open door, the morning sun on her face; she shaded her eyes and peered down the street. Then he spotted a second woman and a third—all squinting their eyes toward the corner at the bottom of the hill.

"What are the women waiting for?"

"The bread truck." Then after a moment, Lupita pointed to a compact van with the back doors sprung open. "There it is."

At the back of the van, a man in his thirties with a flat cap and a white apron was drawing out sticks of French bread from one of three straw baskets. The women were gathered around him like hens pecking at a fertile piece of ground.

At a plateau halfway down the hill, the street opened up to a long rectangular plaza. It was accented with park benches and oak trees and a large fountain at the far end. Seated on the benches were old men in brown sport coats and open collars reading the newspaper or talking passionately with a friend about sports or politics. Some shouted morning greetings to the women standing at the doorways. Sometimes the women shouted back, often with a quip about the old men's impertinence, which made everyone within earshot laugh.

Lupita rolled through the plaza, down the hill, and out of town.

"Where are we going?" Antonio asked.

"I do have other patients, you know," Lupita said, smiling.

"Really. I thought that I was all you could handle."

"Oh, I think I can manage just a tiny bit more."

"I am sure you can."

Lupita had both hands on the wheel, looking like a woman in charge. "I am taking you to a small village. I have a patient to see who is no longer able to leave his home."

"What does he have?"

"Lung cancer. He will most likely die within the month."

"That must be tough for you."

"It is all part of life."

"Still, it has to be difficult."

"Sure. When I lose a patient there is always a time of grief, but never despair. I cannot imagine being a doctor and not having a philosophy of hope. Do you understand?"

"Yes, I think I do."

The village was little more than a single street that traced the side of a mountain. Under a cantilevered section of the mountain was a cave house. Lupita knocked on the front door and entered. "*Hola*, Armando. May we come in?"

The home was small, just three rooms carved into the mountain and thoroughly whitewashed. There were no doors—only rounded archways that Armando's father had chiseled out from the earth a hundred years earlier. Armando was a frail skeleton of a man with a sallow, pocked-face complexion, but despite his years—ninety-two, he claimed—there was mischief in his eyes.

"Ah, Lupita," the old man said, pulling himself up in his bed. "I was wondering when you were going to get around to me."

"How could I forget my favorite patient?"

"It looks like you brought another patient with you this time."

"This is Antonio."

"*Buenas días*, Antonio."

"*Buenas días, señor.*"

"My father was *señor.* You must call me Armando."

Lupita sat down at the side of the bed and drew out a stethoscope from her bag. "Let us hear how those lungs are doing today."

Lupita listened first to the man's heart and then placed her hand behind Armando's back and gently pulled him forward. "Breathe deeply." She listened to the sound of one lung struggling to draw in air and then the other. During this time, Armando's head was bent forward, his forehead resting just below the doctor's neck. With both hands the old man reached up and slowly fondled Lupita's breasts.

Lupita did not move away from Armando, nor did she scold him. In fact, it seemed to Antonio, who witnessed the scene, that Lupita prolonged the examination.

"Big breath," she said. "And again. And one more time."

When she had finished and returned her stethoscope to her bag, Armando said, "Thank you, Lupita."

"You are welcome, Armando. Now do not forget to take your medication. Do you need more?"

"No, I am all right. Thank you."

Lupita glanced at her patient's nightstand and spotted a pack of cigarettes. Armando saw that the doctor had found him out. They exchanged a look, Armando hunching his shoulders as if to say it was all out of his control. Lupita did not berate him—not even with her eyes.

"Is your daughter still coming in to see you every day?" she asked.

"Yes, God bless her."

"Good."

On the road back to Espejo, Antonio asked Lupita about her patient. "I saw what happened back there."

"What did you see?"

"I noticed that you allowed Armando to feel your breasts."

"Does that trouble you?"

"No. I was just wondering what you thought about it."

"He is an old man, Antonio. He does not have long to live. If I can give him pleasure, if I can help him forget his pain for just one moment and remember another time when he was young and lay with a woman, if I can do that, I have done well."

Antonio was silent for a moment. "You are a good woman, Lupita."

The doctor pursed her lips. "I am a woman. I know something about healing and something about the heart."

"Yes," he said, more to himself than to Lupita. "What do you know about *my* heart?"

"I think you are a good man." Then, after a pause, "But it may be too early to say for sure. Are you?"

Antonio looked out the window at the perfectly aligned rows of olive trees. "I do not know what I am. I hope so; I want to be."

"Then you *will* be."

"Is it that easy?"

"Do you not think goodness is a choice?"

"I guess it is. I have never thought about it."

"Then think a moment. All choices come from one of two places: the ego or the heart."

"And your choices with Armando today?"

Lupita smiled. "I will let you decide for yourself. But I will give you this hint: The heart has nothing to prove."

Antonio shook his head in amazement. "How did you learn these things?"

Lupita chuckled. "From my grandfather, of course. He is the man that you must come to know."

"I would like that very much."

Lupita made two other house calls and then suggested they stop at the next town to have lunch. They found a table outside a café facing the village church and began to talk about more personal things.

"Lupita, tell me to mind my own business if I am indiscreet, but I was wondering why you were not married."

"You are indiscreet," Lupita joked, "but I will tell you anyway. Frankly, I have not had the time. After high school, there were six years of medical school and a five-year residency in general surgery, and the next thing I knew, I was . . . how old do you think I am anyway?"

Antonio was thinking how he hated that question, and then he stopped dead.

Lupita immediately saw his expression change. "Antonio, what is it?"

Antonio shook his head. "I do not know. I feel like I have had this conversation before in this exact setting."

"Are you remembering?"

Antonio tried to make sense of it; there was a flash of recognition, and then it drifted into a fog and vanished. "It is gone. There was something, but now it is gone. Damn it."

"That is all right, Antonio. It is a good sign. It will come back. You just need more time."

"But do I have more time? Am I supposed to be somewhere? Am I supposed to be doing something? Who the hell am I?" Antonio grabbed his throat and swallowed hard, knowing that he had pushed his voice beyond its limit.

Lupita reached over the table and covered Antonio's hand. It was the first time that she had touched him outside her medical role, and it made him smile. For one brief moment, he took her hand in his, until Lupita slowly withdrew and, suddenly self-conscious, fidgeted with her hair.

"You are Antonio," she said, finding her composure, "and the rest will come later."

Antonio looked intently at Lupita. "What happened just now?"

"What do you mean?"

"I mean just now, between you and me. What happened?"

Lupita looked away from Antonio a moment, took a breath, and then returned his gaze. "Antonio, I am not sure what I feel for you. I think you know that I like you very much. But I do not know anything about you. I do not know if you are married, if you have children—I know nothing."

"That makes two of us."

"I know." She took in a breath and then added: "I think we should take it slow. All right?"

Antonio smiled a crooked, tight-lipped smile. "All right."

"I NEED TO MAKE A trip to Córdoba. Would you like to keep me company?"

Antonio looked up from his reading at Diego, who was grinning and looking dapper in a brown fedora with the brim turned down full circle.

Antonio snapped his book closed. "I would love to keep you company."

The two men climbed into Diego's work van and rolled down the hill, the vehicle clattering like a wind chime fabricated from pots and pans.

On the half-hour ride to Córdoba, Diego asked Antonio how he was feeling about his stay in Espejo.

"I feel great," he said honestly. "If I could choose a family to be a part of, it would be yours."

"I am glad to hear that. You *are* part of the family. So your wish has already come true."

On the outskirts of Córdoba, Diego followed what appeared to be a familiar route, finally stopping at a stark brick building with a line of small windows and a treeless courtyard. The structure, enclosed by a six-foot high wall, had no redeeming architectural interest.

Diego strode to the front gate and punched in a code on a numerical pad inset into the wall.

As the two men entered the compound, a shriveled man with a sharp nose and pleading eyes tried to slip past Diego and on through the gate before it latched and locked. He was clasping a pillow under his arm as if it were a toddler. Diego took the man by the shoulders and gently reversed his course.

"Ah, Carlos, it is good to see you again. How are you doing these days?"

"I want to go home now."

"You are home, Carlos; this is your new home."

"But . . . I want to go *home*," the man said, giving the word "home" new meaning, more like "heaven" than "a place to reside."

Diego directed the boney man up the stairs and into the building. Antonio noticed the sign at the side of the door: San Lucas Retirement Home.

Once in the building, Diego released the man, who padded down a hallway with his pillow still in arm, muttering, "I want to go home. I am ready to go home now."

Diego turned to Antonio. "That poor man has held the same thought for fifteen years: Escape. I knew him when he was a young buck. He was ornery then, never really happy with his stake in life. Now he yearns for the life he never valued. Sad, is it not?"

Antonio felt a strange pang of grief. "Heartbreaking," he said, hardly able to utter the word.

Diego smiled at a young nun sitting behind the reception desk. Her face was polished and radiant.

"Good morning, Sister Teresa."

"Good morning, Diego. I like your hat."

"Do you now? It makes me look quite handsome, no?"

Diego's response was automatic; it was what he always said when someone complimented his fedora. He considered his lighthearted quip a small tribute to his friend, Juanito, and their first meeting on the road to Granada.

"Yes, indeed. Very handsome."

Diego gave the young nun a wink. The brief exchange was a little game they played each time Diego entered the building.

The nun chuckled. "You rascal," she said, shaking her head. "I think you will find him in the cafeteria."

"Thank you, Sister Teresa."

"You are welcome, Diego."

Diego took Antonio by the arm. "It is this way."

There was a pungent smell about the place, a mixture of disinfectant, cooking oil, and excrement. As the men walked down the hall, they passed a square room full of elderly women with sprouts of whiskers and bloated ankles and, mixed in among them, a few old men swimming in crumpled, mismatched suits and sweaters, one wearing a brown, buttonless suit jacket over a plaid woolen shirt. A small television, mounted seven feet off the floor in the corner of the room, was blaring the news, which from all appearances interested no one.

At the end of the hall was the cafeteria, a mishmash of round and square tables and assorted straight-back chairs. At one of the tables was a man in a padded lounging wheel chair, his hips and legs covered by a knitted green blanket. The man was pale and unshaven with white tufts of unkempt eyebrows, vacuous eyes, and a looseness on the left side of his face that gave testimony to a severe stroke.

The old man faced the wall, having no interest in the world around him. He looked like he had sat in that position immobile, comatose, inanimate for a hundred years. And then he did move; with eyes fixed on the wall, he sliced his hands into the blanket at the sides of his legs as if sealing himself from harm. It was a compulsive ritual that he would mindlessly repeat throughout the visit.

Diego leaned over the man and kissed him on his forehead. "What do you think? Could you use some sunshine today, old man?" Diego wheeled the man to a window, but when the light fell on his face, he bellowed furiously and threw his arms over his eyes as if trying to block the punches of sunlight that jabbed at his head. Diego quickly returned the man to the grim flatness of the blank wall, and he was calm again.

"I am sorry, old man," Diego said. "Maybe some other day, all right?" Diego pulled up a chair and sat beside the man, taking his hand in his. "Do you know me today?"

The man said nothing.

"I am Diego. Remember? Diego?"

The man began to speak, but the words, indecipherable to Antonio, were dark and guttural like a deaf mute trying to form an impossible sentence for the first time and arriving at expelling only gibberish.

"What did he say?" Antonio asked.

Diego leaned his ear to within an inch of the old man's mouth. Again the pale man mumbled something nearly incomprehensible in the back of his throat, Diego repeating after him: "I stand for the holy crusade . . . I stand against the enemies of Christ . . . I stand with Franco, defender of the true Spain."

Diego patted the old man's hand. "Yes, yes, I know, I know."

Diego noticed that the blanket had broken loose from around the man's waist in his tussle with the sunshine, so he tucked the afghan in again, protecting the man's legs from unseen malicious attack. "There, there. That is better."

Then, as if unsatisfied with Diego's motherly effort, the old man chopped his hands into the green blanket for good measure.

"Would you like a drink of water?"

On the table behind the old man was a glass of water and straw. Diego placed the end of the straw on the man's lips, who rejected the plastic tube with a vicious spit, most of the saliva spraying across Diego's face.

"*Bueno, bueno*," Diego said with a bent smile, wiping his face with his shirtsleeve. "It was just an idea; I am not married to it."

Again Diego patted the man's hand. Diego looked for a long moment into the dead eyes of the old man, as if trying to find a remnant of someone he knew and loved from another time.

Finally, Diego heaved a sigh and broke the solemn séance. "I think we can go now," Diego said to Antonio. Then, turning to the old man: "I will see you soon. Maybe next time you will enjoy a little sunshine. Think about it."

The two men retraced their steps down the hallway. At the square room the television was still blaring, and still no one paid any attention.

When Diego reached the reception desk, he planted the fedora on his head and gave the brim a tug as a salute to the young nun.

"*Hasta luego*, Sister Teresa."

"*Hasta luego*, Diego," she said, again shaking her head in amusement.

They left the building. Finally, Antonio could breathe deeply again. He felt that he had emerged from the crypt of the living dead, and he was grateful, nearly gleeful, to gorge his nostrils with warm, untainted air.

On the road back home to Espejo, Diego was strangely quiet.

"Who was that man?" Antonio finally asked.

"One who has suffered greatly."

"How did he suffer?"

"He was a man who sided with Franco and the rebels. One year into the war, he was captured by Republican troops. He was imprisoned in total darkness for two years. His knees were shattered with a sledgehammer. And yet, he was loyal to the end. Rather than divulge the names of Nationalist compatriots, he chewed off his own tongue."

Antonio winced in horror. "My God."

"I learned that he was being held in the Castle of Montjuich in Barcelona. It was not easy, but I made my way to the prison in 1939. I begged for his release. It was granted; after all, he had broken knees and a mutilated tongue; what havoc could the man wreak on a lost Republican cause?"

"What did you do with him?"

"I brought him back to Andalusia in a mule-drawn cart."

"What became of him after the war?"

"He served the Catholic church—mostly as a bookkeeper and librarian."

"Was he a priest?"

"Yes."

"I can tell that you love him very much."

"That has not always been easy. I rarely agree with him; he can be, well . . . inflexible. But he has suffered—as we all have suffered—and he deserves release." Diego paused, as if rehearsing his next sentence. "Yes, I do love him."

"What is his name?"

"Francisco Garcia. He is my brother."

A FEW DAYS LATER, DIEGO offered Antonio another excursion, this time a walk in the orchard. Antonio quickly accepted.

Diego selected an olivewood walking stick from a tall, slender terra-cotta pot at the door. The two men drove the short distance down the hill to the Garcia orchard and pulled off onto a dirt road, which led to a pump house that fed water and fertilizer to the trees. They got out of the car and walked slowly under a serene canopy of green. Although it was only late September—still two months before harvest—the olives were abundant.

As they ambled along, Antonio picked up a dirt clod, crushed it, and brushed his hands clean. "You must love it here."

"For me, there is no other place. My father was born here and his father before him. This earth is part of my blood; I cannot escape it."

"Would you ever want to?" Antonio asked with a smile, knowing the answer.

"No. There is something inspiring about these old olive trees. They are noble and rugged. Did you know that our trees cannot thrive in rich soil? They grow best in poor rocky ground. They can take the driest summer and, although they may suffer for a time, they always come back. We have trees that are 500 years old; a few are a 1,000 years old. Now that is what I call resolve."

"You are like these trees."

"You mean I look like I could be 500 years old?" Diego laughed.

"No. I mean you are tenacious. You flourish in rocky soil."

"That is a great compliment, Antonio. I doubt that I deserve it."

"I think you do."

"Thank you," Diego said gracefully. "Like these trees, I need regular pruning." He suddenly stopped at a massive tree and snapped off a withered twig from a low-hanging branch. "Do you know how to prune an olive tree, Antonio?"

"No. I do not have the slightest idea."

"Let us sit down here," Diego said, patting the trunk of the grand old tree.

Antonio offered his hand to Diego to ease the effort in squatting, and Diego gladly consented, not because he needed the assistance, but because it would have been rude not to accept. Once seated, Diego stretched out his legs and felt the earth. "Sit here beside me," he said, smoothing a piece of ground. "Where were we?"

"You were talking about pruning."

"Ah, yes. You see, an olive branch produces fruit only once every two years. In the spring, we prune the branches that gave fruit in the last harvest. I am a little like that: To be fruitful, I need regular pruning."

"In what way?"

"When we prune a tree, we shape it. It becomes more hardy, more even, more centered. A man is shaped by knowledge. If I want to sustain the cold winters and the dry summers and still bear fruit, I must be obsessive about learning."

"'Obsession' is a pretty strong word, Diego."

"I chose it intentionally." The old man suddenly laughed, which was characteristic of him when he thought of a private joke. "I once read a book about obsession; I must have read it a thousand times."

Antonio shared the laugh. Then, after a pause, he asked, "So, Diego, what is your source of knowledge?"

"One day, I will tell you about my friend, Juanito. He introduced me to the masters of philosophy and literature. That changed everything for me; I began to see the world more clearly—especially the interconnectedness of things."

"Ah, now I understand why your library is so extensive."

"Those books keep me moving in the right direction, but they are not the only source of knowledge, Antonio. We also learn from our successes and, especially, our failures. Although trial and error can be a rude teacher, it can often be life changing."

"So, do you feel that you have been sufficiently pruned over the years?"

Diego laughed. "Just like the olive trees, at least once a year."

Antonio enjoyed the way that Diego was able to poke fun at himself; he was a man who was perfectly at home in his own skin. "You seem like a religious man."

Diego shuddered, as if Antonio had invited him to shake hands with a snake. "No, Antonio. You have misjudged me. In fact, I may be the least religious man on earth. But I would like to think that I am a spiritual man."

"What is the difference?"

"I am seventy-four years old, Antonio, and in my lifetime there is one truth that comes back to me again and again."

"I am listening."

Diego looked skeptically at his young friend. "Are you sure that you want to hear the musings of an old man?"

Antonio considered his question. "Diego, I am a clean slate. I know nothing. Literally." He paused. "I am hungry to learn, and I cannot think of a better teacher than Diego Garcia."

The old man tapped Antonio's leg and grinned. "There are teachers who are more gifted, Antonio, but I am honored to tell you what I know. Here it is then. This is my truth: Dogma divides, principles unite."

"Hmm," Antonio said quietly, mulling over the idea.

"I do not care a wit about dogma. It does not matter to me if Jesus walked on water or if Muhammad split the moon with his finger or if one must be baptized by sprinkling or immersion or not at all. That is all dogma, as far as I am concerned, and it is the root of division. It separates families and drives nations to war.

"For example, the Spanish Inquisition—lasting 300 years, Antonio—was driven by dogma. Its goal was to purge the nation of heretics, meaning anyone who was not Catholic. The crusades were also about dogma. The religious wars in France were about dogma. The Muslims forced out of India and the Hindus out of Pakistan—that, too, was about dogma. And the horror continues to this day."

"So what is the alternative?"

Diego picked up a small green branch. "The alternative is like this twig. If I were to plant this branch in the ground and add a little water, in time it would become an olive tree. That is a principle that you can always count on. And *that* is the alternative to dogma: Principles."

Antonio looked carefully at Diego's face, amazed by the old man's clarity and facility of thought. "Go on."

"Principles are the absolute truths that bridge all religions and all cultures." Diego picked up a small stone and held it in his open palm. "I give you another example from nature. You see this stone? What will happen if I turn my hand over?"

"The stone will fall to the ground?"

"How do you know that?"

"Newtonian physics."

"That is right: Newtonian physics. There are natural laws, like gravity or an olive harvest or the fact that the earth circles the sun, and not the other way around. These physical laws cannot be argued; they are self-evident. But there are also interpersonal laws that influence human relationships: love, tolerance, understanding, forgiveness. These laws are as real as the law of gravity. When we abide by them, they do not diminish our lives; they make them more abundant and more unified. And that is the evidence that makes them true."

"Wait a minute. You talk like love and tolerance and understanding are universal."

"They are."

"But are there not cultures that discount those qualities?"

"Antonio. Do not confuse culture with principles. Culture is very subjective and is influenced by a long history of dogma. Principles, on the other hand, are objective and are not only universal, but also unchangeable. Principles will always be true. You can choose not to believe in gravity if you like, but when I release the stone, it will still fall to the ground."

The two men were silent for a moment.

"A few days ago, I asked Lupita if I was a good man."

"What did she say?"

"She said she thought I was."

"And what do you think?"

"That is the problem. I do not know."

"Then you are not at peace."

"Not even close."

"Antonio, I would like to tell you why I chose to sit here at the base of this very tree. This is a special place for me. This is where I first spoke to the girl who would become my wife. Do you think it is possible to fall in love at first sight?"

Antonio thought of his growing affection for Lupita and Diego. "I am not sure, but I think so."

"I will tell you, it *is* possible, because it has happened to me. I knew instantly that Lupe was a good woman. And I knew that I would marry her."

Antonio smiled.

"I have told you that, because I have the same instinct about you. I believe that in your soul you are a good man. That is why I have chosen you as my friend."

"Thank you for your faith in me, Diego. I will try to honor you."

"Do not honor me, Antonio. Honor yourself. That is all you need to be at peace."

The harvest began the end of November. More than anything, Antonio wanted to help. With the exception of his left shoulder, which still nagged at him, he was physically fit. Still, he knew he could not handle the thirty-pound gas-driven vibrator; it was slung over one shoulder and, once clamped to a three-inch branch, vibrated like a jackhammer; one hour of that would tear his shoulder wide open. But he could drive a tractor, so that is what he did, from sunup to sundown. With a crew of twelve men, it took fifteen days to harvest 8,000 trees.

Almost daily, around midday, Lupita would go to the orchards and sit next to Antonio on the tractor fender. Sometimes she was silent, and sometimes she would shout over the rumble of the engine: "How are you feeling?" or "We will make an olive orchardist out of you yet."

For Antonio, that was the best; the feel of Lupita so close to him was marvelous. He felt like a kid. Then, after a half hour or so, she would kiss him on the cheek, step down from the tractor, and make her way back to the clinic; he would watch her disappear through the trees, feeling a dull ache in his chest—anguish, longing, passion, adoration—the aftermath of each brief and interminable goodbye. He could hardly wait until the end of day, when Lupita, Diego, and he would gather around the kitchen table for the evening meal.

On the fifteenth day of harvest, after the last truck was loaded, Antonio was dead tired, but it was a sweet exhaustion that follows a job well done. Finally, after nearly two months with the Garcia family, he felt like he was carrying his load. He was no longer a patient or a tiresome houseguest, who had overstayed his welcome; he was a friend helping the people he loved.

To celebrate the end of harvest, Antonio invited Lupita and Diego out for dinner. It was Saturday night, and a flamenco guitarist was playing at the plaza restaurant, which was little more than a long bar with three or four tables at the back of the room. But for Antonio, it was perfect: he was with his people.

Lupita and Antonio sat with their backs to the wall with Diego to Antonio's side. The table was covered with a paper red-and-white-checkered tablecloth. In the center of the table was a wine bottle with a stub candle and multicolored wax drippings built up around the neck and down the side. Antonio set the bottle at the end of the table, so that the three could have a clear view of the young guitarist whose fingers were flying over the fretboard of his classical guitar.

The waiter, César, was an old friend of the Garcia family. In fact, his father, whose name was also César, was the schoolboy friend who helped Diego free himself of Lupe's annoying brother with the enticement of rich hot chocolate and two platters of churros. As for young César, when he was a boy, he worked in the orchards with Lupita and, like every other *chico* in the village, had a secret crush on her.

César wore a white dishtowel around his waste, stained with red wine and olive oil. He was a happy fellow, constantly making grand gestures about the fruity flavor of the regional wine or the succulence of his steaks.

"So what will the Garcia family have tonight?"

Antonio felt proud to have been included as a family member in César's greeting. "Why not leave that to you? We are celebrating the end of harvest, so we are ready for a feast. We are in your hands."

César smacked his hands together and scrubbed his open palms. "Excellent. You can trust me. We have the best cook in the province of Córdoba."

"Who is that?" Lupita asked, knowing the answer.

"Why, me, of course!" César hooted, slapping his chest with both fists. "First, we will begin with jumbo shrimp and escargot, sizzling in butter and garlic. Then, an assortment of tapas, ranging from clams to mushrooms to zucchini. Next, I recommend our traditional bean soup with potatoes and blood sausage." César kissed the tips of his fingers.

"That is a lot of food," Lupita said.

"Wait, I am not finished. After that, I will serve a juicy braised chicken with pepper and fresh Andalusian tomatoes. You will see; it is the closest thing to heaven on earth—not counting Lupita, of course."

"Oh, César, you always were a charmer," Lupita said with a wink.

When César disappeared into the kitchen, Antonio noticed that Miguel was sitting alone at the bar, hunched over what looked like a double shot of whiskey.

"Antonio, I want to congratulate you. You worked very hard all through harvest. Do you know what wages we owe you?" Diego asked.

Antonio put his arm around Diego. "You owe me the price of this dinner. I want nothing more."

"Oh, no . . ."

"Diego, I could never repay your kindness. Please grant me this wish."

Diego looked into Antonio's eyes. How could he refuse such a request? "If that is the case, we need to order a very good bottle of wine."

"I could not agree more."

"Tito is right," Lupita said. "You have worked very hard. I am proud of you."

"Lupita, you cannot know how important your words are to me. If I can stand up to your standards—and I know how tough they are—I would be a proud *caballero*."

Lupita fixed her eyes on Antonio. "But you do stand up to my standards."

Diego looked at Antonio and his granddaughter. "What are you two talking about? Antonio, do you love my daughter?"

"I think I fell in love with her the first time I saw her."

"The first time you saw me, you were seeing double," Lupita said laughing.

"All right, then the *second* time I saw you."

"And Lupita," Diego continued, "why are you making jokes? Are you in love with Antonio?"

Lupita took a long time to respond. "Tito, I do love him."

"Oh, Lupita, where is your head? Give me your hand." Diego covered Lupita and Antonio's hands with his own. "Do not tell me; tell Antonio."

Lupita gazed into Antonio's eyes. "I love you, Antonio."

Antonio turned to Diego. "Could I have my hand back now?"

Diego withdrew his hands, freeing Antonio to take Lupita's face in his hands and kiss her softly on the mouth.

Diego slapped the table. "This is a good thing. This is a very good thing."

Recovering from the kiss, Lupita reproached her grandfather. "Tito, do not get too excited. There are still a lot of unanswered questions."

"What questions? We already know the answers to the most important questions: He loves you, and you love him. There are no other questions."

Antonio was the first to see Miguel walking toward their table. The police chief stumbled into a man at the bar and tipped his cap in apology; it was clear that he was more than a little drunk.

"What is the celebration?" he asked in a voice that was too loud for the room.

"We are celebrating the end of harvest," Diego said.

"Ah, the end of harvest. That is good. I like the end of harvest. I am celebrating the end of harvest too. Let us celebrate together."

"I think you have done a little too much celebrating already," Lupita said.

"You do? Why would you say that?" Miguel asked, squinting at Lupita like she was fading in and out of focus.

Lupita offered her left hand to the police chief. "Miguel, please go ba to the bar and sit down," she said gently.

"I do not want to sit down. I want to dance. Do you want to dance with me?" he asked, tugging on Lupita's arm.

Lupita extracted her hand from Miguel's firm grip. "Not right now, Miguel. We have not had our dinners yet. Perhaps after we have eaten."

"All right. After dinner. Now, do not forget. That is a promise, right?"

"That is a promise."

Miguel found his way back to the stool at the bar and ordered another whisky.

"He could be trouble tonight," Diego said.

"He will be all right," Antonio said. "He has just had too much to drink."

César was back with the first course: two-dozen jumbo shrimp sizzling in a frying pan. "Prepare yourselves for the most delectable shrimp in Andalusia. Lupita, you are going to want to marry me after tasting these."

"César, you are already married."

"Details, details. Who says my woman has to know every little thing?"

"César, you know I am not like that."

"I know, I know. But people change their minds."

"Not this time, César," Lupita laughed. "Try back later."

"*Bueno, bueno.*"

César was right. The shrimp were delicious—but then so were the soup and the chicken. Happily, the dessert was a light flan, because all three felt that had eaten enough to hold them through the winter.

By the time the coffee arrived, it was past one in the morning. Antonio glanced at Diego, who was taking a snooze. "It has been a long day for him."

Lupita brushed back an errant thread of hair on her grandfather's head. "Yes, it has. But he is very happy."

"So am I. I do not know anything about my life, but I cannot imagine ever being this happy before." Antonio took Lupita's hands and kissed each palm.

"Antonio, you are sweet."

"God, how I want to hold you."

Antonio looked at the guitarist who was playing a syncopated zapateado.

"Lupita, would you dance with me?"

Lupita did not hesitate. "Of course."

There was no dance floor—just a little space between the tables. Antonio took Lupita's hand and admired her bearing. She wore a white, diaphanous sundress, tied at the waist and seductively unbuttoned at the neck. Her hair was beautifully bundled at the back of her head.

Antonio took Lupita in his arms and inhaled the scent of her skin. They swayed to the music. Antonio could feel Lupita's thigh firmly pressed against his leg, and when he took a step forward, Lupita followed in perfect time and motion. Then, when Antonio stepped back and held Lupita's hand over her head, she placed the other hand on her waist and with her chin up and her shoulders back, she slowly twirled under Antonio's hand, clicking her heel at each quarter turn.

She was so sensual, so indescribably lovely that Antonio stood back in awe, holding his hands over one shoulder and clapping rhythmically to the music. "Ole!"

Lupita drew a long hairpin from her hair and tossed it onto the nearest table. She shook her head, and her hair tumbled down her back. Then, reaching down with one hand, she clasped the hem of her dress and, gathering the skirt, brought her hand to her hip, revealing her long, sinewy thigh and calf. Her other hand was raised over her head, the palm now upturned, now revolving left and right, now following the line of her breast and her waist and her hip.

She closed her eyes. The guitarist was riveted to the dance—as was everyone in the bar—and he accompanied her: Every click of the heel, every swish of her skirt, every delicate gesture of the hand. And she accompanied him, swaying to his music like a slender willow in the wind.

Antonio was so entranced by the dance that he did not notice Miguel, now completely drunk, who swept past him and barged into Lupita. Her eyes closed, Lupita was caught completely off guard and stumbled backward into a table.

"Oh, I am sorry," Miguel slurred. "Did I do that? I did not mean to do that."

"It is all right," Lupita said, pulling herself together.

"How 'bout that dance now?" Miguel grabbed Lupita by the waist and began to march her around the small improvised dance floor, leaning heavily on her to keep his own feet under him.

Lupita looked at Antonio and shrugged, indicating with her eyes that she could handle her drunken friend.

Miguel continued to push Lupita around, now burying his head in the crevice of her neck. He drew Lupita tightly into his body, who responded by prying against his shoulders. Miguel stiffened his grip, and, letting his hand drop, he grabbed Lupita by the rump and pulled her into him.

"No!" Lupita said, not as a shout, but sternly.

Miguel ignored her command.

Antonio stepped in and pulled at Miguel's shoulder, but the drunken policeman shook him off and buried his head deeper into Lupita's neck.

Antonio grabbed Miguel's shoulder again and this time pulled with all his force. "That is enough, Miguel!"

Miguel turned on Antonio and poked two fingers in his chest. "What do you want?"

Antonio turned both hands up as a sign of peace, but Miguel would have nothing of it. He stepped into Antonio, breathing heavily in his face. "You know, I do not like you."

"That is all right. Sometimes I do not like myself either."

"Yeah, but with me, it is different. I do not like you at all. In fact, I curse the day you were born."

"That will do," Lupita said, pulling at Miguel's arm.

Miguel instinctively swung back with his elbow, which caught Lupita in the sternum and sent her colliding into a table.

Antonio's body braced; he grabbed Miguel by his shirt and yanked at him in the direction of the front door. But even in Miguel's drunken state, Antonio was no match for him. The police chief broke Antonio's hold, seized him by the collar, and slammed his fist at the very center of his shoulder wound. Antonio dropped to his knees in agony.

Lupita leapt forward and, with full force, slapped Miguel twice across the face. "Get out!" she screamed. "Get out! Get out!"

Miguel was shaken by the cuffs across his mouth. It was not the impact of the blows that unnerved him; it was the knowledge that Lupita had struck him. He massaged his face, turned, and with head down blundered toward the front door of the restaurant, wildly brushing men aside as he passed.

When he had reached the door, he turned and shouted, "Antonio! I am not through with you!" He paused, his eyes staring blankly and half closed, as if trying to think of something else to add. Then, he turned and pushed hard against the door; when it did not open, he pulled the door open with such momentum that it slammed against the wall and rattled the door's window pane.

When Miguel had left, the bar was strangely silent. Then, first one, then two, then everyone in the room stood and applauded Lupita. "Bravo, Lupita! Bravo."

But the young doctor was in no mood to take bows. She knelt down at Antonio's side, who was already flanked by Diego. She supported his back and chest with her hands. "Are you all right?"

Antonio took in a deep breath. "Well, that hurt like the devil."

"I bet it did," Lupita said. "Let us get you seated. Ready Tito?"

"*Si.*"

The two lifted Antonio up and led him to a chair at their table.

"Once again, you have come to my rescue," Antonio said to Lupita.

"And you came to mine."

"Not very effectively, I am afraid."

"Sometimes the intention is more important than the outcome," Diego said.

The three left the restaurant at two in the morning. Diego was dead on his feet, so Lupita and Antonio led the old man to his bed, pried off his shoes, slipped him out of his shirt and pants, and threw a blanket over him.

Diego snuggled into the mattress. "*Buenas noches*, Lupita. *Buenas noches*, Antonio."

"*Buenas noches*," Lupita said, kissing her grandfather on his forehead.

"Sweet dreams, Diego."

Lupita and Antonio moved to the foot of the bed and fixed their gaze on Diego who was already asleep.

"I love that grand old man," Antonio said. "If I were to be born again, I would ask to come back as Diego Garcia."

"I do not think I want you born again," Lupita said with a playful smile. "You would be much too young for me."

Antonio took Lupita in his arms, and the two kissed long and passionately. In their embrace, Lupita stroked the back of Antonio's head; it was a sweet gesture that he had come to know and adore, and Antonio responded by drawing her closer. Lupita lost her balance for a moment and steadied herself by grasping the footboard of Diego's bed. Just below her hand were the delicate lilies that her grandfather had engraved fifty-five years earlier for his beloved Lupe.

At that instant, Diego snorted in his sleep, which made Antonio and Lupita laugh.

"Maybe we should call it a night," Lupita said.

"Do you really want to?"

"Not really. But I think we *need* to."

"All right."

The two said goodnight and retired to their respective bedrooms. But neither Antonio nor Lupita could sleep. Antonio lay on his back and thought about Lupita: her beauty, yes, but also her grace, her intelligence, her spirit. He could not imagine living a single day without her. Lupita was also in love, but she was more cautious. She adored what she knew of Antonio, but so much remained a mystery. She felt torn apart by passion and reason.

Lupita was still awake when Antonio, wearing only a pair of cotton pants, slowly opened her bedroom door and silently shut it behind him. He walked barefooted to the side of her bed. He could see Lupita's black eyes shinning in the moonlight that streamed through the window. She said nothing, and Antonio gently pulled back the bed quilt. Lupita was wearing her favorite man's dress shirt.

They were motionless for an instant, and then Lupita opened her arms to him. Antonio slipped onto the bed, one leg between hers, and kissed her on the mouth. Lupita rolled his body over hers, turning him onto his back. She straddled him, her hair falling across his face. Antonio undid the first two buttons of her shirt, and Lupita pulled the garment off over her head.

"I want you," she said, running her hands across his chest and stomach. Her mouth was open; she was breathing heavily. Her head swayed as she felt Antonio writhing under her. Then her face suddenly contorted. She straightened her back and lifted herself out of the bed. She picked up the white shirt and pressed it against her breasts, backing up against the window. "I cannot do this."

Antonio lay still, staring at Lupita's silhouette. "What is it?"

"I am sorry. I do not know who you are," her voice said in the dark.

He sat up in the bed. "You do know who I am. I am Antonio."

"Are you?"

"Of course, I am."

"But who is Anthony?"

He was silenced by the incessant question. "I do not know, but when I find out, I will give you all of me."

Lupita bowed her head in the moonlight. "Antonio, I do not want all of you. I just want to know that what I have is real. Right now, tonight, I do not know what is real and what is illusion."

"I understand. But I will not stop loving you."

"I do not want you to stop."

Antonio rolled out of bed, took Lupita's face in his hands, and kissed her quickly on the mouth. "Good night, Lupita."

"Good night, my love."

Antonio had difficulty concentrating on anything other than Lupita; she was all he wanted. Yet, he also knew she was right: their relationship would never be sealed, until the mystery of his own life was unraveled. So, until that time, Antonio decided to throw body and soul into his work in the orchards.

There was always much to be done. The ground between the rows of trees could be turned to better oxygenate the roots. He could snip the suckers sprouting from the base of the trees. And, now that the harvest was over, the trees could be sprayed for pests and fungi.

Diego was Antonio's teacher in all of this—an arrangement that was mutually rewarding. It gave Antonio the chance to better understand the man he so much admired. As for Diego, it was a joy to share his knowledge with such an eager student.

One late morning in mid-December, Diego found Antonio in the orchard, hard at work clipping suckers. He had been at it since sunrise.

The two exchanged warm greetings. Both men were always genuinely happy to be in each other's company.

"How about some hot coffee?" Diego said, settling down at the tree where Antonio had been working.

"You talked me into it."

Diego poured the coffee from an aluminum thermos. They both sat back in silence, sipping their hot drinks, Antonio punching holes in the ground with his heel.

"You seem a little troubled this morning," Diego offered.

Antonio stopped kicking at the dirt. "I have just been thinking about you and Lupita."

"More about Lupita than me, I suspect."

They both smiled.

"Yes, especially about Lupita. I love her Diego."

"I know that."

"But I cannot have her."

Silence for a moment.

"Antonio, do you know what an epiphany is?"

Antonio thought and then replied, "I think so. Is it not God's manifestation on earth?"

"That is right. But there is also a second meaning. An epiphany is a sudden leap of understanding."

"That is what I need, all right: A leap of understanding."

"It is something that we all need. Here in Spain we always celebrate the Epiphany on the fifth and sixth of January in remembrance of the three kings who brought gifts to the infant Jesus. I always participate in that ceremony," Diego said, almost reverently.

Over the months, Diego had shared much of his life with Antonio: his marriage with Lupe, his brother's disapproval, his friendship with Juanito, and his wife's tragic death. He knew about his disdain for the church and found it curious that he would talk about a Christian holiday in such respectful tones. "You surprise me, Diego. I did not think you had anything to do with the church."

"I do not—*except* for the Epiphany. I do not think I ever told you that Lupe was born on the eve of Epiphany. The day is very special for me. It is a day for revelation, just as Lupe was a revelation for me. She taught me how to love and how to be courageous, when my heart was no longer in it. So every year, I think about her, and I pray for new revelations."

"You pray to Jesus?"

"I pray to whatever source of wisdom is beyond my grasp."

"You do not give it a name?"

"Why would I do that? Nations go to war over a name. I just listen."

Antonio sensed that Diego was leading up to something. "Why are you telling me all this?"

"I think you have learned to read my thoughts."

"Well, I just have a hunch that something mischievous is brewing in that great mind of yours."

"You are right, Antonio. I have an idea. On the evening of January fifth, the three kings announce the beginning of Epiphany by entering the square in Espejo and tossing candies to the children. I have been one of those kings, Melchior, for thirty-five years. Miguel has been the second king, Gaspar, ever since he became the chief of police five years ago. And I would like you to be the third king, Balthazar."

"Hold on just one minute. What happened to the old Balthazar?"

"The old Balthazar is praising the King of Kings in heaven. He died of old age last year."

"And why me?"

"Because you have come from afar, like the great King Balthazar from Ethiopia."

"Ethiopia! Then Balthazar is the black king."

Diego grinned.

"Oh, I do not know. For one thing, I am not sure I want to get in a shoving match with King Gaspar."

"That will not happen. Miguel will behave himself. I will see to that."

Antonio still hesitated.

"There is something else," Diego said. "Do not forget the second meaning of epiphany: A leap of understanding."

"I have not forgotten."

"I am sure that if you do this thing for me, you will have an epiphany. You will understand."

Antonio let out a slow breath. "Of course, I will do it. It will be a great honor."

That night Antonio had another bout with his forgotten past, shrouded memories that once again would not be remembered in the morning light.

It was 11:30 when the morning sun cleared the apartments on the opposite side of Pleasant Avenue. A beam of light passed through a hole in a tattered sheet that served as a makeshift window shade. It formed a luminous shaft that awakened the particles of dust in the room, shimmering like a constellation of miniscule stars in another galaxy, and ultimately fell across

Tony's face. The light was not a fanfare to the new summer day; it was a rude reminder of the boy's gnawing hunger.

Tony awakened slowly, pressing his fingertips into the corners of his eyes and stretching the small of his back, which ached as it always did after a restless night on the hardwood floor. Lifting himself to a sitting position, he looked at the single, frameless bed where his mother lay. Tony was never sure if she were dead or alive. He crawled to the edge of the bed and held his hand over her nose and mouth, and then smiled faintly when he felt his mother's warm breath. It was part of his morning ritual: confirming that his mother was still breathing and that he could begin his day.

Tony was already dressed; he was never undressed. He wore a grimy pair of khaki coveralls and a blue and white striped t-shirt that was already two sizes too small for his lean seven-year-old frame.

The boy walked to the kitchen sink and stepped onto an overturned orange crate to reach the tap. He cupped his hands under the stream of water and doused his face and ears. Then he slid his index finger across his front teeth and gums—two, three, four times. Done. That was good enough.

Tony turned and looked again at his mother. He knew she would not get up for three or four more hours, and there were chores to be done. His first morning task was to make his way to the old Negro's basement apartment on 122nd Street and pick up a bottle of moonshine for his mother and her clients. He would take care of that, as he always did, but first he was hungry. He walked across the one room apartment, unlatched the front door, and walked down the three flights of stairs to the street. It was the middle of June in East Harlem, but the boy's bare feet were tough enough to take the heat of the sun on the concrete and asphalt.

Tony walked toward Charlie Ding-Ding's Candy Store on the corner of Pleasant and 118th Street. It was a place that was famous for hosting the block's late-night poker games. Tony already knew about that, but didn't care. He had something else on his mind: a Hershey bar for breakfast, before making the liquor run.

Even for Tony, the concrete was getting hot under his feet, so he picked up his pace.

Mrs. Mancini was sitting in the center of her building's stoop, watching the boys play stickball—the same Mrs. Mancini who was the mother of the terrible Jackoff. She was wearing a flowered, black and white cotton dress.

Tony thought her breasts looked round and plump in the morning sun. With her long, black, curly hair and smiling eyes, she was one of the most beautiful women on the block.

When Tony passed by, she called out to him. "Hey, little Tony. Whacha doin' wid-a no shoes? "'At's-a no good, Sonny."

Tony stopped and looked at Mrs. Mancini, who was smiling back at him with kind eyes. "Hello, Mrs. Mancini," he said, not answering her question.

"You come-a sit wid me," she said, tapping the step at her side.

Tony obeyed. He liked Mrs. Mancini, and he felt at home at her side. When she tousled his hair, he looked up into her eyes and wondered if what he felt at that moment—a warm wave of gratitude and tenderness—was love.

They sat in silence for a long moment. When Mrs. Mancini spoke, it was softly, consolingly. "Tell me, Sonny. You're mama. She is still no feelin' good?"

Tony smiled to himself. He did not fully understand what was wrong with his mother. But he did know that what she had was not something out of her control, like the flu or the measles or the mumps. It was something else: something meaner and inexplicable.

Tony didn't say anything. He just shook his head "no."

"'At's-a no good," she said slowly, pronouncing each word as if it were a line in an Italian ballad. "I'm-a sorry, Sonny." And then, after a pause, "Mia poor lit'le Tony."

Again, the two sat in silence for another moment, when Mrs. Mancini said, "Hey, Tony. You no like-a somethin' to eat maybe? Huh?"

Once again, Tony said nothing. He just looked up into Mrs. Mancini's eyes, smiled, and nodded.

"'At's-a wh'd I t'ought," she said, standing up quickly and smoothing her dress over her hips. "You no move. I-a gotta somet'in' a-good for you. You wait-a see."

Mrs. Mancini escaped into the tenement. In a moment she stuck her torso out the first-floor apartment window. "Now, you no go-a no place, Sonny," she said with a laugh.

Tony just smiled and settled back into the stoop. He had no intention of leaving—certainly not now, with a meal so close at hand.

Five minutes later, Mrs. Mancini opened the front door and again sat down beside Tony. In her lap was a white cloth napkin and a dinner plate, heaping with spaghetti and three enormous meatballs.

Tony's eyes expanded and then began to tear.

"What's da madder?" Mrs. Mancini asked. "You-a no like?"

"I like," Tony said, transferring the plate to his own lap and immediately twisting the fork into the mountain of spaghetti. "Humm," he said, not lifting his eyes from the plate.

Tony ate and ate until he could not possibly take another bite. When he was finished, he wiped his mouth on the cloth napkin and sighed a deep breath of contentment. He had never been so satisfied . . . nor so much in love.

It was within that same week that Mrs. Mancini telephoned New York City Social Services and explained that there was a seven-year-old boy running wild in the streets of East Harlem. Three months later, Tony was sitting in a court room, his chin barely clearing the edge of the defender's long oak table.

"Where is the child's mother?" the judge asked.

The dependency attorney stood up, buttoning his suit jacket in the process. "Mrs. Rossi is not present your honor," he said.

"I can see that," the judge said, mindlessly tapping the tip of the gavel handle on the sound block. "What is her status?" he said with a tinge of irritation in his voice.

The dependency attorney drew out a document from his briefcase. "Your Honor, according to the guardian *ad litem* report, the Mrs. Rossi was recently discharged from Bellevue hospital after undergoing treatment for alcoholism and severe depression."

"Was the mother notified of these proceedings?"

"Yes, your honor, she was."

"I see," the judge said, again punctuating his words with the gavel handle. "Can the State shed any light on this situation?" he asked, turning to the prosecution.

The attorney for the State prosecution was a tall, slender man with a crop of disheveled hair. He wore a crumpled, three-button, charcoal-grey suit; only the lowest jacket button was buttoned. Tony looked at the man as he rose to his feet. He did not like the prosecuting attorney; he thought he had mean eyes.

"Yes, your honor," the State's attorney said, looking not at the judge, but at a document he had fished out of his briefcase. "We, too, have been in consultation with the guardian *ad litem*. We have learned that Mrs. Rossi and the boy live in a one-room apartment in East Harlem. The room is almost entirely without furnishings. There is no bed for the boy. The apartment is described as . . . let me find this." The lawyer turned a page of the document. "Ah, yes, here it is: 'The apartment is unimaginably filthy, cluttered with whiskey bottles, clothing, and newspapers. The stench is almost unbearable.'"

The attorney raised his head and for the first time looked directly at the judge. "Your honor, Mrs. Rossi is a single mother. The father is unknown. She refers to herself as 'Mrs.' for the sake of propriety. 'Rossi' is actually her maiden name. She survives by means of prostitution and the sale of bootleg liquor that, shockingly, is delivered by her son, Tony. In a word, the conditions are 'untenable.'"

The judge turned to the dependency attorney. "Does the defense have anything to add?"

As the lawyer stood, he placed his hand on Tony's shoulder. "Yes, your honor. The attorney for the State is correct. The living conditions are deplorable. We do not argue that point. But a boy of this age belongs with his mother . . ."

"If the mother wants the child," the judge interrupted. "That does not seem to be the case here." The judge then paused. Again, he tapped the gavel sound block with the gavel handle. "It seems to me that this boy has a better chance for survival in a state facility." Another pause. "Does the prosecution have a recommendation as to where the boy should be placed?"

"Yes, your honor," the prosecuting attorney said, leafing through another document. "The Kallman Home for Orphaned Children in Brooklyn, New York."

"I take it there is space for him?"

"Yes, your honor."

"Then so ordered," the judge said, "but with this understanding. Mrs. Rossi has the right to address this court at any time to seek custody of her child. Until that time, the boy will be under the care of the state." With that statement, the judge raised and lowered the gavel. The sound reverberated through the courtroom. "Case closed."

The dependency attorney turned to Tony and placed his hand on his head. "This is probably best for you, young man."

"What happened?" Tony asked, clearly bewildered.

"You are going to a new home," the lawyer said. "You will be fine. You'll see. And one day, when your mother is feeling better, she will come get you."

That day never came. Tony never saw his mother again.

Miguel had been brooding ever since the scuffle at the restaurant. He was keeping a low profile, and although he knew he was in the wrong, he was, for the moment, too embarrassed to apologize to Lupita. As for Antonio, Miguel would never apologize. The police chief was convinced there was something devious about the stranger, and he would find it out. He would uncover his crime, and then Lupita and Diego and the whole village would be grateful to him. All he needed was a break: Just a small piece of evidence to lead him to the real truth.

His chance came in late December. He was on his routine morning rounds, talking to shopkeepers and keeping his eye open for anything unusual. That was his normal mode of operation. He did not attend to the *usual*; in fact, he hardly saw it. He was awakened by the *unusual*: a car without a license plate, a store closed when it should be open, a youngster running down the street during school hours. Those were the things that Miguel noticed.

So when Miguel saw Antonio walk into the village bank on Monday morning, he was on point. Antonio was hardly ever in town and never in the bank. He had no need to be in the bank; he had no money. "What in the world is he up to?" the police chief asked himself.

Miguel waited outside the bank, just down the street at a sidewalk stand of oranges meticulously stacked in front of the Martinez's grocery store.

"Go ahead; have an orange," *Señora* Martinez said.

Miguel was lost in his thoughts. He fingered the pistol at his belt and thought about how he would gun down the *bandido* in the street, if it came to a shootout.

"Have an orange," the shopkeeper repeated.

"What, what?" he said, coming to his senses, but not really seeing the *señora*.

"The oranges: They are very sweet this year."

Just then Antonio came out of the bank. He was counting a handful of bills. Miguel drew out his pistol, but his shooting hand slammed against the orange stand and two or three pieces of fruit began to tumble from the top of the pyramid. Miguel stopped one orange and then another, but more and more started to tumble, culminating in a rumbling cascade of rolling oranges. With all limbs outstretched, he threw his torso over the fruit, his gun still in his hand, now flopping about like a severed high-pressure air hose. The fruit stand collapsed under Miguel's weight, and the chief of police was suddenly rolling about on a cushion of oranges.

The shopkeeper could not stifle a laugh, which only added fuel to Miguel's embarrassment and rage. He scrambled to his feet, but was quickly upended on a carpet of orange "ball bearings" and came crashing down on his backside.

"Easy, Miguel," the shopkeeper said, struggling to keep a straight face. She bent over to give the police chief a hand, but he was in no mood for assistance and jerked his arm away with such authority that it again threw him to the ground. At this point, all pride had evaporated, and he resigned himself to crawling on hands and knees to a clear spot on the pavement, where he was finally able to right himself.

Señora Martinez could not contain herself any longer. A burst of laughter exploded from her sealed lips. "Do not worry, Miguel. I will make orange juice and send you the bill for the rest."

By the time Miguel had regained his composure, Antonio, who had witnessed the knockabout scene, was across the street and entering the hardware store.

Miguel decided to continue his undercover surveillance. Three short, grey-haired women—all with fabric shopping bags stuffed with daily groceries—were standing nearby, still trying to recover from their laughter. Miguel approached them, using them as cover.

"It is a little cloudy today," Miguel said, his eyes fixed on the hardware store across the street.

"Yes, it certainly is," one of the ladies said. She looked at her companions and let out a snort of laughter.

"I do not think it will rain, though," he said, oblivious to the women's losing battle to contain themselves.

"I would be surprised if it did," the second woman mused.

"No, that is right," the third woman said. "You remember, Carmen? We got our last big rain just before the orange harvest."

All three women burst into guffaws, leaning on each other to keep from falling down.

Just then Antonio stepped out of the hardware store with a brown paper sack under one arm. He took a small piece of paper from his pocket, looked at it, crumpled it up, and tossed it into a wastepaper basket attached to the outside wall of the hardware store.

Miguel, surrounded by the three women, dropped to one knee and pretended to tie his shoe. When Antonio looked in his direction, he pulled Carmen's skirt to one side, as if drawing a curtain.

This was not appropriate behavior for any man, not to mention the chief of police, and it both startled and offended Carmen, who unsheathed a loaf of French bread from her shopping bag and whacked Miguel over the head with it, breaking the bread in half in the process.

Meanwhile, Antonio had crossed the street and, passing by the quartet, tipped his head and said, "*Buenos días, señoras. Buenos días*, Miguel."

Miguel, having been reduced to untying and retying his shoe, finally stopped fingering the laces, stood up, and watched Antonio climb the hill toward the Garcias' home.

"Hmm," Miguel grunted.

The police chief then retraced Antonio's steps, going first to the bank. He cut a direct line to the bank teller.

"That tall man who just came in wearing brown shoes, khaki pants, and a black sweater . . ."

The teller, a slender birdlike man, never began business without a proper morning greeting. He looked over the top of his reading glasses. "*Buenos días*, Miguel."

"*Buenos días*, Reynaldo," he said with as much warmth as a clenched fist.

The two men gawked at each other.

"Well?" Miguel said, lengthening the word into three syllables.

"Well, what?" Reynaldo asked, baffled.

Miguel rolled his eyes. "The tall man with the brown shoes, khaki pants, and black sweater," he growled

The teller looked queerly at Miguel.

"And wearing no hat," the police chief added.

Still no recognition.

"Clean shaven."

Reynaldo was still bewildered.

Exasperated, Miguel played his last card reluctantly. "The Garcias' new man."

The teller's face lit up. "Oh, you mean *Antonio*," Reynaldo twittered, as if the stranger were his favorite cousin from Valencia.

"Right, Antonio," Miguel smirked.

"Yes?"

"He was here just a few minutes ago."

"Yes, that is right."

"Well?"

"Well, what, Miguel?"

"Well, what did he want?" he asked loudly.

"Oh, that. He wanted money."

"He wanted money?"

"Yes, that is right. He wanted money."

"So, you gave it to him?" Miguel snapped.

"Of course."

"Did he hold you up?"

Now it was Reynaldo who rolled his eyes. "What are you talking about?"

"He did not hold you up?"

"Of course not."

"Then, you gave him a loan?"

"No, I did not give him a loan."

"Then, what did you do?"

"I gave him 20,000 pesetas from the Garcias' account."

"My God! You gave him money from Diego's account?"

"Of course."

"But in heaven's name why?"

The teller opened the drawer under the counter and fished out a check. "This is why," he said, holding the check in front of Miguel's eyes.

Miguel snatched the check out of Reynaldo's hands. It was made out to "Cash." "This is signed by Diego Garcia."

"I know that. Diego asked Antonio to cash it for him."

"And you believed him?"

"Of course, I believed him. Why would I not believe him? I would do the same thing for you."

"But I am the chief of police!"

"I know that. And Antonio is Diego's friend. So what is the difference?"

Miguel held his head like the top was going to fly off. "Never mind," he said, not knowing whether he wanted to fold his arms across his chest or place them on his hips. "Just never mind."

He stormed out of the bank and marched over to the hardware store. Just as he reached for the door, he remembered that Antonio had tossed a crumpled note into the wastepaper basket. He lowered his head into the basket and then leapt backward, his hand over his mouth and nose.

The fowl smell was Raul's doing, the village drunk, who the night before did what came naturally: As always, he drank until he had to puke, and when he emptied his stomach, he unloaded in his favorite hardware store canister. Miguel stomped around in little circles. "Goddamn it, Raul," he caterwauled. "You goat-smelling son-of-a-bitch."

Miguel cupped a wadded handkerchief over his nose and, cranking his head back as far as possible, reached for the crumpled piece of paper, which to Miguel's disgust was soaked in the day-old vomit.

Miguel carefully unfolded the scrap of paper. "*Caramba!*" He stared at the paper, written with a firm hand in block letters:

$$Zn_3P_2 + NaOH$$

"Yes, yes, yes," Miguel chanted, strutting a kind of chicken dance in front of the hardware store. "I have got you now, you cocky gigolo. I am going to turn you into a gelding."

Miguel held the piece of paper between two fingers and tried to figure out where to put the condemning evidence, reluctantly resorting to wrapping it carefully in his handkerchief and placing it in his shirt pocket. He was so excited with his find that he didn't even bother to interview the hardware store clerk. He finally had all the evidence he needed. There was no question: Antonio was preparing to build a drug lab—meth or crack or any number of designer drugs with the sole purpose of burning up the brains of the village children. Miguel was going to make sure that the stranger rotted in a Spanish prison cell. "He will never see the light of day," he swore under his breath.

Miguel did not waste any time to make the arrest. He immediately drove the squad car to the Garcias' house. He got out of the car and looked left and right. There was no sign of Antonio. He knocked on the front door, his hand on his pistol. There was no answer. This time, Miguel pounded on the door and then leaned his back against the house at the side of the portal.

Diego came to the door, opened it, saw no one, and closed the door.

"Damn," Miguel said. He pounded on the door again, this time drawing the gun out of his holster and holding it with the barrel straight up.

Diego opened the door again and faced Miguel, gun in hand. "For God's sake. You scared the daylights out of me. What are you going to do, Miguel? Shoot me?"

"Where is Antonio?" Miguel whispered.

"I do not know," Diego whispered back. "I think I dozed off. He is probably with the mob, planning his next heist."

"This is no laughing matter," Miguel said, still whispering. "Where is he?"

"My guess is he is in the orchard working. And why are we whispering?"

"Can I come in? I do not have a warrant," Miguel said in full voice.

"Of course, you can come in. You do not need a warrant to come into my house. Since when do you need a warrant?"

"Ever since Antonio started dealing drugs."

Completely bewildered, Diego stared at the chief of police. "I think you better come in."

Miguel stepped through the entry and quickly combed the house—crabbing along in a low crouch and drawing his pistol down at the threshold of each room. When he was sure all was clear, he straightened his legs, which were burning from all the crouching, and returned to the living room. He sat down in an armchair opposite Diego, who was seated on the couch and shaking his head in disbelief.

"All right, Serpico, you want to tell me what this is all about?"

Miguel's gun was still in his hand, and he used it to punctuate each word of his sentence. "What do you know about Antonio?"

"I know he is my friend."

"That is what I thought. Well, he will not be your friend for long. Not after you hear what I have to say."

"Make your point, Miguel. And stop waving that gun around like some kind of brainless cowboy."

"Oh, right," Miguel said, holstering the pistol. He leaned forward over his knees. "Did you know that Antonio is cashing checks in your name at the bank? Huh? Did you know that? I bet you did not know that, did you?"

"You mean the 20,000-peseta check I wrote out today? Is that the check you are talking about?"

"That is the check. Did you know about that?"

"Of course, I knew about that. I wrote it."

"And you gave it to Antonio to cash?"

"Right. I gave it to Antonio. Is that what this is all about?"

"Not so fast. I bet you did not know that Antonio is setting up a drug lab."

"What in the world are you talking about?"

Miguel raised his hand, calling for Diego's patience. He extracted his handkerchief from his shirt pocket and unfolded it carefully on his lap. "You see this?" he said, waving the paper like a tiny flag at a patriotic parade.

"You are saving scraps of paper now, Miguel?"

"No, Diego," he said in a huff. "This is the evidence that is going to put the infamous Antonio away for a very long time."

"Let me see that."

Miguel handed the paper to Diego, who caught a whiff of it and recoiled. "What toilet did you fish this out of?"

"Never mind. Just read it."

Miguel read the symbols and shrugged.

Miguel took the note, wrapped it, and tucked it away in his pocket again. "Those are chemical symbols. Your boy is a drug dealer."

"Wait a minute, Miguel. I think you are jumping to conclusions here. Where did you get this?"

"Antonio tossed it in the garbage."

"I see."

Just then, Antonio walked through the front door.

Miguel flipped around in the chair, dropped to his knees, and drew out his weapon, training it on Antonio's chest.

Antonio raised both hands. "Whoa, whoa, whoa, whoa. What is going on here?"

"Not so fast, big fellow. Turn around. Put your hands on the wall and spread your legs."

Done.

Miguel stepped out from his cover and kicked Anthony's legs back, almost toppling him.

"Now, just a minute," Antonio protested, turning his head toward Miguel.

Miguel shoved his pistol into his back. "Do not move or, I swear, I will blow a hole in your belly."

"*Bueno, bueno.* Just relax a little. I am not going anywhere."

Miguel frisked him thoroughly, even tapping the barrel of this pistol between his legs. "All right. You are clean," he said, putting his gun away. "You can turn around now."

Antonio stepped toward the wall to get his feet under him, turned, and lowered his arms. "You are damned right I am clean. What are you trying to prove?"

"Just sit down."

Antonio sat on the couch beside Diego.

"Miguel has pegged you as a drug dealer," Diego said.

"What?"

"And he has the evidence to prove it."

Antonio gawked in amazement at Miguel. "You want to explain this?"

For the second time, Miguel uncovered the piece of condemning evidence and handed it to Antonio. "Is that yours?"

"Of course, it is mine, but judging from the smell, I cannot imagine where you found it."

"Never mind that. Then you admit it is yours."

"Yes, it is mine. Are you happy now? It is my scrap of paper. I have a desk drawer full of them; I will give you the whole bunch, and you can knock yourself out. "

"Cut the sarcasm."

"All right, all right," Antonio said, trying to gain control of himself. "Just tell me what is going on."

"I will tell you what is going on. You are going to jail," he said smugly. "That is what is going on."

"Okay. But before you throw me in the slammer, may I ask a couple of questions?"

Miguel sat back and folded his arms. "Go ahead."

"Do you know what those chemical symbols represent?"

"I have a pretty good idea."

"Enlighten us."

"Well, I do not know exactly, but I would bet my life that they are drug-related."

"And you would lose that bet. Zn_3P_2 is the symbol for zinc phosphide. And NaOH is the symbol for sodium hydroxide."

"I cannot believe it," Diego said.

"You know those chemicals, Diego?" Miguel asked.

"Yes, I know those chemicals. And you would, too, if you knew anything about olive trees and pest control."

"What do you mean?"

"Zinc phosphide is rat poison. We have a nest somewhere in the house, and I asked Antonio to go down to the hardware store and get a can of the stuff. It works."

"And the sodium whatever it was?"

"Sodium hydroxide," Diego continued. "The common name is caustic soda. We do not produce a lot of table olives, but the ones we *do* produce must be soaked in sodium hydroxide. It is an alkaline solution that removes the bitter acid from the olives. We were running low on the product, and I asked Antonio to order a couple of sacks. All right?"

Miguel suddenly looked more like a sheepish little boy than the chief of police. "So why did you write symbols instead of words?" he asked, more out of curiosity than accusation.

"I do not know. It is faster. Do not ask me how I knew the symbols; I just knew. Maybe I was a chemist in my other life."

"*Bueno*," Miguel said flatly. He walked with heavy feet to the door, opened it, and then turned around. "Could the two of you do me a big favor?"

"What is it?" Diego asked.

"Could you not tell this to Lupita?"

Diego turned to Antonio, who nodded.

"We will not say a word," Diego said.

"It is a promise," Antonio added.

With that, the chief of police walked out the door, closing it silently behind him.

Antonio fell back into the couch. "And this is one of the three kings bearing gifts for the baby Jesus?"

"Yes, indeed," Diego said. "You will see. He looks splendid in a turban."

On the evening of January fifth, Diego, Antonio, and Miguel met at the church to get in costume for the Festival of the Three Kings. All three were in good spirits. Even Miguel seemed less intent in finding fault with Antonio, and, more importantly, he was sober.

It took nearly two hours to dress and apply makeup. Diego, as the venerable Melchior, was by far the most regal of the lot. He wore a long white beard and matching wig, held in place with an ornate gold crown with glass emeralds and rubies. His robe was a lush red and gold paisley print, topped with a white, furry half-cape with black spots.

Miguel played Gaspar, the youngest of the kings. He, too, donned a wig and beard, but black in color. He wore a dark-wine tunic and a rich golden robe that dropped to the floor. Like Diego, he sported a crown, which he meticulously set at a rakish angle over one brow.

As Balthazar, Antonio required the most time to prepare. First, he applied the blackface makeup that squeezed out of a timeworn tube of cream. His robe was white, trimmed with gold cording and a matching sash. His accessories included a magnificent crescent saber, silver snap-on earrings, and a white turban with a gold and ruby brooch and a long tail that wrapped three times around his neck.

When the three had finished dressing, they circled and admired each other.

"In all my years," Diego said, "I have never seen such a handsome trio of kings. We will honor the village."

"The honor is mine," Antonio said.

"Mine too," added Miguel.

"Before we go out, I would like to say a word." Diego offered his hands to form an unbroken circle of kings. "We three come bearing gifts in praise of God who is here among us. Miguel and Antonio, I vow to respect the God that is in you. For there is only one eternal law: To love one another."

Silence.

Diego released the hands of his fellow kings and outstretched his arms. The three men embraced each other—a royal three-king hug.

The three men stuffed their pockets and urns with chocolates and caramels and stepped out the front door under a starry sky to the cheers of the villagers. The kings waved to the crowd and tossed candies to the children, who scurried like mice to gather them up and stuff them into their mouths before their mothers could rebuke them.

Outside the church, three white horses were being held by their owner, a wealthy landowner from Córdoba who wintered in Espejo. "Your steed, King Balthazar," the man pronounced to Antonio, bending low at the waist.

All three mounted like true equestrians. A few villagers made certain the kings' robes were spread out evenly over the flanks of their steeds.

The kings began the slow descent toward the town square, the villagers in procession behind them. Along the way, children popped out of their houses to demand candies, and the kings happily obliged.

At the town square, Christmas lights were strung from tree to tree and along the roof overhangs. When the kings entered, the band—a trumpet, a trombone, a clarinet, and a snare drum—played *Ya Vienen Los Reyes* in tribute to the magi, the crowd singing in full voice.

The kings dismounted and marched one behind the other—Diego, Antonio, and Miguel—with backs straight and their treasures held out before them. The procession moved slowly and in step toward the live manger scene: Mary and Joseph, the baby Jesus, a few shepherds, a goat, a burro, and a star wrapped in tinfoil suspended from a tree branch high overhead. At one point, Miguel accidentally stepped on the hem of Antonio's robe, causing King Balthazar to lose a step.

"I am sorry, Antonio," Miguel whispered.

"*No importa*," Antonio whispered back.

When the kings arrived, all three knelt and, with heads bowed, placed their gifts at the foot of the manger.

Antonio was feeling overwhelmed by the beauty and solemnity of the pageantry and the genuine joy of the villagers. He looked up at the face of the mother of God; it was Lupita, looking more angelic than ever, as she smiled down on him. When he saw her warm eyes, he bowed his head and silently wept.

The kings, shepherds, and holy family remained in position for over an hour, giving the villagers ample opportunity to take photos. All the players stayed in character and reflected on whatever thoughts arise in moments of silent peace.

Even Miguel was saintly. At one point, *Señora* Martinez from the grocery store taunted Miguel: "Oh, I wonder if the kings would like some fresh oranges?"

Miguel neither spoke nor moved. He kept his eyes fixed on the holy infant.

When the band played "Adeste Fideles," it was the actors' cue that they were free to leave the crèche.

And so they did.

The three kings wandered about the square for awhile, distributing their last nuggets of chocolate. When the candy was gone, they escaped into César's restaurant, where the bartender and customers greeted them with enthusiastic cheers. The kings acknowledged the kind reception with deep bows and, as planned, slipped into the small private room behind the bar, where they changed into street clothes.

When they emerged from the restaurant, Antonio turned to Diego. "Would you mind if I left you for a bit? I would like to find Lupita."

"Of course," Diego said. "Miguel and I will help ourselves to some Christmas cake."

Antonio looked at Miguel with questioning eyes.

"Yes, go," he said, offering a hand of friendship.

"Thank you," Antonio said, vigorously shaking Miguel's hand.

"I think I see Lupita at the fountain," Diego said.

Antonio looked in that direction and, yes, she was there, still in costume, a long dark scarf over her head and crisscrossed over both shoulders. "Yes, I see her. She is magnificent."

Antonio walked quickly to Lupita, and the two instantly fell into each other's arms, Lupita's scarf slipping off her head as they embraced. When Antonio stepped back to look into Lupita's eyes, he let go a laugh.

"What is so funny?" she said in mock resentment.

"I forgot I was still wearing blackface makeup. And now you are too." Antonio took a handkerchief from his pant pocket and waved it at Lupita. "Do not worry; it is clean."

"I was not worried."

Antonio dipped the cloth in the fountain and gently rubbed the black smudge off of Lupita's cheek.

"There, good as new."

"Let me return the favor." Lupita rinsed out the handkerchief in the fountain basin and began to wash Antonio's face. She opened up his shirt collar and wiped the front and back of his neck. Then, when she was pleased with her work, she set the cloth aside. As a final pass, she dipped her hands into the fountain and, caressing Antonio's face, kissed him passionately on the mouth.

Suddenly, during that long kiss, Antonio's head was filled with a torrent of images: Savannah and Penelope and Hennessy and Monique and Jean-Pierre Badeau and Harry Tubbs—all of them. His head spinning, he fell completely limp, collapsing to the ground at the base of the fountain.

He began breathing short, agonizing breaths.

Lupita dropped to his side and took his hands in hers. "Antonio, what is it?"

He spoke one word at a time. "I remember. I know who I am."

"Antonio," she said, pulling him into her arms, "that is wonderful."

Antonio's arms lay limp at his sides. When he spoke again, it was soft and vacant like an incantation. "I know who I am . . . and I am no good."

"What do you mean?"

Antonio wrenched away from Lupita's embrace. His jaw was clenched in anguish, his face drawn and gray. His chest was collapsed as if struck by a massive heart attack. He clutched the fabric of his shirt, his fist trembling, the cloth ripping at the seams. And then he bayed like one overcome by Satan. "My God, my God, my God, I am no good."

Nearby villagers stared at Antonio and, not knowing what to do or what to make of it, simply walked away from the tormented man, giving him room to wrestle with his own demons.

Lupita was herself pallid, absorbing the terror of the man she loved. "Please, please let me help you," she pleaded, again taking him in her arms.

Antonio was trembling uncontrollably. Then he began to sob: deep, convulsing wails that expelled from the center of his being.

"I am here," Lupita said, rocking Antonio in her arms.

The band was playing "Silent Night" at the far end of the plaza.

Time passed, the music stopped, and people began returning to their homes.

Gradually, Antonio quieted, drained of all strength.

Lupita asked softly: "Would you like to talk about it, my darling?"

"No," Antonio managed to say. "Not tonight. I cannot . . . I just cannot."

"That is all right, Antonio. You do not have to say a word"

After another moment in Lupita's arms, Antonio said that he would like to go home. The two stood and slowly crossed the now deserted square. They moved silently up the hill to the house. Although they walked arm in arm, Antonio was not at all present. He stared vacantly at the cobblestones under his feet that bled like a nightmare into the streets of the Albaicín. The images came flooding back, beginning with Savannah the evening they left the Franciscan Hotel after a blur of sexual indulgence. The memories were as vivid as yesterday:

After struggling to find a parking place in the city center, Antonio and Savannah set course for the Arab Quarter. On the way Antonio stopped off at an ATM machine to draw out 50,000 pesetas. Savannah pressed in behind him, while he navigated the transaction. She draped one arm around his neck and, standing on tiptoe, hooked one leg around his waist—all this while nibbling on his ear.

A stubby woman with thin white hair and nylons knotted below her knees saw this display of public indecency as she passed with her miniature French poodle. Her mouth dropped so suddenly it loosened her upper dentures, and she set them back in place with the tip of her thumb.

Her small dog strained at its leash, intent on nosing the indiscreet lovers. The old woman gave the dog a quick jerk, knocking the poodle off its feet, who responded with a yelp of indignation. "Naughty dog," the woman scolded and then added, mumbling under her breath, "Shameful, shameful."

Anthony and Savannah finally stepped into the Albaicín as the sun was setting. The Arab Quarter was built like a jumble of blocks on a hillside facing the southwest side of the Alhambra fortress. In this ancient quarter of the city was the Alcaicería, a long, narrow cobblestone passage that had become an oriental bazaar lined with small overstocked souvenir shops. For Anthony, it was too narrow to be called a street; it was more like an alley, with the corners of buildings jutting in and out at random angles. The Alcaicería was a kaleidoscope of color: dresses, shirts, scarves, and carpets in yellow, blue, red, and gold—all hanging from the outside doorways and windows of the narrow shops.

The two meandered slowly up the narrow lane, stopping occasionally to feel a length of fabric or examine an inexpensive piece of Moroccan jewelry. The pungent scent of incense saturated the air.

Finally, Savannah took Anthony by the hand. "Follow me," she said. "I want to show you a shop I adore."

Savannah led Anthony to a side street that was equally narrow, but more somber than the Alcaicería. Except for a run-down van at the end of the grim corridor, the street was abandoned.

"Where are you taking me?" Anthony asked.

"You'll see."

The two walked deeper into the alleyway, their heels clicking on the cobblestones. It was a dark and brooding place. Anthony wondered how a man could live there in the shadows, never feeling the sun on his face. Then he noticed a curious thing: There, above the cornice of an arched doorway was an inset ledge, and on that ledge was a clear vase with a single fresh white lily. It was the only point of softness and beauty in the darkened chasm, and Anthony wondered what soul had taken the time to brighten the otherwise tenebrous doorway—and why.

Then, with sudden and blind impact, Anthony dropped with the full weight of his body to his knees. The air exploded out of his chest, and he slumped forward, struggling to balance himself on his extended arms, his fists pressed into the cobblestones. He felt like his legs were crushed.

Only half conscious, he turned his head to the left to see his assailant and caught a fleeting glimpse of a dark, slender man with black hair and a long length of pipe in his right hand. The assailant slammed his left fist into Anthony's face once, twice, three times. Anthony's arms buckled on the third blow, and he fell unprotected to the ground, his front temple striking the stone passageway with an ugly thud. He lay unconscious like a sack of grain.

When Anthony awakened, the assailant was dragging him by his armpits through the darkened doorway that was graced with the lily above the cornice.

A man with a white stubble beard and a black cat tucked under his arm peered out from his first-floor window on the opposite side of the street.

"What are you looking at?" the assailant snarled.

The inquisitive man quickly dropped the cat and slammed the shutters closed behind him.

The dark stranger propped Anthony up against the corridor wall. Blood was flowing freely from his forehead and mouth.

Savannah stepped out of the dark and straddled Anthony's lap. She withdrew a hand-torn fragment of paper from the cleavage of her camisole and slipped it into Anthony's shirt pocket. Then she gripped his right hand.

Anthony was only half conscious. What was she doing? Savannah appeared out-of-focus in the shadows, and then, slowly, he understood. She was sucking his ring finger, thrusting it deep into her throat. Then, with a muffled scream of effort, she twisted the canary diamond off his finger.

Anthony could barely speak. "Why?"

"You won't need this, love," Savannah said, placing the diamond over her thumb.

"Why?" He murmured again.

"He sounds like he loves you," the assailant said. "You didn't use that 'fuck-me scam' again?"

"Oh, yes," Savannah said, squeezing Anthony's cheeks together with one hand and thrusting her tongue deep into his mouth. She spat out his blood and wiped her mouth with the back of her hand. Then, preparing to stand, she straightened herself and, kneeling on one knee, grabbed Anthony by the crotch and gave it a tug. "I'm going to miss this."

"Stop fooling around," the dark man said. "Let's get the hell out of here."

Through the mental fog, Anthony managed to reach up and grab Savannah by the neck. He pulled her down to him and squeezed with all the strength left in his body, while Savannah pummeled his ribs as best she could. Then Anthony heard the swish of metal, the distinctive sound of a butterfly knife flung open. He ignored it.

The silence of the hallway was shattered by the death scream that ripped from Anthony's throat as the assailant plunged the five-inch blade into Anthony's left shoulder. And still, Anthony gripped Savannah's neck with both hands.

The assailant twisted the knife, and Anthony screamed a second time; the room began spinning, but still he remained conscious. The assailant grabbed the woman by the hair and yanked her backward, slamming her into the opposite wall. Then, in raw anger, he pulled the knife out of Anthony's shoulder and with a deep animal cry swiped the blade across the front of Anthony's neck. Unsatisfied, he grabbed Anthony by the hair and prepared to thrust the blade into his heart.

Savannah lunged forward, falling across the right arm of the dark man. "No," she snapped. "That's enough."

The assailant stared at Savannah and in those three seconds of rage debated between driving the knife into Anthony or swiping the blade across the girl's face. Savannah waited unflinchingly for his verdict. The assailant pulled back his arm to backhand Savannah and then froze, startled by a bellowing voice just outside the open door.

"*¿Quien es? ¿Que Pasa?*"

Savannah and the assailant shot away into the darkness of the hallway, leaving Anthony for dead. They not only took his diamond ring, but also his gold watch, a roll of bills, and a leather shoulder bag, which contained Anthony's passport, credit card, and car keys.

It was there, in the hallway of an abandoned seventeenth-century stone building in the heart of Granada's Albaicín, that Anthony Rossi, president of Transnational Management Services, lay bleeding from head, shoulder, and throat, adrift in the dark comfort and peace of oblivion.

It was also there that Diego Garcia was given a reprieve: Finally, after fifty-five years, he was granted the chance to make peace with his moment of indecision when Juanito faced his executioner.

ANTONIO'S AND LUPITA'S HANDS WERE interlaced at their sides. They kissed each other goodnight, but Antonio's kiss was so distant, so dispassionate that it unnerved Lupita.

"It will be all right," she reassured.

"Thank you, Lupita."

His voice was a world away, and Lupita accepted that. They turne their hands the last to give way, and quietly entered their separate rooms.

Antonio lay fully dressed across the bed. He could not sleep. In the shadows of his room, he saw the faces and heard the voices of the ghosts of his former life. But they were not ghosts; they were real, and he was a part of that other world. His face wrenched with remembrance of that old life; there was nothing that was redeeming—not the bullying, not the power plays, not the abuse he leveled on others—there was nothing that was in harmony with Diego's teachings.

His new life in Spain tugged at him like a warm wave, and he realized that if he waded into the water, the wave could kindly pull him out to sea, away from all that he knew ashore. That would be so easy. But what responsibility did he have to atone for his transgressions? That was the question that nagged at him throughout the night.

Then there was Lupita. Every scene reeling before his eyes came back to her. His love for her was unquestionable. In fact, it was the first time in his pathetic history that he valued another life above his own. But how could he reconcile that love with the chaos that awaited him in Paris?

Before dawn, he got out of bed and silently slipped out of the house. He walked down to the town square just as the sun was rising. The plaza was deserted. He crossed to the fountain and stared into the pool. With no wish in mind, he tossed a coin into the fountain and watched the ripples expand and wash against the basin wall. He thought of Diego and Lupita as that coin: Those whose influence had rippled across the face of his life. He knew only one thing for sure. He wanted every decision to be consistent with the example of his Spanish family.

When he returned to the house, Lupita and Diego were already having breakfast in the kitchen. He followed their voices and pulled up a chair at the table.

"You look like you could use some coffee," Diego said, filling a cup for his friend.

"Yes, thank you."

"How did you sleep last night?" Lupita asked.

Antonio offered a weak smile. "Not very well."

She smoothed an eyebrow. "That makes two of us."

"As for me, I slept like a baby," Diego said. "But then I always sleep like a baby. The older I get, the more I go back to my old ways. I sleep like a baby and think like an adolescent. Right now, I am thinking that you, my dear Antonio, could use a good friend."

"I know I have your friendship, Diego, and I am sure that I will be leaning on you. But first I need to tell you something about myself."

"Antonio, you do not have to tell us anything," Diego said.

"I do. I owe you my life. Sharing my history is the least I can do." Antonio said this with his head down, staring blankly at Lupita's hands folded on the kitchen table. Then he raised his head and gazed into Lupita's beautiful eyes. "My name is Anthony Rossi."

"Then you are Antonio, after all," Diego said. "I knew it."

Antonio smiled. "Yes, I am Antonio. But there is much that you do not know about me. I am an American. I am the president of an international construction management firm with offices in Seattle and Paris. For the last ten years, I have lived in Paris."

There was a moment of silence. Then, Lupita asked the question that had replayed in her head all night long. "Are you married?" The words were almost inaudible.

Antonio paused a few seconds too long, and Lupita withdrew her hand. Antonio closed his eyes and tried to recover from the blow to his heart.

"I am married. But it is not a good marriage; I never really loved her—not in a real sense. It has been breaking up for years. In fact, I think it was breaking up before it began. And, luckily, we have no children."

"I see," Lupita said soberly.

"No, you do not see, Lupita. What I have told you before still stands. There is only one woman who I love, and that woman is you."

Lupita said nothing.

Antonio clawed at his bad shoulder. "Lupita, I am in agony. I would scratch out my eyes, if I thought it would erase the memory of my past. I am ashamed of my life; it is utterly despicable. My marriage is a sham, and my business dealings are unethical, if not illegal. I use and discard people at will. That is what I meant when I said last night that I was no good. But I swear to you, as God is my witness, that is not the man I want to be today—not anymore."

Another long pause.

"What is your wife's name?" Lupita asked.

"Penelope."

"Who is Savannah?"

Antonio tugged at his hair. "She is one of the people I used. And she used me."

"Was she your lover?"

"Yes, but it was not real. It was all a setup. She was the person who lured me into the Arab Quarter in Granada, and it was her partner who nearly killed me."

"But she wrote, 'You were unbelievable.'"

"Yes, but not in the sense you are thinking. I was 'unbelievable' all right: meaning 'I was not credible and not to be trusted.' Do you see?"

Lupita turned and lowered her head, her eyes even more sad.

"Do you want revenge?" Diego asked.

"Regarding Savannah?"

"*Si.*"

Antonio looked long at the old man. "No, Diego. You have taught me better than that. In fact, I want nothing of Savannah or Penelope or my life in Paris."

"Nothing?" Diego asked. It was only a one-word question, but that single word held a world of complexity and challenge.

"My old life holds nothing for me," Antonio said meekly.

"Yes, my son, but what influence does your old life hold on you?"

"What do you mean?"

"You said that you used Savannah."

"Yes."

"Then Savannah holds your soul." Diego took his time, letting the statement sink in. "People are not furniture, Antonio. You do not use them and then discard them, when you grow weary of their novelty."

"It was she who discarded me," Antonio protested.

"That is not the point. I am not talking about her responsibility; I am talking about yours. What responsibility do you have to her?"

Antonio nodded. In his old life the word responsibility had one meaning: commitment to satisfying his own needs. Diego made him realize, perhaps for the first time, that he had never thought about his responsibility to others.

"Now, as to your wife," Diego continued, "you said you never really loved her."

"That is right."

"Did you make her believe that you loved her?"

"Yes. In the beginning."

"Then you lied."

Anthony closed his eyes. His body felt slack and empty. "Yes."

"And later, did you prove to her again and again that you did *not* love her?"

"Yes, Diego, I did that too."

Diego reached over the table and covered Antonio's hand. "Listen, Antonio: That is a terrible thing. There is nothing that you can do to a woman that is more devastating and more dishonorable."

Antonio bowed his head. A tear fell to the table.

"What am I to do?"

Diego touched the knot of his red bandanna. "Antonio, you remember meeting my brother?"

Antonio nodded, picturing the frail priest in his wheel chair staring blankly at a wall.

"I had good reason to despise my brother; he killed my wife. But hate does not make the world flourish; it makes it more frail and puny. It shrivels the soul as it has shriveled the spirit of my brother. I did not want that for myself, and that is why I rescued him from a prison cell in Barcelona."

"How did you have the strength?"

"I listened to Lupe and Juanito. They taught me that only love makes the world richer. And, know this, my son: Without mercy there is no love."

The room was silent for a moment. Then Antonio straightened up in his chair, resolve dawning on his face. He spoke slowly: "Yes, yes. I know now what I must do."

"Good. Just keep listening to your heart."

"I will. I promise."

After a moment, Diego offered to freshen everyone's coffee. All refused.

"I have a question for you," Antonio said to Diego. "Your response will help me plan my life."

"Go ahead."

"I am a very wealthy man. Under the right conditions, would the two of you ever consider living in France or the United States? I could give you both a very comfortable life."

Lupita and Diego looked at each other.

Diego took hold of Antonio's forearm. "My life is already very comfortable. This is my home, Antonio: my earth, my people, my ancestors. No, I could never leave Spain."

"Nor could I," Lupita said. "Espejo is my village. The people need me, and I need them."

Antonio nodded. "Yes. I do not know why I even asked; I knew that would be your answer. Of course, you are right. This is your land," he said, letting the idea go, his mind already drifting to other thoughts.

"What will be your next step?" Diego asked.

"I would like to begin by transferring some money to your account, Diego."

"Why would you do that?"

"To help repay you."

"But we did not take you in for money. We love you; there is no charge for love."

"I know that, Diego. I am not asking this for you; I am asking for me."

"If you want to give us something, Antonio, give us your love. That is all that I cherish."

Antonio turned to Lupita. "I suppose that you feel the same."

"Absolutely," she said, putting her arm around her grandfather.

"I am not sure I know what it means to love. I am only a crude student. But I have the best teachers in the world," he said, grasping both their hands. "My only desire is to love you purely and deeply."

"Then do it," Diego said. "Be the man you are meant to be."

Those words stung, but Antonio knew Diego was right. He had to take charge. If he ever was to love, he would have to be intentional about it.

"What do you need from us?" Diego asked.

Antonio thought for a moment. "First, I would like a little time to think alone. Then, I think I would like to make a call or two to Paris. May I use your telephone?"

"Yes, of course."

Antonio stood, stepped behind Lupita, and kissed her on the cheek. With that kiss, Lupita caressed the side of his face—a warm and tender touch that gave him renewed life.

Antonio moved to the balcony, where he sat for over an hour. Slowly he pieced together his next steps with one thought in mind: to be true to his heart and Diego's standards of honor. He was about to move to the living room to make his telephone calls, when he heard Lupita's voice.

"Would you like some company?" she asked from the doorway.

He turned and looked at Lupita, who looked, all at once, beautiful, courageous, and sad. "Please, come talk with me." He stood up, took her by both hands, and led her to a chair next to his. "I am glad you came; I am always at peace when you are with me."

"What will you do now?" Lupita asked.

"The right thing. I have to do the right thing."

"Yes, I know, Antonio. How long will it take?"

He shook his head. "I do not know. My heart is here, Lupita—you know that—but I have a great deal of work to do. My neglect, my abuse has hurt a lot of people, and I have to make that right; I have to do what is honorable. I need time, Lupita. Can you wait for me?"

"And if it takes a lifetime?"

Antonio did not know how to answer that question. Finally, he said, "Lupita, I cannot imagine my life without you. But can you imagine my life *with* you, if I simply ignored my debts? Diego has asked me to follow my heart, and that is what my heart is telling me. Would you want me to do any differently?"

"No, of course not." Then, after a long pause, she said quietly, "I just do not know if I can ever be happy again without you."

Lupita's words tore at his heart. "Lupita, your happiness is more important to me than my own breath. If there is any way on earth that I can come back to you, I will find it. I put my love for you above all things . . ."

"Except honor," Lupita said, finishing his sentence.

"Yes, except honor."

Telephoning Paris was not easy; it was opening the door to the raw ugliness of his past; and, yet, he knew it must be done. It was the first step in reconciling his past life with his future life.

It did not take Antonio long to decide whom to telephone first. There was only one person he knew he could trust with his life; that was his secretary, Lucy. She was not only fully competent, but, more importantly, she could keep a secret.

Always efficient, she picked up the phone on the first ring. "TMS. How may I help you?"

"Hello Lucy."

"I'm sorry. Who's speaking please?"

Of course, Lucy did not recognize him. The injury to his larynx had changed his voice—now a little breathier, a little raspier.

"I've been in an accident, Lucy. It damaged my voice a bit, but I think you know me. Please don't say my name. This is Antonio . . . Anthony Rossi."

Lucy gasped. "Oh, my. Oh, my God."

"Lucy, I know that you always have a lot of traffic around your desk. Is that the case right now?"

"Yes, sir."

"Is anyone in my office?"

"No."

"Good. Go to my office and pick up this line; I need to talk to you privately."

"Yes, sir. Hold on." Lucy transferred the call to Anthony's office and dashed to his door. "Damn." She had forgotten that she had locked the door and ran back to her desk to find the keys. She fumbled with the keys, until she found the right one and stabbed it into the door lock. Anthony's phone was on the third ring; it would transfer to an answering machine on the fourth ring. Lucy dove across the desk to grab the phone, sending blueprints and reports flying.

"Hello, hello!"

"Yes, Lucy, I'm still here."

"Thank God. I thought I lost you."

"Have you locked the door behind you?"

"No, not yet."

"Do so."

"Okay. Hold on."

"I'm not going anywhere."

Lucy locked the door, circled Anthony's desk, and sat down.

"I'm back."

"All right. Please forgive all the cloak-and-dagger stuff, but I'm not ready for anyone to know that I'm back."

"Where are you?"

"I'm still in Spain. It's a very long and complicated story. I'll take you out to dinner one night and tell you all about it. But for right now, I need your help. All right?"

"Of course."

"I knew I could depend on you. Do you have a pencil and paper?"

Lucy opened the top desk drawer and pulled out a pencil. Then, swiveling half circle, she took out a clean sheet of paper from the printer behind the desk. "I'm ready, Mr. Rossi."

"Good. Are you sitting at my desk?"

"Yes."

"On the bottom right hand side there is a file drawer. Find the folder titled 'Anthony Rossi.'"

Lucy was following his directions as he spoke. "Yes, I've got it."

"Good. Inside that file are photocopies of my birth certificate and my passport."

"Wait a minute. Yes, they're here."

"I want you to overnight both of them to me at this address." He gave the address to the Garcias' home.

"All right. I'm with you."

"Second, what can you tell me about the project with Harry Tubbs in Águilas?"

"Harry didn't know what to do when you didn't come back. He waited for a few days and then sent the contract to Mr. Duncan."

"Has Hennessy signed off on it yet?"

"I think so."

"Has legal signed off on it?"

"I don't know. I don't think so."

"Okay. I don't care how you do it, Lucy, but do not let that contract go out. Find the contract and lose it somewhere. I don't mean destroy it; I mean misplace it for a week or two, until I can get back to the office."

"I can do that."

"I know you can; I'm counting on you. Third, who is running the company?"

"Mr. Duncan."

"How is he doing?"

"He's trying to fill your shoes, but it's a pretty poor imitation."

"Am I still the president of the company?"

"Yes, but I don't know for how long. There has been some discontent among the board members. I think they would like to figure out a way to take your title."

"And do what?"

"I'm not sure. But it doesn't look good for you. Forgive me for saying, Mr. Rossi, but you don't have a lot of friends on the board."

"I know, Lucy. And don't worry; you can speak frankly with me."

"The next board meeting is in three days. I don't know the details, but I do know that legal has been working on a proposal for a new organizational structure, including your role in the company. I wish I could tell you more, Mr. Rossi, but I've been left pretty much in the dark."

"That's all right. Here's your third task. See if you can postpone that board meeting. Tell them there's a critical report that needs to be posted before the meeting. Tell them anything. Just get it postponed for ten days. That's all I need."

"It's done."

"I have a fourth item."

"I'm listening."

"This will be the most difficult for you, but please be absolutely honest with me. What has happened between Hennie and Penelope?"

The phone went silent.

"Lucy?"

"Yes, I'm here. It's not good, Mr. Rossi," Lucy said very slowly.

"What is it?"

"When you fell off the face of the earth, Penelope filed for divorce. I think she figured you were . . . this is very hard for me, Mr. Rossi."

"You're doing fine, Lucy."

"I think she decided you were . . . well, having a romantic interlude in Spain somewhere. Frankly, she had no interest in finding you; she didn't even try. She just wanted out of the marriage."

Now it was Anthony's turn to be silent. The news was not unexpected; in fact, in a way it was what he hoped for. And, yet, he was saddened. It was true that their marriage was in shambles, but he still felt that he owed her something. He owed her respect.

"Mr. Rossi?"

"Yes, Lucy, I'm just taking it in. When did she file for divorce?"

"I'm not absolutely sure, but I think it was in early October. I don't know if you know this, Mr. Rossi, but Washington State law dictates that a divorce cannot be finalized for three months."

Anthony remembered Lucy's divorce. Of course, she would be up on the rules.

"That's right about now."

"Yes."

"But wouldn't she need my consent?"

"Correct. But, given the unusual circumstances—namely your disappearance—Penelope could appeal to the court to grant a divorce in your absence. In fact, I think that is what she has in mind."

"Okay. I'll try to get back before it's finalized."

"There's one other thing, Mr. Rossi."

"Yes?"

"I didn't want to tell you this," Lucy said softly, "but Hennie, I mean Mr. Duncan, has moved in with Penelope."

Anthony felt the grain of his beard. "That doesn't surprise me, Lucy. It's all right. Thanks for telling me."

"Can I do anything else for you?"

"No, I think that will do it. There is just this: Lucy, you are a soldier. No, that's not what I want to say. I called you because you were the only person I could trust. And, frankly, I don't know why you should be loyal to me. I have not always treated you with dignity, and for that I am truly sorry."

"Thank you, Mr. Rossi," Lucy said, her voice breaking up. "Thank you very, very much."

"Goodbye. I'll see you in a week or two. And remember, not a word of this to anyone."

"You have my promise. Goodbye, Mr. Rossi. And please take care of yourself."

Anthony's second call was to his financial consultant, Darby Pecheur. He had handled Anthony's personal account for years; there wasn't anything that he didn't know about his finances.

Darby was the consummate professional: timely, accurate, thorough, and, most importantly, trustworthy. To top it off, he dressed impeccably, always giving Anthony the impression that he went to bed in a dark navy suit.

Anthony did not disclose what had happened over the last four months. As far as Darby knew, his client was taking a long overdue vacation in Spain.

Anthony wanted an accounting of draws made from his credit card since September eighth, the day he was attacked. Darby took a moment to bring up the screen.

"It looks like you have been a busy man," Darby said.

"Why, what do you see?"

"All your withdrawals are from ATM machines. As of today you've drawn out a little over $25,000. You've been hitting the machine about three times a week and always at about $500 a whack, depending on the exchange rate."

Damn. Suddenly Anthony remembered Savannah snuggling up behind him, when he withdrew cash from the ATM in Granada. Sure. She had read his code. She was playing it smart. She could withdraw $500 every day, but that would draw suspicion from the bank.

"Can you tell where the debits were made?"

"Sure. Let's see. Beginning in September, I see draws in—forgive my Spanish—Granada, Jaén, Andújar. For the last week and a half, it's been the same machine: the ATM at the Hotel Glorioso in Córdoba."

Incredible! Savannah was in Córdoba—just thirty minutes away from Espejo! Anthony knew the hotel. It was a magnificent hundred-year-old palace in the heart of the city—an upper-end room costing around $250 a night. Anthony had been paying for Savannah's hotel bill.

"Got it. Thanks, Darby. That's about what I figured. I need one other thing from you. I need you to overnight a new debit card with a new number. But I also want you to keep the old card active. Can you do that for me?"

"Sure. Just give me the address."

Anthony did so.

"Is everything all right?"

"Everything is fine. Having a great time; wish you were here."

"Yeah, I bet."

Anthony hung up. Normally, he would call the credit card company and put a stop on the card, but he didn't want to alert Savannah—not just yet.

Antonio was at a small desk in his bedroom, bent over a notebook.

Diego leaned around the portal and lightly tapped on the open door.

Antonio looked up from his work and hooked his arm on the back of his chair. "Come in, Diego."

"Dinner will be ready in about a half hour."

"Great. Is there something I can do to help?"

"No, everything is simmering," Diego said, stepping into the room. "What are you doing?"

"Oh, I was just trying to get some thoughts down on paper, but it is not easy."

"What are you struggling with?"

"All the basic questions: Where have I been? Where am I going?

Diego sat down on the bed facing Antonio. "Hmm. Antonio, I would like to tell you a story."

Antonio turned his chair around to face Diego directly. These were the moments he cherished the most with his friend. He understood Diego's language: "Telling a story" was code for "imparting wisdom."

"I want to tell you about the death of my friend, Juanito."

Diego slowly revealed the story.

"I have never forgotten his four sacred words: Silence, love, charity, peace. They are the words that I live by. Silence begets love, love begets charity, charity begets peace. It is that simple."

Antonio repeated the words in his head.

"I told you that story for a reason, Antonio."

"Yes, Diego."

"If you choose, you can serve here in Espejo. I believe in you. I believe you would be good for Lupita and good for our village. And I think you would be at peace." Then, after a long breath: "I will not be here forever."

"You are as strong as an ox," Antonio protested.

"Maybe so. Still, no one is immortal. And I would be very happy, if you were to take my place one day."

Suddenly, hearing those words, Antonio could not swallow. "I have never been so honored, Diego."

"Will you think about it?"

"Of course I will."

The next day, Anthony borrowed Diego's van and drove north to Córdoba. During the short drive, he thought about Lupita, of course, but also about Diego's wisdom. He hoped that his words would serve him now.

His first stop was at a fashionable men's clothing store. He was at home in his everyday field clothes; in fact, they gave him a sense of integrity and nobility. So, the idea of exchanging his simple work shirt for a pinstriped business suit was repellent to him. It reeked of his old life. Yet, for what he had in mind, he knew he had to look like a Wall Street banker.

He stepped into the store and selected a classic navy suit, white shirt, and burgundy tie. The salesman called for the tailor: a short man wearing suit pants, suspenders, herringbone shirt, and tie. He was all business. Both sleeves would have to be lengthened, the back pulled in at the waist, and the pants cuffed.

"Could you have that done within the next hour?" Anthony asked.

"Not possible," the tailor said curtly.

Anthony surveyed the suits on display about the store. "If I may ask, *señor*, where did you learn your craft?"

The tailor thought the question strange—a ruse to entrap him perhaps—and he glared at Anthony. "Milan, Paris, London," he said curtly.

"Ah, you must have studied at the Instituto Bianchi."

The tailor's face brightened. "How did you know?"

"Bianchi is the best fashion institute in the world. I see the Bianchi touch in this shop; it could have been nothing else. Besides, my Paris tailor is also a graduate; the give away was your mentioning Milan, Paris, and London: the three Bianchi fashion centers."

"You have a very good eye, *señor*," he said smiling. "Please, let me make your alterations."

"Not without paying for your services; your craftsmanship is too valuable. Would 10,000 pesetas be satisfactory?"

The tailor smiled broadly. "It is too generous, *señor*. Five thousand pesetas will do handsomely, and your suit will be ready in one hour."

"Thank you. You are most kind."

The transaction sealed, Anthony walked a few doors down the street and stepped into a barbershop, where he sat for a shave and a haircut.

When he returned to the men's store, the tailor was brushing down the suit.

"It is a beautiful suit," he said, smiling.

"Yes, it is," Anthony agreed, patting the tailor on the shoulder. "And thank you for being such a master at your craft."

The tailor grinned. "It is a pleasure."

Anthony immediately slipped into the suit. When he looked at himself in the full-length mirror, he could not complain; the suit was impeccably tailored. What he did not like was the fact that he was wearing the suit. Despite its fine texture and drape, it felt like a cloak of disgrace, and he would wear it only long enough to complete the job.

On his way to the car, Anthony passed a tobacco shop and froze, spotting something that attracted his attention in the display window. He went into the shop and made his purchase.

His next stop was the Hotel Glorioso.

Anthony was an actor now—playing an uneasy role to accomplish the task. He walked into the hotel like he owned the place and strolled to the gift shop where he purchased a copy of *El Mundo*. Then he went to the lobby and found a comfortable easy chair that had a perfect view of the elevators and the front entrance. He started to read the paper. An hour later, he was still reading. One of the desk clerks stepped out from behind the counter and, approaching Anthony, asked if he could be of service.

"Thank you. A cup of hot coffee would be very nice," Anthony said.

"Of course. Right away, sir."

Another hour passed, and then it happened. The elevator door opened, and Savannah stepped out. She looked like a million dollars—most of them Anthony's dollars. With the exception of a stunning set of pearls, she was dressed entirely in black: high-waisted wool trousers, a revealing cashmere sweater, a stylish full-length polished rain slicker, and a beaded handbag. She was dressed to kill.

Anthony folded the newspaper and laid it tent-like over his right hand. He cut off Savannah at the center of the lobby, grasping her arm firmly with his left hand. Savannah whipped around and flashed her eyes, outraged by the intrusion. But when she finally looked into Anthony's eyes, the recognition sank in, and all her indignation slowly dissolved into fear. She was paralyzed. Then, like a slow-motion film, Anthony could see an idea dawn in her eyes; her expression turned from terror to defiance, and she opened her mouth, ready to scream.

"I wouldn't do that," Anthony said quickly, thrusting his right hand forward.

Savannah's entire body jerked; what she felt pressed against her ribs could only be the barrel of a pistol.

"A little kiss, my lovely," Anthony said, pecking Savannah on both cheeks.

Savannah stood rigid, staring down at the business section of *El Mundo*.

"Now, we are going to turn, go back to the elevator, and go to your room," Anthony said, as if speaking to a child about the dangers of crossing the street. "I want you to smile for the nice man at the desk."

She complied.

Anthony stood behind Savannah in the elevator. She pushed the button for the fourth floor. As the door was closing, an older American couple, looking like they were dressed for Hawaii, hobbled forward in what for them must have been a dead-out sprint. "Hold that elevator!" the woman shouted, her words snapping like a cookie sheet.

"Sorry, all full up," Anthony said, pressing the "close door" button.

As the doors sealed, the American woman could be heard snarling at her husband. "Why didn't you stop the elevator, Arnold? It wasn't full; it wasn't full at all. You could have stopped it if you wanted to, but, oh no, not you, not Mr. Mamby-Pamby."

The elevator ascended.

Savannah was silent, and Anthony knew her brain was churning.

The elevator stopped at the fourth floor, and the two stepped out, Anthony still standing behind Savannah. "Just march straight to your room. No funny business, please."

Savannah stopped at room 434. A do-not-disturb sign was suspended from the door handle. When she inserted the card into the electronic lock, Anthony slipped his arm around her waist and swung the door open, using Savannah as a shield. The two crabbed along together from the sitting room to the bedroom to the bathroom. The suite was empty.

Anthony released his grip on Savannah, being careful to stand between her and the front door. He canvassed the room. It was richly decorated, but it looked like it had not received maid service for a month. The bed was unmade, and the floor was cluttered with newspapers and a rat's nest of dirty dishes. But most prominent were two plastic bags of white powder in clear view on a small desk.

Anthony poked at one of the bags with two fingers. "What is this? Cocaine?"

Cold silence, Savannah inspecting the polish on her fingernails.

"Where do you get the nerve to set this stuff out in the open?"

"The hotel owner is . . . a customer."

They were the first words Savannah had spoken, and Anthony hardly recognized her voice. There was none of the sweetness that he knew in Granada, but rather a raw abrasiveness: a challenging tone, ready to pick a fight.

"Oh, Savannah, you're hanging out with bad company."

"My name is not Savannah."

"I'm glad you mentioned that. What is your name anyway?"

The ice treatment again.

"I understand; you don't feel like talking. Meanwhile, would you please sit over there?" Anthony said, pointing at two parlor chairs in front of the small balcony.

Savannah sat.

"Maybe I'd be more chatty," she said with a slur, "if you put that gun away."

Anthony looked at the newspaper that was still draped over his right hand. "Oh, you mean this?" he asked. "This is nothing." Anthony drew the newspaper from his hand, revealing a straight-neck briar pipe.

Savannah's shoulders visibly dropped.

Anthony slowly walked about the room, opening drawers and closet doors. Then he moved to the bed. He slipped his hand under one of the pillows and stopped cold, while Savannah suddenly looked like she was one number short of the lotto jackpot. He turned the pillow over, revealing a nickel-plated 32-caliber revolver. "I think I'd better take this," he said, stuffing the gun into his suit side pocket.

His tour finished, he sat down across from Savannah in the second parlor chair.

"May I?" he said, reaching over and snatching the beaded handbag from Savannah's clutches. "Let's see what we've got here." Anthony pulled out an American passport and opened it. A picture of Savannah smiled back at him; she could have been anybody's college sweetheart. "Kelly Sullivan. Place of birth: Las Vegas, Nevada." He looked at Savannah. "Is that who you are: Kelly Sullivan?"

She shrugged her shoulders.

"And you're not from Savannah?"

"No."

"So tell me, Savannah . . . Kelly . . . I don't know what to call you."

Suddenly, her voice softened, becoming more seductive. "Call me Kelly. That's my real name."

"Okay, Kelly. Tell me, what are you about?" he asked, slipping her passport into his suit pocket.

"May I?" she asked, peeling out of her rain slicker.

"Sure."

"I'm about you," she said, stepping forward and dropping to her knees at Anthony's feet. She spread his legs apart and, looking into his eyes, started to unzip his fly. "I know you like this, baby."

Anthony slipped one hand in his suit pocket to protect the revolver. He was repulsed. He literally picked Kelly up off the ground and thumped her into her seat. "No, Kelly, not this time."

She shrugged. "Hey, it was worth a shot."

Anthony turned again to the handbag, this time pulling out a roll of bills. "You won't mind if I keep these," he said, pocketing the money. "I believe they are rightfully mine."

Kelly blinked impassively.

"That's about it. Lipstick, a little change, a subway ticket, but no credit card. Where's my credit card, Kelly? And my passport?"

She looked to one side with infinite boredom.

"Never mind. It doesn't matter," Anthony said.

"If it doesn't matter, why are you here?"

That was the real question. Suddenly, he heard Diego's voice: Without mercy there is no love. "I'm trying to learn the answer to that question," he said slowly.

"Did you want to get even?"

"No, I don't want blood."

"Then what?"

Anthony took a moment, tugging on the lapels of his jacket. "I think I want to understand."

"What's to understand, Sweetheart? You were a mark."

"Please don't call me 'Sweetheart.'"

"Whatever."

"So that was it? I was just a sucker?"

"One born every minute."

"But why me?"

"Why not you? You were rich. I saw you flashing bills at the hotel in Águilas."

"You were at the hotel? I didn't see you."

"No, but I saw you. I knew you were going to Granada; it didn't take long to become a hitchhiker." She smirked. "Damn, that road has a lot of traffic; I swear, I told a dozen horny old men to screw off, before you finally showed up."

"Yeah."

"You seemed to dig the 'baby thing,' so we had a good time." She paused, then added, "But I never believed you."

"Meaning?"

"Meaning you're a lying son-of-a-bitch. Your wife didn't die on you. Ovarian cancer?" she sneered, rolling her eyes. "Give me a fucking break. And you didn't want to be anybody's father. Face it, Anthony, we used each other; I'm just better at it than you."

Kelly hit a raw nerve. She just summed up his life in a phase: He used people. She was right; she was absolutely right. He became sullen.

Kelly could see his pretension dissolve. "What's the matter, Sugar? Did I hurt your feelings?"

"Yeah, you did. Because it is all true."

Kelly squinted at Anthony.

"You know, Kelly, I am grateful to you."

"I bet you are," her voice full of venom.

"It's true. You saved my life," he said evenly. "When your partner was ready to plunge his knife into my heart, you fell over his arm. Even though I used you—and you knew it—still, you risked your life to save mine. Why did you do it?"

"I don't like blood," she said, the surliness fading from her voice.

"No, it's more than that, Kelly. You're not as tough as you pretend to be. I hate to be the one to tell you, Kid, but you have principles. Sure, they're plenty rusty for lack of use, but they have not disappeared altogether; they're just hidden away somewhere in the depth of your soul."

"You're not going to start singing 'Kum Ba Ya,' I hope."

Anthony smiled. "You know, it might not hurt. The point is we both know better, don't we? That's why I came, Kelly: Not for revenge, but to thank you, to tell you I'm sorry for how I used you." He searched for the right phrase. He started, stopped, and started again. "What if . . . ? Look, it's like this. We can both do a helluva lot better."

Kelly didn't answer, but her eyes did not look as mean.

There was no time to say more. Someone was opening the front door. Anthony pulled the gun out of his pocket and tucked it under his armpit out of view.

An angry voice called out: "Kelly, where the . . ."

The man stopped dead. He was thirty, maybe thirty-five years old. He had a slender waist and firm, muscular build. He looked quick as a cat, but also strung out, like he was sampling his own drugs—the vacancy in his eyes giving him away. He looked to be Arab.

He walked slowly into the room and then bolted for the bed, flinging the first pillow back, then the second, then the spread. He cursed in Arabic.

"Looking for this?" Anthony said, presenting the pistol.

The Arab stopped moving and looked down to one side, the picture of dejection.

"You don't like it when someone else has the advantage, do you?"

"What do you want?" he said in a guttural English, his tone coarse and scowling.

"First, to be treated with a little respect. Okay?"

The Arab said nothing.

Anthony looked hard at the cold assailant and considered his options. Then he pointed the barrel of the pistol at the bags of cocaine on the desk. "You realize, of course, that your—merchandise—changes everything." He pursed his lips and slowly nodded his head. "I think I know what I need to do here."

Anthony stood, motioning to the Arab to back up. He took the telephone from the desk and returned to his seat. "You'll excuse me." With both eyes on his prisoners, he picked up the receiver and dialed a number. He waited a moment, smiling demurely at Kelly and the Arab. "Ah, good, you are in . . . I need your help . . . well, it is a somewhat delicate task, and you are the only man for the job . . . I have made the acquaintance of a rather ugly pair of thugs—drug dealers actually . . ."

The Arab's body slowly shrank as if preparing to pounce. "Ah, ah, ah," Anthony warned, waving his gun at the Arab, who grudgingly straightened his spine.

Anthony returned to his telephone conversation. "No, I am still here . . . the Hotel Glorioso in Córdoba, room 434 . . . maybe. I would come armed . . . good. Thirty minutes it is. *Adiós* and thank you."

"It doesn't have to be this way," the Arab said.

"You are in no place to negotiate."

"What do you want? Do you want the goods?" he asked, pointing his head at the cocaine. "You've got it."

The proposal was so outlandish that it made Anthony smile in disbelief. "No, I don't think so. I'll tell you what, though, I am interested in that beautiful diamond ring you have on your index finger. I believe that belongs to me. Just set it on the desk nice and easy next to your precious bags of cocaine."

The Arab pulled on his finger, put the ring in the palm of his hand, and slapped it down hard on the desk as if it were a domino.

"Please, I said 'nice and easy.'"

The Arab stood there, his mouth slightly open, feeling the inside of his lower lip with his tongue. He was the kind of punk you wanted to slap across the face.

"I'll also take the Rolex. On the desk—*easy* this time, if you please."

He did so.

"Good. Now empty your pockets."

Done.

"And now take off your clothes. They don't belong to you; they belong to me."

The Arab flashed a cold look and stripped to his undershorts and socks.

"The socks, please."

The socks came off.

Anthony thought for a moment. His ego and spirit were brawling. Shaming the thug was tempting—very tempting—and yet, at the same time, revolting. He took a long pause, finally deciding that humiliation was too easy and too sordid. Of course, Diego was right: The visit could not be about revenge. For Kelly it would be about forgiveness; for the Arab—that was different—something else was at sake: justice and the protection of innocence.

"You can keep the shorts; they're not my style."

The Arab expelled a breath of relief. He actually tipped his head fractionally in gratitude to his captor for the small consolation.

"Now, on your knees."

Anthony stood up and, never taking his eyes off the Arab, opened the French doors to the balcony. Then he stepped back, distancing himself from Kelly and the Arab.

"Kelly, gather his clothes and shoes and throw them over the balcony."

"Is this necessary?" she protested.

"Please do as I say, Kelly."

She followed the instruction and returned to her chair.

"Now you," Anthony said, wielding his gun at the Arab. "That must be uncomfortable on your knees. If you will be so kind, please take my chair."

The Arab stood up, walked to the chair opposite Kelly and sat down. He felt a chill from the open doors and wrapped his arms around himself.

Anthony moved to the desk, giving his two captives a wide berth. He put the diamond on his finger and, not wanting to fumble with the band, stuffed the watch in his pocket. He sat on the desk and planted his feet on the seat of the desk chair.

On the desktop were a wallet, a set of keys, some change, and a butterfly knife—the same blade that had ripped a hole into his shoulder. He opened the wallet with one hand and struck it rich. There were at least a hundred thousand pesetas (about $1,000) in new bills, a debit card with the name 'Anthony Rossi,' and an Algerian passport. Anthony thumbed through the passport.

"Abdul-Khaliq Ben-Salem. A beautiful name. What does it mean, if I may ask?"

"Servant of the creator," the Arab muttered.

"Servant of the creator," Anthony repeated slowly. Suddenly, he was saddened by the untold story of a wasted life. "How tragic. What a mockery. You have dishonored your parents, Abdul."

The Arab's face was vacant.

Anthony continued to scrutinize the passport. "Did you know your visa has expired? This is not good, Abdul. I'm sure the Spanish government would frown on this."

Anthony crammed the passport, the wallet, and the knife into his pocket. "You know, I don't see my passport in all of this."

"We sold it," Ben-Salem said quickly, beginning to shiver.

"Hmm. What is the market for an American passport these days?"

"A lot," the Arab said with cold eyes, "if you know the right people."

"And you know the right people."

Ben-Salem suddenly shut up.

"Right."

Anthony nudged the chair under his feet to one side, stood up, and arched his back. "I think I've had enough of this." He put one bag of cocaine in his pocket and began to backtrack toward the front door. "Kelly, come here."

Kelly walked to Anthony, and Ben-Salem started to follow.

"No, not you," Anthony said, pointing the pistol at the Arab. "You stay right where you are."

The Arab sat.

Anthony drew out Kelly's passport and a wad of bills and, without ceremony, handed both to her. "Kelly, I want you to run as fast as you can. Do not look back. Go home and make something of yourself; you are worth it."

Kelly was stunned. She looked first at the passport and money clutched in her hands and then at Anthony, searching his eyes for understanding.

Anthony smiled at her. "It's all right, Kelly. Get the hell out of here."

Kelly smiled, heaved a sigh of relief, and kissed Anthony on the cheek. "Thank you," she said with genuine gratitude. Then, in the next instant, she was through the door and gone, closing the door behind her.

Anthony turned his attention back to the Arab. "It's been a pleasure, Mr. Ben-Salem."

With his back to the door, Anthony unlatched the lock. He took a handkerchief from his hip pocket, wiped down the gun, opened the chamber, and dropped the bullets into his hand. He then gripped the revolver by the barrel and pitched it into the middle of the room.

The Arab started to rush toward him.

"Hey, hey, hey!" Anthony shouted, drawing a hand grenade out of his suit pocket. He held the grenade at arms length between thumb and forefinger.

The Arab's feet stopped moving.

"Why don't you sit back down? You look a little strange standing there in your underwear."

The Arab retreated to his chair.

"I'm so sorry; I almost forgot," Anthony said, tapping the side of his head with the grenade. "I had this little gift for you. Have a nice day."

He pulled the pin and tossed the grenade into the room. It bounced once and rolled within three feet of the Arab, who leapt from his chair and dove through the French doors onto the balcony, pressing his back against the outside wall.

Anthony backed out of the room, shut the door, and took the elevator to the lobby. He walked directly to the front desk.

"May I help you, sir?" asked the desk clerk.

Anthony placed the confiscated passport, wallet, bullets, knife, and bag of cocaine on the desk. He spoke with absolute calm. "I believe yours is a respectable hotel."

"Without a question, sir," the clerk said, clearly confused.

"Then you have work to do. There is a drug kingpin in room 434. All of this belongs to him," he said, passing his hand over the goods. "I have already called the police. Please make sure they get this."

That said, he turned and strode out of the hotel, loosening his tie and unbuttoning his collar as he walked. On his way to his car, he looked up at the fourth-floor balcony where the Arab was still sealed to the wall. He put two fingers to his mouth, blasted a shrill whistle, and waved. The balcony captive looked at Anthony and then peeked around the corner at the grenade.

Anthony got into his car and started the engine. "Without mercy there is no love," he said to himself, quoting Diego. Then he added: "But without remorse, mercy is best left to heaven."

He could hear approaching sirens as he pulled out of the driveway and headed back to Espejo. As soon as he left the Córdoba city limits, he pulled the car off to the side of the road and changed clothes, feeling out of sorts in the new business suit. At home again in his field clothes, he settled in behind the wheel and pictured Lupita's smile.

After ten minutes on the balcony, the Arab decided the grenade was a dud. He stepped into the room. His plan was to fling the grenade over the balcony railing, but when he lifted the bomb it felt strange—too light to be a real grenade.

He looked confoundedly at the object and, tentatively, pressed a lever at the crown. A one-inch flame sprang to life. It was a cigarette lighter, and the Arab flung the "grenade" through the open French doors, his enraged scream dissolving into a police siren.

At that instant, there was a crushing blow to the door.

Abdul-Khaliq Ben-Salem stood shivering in the middle of the room in his undershorts. A pause and then a very slow "Shit."

He had a big problem, and his mind scrambled for a solution. He saw the kilo of cocaine on the desk, pounced on the bag, and flung it like a discus toward the open balcony doors, but he missed his mark, and the bag smacked hard against the sharp edge of the door jam and exploded, filling the room in white dust.

A second blow breached the door, and a pair of armored policemen rushed into the room. And there, behind the SWAT team, in the mist of cocaine dust and door fragments stood Miguel—his feet set apart, his weapon drawn, and his eye trained down the barrel of his gun. When the policemen had pinned the Arab to the floor, Miguel lowered his pistol, stepped into the room, and cuffed the prisoner. It was done. The sacred, unspoken dream he had guarded for so long had finally come true: a genuine, unequivocal felony bust! The Espejo chief of police unleashed a smile that uncovered all his teeth.

IV

THE RETURN

It was winter in East Harlem, and Little Tony, just five years old, was once again locked out of the Pleasant Avenue apartment. It happened every time his mother left the flat in the late afternoon. She always locked the door behind her, and she had the only key. If Tony was outside at the moment, as he was this day, he was stranded. He would not gain entry into the apartment, until his mother returned sometime in the early morning.

Tony wedged his back into the corner of the stoop landing. He drew his knees to his chest for warmth, wrapping his arms around his spindly legs and tucking his fingertips inside the crevices of his elbows. It was 2:30 in the morning, and the snow was falling. He watched the crystalline flakes wafting from above the streetlights, a kaleidoscope of white against a black sky. The flakes perched on his tennis shoes for just an instant, before melting into the frayed canvas. How short-lived were these delicate flecks of ice.

Tony's teeth were chattering, so he locked his jaw, his mouth becoming a thin line of determination. He would survive and survive on his own. He could knock on any apartment door and immediately be escorted into a neighbor's warm apartment. He would be offered hot chocolate and a cookie—maybe an oatmeal and raisin cookie that was chewy on the top, but crispy on the bottom. Yes, he could be eating cookies right now, but he would not allow himself that luxury; he would not even allow himself to think about it. As cold as he was, he could not bear to look into the eyes of a well-meaning benefactor: eyes of judgment or shock or, worst of all, pity. He would rather fall asleep in the drifting snow than endure that awful scrutiny.

And so he waited. At 4:45 in the morning, a yellow cab pulled alongside the curb in front of Tony's tenement. A brown-faced man with a white woven skullcap stepped out from behind the wheel and circled the rear of the car. He opened the curbside passenger door and reached into the darkened interior. He had Tony's mother by the wrist. It was not a polite touch; it was a white-knuckled grasp, as if, with utter repulsion, he were squeezing the life out of a snake.

Mrs. Rossi's head did not clear the door opening and made a clunking noise as bone collided with metal. She did not react to the blow. She swung her legs out of the cab and onto the street, but one ankle lay precariously on its side. When she emerged from the car, the ankle gave out. She collapsed like a house of cards, landing face down in the snow.

The cab driver threw his hands over his shoulders in a gesture of detachment and moral innocence. He shut the door with a flick of his wrist and turned his back on the woman crumpled in the snow. When he had rounded the cab again and opened the door, he placed one hand on the edge of the door and the other on the roof. From that vantage point, he took one last look at Tony's mother and said, "*Masha'allah*"—God has willed it. When he drove away, the wheels spun and slid left and right, before grabbing traction in the middle of the street.

At five foot even and ninety pounds, Mrs. Rossi looked less like a human being and more like a dead dog left to rot on the street. Tony rushed to his mother's side and pulled on the shoulders of her cotton coat. His mother's head fell forward.

Tony tugged harder on the thin coat. "Momma, Momma, get up," he cried. "Please, Momma, get up. You gotta get up now."

Somehow Mrs. Rossi managed to open her eyes ever so slightly. "Hafta get up," she said, half comatose.

"I hold you," Tony said, now wrapping his arms around his mother's waist. The woman lifted herself to her knees and then, pressing down on Tony's shoulder, got both feet under her. She was more stooped than standing, but with her arm around Tony's neck, she was able to shuffle her feet forward. Like a little soldier, Tony tried to stand tall and straight. In what seemed an eternity, mother and child inched their way up the stairs to the tenement's front door. The woman leaned against the door as Tony held his breath and rummaged through her coat pockets. He expelled a blast of air, when he found the key. The boy unlocked the door, and when he turned the knob, the door flew open and the two of them fell across the threshold in a heap.

"No, Momma," Tony said. "We no be home. You gotta get up, Momma."

The woman did not move. "Sleep," she said. *"Lo vado a dormire,* I go to sleep now."

"No, Momma. You no can sleep, Momma. You no can sleep."

Tony straddled his mother, again cupping his hands under her waist. He squatted over her and then lifted with his legs, his head tipped back, heaving with all the strength of his little body.

The woman responded. Again, she dragged herself to her feet, and finally—step by step, flight by flight—the two tugged and towed themselves to the third-floor apartment. When Tony had opened the door, the two of them lurched into the room. The boy directed his mother to the single rumpled bed, where she immediately collapsed like a corpse.

Tony was dead tired himself. He rolled his mother to one side to dislodge the only blanket they owned. They would need it; the apartment was unheated, and the frost had crystallized on the window that overlooked the alley below.

The boy pulled off his mother's shoes. Then he sat down on the edge of the bed and with a grunt tugged off his sneakers. He lay down beside his mother and then snapped the blanket so that it fell equally across their bodies. Then he pressed his rump into the curve of his mother's midsection and pulled her arm across his body. Finally, he placed the palm of her hand over his heart, covering her slender fingers with his own little hands. His mother did not move, did not respond to the warmth of his body, and the boy immediately fell asleep.

Tony was awakened, not by light, for the sun had not yet risen, but by moisture and the smell of urine. He felt his coveralls between his legs; he was dry. He then felt the mattress under his mother's thigh; it was soaked through.

Half asleep, the boy walked across the cold floor to the bathroom and lifted the soiled and threadbare bath towel from the hook behind the door. He returned to the bed. He rolled his mother to one side and wedged the towel under her hips.

Mrs. Rossi was still drunk, still unconscious or at least almost unconscious. She moaned, not in her own voice, but in a voice that was husky and yearning. "I know whacha you like-a," she said in the fog of her own nightmares. "Come to you liddle bitch."

"No, Momma. It's me, Tony," he said, still pressing the towel into the wet mattress under his mother's hips. "You go back to sleep, Momma."

But Mrs. Rossi did not go back to sleep—not really. She took Tony's head in both hands and, with legs akimbo, pressed his face down, under her dress, and into her crotch. She was not wearing underwear, and the smell of urine and semen made Tony gag. He was suffocating. At that moment, he could feel his spirit leaving his body—his nascent soul drained and then refilled with depravity and torment. He struggled to escape her hold, but the more he wrestled to release himself from her hold, the more she pulled the boy into her genitals, writhing in his face.

Then, with all his power, Tony lowered his chin and wrenched his head out from under the grasp of his mother's steel grip. He was screaming, "Noooo!" He stood now at the side of the bed, his body shaking, his head jerking again and again. As he wiped his mouth with the back of his hand, he stared down at the woman in the bed. He did not know her; she was a stranger to him: a dark and hollow intruder. And then the boy was sick; his stomach convulsed and he threw up, the discharge spewing in the bed where the stranger lay.

His mother did not respond. Again, she intoned that strange, seductive moan and curled into a fetal position, as if waiting to be reborn, to start anew, to take her chances one more time in the iniquitous family of humanity.

Still standing there by the bed—shivering, shuddering—Tony replayed the horror of the night in his mind, and his eyes turned to stone. Then, as if in a declaration of a new way of being, he opened his mouth and howled again, "Noooo!"

When Antonio awakened, he was in a cold sweat. The word "no" was still reverberating in his head. Of all the nightmares that he had lived and relived in the last year, this dream was the most vivid, the most real, and the most telling.

And it was remembered—every second of it and every decision that grew out of it. It would be the last night that he shared a bed with his mother; for the next two years, before entering the Brooklyn orphanage, he would sleep in a bundle of clothes and newspapers on the hardwood floor.

It was also the last time he would genuinely declare his love to his mother or anyone else in the world, with, of course, two unequivocal exceptions: Diego and Lupita. Now he knew, more than ever before, he had to face every last ghost of his life. He had to close the door to his past, before he could open the door to his future. It was not what he wanted—it would have been so much easier to stay in Espejo and work the olive orchards with Diego—but he knew he could not. In time, the ghosts would destroy him and his life with Lupita, and he would not allow that to happen.

Antonio looked at the alarm clock on the table beside the bed; it was 5:30 in the morning. His bag was packed and placed at the front door. It was time to say goodbye, and it would not be easy. He did not know when, if at all, he would return, and the thought of never seeing Diego and Lupita again brought tears to his eyes.

Antonio walked out into the living room and found Diego already waiting for him. The gentle Spaniard had left his bed even before Antonio that morning. He would not be denied a final embrace.

"*Buenos días,* Diego."

"*Buenos días,* Antonio."

Antonio looked at Diego. He could not put his finger on it, but there was something different and unsettling about him. He puzzled about it an instant and then shook off the feeling. "All night I tried to think how to thank you," Antonio said. "I do not have the words. Every phrase seems inadequate. All I know for sure is that I love you with . . ." Antonio began to break down.

"Yes, yes, I know, my son. I feel the same way. Do not worry. I will be with you, wherever you are. If you listen hard enough, I will speak to you."

Diego took Antonio in his arms.

Lupita stood by quietly, watching the men she loved say goodbye, finally turning away to tame her emotions.

When the men broke their embrace, Diego said, "I have a small gift for you, Antonio."

Diego took a red bandanna out of his pocket. It was folded and knotted. "The first day I met you, I wrapped this bandanna around your neck. I did not know what I was doing then, but I thought it could serve as a kind of compress.

"It is no ordinary scarf. It once belonged to my friend, Juanito. He wore it as a protest against tyranny, and I after him."

Suddenly, Antonio understood what had unsettled him earlier: Diego's neck was bare of the ever-present red cloth.

"It represents all that is noble in humankind. Now it is yours. I have washed the bandanna, but the stains will not come out. It clings to your blood and the blood of Spain. We are part of the same fabric, you and I. Your blood is intermingled with my blood, and there is nothing that time or any person can do to change that."

Antonio was silently weeping now without shame. He looked intensely into Diego's eyes, which were also filled with tears. He did not see the crow's feet at the corner of his eyes or his unwieldy white brows; he saw only the eyes of the father he had always longed for. He wrapped his arms around the old man. He did not pat him on the back; he held him firmly and quietly. "Thank you, Diego. Thank you, thank you."

"It is I who thank you, my son."

The two separated, and Antonio stood for a moment, his head down. He fingered the bandanna and suddenly realized that there was something flat and round inside. "There is something here," Antonio said.

"Yes, it is for you," Diego said, "but I want you to open it when you are in the plane. Would you do that for me?"

"Of course, I will." Antonio gently folded the bandanna and slipped it into his pant pocket.

"There is one other thing, Antonio."

"Yes, Diego."

"Our door is never locked, and you need never knock. This is your home. Would you remember that?"

"Yes, Diego. I will remember."

Antonio hugged his friend one last time.

"We need to be going," Lupita said softly.

Antonio walked to the door, picked up his bag, and then turned to say goodbye. Diego was no longer there. Antonio could see the back of his friend through the doors of the terrace, leaning over the railing and surveying the orchards that he loved so much. He was softly humming a haunting tune.

The melody was vaguely familiar to Antonio. He turned to Lupita. "What is that song?"

Lupita listened for a moment and smiled. "It is '*La Violetera*.' He sings it when he is very happy or very sad."

Antonio had to look away. He held the door open for Lupita, who, as she passed through, reached up to caress Antonio's face and with her thumb wiped a tear from his cheek. Antonio stepped through the threshold and pulled the door closed, hearing the latch click into place.

Antonio and Lupita were unusually quiet during the first moments of the two-hour drive to the Granada airport. Lupita was driving, her eyes fixed on the road.

Antonio would occasionally glance at Lupita's profile, and each time he did, he was swept away by her beauty.

Finally, Lupita said, "I want to know something."

"Yes. Anything."

"Are you free of Savannah?"

"Oh, yes, Lupita. Córdoba was cleansing for me. I had to go. I had to understand. How can I say this? I went to Córdoba because I was ashamed of myself—ashamed of the lies. Savannah helped me face up to my own guilt. For that I am deeply grateful. I know now who I want to be. But that is all, Lupita. There is no love there—only self-reproach, and it will take some time to forgive myself."

Lupita nodded. "There is something I must tell you."

Antonio turned his body around to look fully at Lupita. "Yes?"

"Miguel has asked me to marry him," she said without a smile.

Antonio felt like the wind was knocked out of him. "What did you say?"

"He was very sweet; he actually got down on his knees. I said I was flattered and that I would have to think about it."

"You are not serious." It was more an accusation than a question.

"Stop right there, Antonio. Who do you think you are? You are not the only *caballero* on the face of the earth, you know."

"Yes, of course, I know that. But Miguel? I have come to like him, but, still . . . would you truly consider marrying Miguel?"

Lupita took the wheel by both hands and arched her back. "I do not know . . . no . . . maybe . . . I do not know. That is not the point."

"What is the point?"

"The point is that I am in my prime. There are men who desire me. They have always desired me. I have known that ever since I was sixteen years old, and I will not wait forever."

"I know, Lupita. Believe me, I know. I do not take you for granted—not for an instant. You are the most incredible woman I have ever known. God knows I wish I could take you in my arms right now and never let you go. But I cannot do that. I just cannot. I have to go back to Paris."

Lupita patted Antonio's knee. Antonio took her hand and kissed it three times, holding the third kiss for a long moment.

When they reached the airport, Lupita insisted on saying goodbye at the car. They embraced and Antonio felt that his heart would break.

"Do not come back unless you plan to stay for good," Lupita said in his ear.

"Lupita."

"Promise me."

"I promise you."

Before going through security, Anthony walked into the men's room and changed into his suit. He was going into battle now, and the Bianchi-tailored suit was his armor. He repacked his bag. The last items to go in were his Spanish work clothes, a pair of canvass pants and a blue denim shirt; he carefully smoothed and folded the garments, setting them in the suitcase with a quiet affection.

The 9:30 a.m. plane took off on time. Anthony would make connections in Barcelona and land at the Charles De Gaulle Airport at 6:15 p.m. Anthony had lots of time to think about his life in Spain, and the life he was returning to in Paris.

When the plane left the ground at Granada, Anthony took the red bandanna from his pocket. He unknotted the kerchief and laid it out on the fold-down tray. There, in the center of the cloth, was a cross section of an olive branch the diameter of a silver dollar and twice as thick. It had been hand rubbed to a smooth, glossy finish.

Anthony picked up the olive medallion and examined it closer. It felt good to the touch: silky and yet firm, like a flat stone polished by sea and sand. There was a delicate carving of a lily with a straight stem and petals that curled like a seashell around its stamen. It must have taken Diego hours to get it just right.

Anthony turned the olive piece over and read four words burned in a graceful script along the rounded perimeter of the medallion:

Silence, love, charity, peace.

Anthony smiled and slowly turned the medallion in his hand. At that moment, a flight attendant paused at Anthony's aisle seat. "That's lovely," she said. "Was it a gift?"

"Yes," Anthony said, handing the piece to the attendant.

She read the inscription. "From someone who loves you very much, I imagine," she said, returning the amulet.

"Oh, yes."

"And now it is your good luck charm."

"That's right—and much more."

The attendant patted Anthony on the shoulder and smiled sweetly. "Have a pleasant flight."

"Thank you very much."

Nine hours later, Anthony's plane touched down in Paris. He hired a taxi to drive him to his home in the seventh *arronndissement*, a stylish, nineteenth-century apartment overlooking *La Seine*—a half-hour ride with good traffic.

"Soyez le bienvenu à Paris," the driver said, unusually friendly for a Parisian chauffeur.

"*Merci.*"

"Are you coming home or just visiting?"

Anthony was stumped. "I don't know," he finally uttered.

The driver glanced at his passenger in the rearview mirror. "That is a strange response."

"I am in a kind of strange period in my life."

"Well, I hope it will go well for you."

"Thank you. How are things going for you?"

The driver was taken back by the question. Normally, his customers had little interest in his state of mind. "I am doing all right. It can be difficult working nights, but I think we will survive."

"You have a family then."

"Yes, a wife and two kids." The driver flipped down his sun visor, slipped out three photos, and passed them back to Anthony.

"It is a beautiful family," Anthony said truthfully.

He returned the photos.

"*Ouais,* I am proud of my family. They make everything worthwhile."

"I understand completely," Anthony said, thinking of Lupita and Diego.

"Do you?"

"Yes, I think I do."

"Then you are a lucky man, *monsieur*."

Anthony stepped up to the arched doorway of the apartment house. He twisted the knob that was centered in the middle of the door, but it was locked, of course. He instinctively patted his pocket and then laughed at himself; the key was long lost. Just then, a French woman bundled in a sable coat opened the door. They had seen each other many times before over the years, but had never spoken. Anthony was sure the woman had no idea that he had been gone for four months. They nodded and smiled politely, and Anthony slipped through the opening. The vestibule light switched off just as he reached the elevator. He stepped in and pushed the button for the fifth-floor. A moment later he was facing his front door. He took in a deep breath and rang the doorbell.

Inside, Hennessy was just stepping out of the sauna—a luxury seldom found in a Parisian apartment. Hennessy loved that sauna; he always felt that twenty minutes in the steamer opened his pores and made him a new man.

Meanwhile, Penelope was sitting at her dressing table, applying a creamy green mask to her face and neck.

"Can you get that?" Hennessy shouted, sure that it must be someone from work dropping off a contract or a set of blueprints for his approval.

"I'm cleansing and exfoliating," Penelope shouted back.

Hennessy cursed under his breath. He wrapped a bathrobe around himself, stepped into a pair of slippers, and jammed his glasses on his face, which, with the steam from the sauna, did not improve his vision. In fact, all he could make out were hazy shapes.

Anthony rang a second time.

"Okay, okay, I hear you, for Pete's sake." Hennessy quickened his pace. When he opened the door, the cold front from the outside collided with the hot front behind his glasses, creating an impenetrable fog bank. In short, Hennessy was blind.

Nor did it help that the hall light had, predictably, snapped off. Anthony spoke from the shadows: "Good evening, Hennie."

Although Hennessy was blind, he was not deaf, and he knew that voice. He feverishly swiped his fingers across the lens of his glasses, which only smeared the condensation.

"May I come in?" Anthony asked.

Hennessy tipped his head down and looked over the top of his spectacles. "Holy cripes," he said, stumbling back, his arms backstroking, which threw open his bathrobe, revealing his nakedness.

Hennessy fumbled for his glasses planted cockeyed on his face and perched them on top of his head. "Is that you, Anthony?"

"It's me."

Hennessy just stared into Anthony's face. He didn't know how to react. How do you behave when you're caught red-handed sleeping with your best friend's wife? His head was bobbing like it would spin off his shoulders at any moment.

"Aren't you going to give me a hug?" Anthony asked.

"Well . . . you're damn right I am," Hennessy roared, throwing his arms wide open, which again unveiled his bare body.

"I don't know," Anthony quipped, "I don't think we've been dating long enough."

"Huh?"

"Oh, what the hell."

Anthony threw his arms around his schoolboy friend.

"What is going on out here?" Penelope said, appearing barefooted in the living room. She was wearing a satin lounging robe and an avocado-green face that was beginning to dry and crack at the seams. "Oh, my God," she said, recognizing Anthony.

"Hello, Penelope."

Her feet were planted. She spoke like she was under hypnosis. "You're back. I can't believe it."

Anthony shrugged. "Yep. I'm back."

Penelope snapped out of her trance, stomped up to Anthony, and smacked him across the face. "Where have you been hiding out? We thought you were dead. Why didn't you call? What happened to you? Were you in an accident? Were you trying to find yourself? What?"

Anthony rubbed his face. "Let's see. That would be yes, yes, no, yes, no, no, yes."

"Don't you dare be smart with me," she said, lightly punching Anthony in the chest. "Come here."

Penelope put her arms out for an embrace.

Anthony stiff-armed her and screwed up his face. "I don't know."

"What?"

Anthony pointed at the framed mirror hanging above a Japanese accent table.

"What?" Penelope said again, this time with heavy irritation. She turned and looked at herself, screamed, and bolted for the bedroom.

Meanwhile, Hennessy was still standing dumbfounded in the center of the living room. "I still can't believe it is you. And I greet you at the door in my bathrobe."

"It's a very nice bathrobe. I've always liked it."

"Oh . . . yeah . . . that's right. I forgot." Hennessy cinched the robe tighter around his waist. He scratched one side of his face and then the other. "Listen, Anthony, I think it would be best if I left. You and Penelope must have a ton of things to talk about." He looked at his watch, not for the time, but because he didn't know where else to look at the moment. "Wow, what am I thinking? I have a stack of work to do," he said, throwing his arms in the air and smacking himself on the side of the head. "I'll just . . ."

He started moving toward the master bedroom and then circled back to finish his sentence. "I'll just pick up a few things and be on my way. Give me two minutes—less than two minutes; give me sixty seconds."

"Relax, Hennessy. There's no reason to run off. You probably have more right to be here than I do."

"No. Absolutely not. I'm out of here."

Hennessy escaped into the bedroom. Anthony could hear a few clunks, which must have been Hennessy banging into a lamp or a night table.

Anthony surveyed the room, admiring the transformation. Everything was new: the couch, the love seat, the coffee table—everything. Penelope loved to redecorate. She could spend hours poring over furniture catalogs and consulting with designers.

Hennessy blasted out of the bedroom. He was a man of his word; he was out in under a minute. He was now wearing pants with suspenders hanging down from the waist, an unbuttoned dress shirt, unlaced shoes, and no socks. He had an armload of rolled blueprints, a suit jacket, a topcoat, a pair of socks, a shaving kit, Anthony's bathrobe, and, for a reason unknown even to Hennessy, a black umbrella. The entire bundle was precariously held in place under the crook of his chin.

"So, I'll be going now. Great to see you, Anthony. We'll have to talk. Lots to talk about. Here's your bathrobe." Hennessy tried to strip the bathrobe from the twisted pile in his arms, and the blueprints tumbled to the floor. "Damn." He bent over to retrieve the blueprints and managed to get them stacked in his arms, but his foot was on the tail of his topcoat, and when he stood up the coat pulled out, taking with it the lion share of the laundry.

Hennessy stared down at the limp pile of clothing like it was a coffin being lowered into a grave. He relaxed his arms and let the remaining jumble flop to the floor. With arms hanging loosely at his sides, he stood numbly for a moment as if offering a prayer of bereavement. Then, on its own volition, the umbrella exploded open. Hennessy, still mourning the "deceased," heaved a long, slow sigh. "I'll just pick this stuff up tomorrow sometime," he said, giving the mound a timid sidekick. "Yeah, that's what I'll do. Is that okay? I hope that's okay."

"It's okay, Hennie."

"Good. Then that's what I'll do."

Hennessy turned for the door and then suddenly spun back around. "It was good to see you, Anthony," he said pumping his partner's hand, "real good to see you." He paused and placed his hands on his hips and, not knowing what to add, repeated, "Real good to see you." He looked at the pile again and shook his head. "Oh, you know, I need this," he said, picking up a single blueprint at random. Got to have this one; big job, this one is."

"Well, bye for now," Hennessy said, making for the door.

"Goodbye, Hennie."

Hennessy whisked out the door.

There was a moment of silence in the house. Then Anthony could hear his vice president unleashing a string of curses. The doorbell rang, and Anthony opened the door.

Hennessy was standing with his arms propped against the door jam like he was being frisked. "I forgot my glasses. I can't see a thing without my glasses."

Anthony pointed at Hennessy's spectacles, still perched on his head.

"Huh? Oh, yeah," Hennessy said, groping for the eyewear. He snatched the glasses and stuck them on his face. "Got 'em." He shook Anthony's hand again. "Well, see you soon."

"See you soon, Tiger."

"Right," Hennessy said, snapping an about-face. With his chin in advance, he strode down the hallway, as if he were marching off to war.

Again, Anthony closed the door and turned into the room. Then he noticed Hennessy's car keys on the small table at the door. He picked up the keys just as the doorbell rang again. He opened the door, dangling the keys by the leather BMW key ring as if he were holding a mouse by the tail.

Hennessy had his mouth open and a finger raised to the sky for exclamation. Anthony gave the keys a jingle.

Hennessy said nothing, but the muscle under his right eye twitched. He delicately took the "mouse" by the tail.

"Thank you."

"You're welcome."

Anthony closed the door and collapsed into one of Penelope's new armchairs. He had to smile at poor Hennessy; he never was very good under pressure. But, for the first time in his life, Anthony realized that it was that very quality—that bungling schoolboy enthusiasm—that Anthony cherished in his friend.

"Who was that at the door?" Penelope asked, gliding into the room like a runway model. She was looking very proper and Katherine Hepburnesque in a pair of wool trousers and a long-sleeve, high-neck blouse.

"Oh, that was Hennie leaving."

"Hennessy left?"

"Yeah, he said that he had a lot of work to do."

Penelope sat down in the loveseat across the room, keeping plenty of distance between the two of them. "It's more likely that he was embarrassed."

"I suppose there was that too."

A pause.

"You're looking good, Penelope. Beautiful as ever."

"Thank you," she said, not sure how to take the compliment. In fact, she was not sure how to take the whole situation. For months, all she could think about was the divorce, but now that Anthony was sitting there in the same room, she felt confused and unsettled.

"Well, where do we start?" Penelope asked.

"Penelope, if you don't mind, I don't think I have the strength to start anything tonight. I know it's still early, but could we hold off until tomorrow? I'm hanging on here by a thread."

Penelope's familiar sarcasm crept back into her voice. "Sure, why not? I haven't heard a word from you in four months. What's another night?"

"I'm sorry, Penelope. Really, I do want to talk to you." He furrowed his brow. "What day is today? I've lost all track of time."

"It's Friday."

"Good. What have you got planned for tomorrow?"

"Nothing much. I was going to do a little shopping for the apartment."

"It looks terrific, by the way."

"Thank you." Penelope looked sideways at Anthony. He had never praised her about anything, and this was the second compliment within two minutes. She wondered what he was plotting.

"I'll tell you what. Remember how we used to love to visit Île de Ré?" Anthony was referring to the picturesque, low-lying island in the Atlantic, just off the coast from La Rochelle.

"That was a very long time ago."

"Come on. It'll be fun. If we leave at eight o'clock, we can be there by noon easy. What do you say? We'll shop to your heart's content in Saint-Martin-de-Ré. We'll make a day of it and return Sunday morning."

"It's the off season," she said, continuing to protest.

Anthony smiled. "It doesn't matter."

Penelope looked at Anthony as if trying to place the name of someone who was vaguely familiar. "OK. You've talked me into it."

"Good," Anthony said, boosting himself out of the armchair. "I like that easy chair."

Penelope counted the third compliment.

"I'm going to crash," Anthony said. "I think I'll take the bed in the guest bedroom, if that's all right with you."

"That'll be fine."

"Goodnight then," Anthony said, giving Penelope a peck on the cheek.

"Goodnight, Anthony."

Penelope sat alone and thought a long time about Anthony and Hennessy and her life in general. Then she went to the bedroom and set the alarm for 7:00 a.m.—a God-awful hour, she thought. She propped herself up in bed, read for a couple of hours—at least pretended to read—and then drifted off into a restless sleep.

Anthony and Penelope left the house on time, beginning their excursion to Île de Ré. They drove southwest, past the gothic twin spires of the cathedral of Chartres, through the Loire Valley from Orléans to Tours, and from there on to the Atlantic. It was a four-hour drive, and Anthony took every moment of it to unravel the mystery of his four-month absence, glossing over the details of his flirtation with Savannah and romance with Lupita. Penelope listened intently, only asking a question now and then for clarity. By the time they crossed the graceful three-kilometer bridge that connected the port of La Rochelle to the island, Anthony was winding up the story of his Iberian odyssey.

After crossing the bridge, they drove directly to the renaissance fishing harbor at Saint-Martin-de-Ré. The sky was blue and the air crisp. Despite the cool temperature, they both elected to eat outside. They found a table at a harbor-view café with blue shutters and a white canopy.

When they had placed their order for lunch, Anthony began to talk about his affection for Diego. He took the olive medallion out of his pocket and handed it to Penelope.

She read the inscription out loud. "Silence, love, charity, peace." Penelope puzzled over the words. "What does it mean?"

"It means a lot of things, but mostly it is a reminder for me to do the right thing—to listen to my conscience."

"And is that what you are doing today?"

"I hope so. I'm trying." Anthony shifted his body toward Penelope, hooking his arm over the back of his chair. "Look, I know our marriage has been a disaster for a very long time."

"No thanks to you, I might add."

"You're right. I was unfair to you. No, that word is not strong enough; I was 'cruel.' And I certainly wasn't faithful."

"I suspected that for years."

"I know, and at the time I was totally indifferent. I did exactly what I wanted and could have cared less about your feelings."

"I didn't do much better," she admitted.

"We both messed up."

"So where does that leave us?" Penelope asked.

"I'm not sure. I know that two key events have happened in the last four months. First, I know that you have filed for a divorce."

Penelope's neck stiffened. "How do you know that?"

"Lucy told me."

"When did she tell you?"

"A couple of weeks ago."

Penelope glared at Anthony.

"I know. Why should I talk to her and not to you?"

"Exactly," Penelope huffed.

"I called Lucy, because I knew I could trust her. I wasn't sure I could trust you—not after living through our cold war. Lucy helped me get a new passport and updated me on news from the home front. I wish I could have trusted you, but I didn't."

Penelope nodded, knowing that he was right. "You said two events have happened in the last four months. What was the second thing?"

Anthony looked past Penelope at a gleaming luxury sailboat easing into the harbor. At the wheel was a man with a white captain's cap and a pipe clenched between his teeth, the bowl hanging upside-down. At his side was a blond beauty—unnaturally tanned for the month of January. She was not wearing a rain slicker or a squall jacket, but a full-length, artic-white fur coat, clutching its uplifted collar at her neck.

"Penelope, take a look at the skipper on that sailboat coming in just now."

"The one with the trophy wife?"

"Yeah."

"What about him?"

"That was me four months ago: A man with the world by the nape of the neck."

Penelope looked again at the boat. "And I suppose I'm the bimbo."

"No. Please, Penelope. I'm not talking about you. I'm talking about me—about my spirit: the greed, the ego, the self-indulgence. All that has changed now; I want a new life for myself."

"What kind of life?"

"A simple life. I don't want to prove that I'm the toughest, meanest son-of-a-bitch on the block anymore. I hate that."

Penelope searched Anthony's face. "What are you talking about? What does that mean?"

"It means I don't have to make a million dollars a year for one thing. I don't even have to make a hundred thousand. In fact, I'd be happy just getting by on practically nothing, if I loved my work and my family."

Penelope blew a toneless whistle and spoke very slowly, drawing out the words. "Oh, I don't know about that."

"I know, Penelope. We get used to the easy life. We think we can't get by without this year's Mercedes or the chateau on the lake or the apartment on the Côte d'Azur." Anthony took Penelope's hand. His words quivered with fervor: "But you can. That's what I've discovered. You can say goodbye to the excess and be incredibly happy."

Penelope withdrew her hand. She spoke slowly at first, but then her pace gradually quickened, and by the end of her speech, she was preaching to him. "But I like the excess. I like my life the way it is: my $100 body massages, my vacations in Venice, my diamonds and furs and outrageously expensive shoes. I don't want to give that up, Anthony, because you suddenly got religion."

Anthony searched for the right words to say and could find none. The silence was interrupted by the waiter, who stepped to their table and asked if he could serve more wine.

"Non, merci." Anthony said. He paid the bill and looked at his watch. It was two o'clock; the stores would be reopening soon. "Why don't we visit some of your favorite shops?"

Penelope beamed. "You know I want to."

"Oh, yes," Anthony sang out with a smile.

They strolled through an archway and onto a cobblestone side street with a treasure house of galleries, clothing boutiques, and high-end antique shops. Penelope was in her element: trying on hats, selecting a few leather-bound books for the library, poring over a collection of original gold jewelry. But she spent the most time in an import shop that featured racks of Oriental and European tapestries. She was determined to find just the right piece to hang over the fireplace in the apartment den. She sought out the salesclerk, who was refolding a stack of fisherman-knit sweaters: a twenty-something woman with a floral scarf and a silk dress over a faded pair of jeans.

"Could you help us please?"

The clerk offered a patronizing smile, clearly preferring to be left alone.

If Penelope saw that the clerk was put out, she ignored it. She made the salesclerk show her everything, which turned the young woman's patronizing smile into a feebly disguised sneer.

"I don't know," she would say, pondering over an English foxhunt tapestry or a French hanging of a medieval fortress with approaching riders. She would step back and hold her chin and ask Anthony what he thought about the choices.

Anthony gave his best perspective, commenting on how the color of one might better match the leather chairs or how the design of another was in keeping with the theme of the room.

In the end, Penelope was unconvinced and thanked the salesclerk for her time.

"Je vous remercie, madame," the clerk said, in a tone that sounded nearly civil.

Penelope left the shop without a purchase, but that didn't seem to matter. It was the thrill of the hunt that excited her.

Before they knew it, the shops were closing and the day was gone. They found their car, placed their packages in the trunk, and took one last tour around the harbor at that magical time of the evening when the sun was setting and laid a veil of muted gold over the whitewashed cafés and storefronts.

The air was noticeably cooler now, and they stepped into a restaurant to warm up.

When they settled into their chairs, Penelope looked long and quizzically at Anthony. "You were wonderful today," she finally said.

Anthony smiled. "I never realized how passionate you are about shopping. My goodness, you're a world-class athlete."

Penelope laughed. "It's all in the conditioning."

"So what did you think of the day?" Anthony asked.

"I loved it. And I adored you. I've never seen you so patient, so much in the moment. It made me wonder if I had made a mistake in filing for the divorce."

"One day does not make a marriage."

"No, that's true. But you were wonderful. What has changed?"

Anthony squared up on Penelope. "I haven't told you about the second key event."

"What are you talking about?"

"Remember, I said that there were two key events during the last four months."

"That's right; I forgot. What is it?"

Anthony paused and Penelope did not break the silence.

"I have fallen in love."

"The Spanish girl?"

"Yes. Lupita."

"I see. Are you happy?"

"It's incredible. There is a spiritual connection that I cannot explain. I feel like we were perfectly designed for each other."

"I bet she has nice tits too." It was a cheap shot, and Penelope knew it. Quickly, before Anthony could respond, she said, "I'm sorry. I didn't mean that. I guess I'm a little jealous. No, I'm a lot jealous. That's what I want; it's what I have always wanted."

"I'm sorry, Penelope."

"Then why today? Why did we do this?"

"I wasn't sure. I wanted to find out about us."

"And are you sure now?"

"I think I am."

"You *think* you are."

"Yes."

Penelope took his hand. "And what if I decided to fight for you?"

Anthony half smiled. "I can't control what decisions you make for yourself."

Penelope fingered her wedding ring. "I wonder if you can do me a favor?"

"I can try."

"Unless contested, the court will finalize the divorce next Thursday, January twenty-fourth. That is just five days away."

"Okay. What's the favor?"

"Would you wait until that day to make your decision?"

Anthony thought for a moment. "Yes, I can do that. But I have a favor to ask of you. Actually, I'd like us to be agreed about something. If either one of us decides to go ahead with the divorce, the other must honor that decision. Whatever the outcome, I would like us to be civil—more than that, I would like us to be friends. Are we agreed?"

"I agree."

"No hedging?"

Penelope smiled. "No hedging, Anthony. You have my word."

After dinner, the two walked to the Hotel de Toiras, a small but lovely port hotel with fine furnishings and an attentive staff. They got separate rooms. When Anthony walked Penelope to her door, she lifted her eyes, looked at him dreamily, and stepped forward

Anthony took a step back. "No, Nel," he said. "It's been a wonderful day, but let's not confuse things."

Penelope's face darkened. The rebuff smarted, and Anthony knew it.

"All right," she said without embellishment. She turned and slipped into her room.

The next morning they drove back to Paris, often with long stretches of silence, both mulling over their past lives and their lives to come.

On Sunday, Anthony packed his bag and left his lavish apartment to Penelope. In the old days, he would have moved into a suite at the Hotel de Crillon, overlooking the Place de la Concorde. Now, his choice was much less pretentious: a small two-room apartment above a bakery near the office.

Anthony had good reason to leave: He wanted to be away from Penelope, to allow his mind freedom to reason. There was much to think about. He walked for hours, mostly along the Left Bank, trying to put all the pieces together.

On one of those walks, he stopped midway across his favorite bridge, the *Pont Neuf* that spanned the western tip of the *Île de la Cité*, the island that was the medieval center of Paris. He leaned over the west railing, staring into the Seine and the dark water that escaped under the arches of the bridge like time dissolving into eternity. The moment reminded him of Diego and how the two of them hunched over his balcony and talked about philosophy and the revelations of life. He took out the olive amulet from his pocket and felt its smooth surface. And in that instant, Diego appeared.

"*Buenos días*, my son," Diego said.

Antonio was not troubled that Diego was suddenly there at his side; he was simply delighted to be in his company—even the spirit of his company. "*Buenos días*, Diego," he said with a sad grin.

"You seem troubled, Antonio. Have you lost your way?"

"It is easier in Spain."

"Easy will not make a righteous man of you."

Antonio smiled. "If that is true, I should be a saint when I am through with this."

"You do not need to be a saint, my son—only a man of truth. Speak what is honorable, do what is right. Take care of those you have injured. All the rest will fall into place."

"And if I am not able?"

"You *are* able. You are my son."

"If that is true, then you are my father."

"Did you ever doubt it?" Diego asked with a smile. "*Hasta luego*, Antonio."

Antonio turned and reached out to Diego, his hand passing freely though space. "Must you go?"

"There are olive trees to tend to," he said with a smile and a wink, "but do not worry, my son: I am always with you."

On Monday morning, Anthony telephoned Lucy.

"Mr. Duncan told me you were back," she said.

"Then that means everyone knows."

"I'm afraid so."

"It doesn't matter any more."

"How can I help you, Mr. Rossi?"

"Were you able to postpone the board meeting?"

"I was."

"That's great. Here's what I'd like you to do. I know it's short notice, but I'd like you to set up a meeting with the board members and executive staff for five o'clock tomorrow evening."

"Done."

"Do you know if Harry Tubbs is in Paris?"

"I'm not sure, but I can find out."

"If he is, I would like him at the meeting as well."

"I can do that."

"Also, could you have the contract for the Águilas job on my desk by noon tomorrow?"

"Yes, sir."

"Good. Is there anything else that I should know about?"

"Yes, there is one thing. We have a problem."

"What's that?"

"You remember the seven-story parking-lot project."

"The one Jean-Pierre Badeau was heading up?"

"Yes."

"What about it?"

"This is not good news, Mr. Rossi. Last Wednesday, one of the columns on the ground floor buckled."

"My God. Was anyone hurt?"

"No. But it was close. There were three electricians working in the area, and they just barely escaped. Naturally, the job has been shut down. The whole thing is a mess."

"Okay. We'll figure it out."

Lucy took in a breath. "Mr. Rossi, there is something else."

"Yes. What is it?"

"It's Jean-Pierre."

The face of the nervous manager flashed before his eyes. "What about him, Lucy?"

"You know he's a very good friend of mine."

"I believe I knew that."

"He's not doing well."

"What do you mean?"

"He did not take the accident well. He blames himself. And he's behaving very strangely."

"In what way?" Anthony asked, genuinely concerned.

"When you talk to him, he acts like he doesn't hear you. It's as if he's in another world. It's very scary, Mr. Rossi; I'm very worried about him."

"Okay. Make sure he is at the Tuesday meeting. I want to talk to him."

"All right. I'll try, but I can't guarantee that he'll be there. He's been missing a lot of work, and he is not answering phone calls, not even mine."

"Do the best you can. That's all I can ask."

Anthony called Monique Ducros on her cellular phone. She was shocked to hear his voice, and when he asked if they could meet, she hesitated.

"I am not sure," she said. "*Á quoi bon?* What good would it do?"

"Maybe nothing. I just feel like I need to talk with you."

They agreed to meet for coffee at a favorite bistro on rue Saint Dominique, Le Café Thoumieux.

Anthony arrived first and found their usual table at the back of the cafe. When Monique walked in, he stood up and took her coat. She was dressed simply in jeans and a V-neck pullover. But despite her casual attire, she could not disguise her natural beauty. She was still ravishing, even without makeup.

"Thank you for coming, Monique. I wasn't sure that you would make it."

"I almost did not."

"What changed your mind?"

She pondered a moment. "*Je ne sais pas.* I do not know."

"That's okay," he said, letting it go.

"*J'ai changé d'avis*—I changed my mind. I do know why I came. It was pity."

Anthony held his breath, as if not breathing could stop her words from breaking his heart. "Yeah," he said softly, recognizing the truth.

"What are you wanting, Anthony?"

"I'm not going to ask you to forgive me, Monique. That's too much to ask. But I do want you to know that I am deeply, deeply sorry. What I did to you was unconscionable."

A waiter came to their table, and they ordered espressos.

After a long silence, Monique said quietly, "What you did was *méprisable*—how do you say?—despicable. I hated you for a long time. I cannot decide if I still hate you. I am trying to forget all that."

"I understand. How are you doing now?"

"*Ça va.* I am managing."

"Have you met someone?"

She smiled faintly. "*Oui.*"

"I hope he appreciates you. You have such a good heart; you deserve the best."

"He is a good man."

"Is he French?"

"Yes. He is not as rich as you, but he knows how to treat a woman."

"I'm very glad to hear that."

"And he is not married," she added.

Anthony nodded and, lightly placing his fingers on her forearm, asked, "Is there anything that I can do to help you? Anything at all."

She cringed away from him. "Nothing. There is nothing you can do."

There was a moment of silence, while Monique sat transfixed, hardly blinking.

Anthony could hear the big clock on the wall tick away a minute.

"I think I will be going now," Monique said.

Anthony started to stand.

"*Non. Ne bouge pas.* Do not get up," Monique said, throwing her coat over her arm. She stood and started to turn for the door and then faced Anthony. "I have decided that I do not hate you, Anthony. I feel sorry for you. You are *vide*—a hollow man. I am hoping you find your way."

Monique turned and was gone.

Anthony sat quietly. Then the waiter appeared and set two espressos on the table.

"Merci," Anthony said, without looking up.

"Will there be anything else?"

Anthony finally looked at the waiter. *"Non, merci—merci beaucoup."*

The man scribbled a number and left the bill at the table. *"De rien, monsieur."*

Anthony lingered a moment longer. He raised the cup of coffee to his mouth and paused, his mind lost in silence. Finally, he took a slow sip, but tasted nothing. He paid the bill and left.

ANTHONY WENT TO THE OFFICE on Tuesday, arriving at 2:00 p.m. For the first time in their long business association, he gave Lucy an exuberant hug, which rattled her, a deep blush sweeping across her face and down her neck.

"Thank you, Lucy. You're the best. I don't know what I would do without you."

Lucy nervously tugged at the hem of her grey pin-stripped suit jacket. "You're welcome, Mr. Rossi."

Anthony asked not to be disturbed until the board meeting. He wanted to study the Águilas contract. Then, at precisely five o'clock, with contract in hand, he walked to Lucy's desk.

"Well, what do you think, Lucy? Ready to face the lions?"

"Yes, sir," she said, collecting her pencil and steno pad.

The two walked to the conference room, where everyone had been waiting for at least ten minutes. When Anthony entered, the men stood and applauded.

Acknowledging the greeting, Anthony took his chair at the head of the table, placed the Águilas contract in front of him, and asked everyone to be seated. The board members, twelve in all, surrounded the conference table. The executive staff was seated along the side walls behind the board. Hennessy was in his traditional position at the end of the table opposite Anthony.

"I'm not sure if you are applauding my return or my near demise."

There was a ripple of nervous laughter.

"I realize that there's a lot a mystery surrounding my absence. Some thought I was dead. Some thought I was just having a good time on a beach somewhere in Southern Spain."

More polite laughter.

"It's a long story that we'll save for another time. The important thing is that I am back, and I want to take care of business."

That statement was answered with deafening silence.

Anthony stood up and stepped to one side of his chair. "We haven't spoken much about values in this company. And I think that has been a critical lacking. I don't think we know who we are." Anthony looked at Jack Benson, the chairman of the board. "Jack, do you know who we are?"

"We are a construction management company," Jack said without hesitation.

"And what is our purpose?"

"To make our shareholders obscenely wealthy."

One of the French board members chuckled and, seeing he was alone, quickly swallowed his laugh.

"That's where you're wrong, Jack. That's not our purpose; that's our bottom line. Our purpose is to serve humanity; and if we do that well, we will be amply compensated. For too long, we have been in the business of making a fast buck. That's fine; we all have families to feed and mortgages to pay. But it loses sight of our real mission."

"And that is?" asked Jack.

"Our real mission is to build bridges—to help people get from one place to another with ease. Our mission is to construct offices that are so safe and so pleasing that people will be eager to go to work on Monday morning. Our mission is to make a positive difference in the lives of the people we serve.

"Let me give you an example of what I mean. You all know Harry Tubbs. Harry, how are you doing?"

"Damn fine. Good to see ya, old man."

"Harry has been trying to tie up a contract for a prime piece of land in Águilas, Spain. This is the contract." Anthony picked up the document and tossed it onto the center of the table. "It's designed to swindle an old Spanish fisherman out of millions of dollars."

"Hold on there, buckaroo. You helped me write that contract."

"I know I did, Harry, but I was wrong. That contract is a disgrace. And as long as I am president of this company, we will never do business that way. That is my promise to the company."

There was a pause.

"Wait a minute," Jack said. "I'm not sure how I feel about all this. It sounds awfully soft to me. That's not the kind of language our stockholders like to hear. They want a leader with a killer instinct—someone like the old Anthony."

"The old Anthony is dead. He was buried in Spain. This is the new Anthony. Can you live with him?"

Jack was surveying the room. The board members were squirming in their seats. "Well, the Anthony that you buried in Spain knew how to make money. Now, the way you're talking, I'm not sure you could pay for my suit. I'm sorry, Anthony, but I don't think this company needs a frickin' missionary." He looked around the room. "Am I wrong here? Hennessy, what do you think?"

All heads turned toward the vice president who looked uncomfortable in the spotlight. "I think you're right, Jack. I think our company needs someone who can swim with the sharks. In fact, I'd say they want the biggest, baddest shark in the pond."

"Are you the man for that job, Hennie?" Anthony asked without any hint of sarcasm.

Hennessy was starting to sweat. He was way outside his element. "Yeah, I think I may be. I mean, yes, I am."

"I see. Well, before you take over the helm, you might want to check the weather. The horizon looks very threatening." Anthony looked around the room. "Lucy, were you able to reach Jean-Pierre Badeau?"

"No, sir. I could not locate him. He does not answer his home phone or his mobile."

Anthony's voice became even more deliberate. "Would you like to know why Jean-Pierre can't be found? He's in a world of hurt. He's one of our own, and we're not taking care of him. He has a job that is in deep trouble; we all know it, and we haven't done anything to help him.

"That's going to change right now. We will not leave Jean-Pierre in the cold. And we will not do shoddy work—not anymore. I don't care if we have to tear the whole thing down and start from scratch. This company will not put our people or our clients at risk. Not on my watch."

Jack took in the room again. There were a few nods. "Well, that's fine and dandy, Anthony, but that costs money, and that is something we have not been making a lot of recently. And, if you don't mind my saying, your . . . little diversion in Spain has not helped any."

"I want to say something about that."

"I'm not finished. We're taking the company over, Anthony. We are buying out your stock options—and, believe me, we've got the lawyers to do it. If we do decide to keep you on—and, understand, that is a whopping 'if'—you will be a puppet for the board of directors."

There was a firm knock on the door, and the secretary who was covering for Lucy rushed into the conference room. "I am sorry. *C'est une urgence absolue*—an emergency. *Monsieur* Rossi, you need to take the call on line one."

Anthony picked up the handset. "*Je suis Anthony Rossi. . . . Oui. . . . C'est exact. . . . Où ça. . . .? Je peux être là dans quinze minutes.*"

Anthony dropped the receiver. "I've got to go," he said, rushing to the door.

"Stop right there," Jack said. "We are not through here. You leave this room, and you will never run this company again. We will sue your butt for breach of contract. We'll have you tied up in court so long, you'll wish you never came back."

Anthony paused only briefly. "Do what you must, Jack. If I do not leave, I could lose a good man, and right now that is more important to me than losing a company."

With that, Anthony lurched out of the conference room and bolted for the elevators. He pounded on the down button. "Come on, come on, come on!"

Finally, the elevator doors opened and Anthony lunged in and pressed the button for basement parking. When the elevator doors eased open, he squeezed through the gap sideways and sprinted to his car. Seconds later, his Mercedes was screaming up the ramp toward the city street. He crashed the security barrier and squealed onto the Avenue du Maine, fishtailing as he made the corner.

At the first light, Anthony was behind traffic in all lanes. He laid on his horn and took the sidewalk—people scattering like cats. He crashed the red light and was clipped on the rear end by a delivery van. The collision spun his car ninety degrees to the right, but he jammed on the accelerator and was off again, careening across the *Pont Neuf* at breakneck speed. He took a hard right on the Right Bank and then a hard left on Rue Quincampoix, barreling past the *Gare de l'Est.*

The traffic came to an abrupt halt at a crosswalk, which was strange because Anthony had rarely seen a Parisian stop for a pedestrian. He glanced at the stalled car's license plate; it was English; that explained everything. He skimmed past the Brit and, tires squealing, swerved around the pedestrian. The walker—an old veteran wearing a black beret—responded with a profane three-tier gesture: slapping first the wrist of his closed fist, then the bicep, then the shoulder, his quivering arm now high overhead, banging the sky.

Anthony spotted the police cars first, their blue and yellow lights flashing at the side of the street. He raced forward, weaving in and out of traffic. When he reached the construction site, he slammed on his brakes with such force that his car nosedived and then spun out of control, crashing into the side of a compact patrol car.

A police officer was in the lightweight car, talking on the radio at the moment of impact. Although the policeman was uninjured, it threw him to the opposite side of the car and contracted every muscle in his body. He exploded from the vehicle, drew his weapon, lay over the hood, and targeted Anthony, who was scrambling out of his car.

"Halt!" the officer shouted.

Anthony stopped dead and threw his hands into the air. "I'm Anthony Rossi!"

"I do not care if you are François Mitterrand. Put both hands on the car and spread your legs."

"Look, officer . . ."

"*La ferme!* Do it."

Anthony leaned against the car spread eagle.

Then there was another commanding voice: "*Qui êtes-vous?* Who are you?" Anthony turned his head and saw a tall man in a suit and topcoat, carrying a bullhorn.

"I'm Rossi. Anthony Rossi."

"Stand up, Mr. Rossi. We have been waiting for you. I am Inspector Benoît Garrone," he said, flashing his badge.

"But he rammed my car," the police officer whined.

"It is all right, Dupuy. I will take it from here."

Looking forlorn, Dupuy holstered his gun and examined the raw-metal scrape that fell across the entire side of the patrol car. In revenge, he gave Anthony's car a swift kick, which reshuffled the bones in his foot, and he leaned two hands against the car to recover.

"Ça va?" another officer asked with a smile.

Dupuy straightened up and for no reason adjusted his tie. "He rammed my car," he mumbled.

Meanwhile, Anthony and Inspector Garrone rushed up the stairwell to the top floor of the seven-story parking lot.

"We will be as close as we can without being detected," Garrone said out of breath. "If I can, I will try to stay with you, but he is *catégorique*: He only wants to talk to you."

"What do I do?"

"Rely on your best instincts. That is all anyone can do."

In the next moment, the two men emerged from the stairwell onto the final open-air floor. Anthony felt the cold wind smack his face, and his body shivered.

Jean-Pierre Badeau was balanced on a corner of the three-foot high concrete barrier. One short step backward and he would fall to his death on a heap of steel beams. The wind was gusting and the thin man looked cold and fragile, despite the benefit of his down parka. "Only Rossi. I only want to talk to Rossi. You go away."

"We are here to help you," the inspector said softly.

"Only Rossi!" Badeau screamed, belting the words with such force that his body tilted backward, and he flapped his arms to regain his balance.

"*D'accord*, I am going," the inspector said, backing down the stairwell. *"Bonne chance,"* he whispered from below.

Anthony eased forward, one step at a time. He got within ten feet of Badeau.

"Stop! That is far enough, *Monsieur* Rossi."

"Okay, Jean-Pierre. I'll stay right here. Let's just talk."

"You want to talk now?" Badeau asked, his voice shaking from a mix of cold and raw emotion. "You do not talk, *Monsieur* Rossi. You rant, you moralize, you ridicule. You are very good at that, but you do not talk."

"I know, Jean-Pierre. . . ."

"I am talking now," he shouted. "It is not your turn to talk; you talk all the time. I am talking. You think you know everything. You think you are so *malin*, so smart: the all-knowing, all-powerful American, *Monsieur* Rossi. But, you know what, *vous ne comprenez rien du tout*. You do not understand anything." Badeau suddenly changed his voice to a half whisper. "In fact, I think you are the most stupid person I know." Badeau pivoted on the barrier and flung his arms out. "Anthony Rossi *est un parfait idiot*!" he screamed to the world.

Anthony rushed forward, and then Badeau flipped back around.

"Stop! Not another step, you *espèce de* . . ."

Anthony pulled up short, having gained five feet on Badeau.

"Okay. May I talk now, Jean-Pierre?"

"I do not know, *Monsieur* Rossi. What are you going to say? Are you going to tell me I am not *à la hauteur*? I am not good enough? Are you going to tell me I don't know how to do my job? Maybe you want to tell me to stop farting. *Eh, oui, c'est ça!* You want me to stop farting, *n'est pas*? Well, I am sorry if I have offended you, *Monsieur* Rossi, but that is what I do. I fart. I am a farter. Some people are born musicians. But not me; I am a born farter. And if that does not please you, *Monsieur* Rossi, you can . . . you can . . ." Badeau could not finish his sentence; even in his rage he could not curse at another human being.

"You're right, Jean-Pierre. I have been a bastard. I know my treatment of you has been a disappointment."

"A disappointment! A disappointment! No, a cola soft drink is a disappointment. An over-cooked steak is a disappointment. No wine with your bread and cheese is a disappointment. But what you do is something else, *Monsieur* Rossi. What you do is . . . *honteux* . . . disgraceful! A disappointment? No, you treat me like *la merde*."

Anthony made no effort to defend himself.

"Why do you do that?" Badeau asked. "Why do you ridicule people? Do you want them to be humiliated? Does that make you feel important?" Badeau was suddenly crying through his words. "Do you think that I am not trying? Do you think I want to be *incompétent*, *Monsieur* Rossi? Is that what you think?"

"No, of course not."

"*Bien sûr que non*. You know I cannot sleep at night, *Monsieur* Rossi? Did you know that? You know why? Because I am thinking about the job. I'm thinking about your *putain* job, and I cannot tolerate it anymore." Badeau bowed his head and wiped the tears from his closed eyes.

Anthony sprung forward, his arms outstretched. At the same instant, Badeau opened his eyes, saw Anthony rushing toward him, and took one step backward. Anthony plunged forward and wrapped his arms around Badeau, catching him just under the armpits. Badeau was dangling over the side, and Anthony's grip was slipping on the slick nylon of Badeau's parka. The crowd screamed from the street below.

"Hold on!" Anthony shouted.

His grasp around Badeau's chest gave way. For one second, there was a flurry of arms, and with a shout from his gut, Anthony snagged one sleeve and then the second. Almost immediately Badeau started to slip out of his parka. Anthony quickly adjusted his grip—grabbing Badeau's left wrist and, with that anchor held firm, the right wrist.

Anthony looked into Badeau's eyes, and he saw the face of terror. He saw a man who was driven to desperation, but in the end, a man who still clung to life.

"*Au secours!* I do not want to die," Badeau said, his legs flopping about trying in vain to find a foothold.

"You are not going to die," Anthony said almost matter-of-factly and with all his strength hoisted Badeau's upper body over the barrier.

The inspector was now at Anthony's side, and he reached over the barrier and clutched Badeau by the belt; together they pulled the thin man over the wall, where he collapsed on the floor.

Anthony threw his arms around the sobbing Badeau. "I've got you, Jean-Pierre. You're okay. From now on everything will be okay."

The medics were there. They put Jean-Pierre on a stretcher and tied him in. Then they headed down the stairs, Anthony holding Badeau's hand all the way down to the ground floor.

At the ambulance, Anthony saw Hennessy, Lucy, and Jack. They all looked shaken.

"I'm going with him," Anthony said to Hennessy. "Would you drive the Mercedes to the hospital? The keys are still in the car." He spotted the name of the hospital on the side panel of the ambulance. "It looks like we're going to the *Hôpital Saint-Louis.*"

There were tears in Hennessy's eyes. "Sure," he said, his throat tight. "I'll take care of it. Thank you, Anthony, thank you."

Anthony placed his hand over Hennessy's heart as a sign of gratitude and started to step into the ambulance.

"We cannot allow that, sir. *C'est interdit,*" the medic said, wagging his finger in Anthony's face.

Inspector Garrone showed the medic his badge. "Let him go. I will take responsibility."

"But it is *interdit*!" the medic protested again.

At that point, the inspector surprised Anthony. The American had lived among Parisians long enough to know many of their conventions. For example, given a choice, a Frenchman will predictably protest his anonymity, especially after violating a bureaucratic policy—after all, an unnamed offender cannot be held accountable. So, the inspector broke national character when he stepped up to the medic, leaned into his face, and spoke in stern, staccato syllables. "Listen. My name is Inspector Benoît Garrone—that is spelled G-a-r-r-o-n-e; I will tell you one last time: I take responsibility. *D'accord?*"

The medic finally relented: *"D'accord.* Agreed.*"*

"I'm going with you," Lucy said to Anthony.

Anthony looked at his secretary and then the ambulance driver.

"You take responsibility for her too?" the driver asked the inspector.

"Yes, yes. Go!"

Anthony and Lucy got in the ambulance and sat down beside Badeau, who had an oxygen mask over his nose and mouth.

"You're going to be all right, Jean-Pierre. I'm going to see to it," Anthony said.

Badeau nodded.

Lucy leaned forward and took Badeau's hand. "Jean-Pierre, *c'est moi*, Lucy. We're here for you."

Badeau tried to say something, which made him choke.

"*Ça suffit!*—that's enough!" the medic said, adjusting his patient's mask. "Let him rest."

Anthony and Lucy leaned back against the wall of the van, Anthony folding his arms across his chest in a vain effort to control his trembling hands.

"You're right, Lucy. We are here for him." Then after a long pause, he added, "But it can't stop with Jean-Pierre. The company has to take care of all its employees." Then, suddenly, it was almost as if Anthony had become his old self, barking out orders. But this time his "barking" was driven by raw passion, not meanness. "I have an idea, Lucy. If I have any influence left in this company, I am going to create a new position—call it employee advocacy—and you will be its director." The excitement was building up in his eyes. "Yeah, that's it. You'll make sure that every employee is treated like—here's a novel idea—a human being. You'll create career development programs, health programs, communication programs. You know how to do that kind of stuff." Anthony paused as if he were visualizing the transformation. "Damn, this feels good to me. What do you think, Lucy."

The secretary actually giggled.

"I know, I sound crazy."

"No, you sound on fire."

"I do, don't I? More than anything, I'm excited about you. Lucy, you are going to change the image of TMS. I'm not talking about a new mission statement; that's fluff. I'm talking about a new culture. Employee driven." Anthony turned and faced Lucy straight on, his eyes still dancing. "What d'you say? Are you up for it?"

Lucy looked at Anthony with a sense of wonder and renewed admiration. "Yes, Mr. Rossi, I think I am. . . . think I am."

After a cursory examination in emergency, Badeau was admitted to the hospital for more intensive tests. When Anthony visited his room, he found the project manager sedated and sleeping soundly on his back. He pulled up a chair and took Badeau's hand.

"I don't know if you can hear me, Jean-Pierre. I want you to know that I'm sorry. You were right about everything; I was such a shit. You are one courageous manager, Jean-Pierre, you crazy, out-of-control Frenchman."

Anthony dropped his head, closed his eyes, and listened. Then, after several minutes, he looked up at Badeau again. "Don't worry about a thing, Bud. We've got you covered. You just rest up now . . . you hear?"

The door to the hospital room flew open, and Badeau's wife, Nicole, stormed in, a nurse on her arm, struggling hopelessly to calm the hysterical woman. Immediately sizing up the situation, Anthony took the woman by both shoulders and backed her out the door.

"Calm yourself, Nicole. You're no good to him this way."

"Do not tell me what to do. This is your fault." She broke away from Anthony's grip and beat her fists into his chest.

Anthony let her pound on him, until, in total exhaustion, she fell limp into his arms. Anthony led her to a couch in the adjacent waiting room, where they both sat down side by side.

"You did this," she hissed. "*Vous l'avez rendu fou*—you drove him crazy. He could never please you."

"I know, Nicole. He was right; I was wrong. That will change. Everything will change."

"*Oui, c'est certain*," she said sarcastically.

"People do change, Nicole. It is possible to become a better person. I know that now. Give me a chance; give me a chance to make things right."

"And Jean-Pierre? What about Jean-Pierre?"

"Jean-Pierre will be fine. There will always be a place for him in our company. We will not run from our people; we will see this problem through. You'll see. Jean-Pierre will bounce back, and he will be free choose whatever work he wants for himself and his family. *D'accord*?"

"C'est promis?"

"That's a promise."

Nicole took off her glasses and swept the tears from her eyes, breathing long, disjointed sighs.

Anthony looked into her eyes. "Now, do you think you would like to see Jean-Pierre? He's been sedated and is resting peacefully, but I bet he can still feel the warmth of your hand. Talk to him; he will hear you. Tell him you love him; it's the best medicine on earth."

"Yes. I would like to see him."

Anthony led Nicole back to Badeau's room, where he left her, sitting by her husband's side, his hand in hers.

When Anthony left the room, Hennessy was waiting for him in the hallway. He had witnessed the scene with Nicole and was flooded with emotion. The two men stood silently for a moment in the center of the hall. Hennessy looked into Anthony's eyes and shook his head in wonderment. They embraced.

"Incredible," Hennessy said. "You're incredible."

"What do you say we call it a day?"

The two men walked to the elevators and on to the parking lot.

Hennessy gave Anthony his car keys. "You did a number on the Benz, but it still rolls."

"That's what counts."

"Listen, Anthony. There's something . . . well, something I'd like to say."

"Hennessy, I'm really bushed. Can it wait until tomorrow? I'd really like to be able to give you my full attention, and right now I'm running on empty."

"Sure. As a matter of fact, Jack and I were hoping that we could both drop into your office tomorrow morning sometime."

"That would be fine."

"How about ten o'clock?"

"Good. I'll see you then."

Anthony drove straight to his small apartment. Once in his room, he took one brief look at the narrow street below: the compact French cars parked bumper-to-bumper and pressed against the eighteenth-century storefronts, two wheels on the road, two wheels perched on the sidewalk. He then lay on the bed, his hands behind his head, staring at the ceiling. The following day would demand a hundred decisions. What would be his place in the company? Would he even stay on? What about Penelope? And—always first in his heart—what about Lupita and Diego and his life in Spain?

His head turned over all the options. Sometimes he thought he had all the pieces in place, and then everything fell apart, and he started all over again. Everything was riding on the next day.

In the shadows of his sleep, Anthony heard someone whistling a lilting melody. He knew that tune; it was "*La Violetera*." He searched the darkness for Diego, hearing his voice before he saw him.

"*Hola*, Antonio."

"Where are you, Diego?"

"I am here," he said, stepping out of the shadows.

But Diego's eyes were cast down, and Antonio did not recognize him. "Who are you?"

"Do you not know me?" Diego asked, raising his head.

It was true; it was Diego, but a young Diego—a man of twenty. His back was straight, his hair pitch black, and his smile gleaming. He was the most beautiful man he had ever seen.

Antonio smiled and threw himself at his friend, wrapping his arms around his waist and lifting his feet off the ground. "Diego! You are so young and handsome!"

"I have not always been old," Diego said with a warm laugh. He held Antonio by the shoulders, inspecting him at arm's length. "There is someone that I would like you to meet," he said, looking over his shoulder at someone in the dark.

Anthony squinted, trying to make out the figure, who finally stepped into the light. It was a brown-skinned, barefooted woman in white—exquisitely beautiful. She had a luminescence about her that was overwhelming. At first he thought it was Lupita, and he nearly swept her up in his arms. But it was not Lupita.

Young Diego spoke: "Antonio, may I have the honor of presenting the love of my life, Lupe."

Antonio was speechless. Tears came to his eyes. He looked at Diego, who only smiled. Antonio stepped forward, took Lupe's hand, and kissed it tenderly.

"Oh, no Antonio," Lupe said. "You must give me a hug," and she took Antonio in her arms, caressing the back of his head, as was Lupita's way.

"I am so honored to meet you, Lupe," he said.

"And I am honored to meet you."

"We are all honored," Diego said, putting his arms around Lupe and Antonio.

"I am so glad that you have come," Antonio said.

"We thought you might need our advice," Diego said with a smile.

"Oh, yes, yes!" Antonio said.

"Is it so difficult?" Diego asked. "You already possess everything you need: Silence, love, charity, and peace."

"Yes, but what should I do?"

"You must answer that for yourself," Lupe said. "With whom do you stand? Do you stand with the rebels, who have no rules, no conscience, no trust in elections—with those who believe only in bayonets and blood?"

"Or will you stand with the people?" Diego continued, as if his thoughts were a natural extension of Lupe's thoughts. "Will you think deeply, love profoundly, serve completely, and harvest peace?"

Diego moved to Antonio and cupped his son's face in his hands: "Do not make this more difficult than it is: Are you Anthony or are you Antonio?" Then, the young Diego kissed his son on both cheeks, smiled a calming, paternal smile, and then withdrew a step.

Anthony began to ask another question, but the images of Diego and Lupe began to fade, becoming more and more transparent.

"No, no . . . please, do not leave!" Anthony pleaded. "I have so much to ask you both."

"You do not require us," Lupe said, her sweet voice quickly vanishing. "You have all you need to know."

Then, drifting in from the darkness, in the softest of whispers, were Diego's last words: "Listen to your heart, my son."

Anthony was staring out his office window at the sea of Parisian rooftops. He unconsciously massaged his left shoulder. Then he reached into his pocket, drew out the olive medallion, and fingered the rounded edges.

There was a tentative tap at his door. Anthony pocketed the amulet.

"Come in."

It was Hennessy and Jack Benson.

"Are you ready for us?" Hennessy asked.

"You bet. Have a seat."

Anthony rounded the desk and sat down on the leather couch opposite his guests, who were seated in two fabric club chairs across a coffee table.

"Whose meeting is this?" Anthony asked.

"Maybe I should start," Jack said. He held his hands together, as if in a prayer, and then polished the palms. "I was out of line yesterday." He paused. "I'll level with you, Anthony: The board wanted you out. There has been talk about—what's the best word—your 'abrasiveness' for a number of years. When you disappeared, we saw it as the perfect opportunity to have a changing of the guard. Then, yesterday, when you talked about a new mission, I used it against you. At that point, you could have talked about rescuing stray dogs and homeless mothers, and I still would have attacked you."

"I think I knew that."

"But, after yesterday—especially the thing with Badeau—I have a different take. I'm speaking for the board, when I say that we would like to keep you on. We don't think we could find a better man for the job."

"I see. And Hennie, what do you think about all this?"

Hennessy leaned forward, his hands on his knees. "I've had a change of heart too, Anthony. I have to admit that I liked the idea of being the president of TMS. It . . . well, it made me feel important—like I was somebody. But you have changed that. Yesterday, I saw a new Anthony—the kind of man that I would like to work for."

"To underscore what Hennessy is saying, the board is ready to make your package a little sweeter," Benson added. "We were thinking a $200,000 bump in annual salary."

"That's a pretty hefty bump, Jack. Maybe about two-hundred K more than I deserve."

"What do you mean?"

"Look, I appreciate your offer. I really do. But, frankly, I'm not sure I want to take it. I've been exploring some other ideas."

"For instance?"

"For instance, the leadership of this corporation." He shifted his body to face Hennessy straight on. "Hennie, I owe you a long-overdue apology. I will be absolutely honest with you: I am ashamed of myself. I have been manipulating you for years, keeping you on the sidelines, exactly where I wanted you."

"Yes, I know that."

Anthony tapped his pant pocket, feeling the amulet under his hand. "I was wrong—my God, how I was wrong. My arrogance squashed your potential for greatness. *Your* potential for greatness," he said, repeating the words slowly for impact. "That was unforgivable."

"Thank you for saying that, Anthony."

"So, I want to start from the beginning," he said, moving to the edge of his seat. "I'd like to ask you a very important question, and I want you to be drop-dead honest with me: In a perfect world, what role would you have at TMS?"

Hennessy took his time. Then, his expression became more self-assured, almost heroic. "I would run the company," he said unfalteringly.

Anthony reached over and grabbed Hennessey by the knee. "Then run it! You can do it, my friend. You've always had the capability; I just would not let you believe it. I made you think that you were inadequate. You are not inadequate, Hennie; in fact, between the two of us, you have always been the better man. You had the heart; I only provided the grit. And with Jack here at your side, you have more grit than any human being should be allowed to have—no offense Jack."

"None taken," Jack said with a smile, knowing Anthony spoke the truth.

"So, do it, Hennie. Run the company. Send me a dividend check once a year. Take care of the corporation, take care of the people—and, by the way, you will find that Lucy can help you accomplish that—and, for Pete's sake, take care of yourself."

"Does this mean that you are stepping down?" Jack asked.

"Yes." He looked at Hennessy. "But I'm leaving the company in great hands. I have looked at the books from the last quarter, and, yes, the numbers are down, but that's because Hennie was trying to do the job with one arm tied behind his back. That's not the case anymore; he's now in charge. Just watch the company take off."

"That's good enough for me," Jack said, jumping to his feet like a man with a lineup of pressing back-to-back meetings.

Anthony and Hennessy stood up. There was a round of hearty handshakes.

"I will leave you two to your devices," Jack said. He walked to the door, opened it, and then turned back for one last word. "Have fun, both of you. And damn it, Hennie, make the company an obscene bundle of money."

"I'll do my best, Jack," Hennessy said.

The two men sat down again.

Anthony smiled at Hennessy, who had a troubled look on his face, like someone needing to make an apology. "Hennie? What are you thinking?"

It took a moment for the new president to respond. Anthony watched him rehearse his speech in his head.

"Anthony, I'd like to talk to you about Penelope."

"I know, Hennie."

"This is not easy," he said, his eyes fixed on the carpet.

Anthony reached over and gave Hennessy a pat on his knee. "It's okay, Hennie. Whatever it is, it's all right."

Hennessy looked up. "I love her, Anthony; I've always loved her. I feel like an absolute jerk for saying it, but that's the way it is."

"I have just one question for you: Is it real?"

"It couldn't be any more real." Hennessy paused. "Do you hate me for that?"

"You're my friend, Hennie. No, I don't hate you; I want the best for you. I want you to be happy. Are you happy with Penelope?"

"Anthony, the last four months have been unbelievable. Penelope is a dream come true for me."

"You know she can be expensive," Anthony said with a smile.

"Sure. I know that. But that doesn't bother me. I like expensive things too. In that respect, we're two of a kind."

"And how does she feel about all this?"

Hennessy bit his bottom lip. "I'd like you to ask her for yourself. She's in my office right now. May I ask her to come in?"

Anthony smiled. "Sure, have her join us."

"Good. I'll be right back."

Hennessy stepped out of Anthony's office, leaving the door open.

Anthony stood and walked to the window, his eyes tracing the web of tree-lined Parisian streets, his gaze finally resting on the gilded Church of the Dome, which sheltered Napoleon's sarcophagus. It was an awe-inspiring chapel: the red porphyry tomb on a massive green granite base under a canopy of frescoes of Christ and Saint Louis. Anthony used to love visiting the church and imagine that he, like Napoleon, was the mighty emperor of his own realm. He shook his head in remembrance of his own contemptuous pride. Again, he took the olive medallion from his pocket and turned it over in his hand.

Penelope's voice interrupted his thoughts.

"Here we are again: The three of us—just like the old days."

"Hi, Penelope."

Hennessy was at the door. "I think I'll leave you two alone. Give me a holler if you need me."

"Okay, Hennie. Thanks. I appreciate that. I'll catch up with you in a bit."

"Don't go too far, Sweetheart," Penelope added with affection.

Anthony came around to the front of his desk, sitting down on the edge. Penelope crossed the room and took both his hands. She was wearing a white silk blouse open at the neck, a single diamond at her throat. As usual, she looked elegant. It was one of the things that Anthony had always admired about her: She was a very classy woman.

Penelope smiled at her husband.

"Hennie tells me that he's madly in love with you."

She smiled even more broadly. "Yes."

"And how do you feel?"

Penelope kissed Anthony on the cheek and sat at his side on the edge of the desk. "I feel like I am a lucky woman: To have had two men head-over-heels in love with me in a single lifetime."

"Oh? I know about Hennie. Who was the other guy?"

Penelope gave Anthony a light jab to his thigh. "You did love me once."

"Yes, I did. And I love you still, but in a different way."

"Meaning?"

"I love your will, your feistiness, your ferocious independence."

"But do you love *me*?"

"Yes, I do love you; I have always loved you, but not as a woman needs to be loved." Anthony felt the searing anguish of his past. "My sweet Penelope, you were a prize for me, like a new car or a fancy house. I was never faithful to you, almost from the very beginning. Yes, I loved you; at least, I loved the *idea* of you, but I was never *in* love with you."

Penelope's eyes were brimming with tears. "I guess I always knew that; I just did not want to admit it to myself."

"I am so sorry, Penelope. I wish there were something I could do to make it right."

Penelope smiled softly. "When we came back from Île de Ré, I asked for five days."

"I remember."

"I saw something in you that was exciting: A man with a heart, a man with compassion. It was the person I knew when we were first married, before you became cool and cynical. Now the compassion is back, and for a moment I think I fell in love with you all over again, despite myself."

"Penelope," Anthony said, pronouncing her name sadly, apologetically.

She raised her hand and shook her head. "No, let me finish. The compassion is back, but you are gone. I know that. You are somewhere else—in Spain, I suspect—and there is nothing I can do about it."

Anthony stood up and faced Penelope. He took her by the shoulders. "I'm sorry."

"No, it's all right." She collected herself. "It really is all right. You asked if there was something you could do to make it right."

"Yes, anything."

"You can give me your blessing. Hennie has asked me to marry him."

"Oh, Penelope, you have it. I'm happy for you; I could not have chosen a better man."

Anthony gave Penelope a long, warm embrace. Finally, when he relaxed his hold on her, Penelope pulled him back in—a lingering hug, like the interlacing of young lovers at a train station, reluctant to say goodbye.

Penelope finally broke the embrace and wiped a tear from her cheek. Then she laughed. "Guess who Hennie wants for his best man?"

"No idea."

"You, of course. He says that you are still the *best* man, but that he is the *luckiest* man."

"You've got to love the guy."

"I do love him; I really do."

Two weeks passed. In that time, Anthony turned over the reins of the company to Hennessy. Together, they charted the direction of the corporation: a more caring company with Hennie as president, Lucy as director of employee advocacy, and, to keep Jack Benson and the board of directors happy, a possible expansion of the firm's European division with a new office in Spain.

On the second Friday of the week, Anthony was alone in the office. He went to the closet, pulled out his suitcase, and placed the bag on his desktop. He opened the lid and smiled at its contents. In the next few moments, he took off the mantle of business, the wool suit and the silk tie, and replaced it with his simple Spanish work clothes. He looked approvingly in the mirror. Then, he lifted Diego's red bandanna from the suitcase and laid it across his open hands like an offering, reflecting on the sacred significance of the stained fabric. He knotted the kerchief around his neck with solemn reverence.

Anthony closed the suitcase and walked out of his old fortress.

Lucy was still at her desk, when Anthony emerged from his office. She stood up, taking in his strange garb.

"You are leaving," she said resolutely.

Anthony was beaming. "Yes. I'm going now."

The two friends hugged one last time.

Lucy smoothed her suit jacket. She swallowed hard. "If I may ask, Mr. Rossi, where are you going?"

Anthony smiled at his secretary. "Home. I'm going home."

The sun was beginning to rise as Antonio approached Espejo. The olive trees stretched out over the rolling hills. He lowered the car window and breathed in the morning Andalusian air. In the next moment, he could make out the church steeple glimmering yellow in the sunlight.

Antonio rolled slowly up the cobblestone road to the top of the hill. He parked the car just shy of the Garcias' home and walked the last few steps, not wanting the sound of his rumbling wheels to give away the surprise.

He turned the doorknob and grinned. The door was open, as he knew it would be. He silently stepped into the house and immediately saw Diego huddled over the balcony railing, his morning coffee cupped in both hands. He found him as he had left him: whistling the melody to "*La Violetera.*" Antonio eased up behind him, stopping at the doorway.

Diego felt Antonio's presence, but still did not stir. A slow smile brightened his face, as he watched the sun awaken the leaves of the olive trees in the valley below.

"Welcome home, my son," he said, as calmly as awaking from a pleasant siesta.

Antonio leaned over the railing at Diego's side. "It is good to be home, father," he said putting his arm around Diego's shoulder. "It is so good to be home."

For a long moment, the two stayed that way, both watching the morning light dance on the rooftops.

Finally, Antonio could not contain himself any longer. "Where is Lupita, father?"

Diego hesitated. "She is with Miguel," he said, his face expressionless.

"With Miguel?"

"Of course. It is only right. They were married last Sunday, you know," Diego said, sedately sipping his coffee.

Antonio stared at him in horror, and Diego stared back, and for one instant the world stopped. Finally, Diego's eyes gave his mischief away, and they both laughed at once, falling into each other's arms.

"Oh, you old rascal," Antonio said, grabbing his father by the shoulders and giving him a playful shake. "Now tell me—and no tricks—where is Lupita?"

"She is at the church. It is where she has gone every morning since you went away."

"Good," Antonio said, shaking his finger at Diego as one last scolding. "You . . . you will get yours," he warned.

Antonio rushed to the front door.

"Antonio!"

He turned to Diego. "Yes, father."

Diego slowly took in his friend, and then placed both hands over his heart. "I am the happiest man on earth."

Antonio shook his head, his heart too full of emotion to respond. He turned, bolted out of the house, and bounded up the stone treads to the church, taking two steps at a time. He paused at the massive church door to catch his breath. Then he slowly opened the door and stepped through the portal.

Lupita was kneeling at the front of the sanctuary, her hands clasped before her. She was dressed in white, a lace shawl over her head. A band of morning light streamed through a stained-glass window and fell across her face. Antonio walked to her in quiet reverence and knelt beside her.

Lupita turned to him. Tears were streaming down her face.

"I am home," Antonio said softly.

Lupita threw her arms around her lover's neck. "Antonio, Antonio, Antonio," she whispered again and again, the sound of his name resounding like muted bells in the old stone church. There they held each other, as Diego had once held Lupe, as all lovers embrace the exquisite belief that no one has loved as deeply as they have loved. And then the church bells did peal, all at once an invitation to morning mass and a sacred reception for one who was asleep and now, at long last, was awakened.

ALLEN JOHNSON IS A NATIONALLY acclaimed keynote-speaker, consultant, author, and photographer. He holds a master's in speech from the University of Washington and a PhD in counseling psychology from Washington State University. In addition to writing, his diverse passions include acting, cycling, painting, creating video documentaries, and singing jazz standards to his own piano accompaniment.

Allen is also the author of the following non-fiction books:

The Power Within: The Five Disciplines of Personal Effectiveness

This Side of Crazy: 54 Lessons on Living From Someone Who Should Know Better But Keeps Messing Up Anyway

To learn more about the making of *The Awakening*, as well as other titles, please visit Allen's author website: booksbyallen.com.

Allen and his wife Nita divide their time between their primary home in Richland, Washington, and their adopted home in Pérols, France.